DEFENSIVE HEART

THE DONNELLYS
BOOK TWO

DOROTHY F. SHAW

PRAISE FOR DOROTHY F. SHAW

"*Unworthy Heart* reminded me of what I love about the romance genre."—The Book Tart

"*Unworthy Heart* by Dorothy F. Shaw made me think, made my heart happy, made me tear up and made me sigh in happiness. Shaw combines heat with heart almost flawlessly. I cannot wait for the follow-up books in this series."—Romance Novel News

"I fell in love with the series from book one…Grab your copy and buckle up for the ride. Dorothy Shaw doesn't do anything halfway."—Beyond the Valley of the Books on *Defensive Heart*

"Holy smokes, can Dorothy Shaw write a freaking awesome sex scene…"—Wicked Good Reads on *Defensive Heart*

"*Defensive Heart* by Dorothy F. Shaw is a good read which gives credence to the statement that opposites do attract."—Harlequin Junkie

"Even though there is plenty of sex in *Shattered Heart*, the author does not neglect the storyline at all – packing it full of romance, danger, trauma, healing, laughs, and the Donnelly family."—Crystal's Many Reviewers

"*Shattered Heart* is an emotional tear-jerker of a romance that had me reaching for the tissues on more than one occasion."—Romance Novel News

"Wow! What a sexy, steamy story that kept me reading from the first page."—Crystal's Many Reviewers on *Stripped Bounty*

"If you are into vanilla, forget this book! Characters larger than life and sex to die for. Dorothy F. Shaw painted a canvas that is both intriguing and close to hardcore."—Amazon Reviewer on *Stripped Bounty*

"Epic story! Rosie and Badger are amazing characters that pull you into the story. The sex is HOT and the ending is perfect!"—Book Addicts PR on *Stripped Bounty*

"I was blown away by how easily the story was told by Dorothy F. Shaw"—CeeriJays Smexy HotReads on *A Few More Rules*

"*A Few More Rules* (a femdom novella) is a super-hot romance that sets the foundation well for a probable HEA between Rig and Beth. This story is a winner."—Romance Novel News

"WOW!!! This erotic, sensual short story will have you panting for more! These two beauties are more than fang bangers. The dark world of lust and sex will feed any appetite you desire."—Bookaholic and More Blog on *Playtime*

"I like books that grab my attention so much that I read a line and end up gasping or commenting out loud... and this one did just that - a few times! I'll definitely be reading it again."—Goodreads Reviewer on *Playtime*

"True to Dorothy Shaw's form, *Avoiding the Badge* is full of everything I love about her writing."—Amanda at Wicked Good Reads

"I liked the way the author brought about the truths that they had been keeping from each other, and I really enjoyed the steps that the two characters took in order to overcome the troubles in their path."—Amazon reviewer on *Avoiding the Badge*

"*Redeeming the Badge* is a second chance romance that is hot as Hades and with a backstory that will twist your heartstrings." —Amazon Reviewer

"This is a tale of love and heartache, dealing with some tough issues such as infertility, endometriosis, and miscarriage. It will tear at your heartstrings and make you believe in true love." —Amazon Reviewer on *Redeeming the Badge*

"Jeff and Tish are a good couple with incredible chemistry that makes you jealous. I can't recommend this series enough." —Amazon Reviewer on *Trusting the Badge*

"*Trusting the Badge* is a quick read for readers who enjoy a focus on relationship building, characters with tragic backstories, and some steamy moments." —Amazon Reviewer

"It was written in a way that I got very emotional reading it, most books don't make me cry. This one did."—Amazon reviewer on *Jaded Heart*

"As usual, Shaw creates characters that can be hard to like. Garrett is not easy to connect to. He treats Angie like crap, but Angie keeps fighting for them. Their flameout moment is painful to read about but very necessary. Garrett has to deal with his past, which he has been avoiding for years and years. With all of this, I still couldn't put the book down."—Romance Novel News on *Jaded Heart*

Defensive Heart

The Donnellys Book 2
© 2019 Dorothy F. Shaw

Uptown girl, tattooed bad boy. Think you know which one is wild? You'd be wrong.

Greenwich Village is home to successful artist Jimmy Donnelly, and the world is his playground. A broken heart in college left him with zero interest in being tied down. But when he meets a sexy, quick-witted Manhattan attorney, he reconsiders his bad boy ways.

Sonja Martin's life is filled with work, an ex-husband who refuses to stay gone, and a teenage daughter who won't follow the rules. Jimmy, with his myriad of tattoos and piercings, looks more like one of her clients than a potential lover. But when every argument between them feels more like foreplay, she can't seem to stay out of his bed.

The heat burns through whatever defenses Sonja thought she had. And Jimmy finds his every fantasy fulfilled—and exceeded—by a woman whose fire burns as bright as her fiercely guarded vulnerability.

But his case for breaking her out of her self-imposed mold might just be dismissed. And he'll lose the best thing he's ever found.

DEDICATION

To my unicorn, you wove your way deep into my heart and mind—my very soul.
You changed everything, and I will never be the same.

ACKNOWLEDGMENTS

Shout out to my beta readers: Dawn Vaeoso, Alissa Dawn, Tere Harden, Trenda London and my cousin, Sherri Zak. Thank you so much, as always, your feedback was invaluable. And, Sherri, you are my typo-finding queen! To my friend, Amy Wilson, an incredible nurse…thank you for your help with the medical scenes. To Richie "the kid" Hammer, for your help with the NYPD officer scenes, but also, thank you for remaining a part of my life.

And for author, Shawna (Thomas) Guzman… Chica, I could thank you a thousand times, plus a thousand times more, and it would never be enough. You took me by the hand and molded, shaped, taught and then, with a soft heart but firm hand, taught some more. I could not have made it this far without you. I still have so far to go, but I will forever be grateful for you.

**Added with 3rd version re-release: Special thanks to Sunnie Andrews (badass aspiring author and friend) for being an awesome PA and proofreader/beta reader. And fetching coffee and getting my ass to signings ALMOST on time. <3

This book might piss you off. But if I've done my job, while you're busy being pissed off, you'll also fall in love with the hero and the heroine. May contain: A pompous, misogynistic ex-husband. A rebellious teenager. A ton of sex. Adventurous sex. Make-up sex. Desperate-OMG-GET-YOUR-CLOTHES-OFF sex… Did I mention there's a lot of sex?

PLAYLIST

Stone Sour - *Made of Scars*
Tchaikovsky - *Romeo and Juliet*
Otis Redding - *These Arms of Mine*
Type O Negative - *Anesthesia*
Type O Negative - *Burnt Flowers Fallen*
Godsmack - *Whatever*
Jason DeVore - *Wait*
Lana Del Rey - *Burning Desire*

CHAPTER ONE

JIMMY DONNELLY'S SHOULDER JERKED FORWARD. *What the—*

"Pardon me. Crap! Ugh."

He glanced to see who'd bumped him, and his mouth dropped open. *Whoa!* "No problem," he managed to mumble after he'd gotten his jaw working. The woman was gorgeous—and tall. Holy crap, she was tall.

"Thanks." She looked down. "Oh my God! No!" She swiped her hands down her white suit jacket.

"Shit. Let me get you a towel." Jimmy signaled the barback and then handed her the clean rag. "Was that your drink or his?"

"*His.* I was just coming to get my own. Ugh! That guy didn't even apologize." Her tone was filled with annoyance as she swiped at the front of the jacket, then down one thigh.

Jimmy let his gaze roam down her body. She was tall but also petite—a complete oxymoron, but the perfect description nonetheless. He took in the white formal pantsuit she wore and continued down to her beige, very expensive-looking—*holy shit*—stiletto pumps. Jimmy whistled low. Classy for sure, but completely out of place in a dance club like Tangled. He rested his elbow on the bar. "Could be worse. Could be red wine."

She pinned him with a glare cold enough to freeze hell. "Let me know if you have anything useful to say. That's really not helping." She went back to swiping at her clothes.

"Uh…" He cleared his throat. "Yeah, sorry." Talk about feeling like his mother just scolded him. Jimmy smiled, trying to hide the sudden nervous energy filling his belly and rocketing up his throat. It made his tongue feel like someone had spread a layer of rubber cement on it. He turned away and resumed his wait for the bartender.

A few minutes later, she slid into the small space between him and another patron. Like a magnet drawn to the pull of another, Jimmy couldn't help himself and looked over, taking in her profile. Man, she really was beautiful.

She glanced at him, nodded, then turned away. After a few beats, she looked back. "You're staring."

Jimmy cringed. "Sorry." He focused back on the bartender, but after another few moments, curiosity took over, and he risked another peek. Her blonde hair was pulled up in a twist on the back of her head, appearing to defy the laws of gravity, and she had the brightest sky-blue eyes he'd ever seen. She wore little makeup and had one of those faces with skin so milky white and perfect it looked like it'd been scooped out of whipped cream.

She hit him with another glare and shifted to face him. "Is there a problem?"

He bristled at her annoyed tone, layered with a hint of a New York accent. Yup, he'd been staring, but Jesus, she didn't need to be so nasty. Jimmy looked her up and down, damn ready to give it right back to her. Being of Irish descent, he normally let things slide, but she'd definitely riled his temper. The crowd pressed in closer, and someone muscled in behind her, forcing their bodies to almost touch. "You're a little overdressed for a place like this, don't you think?"

She raised a single brow. "Aren't you a master of observation."

"Usually." Jimmy smirked. Jesus, she smelled good. "If you don't mind me saying, you're…stunning."

She cocked her head to the side with a smirk rivaling his own. "Great, thanks."

Stunning *with* an attitude. A little like fire and ice. How intriguing. Unable to resist a good game of tit-for-tat, he leaned toward her. "Nice shoes. You mug someone in a back alley to score them?"

She took a small step back and bumped the guy behind her. "Hardly."

"I'm striking out here, aren't I?"

"That's assuming you ever actually made it up to bat."

"Ouch." Jimmy rubbed the center of his chest. "Look, let me start over." She mumbled something sounding a lot like, "Do I have a choice?" but he ignored it. Jimmy held out his hand. "Hi, I'm James Donnelly. Let me buy you a drink. To— you know—make up for my sarcasm."

"I think I can manage the purchase of my own drink. Thank you anyway." She didn't take his offered hand, just turned back toward the bar.

Jimmy laid his neglected palm on the bar top and leaned close enough to almost touch her ear with his lips. "That was rude."

She jerked away as if he'd slapped her. "What was rude?"

"I got you a towel so you could wipe up a drink *I* didn't spill on you. Then I tried to apologize for staring at you, which, again, wasn't trying to be rude…then I tried to start over with you and shake your hand, and you snubbed me."

Screw this lady. He drummed his fingertips on the counter.

"I beg your pardon?" She faced him, one hand on her hip and annoyance clear in her expression. "I thanked you for the towel. Ugh, forget it. Why are you talking to me?"

"Exactly." He shrugged and turned away. Why waste time

and energy on someone with an entire stick up her ass? He wanted to ask her where her broom was, but figured she'd turn him into a toad—or worse. He loved a little fire and ice in a woman, but she wasn't full of fire *or* ice. The woman appeared to be merely a regular bitch.

"Now who's rude?" She tugged on his arm, and he glanced over his shoulder at her. "Fine. Buy me a drink." She sighed. "Vodka tonic, with a lime."

Interesting. Maybe the stick wasn't embedded as deep as he thought. He faced her again. With a broad smile, he smoothed his hands down the front of his white button-up shirt. "Tell me your name first."

WHO IN THE *hell* did this lunatic think he was? Sonja Martin stood, hand planted on one hip, studying the boy standing before her. Yes, *boy*. She took a moment to appraise his features: A head full of dark, almost black, spiky and tangled hair fell over his forehead and covered the tops of his ears, both of which were pierced. Equally dark brows framed a set of pale hazel eyes. His nose, with one nostril pierced, was thin and straight but curved slightly down at the tip. A thin goatee framed his full mouth and merged into a thin strip down his squared, narrow chin.

Plenty good-looking, no denying it, but his features weren't perfect either. He was younger than her, but then again, who wasn't in a place like this? Giving in, she held out her hand. "Sonja Martin."

He wrapped his fingers around her hand in a firm but not excessive grip. "Nice to meet you. Can't say it's been a plea-sure so far, but maybe there's hope." He winked and smiled, revealing a set of straight, white teeth and a pair of dimples some would kill for.

The smile was potent, and her breath caught in her throat. "You really know how to turn on the charm, don't you?"

"Oh, come on. Lighten up, will ya? We need a shot."

"I'm not doing a shot with you, Mr. Donnelly."

"Sure you are. Good memory with the name, by the way." He rubbed his hands together. "I'm going to order two shots along with your drink, then we'll drink them. Simple."

Sonja couldn't quite believe this guy. He was either already drunk or just plain stupid. Never mind rude, annoying and downright egotistical. She could go on and on, and should've already walked away from him. Yet she stood there, like some sort of subservient sheep—*how typical of me*—and let him order them shots and drinks.

Sonja shook her head, clenching her teeth in complete annoyance. Thing was, she wasn't sure who she was more agitated with, herself or him. Just what she needed, another pompous ass ordering her around. *Spare me. I'm full up.* The bartender returned with her vodka tonic (minus the lime), two shot glasses filled with dark fluid, and a glass of what appeared to be Guinness. When her unwelcome and distracting company slid the shot in front of her, Sonja eyed the nearly black liquid and frowned. "What is it?"

"Jägermeister." He raised his shot glass. "Come on, lift it. What shall we drink to?"

She waved her hand, signaling the bartender. She needed the lime for her drink. "I'm not drinking that."

He picked up the other shot and held it in front of her. "Sure you are."

"Mr. Donnel—"

"James. Take the shot."

"James. Whatever. You can have both." The bartender appeared. Finally. "You forgot my lime."

"It's been a while, hasn't it?" James chuckled.

"Excuse me?"

He set the shot intended for her on the bar top. "Safe to

assume you're single. It's been a while since you've gotten laid, huh? Must be it."

"It has no—" Heat flooded her cheeks, and agitation pulsed through her. She was single, but her relationship status or sex life was none of his damn business. And besides, it hadn't been *that* long. Had it?

Cupping her elbow in his hand, he bent close to her ear. "You are, and it has. Drink the shot, Sonja. Trust me, you need it." His hot breath feathered over her neck, and she shivered.

Sonja cursed her body for responding in any way, shape or form to him. She should slap him, not get aroused by him. Breathing deep, Sonja sought for some measure of calm and came up short when his masculine scent flowed through her senses like a cool stream, making her shiver again. *Crap.* Always such a sucker for the aroma of clean soap and cologne. The bartender placed a lime on the edge of her drink, and she shifted, pulling away from James. "Thanks."

James held her shot glass up in front of her again. "Drink up."

"You don't give up, do you?"

"Once I sink my teeth in, I don't let go."

Knowing it was a bad idea, Sonja took the glass from him. "Is that it? You think you've sunk your teeth in?"

"The bite is so much more pleasurable if you relax and go with it." He smiled and raised his shot. "To being stunning, Ms. Martin." He tapped her glass with the edge of his.

She paused and took in his dimples, the curve of his lips. He was too sexy. A prize chock-full of wickedness, she wasn't quite sure she wanted to collect on. "Are you trying to seduce me, James?"

"Do you want to be seduced?"

"Not particularly." With a laugh, Sonja tilted the shot to her lips. She closed her eyes and swallowed the dark liquid; the sweet licorice flavor spread over her tongue and burned on its way down her throat. When she opened her eyes, he was watching her, his gaze fixated on her lips. She licked them… slowly. *Two can play at this game.*

James's eyes flared before narrowing. He tapped the bottom of the shot glass on the bar top and drank it down.

Was that some sort of shot ritual she wasn't aware of? Hmm. "How old are you?"

He hissed through his teeth and set his glass down. "Old enough to know and still young enough to do something about it."

"How very cliché."

"And how old are you?" A smooth grin tipped the corners of his lips.

"How very impolite." She raised a brow and squeezed the lime into her vodka tonic. "Too old for you. What are you, twenty-five? Twenty-six?" She licked the remnants of lime juice from her fingertips.

"Are you trying to seduce me, Sonja?"

"Only in your wet dreams."

He leaned close again, placed his hand on her lower back and pulled her against him. "Keep licking your lips and fingers like that, honey, and you'll be the star in my wet dream tonight."

Sonja tensed, trying and failing to ignore his words and warm breath on her ear. The heat of his hand burned through her clothes, and she trembled against his hard chest. James dragged his hand from her lower back to her waist, framed it for a moment between his thumb and fingers, squeezed, then let go of her. A beat of arousal pumped through her and settled between her thighs. Sonja swallowed past the lump in her throat. Why was she letting him get to her this much?

He waved for the bartender. "I think we need another shot."

"No. No, we don't."

He smiled and winked at her. "Shh. I got this."

"I bet that smile gets you into a lot of beds, doesn't it?" She sipped her drink.

"Will it get me into yours?"

A laugh she couldn't suppress bubbled up, and she sucked the liquid down the wrong pipe. Talk about a cold splash of water. Her libido went silent as she attempted to breathe.

"Shit. Sorry." James grabbed a napkin and handed it to her, and then rubbed her back while she tried like hell to appear dignified while coughing up a lung.

Sonja wiped her mouth with the napkin. "No. Not likely." She coughed again and cleared her throat. "Don't you have a girlfriend around here somewhere you should be annoying?"

He grabbed the freshly delivered shots. "Nope. I'm all yours. Here."

"Oh God. Are you trying to get me drunk?"

"Will it get me into your bed?"

"Not a chance." She smirked but took the shot and tossed it back, this time with no hesitation.

He shook his head. "You didn't wait for the toast. Bad form, Sonja. Bad form."

"Aw. You'll get over it." She patted his shoulder.

"Nope. You've wounded my heart. How much of a beating do you think a guy can take?" He placed his hand over his chest. As he did, the sleeve of his shirt rose, revealing tattoo work on his wrist.

"Oh my, this wounded puppy thing is pretty pathetic. Go ahead, make a toast. I'll sip my drink while you toss back the second shot you insisted on having."

"Wounded puppy? *You are* relentless." He grinned. "I think you should make the toast this time."

Thanks to the alcohol kicking in, Sonja's tongue was getting looser and looser. Where were her friends, anyway? Weren't they supposed to be there to save her from situations like this? However, Sonja's libido didn't want her to be saved at this point.

The guy looked more like the clients she represented back home in Manhattan than any type of man she'd ever consider going to bed with. There was something about him, though. It made her go weak in the knees, which was more troubling than anything else. "Okay, fine." She raised her drink. "To your bedroom eyes, dimples, and wicked smile created to drop panties…though surely not mine." She nodded, feeling quite pleased with herself.

He dipped his chin and raised one brow. "Clever. Very clever."

"Thanks. Glad you liked it."

He repeated the actions from before: tapped the bottom of his glass on the bar, raised it to his lips and swallowed the alcohol. When he did, she caught a glimpse of a tattoo snaking up his neck, visible just above the collar of his shirt. She intended to ask about the little ritual with the shot, but was so distracted by the tantalizing peek of his ink all rational thought left her mind.

He set the empty shot glass upside down on the bar. "I'm thirty."

Holy shit.

CHAPTER TWO

JIMMY WATCHED HER EXPRESSION CHANGE WHEN HE TOLD HER his age. She'd asked how old he was and guessed wrong, yet hadn't told him hers. The look on her face was proof enough she had to be older. "Problem, Sonja?"

"You're older than I thought, but still young." She brushed some invisible lint off the sleeve of her jacket.

He leaned forward. "Is this where you tell me you're too old for me?"

She laughed. "I *am* too old for you."

"Let's do another shot and discuss it." He took a swig of his Guinness.

"No. Oh God, no." She placed the palm of her left hand on his chest.

He glanced at it. Smooth alabaster skin, long French-manicured nails, and, like he noticed already, no wedding ring. No mark from one either. He placed his hand over hers and met her gaze. "Okay, no shot. Let's discuss it anyway."

"How many tattoos do you have?"

He smirked and traced her fingers. "One."

Sonja pulled her hand away and let out a nervous laugh as she turned and stared toward the dance floor.

"You don't have any, huh?"

"You have more than one." She looked back at him and traced the dragon's tail swooping up the side of his neck.

Her cool fingers on his skin lit his blood on fire. He stood stock still, but his pulse pounded like a drum in time with the music, and he tightened his grip on his beer glass. "I'll let you count them if you want."

She licked her lips. "No, I don't have any."

The shots of liquor had worked their magic and loosened her right up. He wasn't trying to get her naked—not that he'd turn her down if she offered—he just wanted to help her relax. Honestly, she intrigued him. She was such an anomaly in this club, with her white dressy business suit, her perfect blonde hair and her bottomless blue eyes. He wanted to know more about her. "Do you live here?"

"No. I live in Manhattan." She ran her fingertips down the buttons of his shirt. "I'm here partly for business, partly for a visit with a friend." She pulled her hand away. "Do you?"

"That explains the suit." He moved his hand to her hip. Point for him on the Manhattan info. "I don't live here either."

She glanced at his hand but didn't pull it away. Yup, bless the Jäger gods. *Sweet.* They were doing their job nicely.

She scraped her teeth over her bottom lip. "I should go find my friends."

"If you insist." He tilted his head to the side. "It was a pleasure to meet you, Sonja Martin." Taking her hand in his, he kissed her palm.

Sonja blinked her big blue eyes and swallowed—her throat bounced with the action, then she licked her lips. He was getting to her. And as blood flow found its way south to his less logical head, she was getting to him, too.

"Thanks for the drink—drinks." She giggled, then abruptly pulled her hand away and covered her mouth with it, eyes wide with a full blush coloring her cheeks—as if shocked the sound came from her.

"I like the giggle. Not something you do often, is it?"

She shook her head. "I better go."

"Yeah, you said that." He leaned on the bar, enjoying her flustered reactions.

She picked up her drink. "Okay, I'm going. Really, it was nice meeting you, too."

He nodded, and she stepped away, making her way through the crowd in the direction of the tables. He wanted to follow her, but didn't.

Turning, he glanced up at the balcony. Jimmy scanned the mahogany railing bordering the circular area, searching for his brother Ryan. With no sign of him, he let his gaze wander around the surrounding walls there and then downstairs. Jimmy smiled. He loved this club. The place looked like the love child of a gothic-style building and an old Victorian house. Complete with a full head of industrial-style art decorating the walls. His art, to be specific. And Jimmy never got tired of seeing his art decorating walls. *Starving artist, my ass.* The display was a sweet reminder of how far he'd come.

Pulling his cell from his back pocket, Jimmy texted his brother.

Sonja's head buzzed from the two shots of Jägermeister in addition to the drinks she'd had before she met James. She found her friends and took a seat at the table they'd all been congregating around.

"Where'd you disappear to?" her friend Ginny asked.

Sonja ran her hand up the back of her hair, smoothing it. "Nowhere. Just up at the bar."

"All this time? Someone try and pick you up?" Ginny sipped her beer.

"Someone tried to pick you up?" Sandra butted in. "Was he hot?"

Ginny elbowed Sandra. "I just asked her that. She hasn't answered yet."

"Well?" they both asked in unison.

Sonja shrugged. "I…I don't know. Maybe."

"Woo hoo! What'd he look like?" Ginny sat next to her.

Sandra looked around. "Where is he?"

"My goodness, you two sound like a couple of cackling hens." She laughed and took a gulp of her drink. Maybe he *was* trying to pick her up. She thought back to his smile, those damn dimples, and the hot brand of his hand on her lower back and, later, on her hip. He'd touched her more than a few times.

When he kissed her palm, heat pooled low in her belly, and she'd clenched her thighs together. God, she was *never* attracted to men who looked like him. She knew plenty who acted like him, but piercings and tattoos were always a turn-off for her, and yet, all she wanted to do was trace the lines of the ink on his neck leading to his chest. How far down did it go? What was it? Could she lick it? Sonja fanned her face and shook her head. A few drinks, and she was acting like she was in heat.

Ginny's hand waved in front of her face, interrupting her tattooed James fantasy. "Earth to Sonja."

She cleared her throat. "I guess some might find him attractive, but he wasn't my type." She took another swallow of her drink. "He had tattoos." She sneered. "And piercings."

Both her friends laughed. Ginny tossed her hair over her shoulder. "Definitely not your type, Sonja."

Sonja shrugged and downed the rest of her vodka tonic. How many places on his body were pierced? She hadn't thought to ask him. Now, she wished she had. Sonja looked across the crowd and caught sight of him climbing the staircase. She zeroed in on his long, lean body, and her breath seized in her throat. His white dress shirt fell just below his hips, blocking the view of his denim-clad butt. *Damn.* She watched as his nice, long legs carried him up the stairs and out of her range of sight.

The guy had to be over six feet tall. She was far from short, and her spike-heeled pumps brought her almost eye-to-eye with him. Yes, a generous amount over six feet tall for sure. Sonja stared up at the balcony. He'd probably gone on to his next victim, she supposed—if she considered herself a victim. Maybe the next lucky contestant?

"Ohh!" Sandra squealed and clapped her hands. "I looooove this song! Let's go dance." She grabbed Sonja by the arm and pulled her from her seat.

"Oy vey." Sonja trailed after her. Some modern dance song she didn't know blasted through the dance club's speakers. Ginny came up behind her and Sandra, spinning and bopping her hips from side to side.

Odd how easy she'd forgotten what fun they'd all had in college dancing on the weekends. Had it really been twenty years since she was in law school? Where had the time gone? Sonja tamped down the wave of nostalgia and spun around her friends. She shimmied her hips, letting the music and the crowds take her away.

"Shake it, Sonja," Sandra shouted, a huge grin adorning her lips.

Ginny giggled and came up behind Sonja, pinning Sonja between herself and their other friend. Laughing, Sonja rocked her hips with her hands swaying above her head. She needed to get out and do this more often.

Regardless of the fun, her mind wandered back to James. He was thirty. Eleven years her junior, which would make her one of those cougars she heard people talk about. Sonja cringed, and embarrassment pulsed through her at her foolishness. What the hell would a thirty-year-old playboy want with her old flat butt? Not much, she was willing to bet. She looked young for her age, but not *that* young.

When the song changed, Ginny grabbed Sonja and led her toward the bar, hollering over her shoulder about another birthday shot. Why not, right? They were in Vegas. She'd finished her business today, and this *was* a birthday party, after all. Another shot of Jäger went down smooth—Ginny and Sandra scoffed when she'd requested it instead of their normal lemon drops, but they drank them anyway and migrated back to their table.

Then…he was there. Appearing out of nowhere. *Damn, he's pretty.*

James clasped her hand, tugged her close and bent his head to her ear. "I need to leave now."

She pulled back to focus on his face and then his lips. "Is your tongue pierced?"

He smiled, chuckling. "You thinking about taking a walk on the wild side?"

Yes. "I'm a little drunk." A walk sounded like an amazing idea.

He wrapped an arm around her waist and drew her flush against his body. "So, is that a yes or a no?"

Sonja's stomach tightened when her pelvis met his. My God, he felt good and smelled like heaven on a stick. It was almost enough to sober her right up. Almost. "I don't take walks on the wild side." It wasn't a lie. Sonja didn't do the wild side. Ever. She ran her hands up his arms, feeling the muscles beneath his shirtsleeves, resisting the urge to squeeze them.

James opened his mouth and revealed the piercing, rolling the barbell in his tongue around for her to see. She hadn't noticed it earlier, but she sure as hell noticed it now. What would it feel like against her nipples? Her clit? A gasp escaped, and said body parts throbbed in time with her pulse. Her physical reactions to him shocked her, but she dismissed them.

The alcohol was the cause. At least, that's what she told herself.

"Maybe you should think about it. Might be worth your while."

She smiled, a witty retort poised on the end of her tongue, but took a step back when she noticed Ginny approaching.

"Who's your friend?" Ginny asked and then whispered in Sonja's ear, "Thought you might need a rescue."

Sonja cleared her throat. "Ginny Freeman, this is James Donnelly."

Ginny grabbed his hand and shook it. "No shit? *The* James Donnelly?"

His lips spread into a genuine smile, and he laughed. "Depends on which James Donnelly you mean. I'm betting there's more than one. Pleasure to meet you."

Sonja looked back and forth between the two of them. What the hell was Ginny talking about?

"The artist, of course. Your art's all over this bar, am I right?" Ginny beamed.

"That'd be me. Live and in person." His smiled widened, and his eyes crinkled at the corners.

Sonja touched his arm. "You're an artist?"

"How do you *not* know who he is, Sonja? He lives in the Village, for fuck's sake." Ginny laughed. "I swear you reside in that courtroom."

Sonja didn't know what to say. Heat swamped her face, and embarrassment flooded her chest. She'd never heard of him. He lived in Greenwich Village? *Holy hell.* She'd mentioned she was from Manhattan, but he hadn't said anything about being from there, too. Finding her voice, she narrowed her gaze on Ginny. "Thanks for pointing that out. You may be excused from class now." She smiled and nodded in the direction of their table.

"Well, all right then. It's awesome to meet you, Mr.

Donnelly. I *looove* your work." Ginny shook James's hand again before finally walking off.

Sonja motioned around them. "This is really your art on the walls here?"

"Yeah. No big deal." He put his hands in his front pockets and looked around. "It's what I do."

Someone tapped his shoulder, and James turned around and spoke with him.

For God's sake, was everyone in the bar on a mission to interrupt them? She caught sight of the man. Definitely handsome with sandy-brown hair and light eyes. He and James appeared to be about the same age, but the man was more in line with her preferred style of dress and clean-cut looks.

He said something to James about paying the bill, then glanced over at her. James cleared his throat and stepped aside. "Ryan, this is Sonja Martin. She's in town for business."

"Nice to meet you." She smiled and shook his hand.

Ryan paused, still holding her hand, before finally speaking. "Nice to meet you, too." He excused himself and walked away.

"Where were we?" James circled her upper arm in his hand.

A zing of arousal bounced through her at the contact, and she tamped it down. "Your friend seems nice."

"He's my brother."

"Really? You don't look anything alike."

"Yeah, we get that a lot. So, where are you in the City?"

"Upper East Side."

"Ah, the high-rent district. Nice."

She waved her hand at him. "Whatever."

"About that walk we talked about." The corner of his lips quirked in a devilish smile. "Give me your card."

She paused and bit her bottom lip.

"Come on, Sonja." He slid his palm down to her forearm

to her hand and laced his fingers with hers. "I want to be able to talk again, have coffee or something."

A shiver ran through her. At a loss for how to respond, she untangled her fingers from his and took a seat at the table. Jimmy folded his long body into the seat beside hers. Sonja picked up her drink and swirled the small straw in it. "Why don't you stay and hang out longer?"

"Wish I could." He leaned forward and ran a finger along the back of her hand. "My brother is ready to go, and I guess he ran into someone he knows from work here."

Her skin tingled from his touch, and for the love of heaven and all things holy, she wanted him to touch her again. "We live in two different worlds."

He shrugged, sat back and crossed his arms. "And?"

"I'm too old. Why would you want to call me or have coffee with me?"

"Bah, with the too-old excuse. What are you? Eighty?"

She laughed and shook her head. When she first ran into him—literally—he'd pissed her off, and now he kept making her laugh. It intrigued her. Made her *want* him to call her. But that wasn't a good idea. In fact, it was a really foolish one. "I'm forty-one, divorced, and I have a fifteen-year-old daughter." There. She'd said it. "Still want my number?" Sonja sipped her drink, pleased with herself and quite sure he'd run as fast as lightning in the other direction. But she also thought it might suck if he did run. *What. The. Hell.* Had to be the booze scrambling her mind, making it bounce back and forth like a damn ping-pong ball, and sending her hormones into overdrive.

He grinned and leaned forward. "You're looking kinda smug right now."

She giggled and then groaned, rolling her eyes. *Jeez, I sound like I'm fourteen. Enough with the giggles.*

He laughed, too, his eyes smiling along with his lips. They debated the issue of seeing each other beyond this little encounter until his brother approached them again and attempted to drag James out of his seat. She realized he'd called him Jimmy.

James stood and held out his hand. "Card, Sonja. New York is a big city. Don't make me have to track you down."

"You think you could?"

"Count on it. Card."

"Fine." She pulled her purse from beneath the pile of sweaters and other purses in the center of the table. "I can't believe I'm doing this." She shook her head and handed him the business card.

"Bergman and Bergman. Sonja Martin, Criminal Defense Attorney. Well, that sure as hell explains a lot." He snorted.

She frowned and stood. "What's that supposed to mean?"

"Fire and ice, baby." He kissed her cheek. "Talk to you soon, Sonja-the-lawyer."

"If you must, James-the-artist." She gazed into his eyes. "What the hell does fire and ice mean?"

"You'll see." He smirked and walked away.

She touched her cheek where he'd kissed her. Had she just given her business card and phone number to a thirty-year-old tattooed and pierced artist? Yes, she most certainly had. Sonja shook her head, blew out a harsh breath and watched him disappear into the crowd.

CHAPTER THREE

Jimmy settled into an alcohol-induced haze, sitting next to a hot little brunette at the diner he'd gone to with his brother and Maiya. Both women were covered in tats, which was no big thing to him. What *was* fucking weird was Ryan, aka Mr. Abercrombie & Fitch, down to his toes, flirting and looking at the chick, Maiya, like she was the only woman on earth.

Since Ryan had gained custody of his son, his brother rarely dated. Maybe Ryan was looking to take his own walk on the wild side because this girl was *not* his brother's type whatsoever. But watching Ryan tease and flirt with the red-haired beauty next to him brought Sonja front and center in his cranium—not that he'd stopped thinking about her much since leaving Tangled.

"So, what do you do for a living?" the girl next to him asked.

What was her name again? *Oh yeah. Heather.* He stretched his arm out along the back of the booth. "You into art, Heather?"

"Dunno." She shrugged and leaned her head back onto his arm. "What kind of art?"

"All kinds, any kind. Art's not for everyone." His gaze wandered over her features. She had long, dark-brown, curly hair with a set of chocolate-brown eyes. Pretty, definitely pretty.

A vision of Sonja passed through his mind. She was tall, slender and blonde. Ryan had teased in the car on the way to the diner that she was *way* out of his league. He was right. But man, something about her sucker punched him right in the gut. And Christ, she was a real bitch at first, too, but it'd only served to spark his interest more. Jimmy shifted in the booth and swiped his hand through his hair.

"I like the art at Tangled. Does that count?"

"You get a gold star." He touched the tip of her nose. "That'd be what I do."

"No shit, really? How fucking cool." She smoothed her palm up his thigh.

He looked at her hand and then back to her face. "Find something you like there?"

"Mmhmm, yeah."

Jimmy ran his hand through his hair again, torn for the first time about fucking a woman. Shit, Heather was fine enough: nice body, pretty face, tats and piercings. The whole package—his *usual* one-night-stand package. No fuss, no muss. Pushing all thoughts of Sonja out of his mind, he slid Heather's hand higher on his thigh.

"You 'bout ready to get out of here?" Ryan asked.

"I'm gonna catch a ride with Heather back to the hotel. You planning on meeting me there?" Jimmy pulled his wallet from his back pocket.

Ryan looked at Maiya. "I don't know. Maiya, am I meeting him there later?" She smiled but said nothing. "Tell you what." Ryan glanced at Jimmy again. "I'll shoot you a text if I am heading your way, cool?"

"I'll leave my phone on." Jimmy tossed thirty bucks on the table and got up, pulling Heather with him.

"Talk to you later, Heather," Maiya said.

"Count on it," Heather called out behind them.

Jimmy fussed with the radio while Heather drove in the direction of his hotel. She chattered on, oblivious to his apparent lack of attention to what she was saying.

When they arrived, he dragged her into the bar, did a shot and drank another Guinness. May as well prime his buzz again. He had a feeling that if he didn't, he was going to send this bundle of hotness back where she came from. Heather smiled and giggled about everything he said. Was he always this funny? Nope, probably not.

"Let's go." Taking her by the hand, he led her to his room. After getting the door open and pulling her inside, he closed them in and stepped toward her.

A coy smile arched Heather's lips. "What next?"

"How flexible are you?"

"I can do a split. Does that count?"

"Can you now?" Jimmy pressed close to her body and ran his hands down her lower back to her ass. He bent forward and gripped the underside of her ass cheeks, picked her up and urged her thighs around his hips. Then he kissed her.

Sonja's face slammed into his mind, and the feel of her fingertip tracing the ink on his neck rolled through him—the recollection so vivid his skin tingled.

Heather hiked herself up higher, using his shoulders for leverage and chased after his tongue with her own.

Nope. No.

Not happening.

Shit.

Come on! Don't be a dumbass! Jimmy broke the kiss and laid her on the bed. He pulled away and removed his shirt. He was fucking doing this!

"Holy fuck! Those are incredible." Sitting up, Heather raised her hand to his chest. "I had no idea you had this much work hiding under your clothes."

"Thanks." He looked at her fingers on his skin and then up at the ceiling. They didn't feel anything like Sonja's. *Fuck me.*

Heather traced the intricate lines of the Asian dragon's tail inked into the flesh of his neck and down over the dragon's body, adorning his shoulder and chest. She continued her exploration to his abs, and when her fingers met the top of his pants, she tugged open his belt.

He grabbed her hand, stopping her. "You know, honey. I think maybe…"

"Maybe what?"

Dammit. Frustration burned through him. Bending forward, he kissed her again, trying for all it was worth to get the damn lawyer out of his head. Yet there she was. Front and fucking center, smiling with her blue eyes. *What the hell?* Jimmy kissed Heather harder but abruptly pulled away when she moaned. Christ, his dick wasn't even hard. Nope. This was *not* happening. "I think maybe you should go."

"But… I thought…"

"Yeah, I know." He pulled her up from the bed. "I'm sorry. A little too much booze. You know how that is, right? Totally not you." He walked her to the hotel room door.

"But… Are you sure? I mean, I can try and…" She turned and cupped his dick through his jeans. "I'd be happy to—"

Jimmy cringed and pulled her hand away. "I bet you would. That's not necessary, though. But, hey, thanks for the offer." He forced a smile and opened the door.

"Oh… Um…" She shrugged, a confused look on her face. "Well, it was really nice meeting you."

Damn, the last thing he wanted to do was hurt this chick's feelings, but it wasn't going to happen tonight. Or ever, actually. "It was really nice meeting you, too. You'll be okay getting home, right? You good to drive, or should I call you a cab?"

"Nah, I'm good." She gave him a crooked smile and walked out of the room.

Jimmy watched while she made her way down the hotel corridor. She didn't look back, and that was for the best. He blew out a breath and closed the door. Pressing his back against the cold metal panel, he ran his fingers through his hair.

Damn. Did he really just do that? Turn down sex with a hot chick? *I sure as hell did.* Jimmy walked deeper into the room and stripped off the rest of his clothes. He stretched out in the empty bed, propped his hands beneath his head and stared up at the white ceiling. What was Sonja-the-lawyer doing right now? With any luck, she was thinking about him, like he was her. A woman like that—Jimmy's heart pounded in his ears—out of his league for sure, but damn if that made one bit of difference.

CHAPTER FOUR

SONJA LEANED BACK IN THE FIRST-CLASS SEAT ON HER FLIGHT home and closed her eyes. Ginny hadn't stopped talking since takeoff but had finally—thank God—started reading a magazine. Bless the silence because she needed a nap. After drinking too much and being up half the night, Sonja had reached her limit.

"He's definitely going to call you."

That didn't last long. Irritation prickled the back of Sonja's neck. "Will you drop it already, Ginny?"

"You're not interested; it's fine. Give him my number when he calls."

Sonja opened her eyes and glared at her friend. "You have *got* to be kidding me, right?"

"What? I'm totally serious. He's James Donnelly, for God's sake. You don't want him. He's not even your type; you said so yourself. I'll take him off your hands." Ginny faced forward again, brushed her long auburn hair over her shoulder and flipped another page of her magazine. "Consider it a favor."

"I didn't... I am not... I can't believe you just..." Sonja snapped her head forward and glared at the back of the seat in front of her. "Seriously? A favor?" Frustration pulsed through her. She pinched the bridge of her nose and blew out a breath. "Really? Stop talking. Just stop."

"You're so touchy. Take a nap, okay?" She patted Sonja's hand.

Sonja jerked her hand away. "That's exactly what I've been trying to do for the last hour, except you won't shut up about the *spectacular* James Donnelly. For the last time, will you just drop it, please?"

"Soorrryyy! Jeez, Sonja." Ginny frowned and looked back at her magazine.

"I'll be right back." Sonja stood and headed for the bathroom. Once inside, she splashed cold water on her face and took a couple deep breaths. She wasn't going to hear from him; she was quite sure. She didn't intend to contact him—not like she could anyway—he hadn't given her his number or business card. *Typical playboy.* Though she hadn't asked him for it either.

Once they landed at JFK, Sonja said goodbye to Ginny. After retrieving her luggage from baggage claim, she made her way outside and let out a sigh when she saw the limo driver waiting, sign in hand with her name on it.

"Ms. Martin." He nodded and grabbed her bags from her.

Sonja took in his salt-and-pepper hair, his broad shoulders and solid frame. He was a good-looking man, at least six feet tall. No tattoos. However, he could be hiding them. No visible piercings—doubtful he had any of those hiding. Nothing colorful about him at all, really.

He was probably older than she was, too. The man was, without a doubt, more her type than James Donnelly had been. Although she'd noticed and appreciated the limo driver's good looks, Sonja was thoroughly uninterested.

Once they were on their way, she busied herself perusing the many emails that had arrived during the five-hour flight from Vegas. After she flagged the ones needing attention,

Sonja set her phone down and stared out the window at the city lights whizzing by.

She'd been gone since Wednesday evening, and her live-in housekeeper and occasional babysitter had been keeping an eye on her daughter. Maybe Casey would come out of her room and enjoy some ice cream with her. A little mother-daughter time to catch up on anything going on at school or whatever else her daughter might be inclined to share. Which wasn't usually much.

They pulled into the underground garage of her building on Park Avenue, and Sonja let out a sigh. The driver insisted on walking her upstairs so she didn't have to pull her suitcase herself. It wasn't necessary, but she didn't argue. It was just easier to go along with what he wanted.

The elevator dinged when they reached the fifteenth floor, and Sonja stepped off, heading for her front door. She'd grown up in this co-op, and her father had transferred it to her name when he retired and moved to Connecticut six years ago.

Setting her keys in the small crystal dish on the sideboard in the entryway, she turned and took her suitcase from the driver and handed him a generous tip. "Thank you. I can manage from here."

He smiled, his warm brown eyes crinkling at the edges. "Quite welcome. Will you be needing anything else tonight?"

"Thank you. No." She tilted her head to the side, taking in his features again. Yes, still handsome. No, still no spark.

Nodding, he stepped back from the door. "Have a good night, Ms. Martin."

"You as well." The house was quiet, as usual. Maybe the maid was in the kitchen or asleep in her room. It was a little past nine o'clock—too early for Casey to be asleep yet.

Once in her bedroom, Sonja made quick work of unpacking before removing her clothes and then went into the bathroom and took her hair down from the up-twist it'd been in all day—but then pulled it into a loose ponytail. She rarely wore it down. After she finished, Sonja made her way down the long hall to her daughter's bedroom and knocked. She opened the door and peeked in. "Casey?"

"Yeah?" Casey glanced up for a brief moment from the iPad positioned on top of a pillow on her lap.

"I'm home." Sonja stepped in and, closed the door and then took a seat on the edge of the bed.

Casey's long hair hung loosely around her shoulders. She was a brunette, like her father, but the teenage years had hit hard, and Casey had started coloring her hair black with all sorts of other colors mixed in. This month, it was bright, electric blue.

Casey brushed her bangs out of her eyes. "I heard the door."

"I missed you. Did you have a good weekend?"

Her daughter shrugged, keeping her attention on the screen. "It was all right, I guess."

"Did you go to synagogue on Friday night?"

"No. I didn't feel like it." Casey tapped the device with her fingertips, typing something Sonja couldn't see.

Sonja sighed. "Honey, you know it's important you go."

Her daughter shrugged again, apparently uninterested in anything Sonja was saying. Girls, more specifically teenaged girls, could be a handful. Hormones and whatever else they happened to have issue with at the moment made for difficult relations. After a few beats of uncomfortable silence, Sonja stood and gathered a pile of dirty clothes from the floor and tossed them in the hamper in Casey's closet.

Turning, she looked around her daughter's bedroom. Posters of bands she'd never heard of littered the walls. Walls that at one time had been pink when Sonja occupied it as a child on through her young adult years, until she'd gone to college.

Now, the walls were a muted gray color. Drab and depressing, but what her daughter had requested two years ago. Sonja had protested, but in the end, she'd had the room painted for her. It was just easier. Same went for the hair *and* the thick, dark eyeliner Casey wore around her eyes. It was a phase. That's what Sonja kept telling herself anyway. It was only a phase. Normal for kids these days. "Want to have some ice cream with me?"

The offer got Casey's attention. She paused her typing and looked at Sonja. Her pale, ice-blue eyes, lined like a cat's, sparkled in the dim light of the room. "I guess." Casey set the pad aside and moved off the bed.

Sonja smiled and opened the door for them. "I think we have some chocolate syrup in the fridge still."

After dishing up two big bowls of cookie dough ice cream, she covered both with a generous layer of warmed chocolate syrup. She topped them with whipped cream and a cherry and slid Casey's across the center island to her.

Casey grabbed a spoon, stuck it in the mountain of ice cream and moved toward the door with a mumbled, "Thanks."

"Wait. Don't you want to eat it in here with me? I was…" Sonja set her own bowl on the counter. "I was hoping we might sit and chat."

Casey turned around. "About what?" She spooned some whipped cream into her mouth.

"I don't know. Anything, I guess. About your week or mine, maybe?" Sonja felt at a complete loss, and disappointment settled heavy in her stomach. The gap between her and Casey stretched wider every day. Sonja had no idea how to navigate it. When her daughter started acting out last year, Sonja had gotten her into therapy, but it wasn't working. Things were not getting better.

"Nah." Casey spooned in a mouthful of ice cream and swallowed. "Maybe another time. I'm gonna go back to my room."

"All right." Sonja let out a resigned sigh and sat at the island. "You're welcome."

"Yeah. Thanks for the ice cream, Mom." Casey licked her spoon and left the room.

Things were definitely not getting better.

CHAPTER FIVE

JIMMY STEPPED INTO HIS APARTMENT IN GREENWICH VILLAGE after an exhausting flight from Los Angeles. Actually, the flight wasn't too bad, but the last week in L.A. had been tiring. He'd ended up being in Los Angeles just over four weeks.

He'd stayed an additional week to take care of his nephew, Jacob, while Ryan ran out to Vegas to help his girl—at least she was supposed to be his girl. Jimmy wasn't sure if his brother was going to figure out the mess Ryan called a relationship or not.

Since his brother had finally let go of his fear of getting involved with someone again, he seemed to know what and who he wanted. Now Ryan's chickie, Maiya, needed to figure her side out. Hopefully, they'd get it all together, and shit would work out for them. Sure would be nice to see his brother happy and settled after so many years of madness. Ryan deserved it.

Jimmy climbed the spiral metal stairs leading to his loft bedroom, dropped his bag in front of his dresser and flopped on his bed, intent on closing his eyes for only a minute. He'd taken a red-eye home, and it was barely ten in the morning.

Shit, he didn't even get up this early after getting a full night's sleep.

Norton, his cat, jumped up next to him and started mewling with requests for attention and probably food. His neighbor, Mrs. Lansky, had been taking care of the cat while he'd been away. Stroking Norton's black fur from his head to tail, he then scratched under his chin. The cat rewarded him with a resounding purr and kneaded Jimmy's belly. After a few minutes, Norton finally settled, curling up in the crook of Jimmy's arm.

The next thing Jimmy heard was the sound of his cell ringing. Rubbing his eyes, he peered at the clock on his bedside table. Two p.m. He snorted. *Damn, long minute.* Rolling to his side, he reached for the phone, which had stopped ringing. He swiped his thumb across the screen, and Norton jumped off the bed. Jimmy pulled up the missed calls and saw it was his brother. Hitting the *Send* button, he rose from the bed and walked downstairs.

"Thanks for letting me know you got home okay."

Jimmy chuckled. "Sorry, *Dad*. I fell asleep when I got home."

"Whatever. You're lucky I didn't call Mom and let her know I hadn't heard from you."

"You're right. Totally lucky." He stifled a yawn behind his palm. "Seriously, though, I did fall asleep, and it was too early to call you anyway."

"I figured."

Jimmy knew the resigned tone he heard in his brother's voice had more to do with his chickie than it did him. It worried him. "You hear from her yet?"

His brother sighed. "Nope."

"Sorry, man. That sucks." Jimmy picked at the pile of mail on his countertop.

"Is what it is."

"Yeah, I guess so. All right, let me go. I got a pile of mail I need to sort. Hungry too. Give Jacob a hug from me?"

"Will do."

"Hey, Ry?"

"Hmm?"

"Keep your head up."

"Thanks."

Jimmy disconnected the call and set the phone down. He scooped up the pile of mail and moved to the small dining table. Pulling his wallet from his back pocket, he tossed it on the table. The end of a white business card sticking out of his billfold caught his eye. He slid the card from its hiding place.

Bergman and Bergman. Sonja Martin, Esq. Criminal Defense.

He'd thought about Sonja-the-lawyer several times over the last four weeks, but he hadn't called her. Not that he'd forgotten about it, just that whole out-of-sight, out-of-mind thing. Maybe she'd be up for dinner. Hell, it was worth a shot, right? Scooping up his phone, Jimmy stared at the card in his hand. He hesitated a moment—*chicken shit*—and dialed the office line rather than her cell.

"Bergman and Bergman. How may I direct your call?"

"Ah, yeah. Sonja Martin, please?" Jimmy rose from his seat.

"I'm sorry; she's in court. Would you like to leave a message?"

"Which court?"

"Are you one of her clients?"

"No, ma'am." He cleared his throat. "My name is James Donnelly. She was interested in commissioning a piece of art from me." *What's a little white lie, right?*

"Why don't I take your number, and I'll let her know you called?"

Jimmy pinched the bridge of his nose. *Think. Think.* "Sure, that'd be fine. I just figured… Wait, it's public record, isn't it? I mean…the court cases and stuff. I want to—you know what? I'll just call her cell. Thanks."

"As you wish, Mr. Donnelly. Anything else I can—"

Jimmy disconnected the call before the receptionist finished speaking. Not that he wanted to be rude, but he needed to mentally prep for his next move. Pacing the entryway hall, he wiped his sweating palm on his thigh and dialed her cell.

The phone rang in his ear, and nervous tension raced through his blood. What the hell was his problem? What was with this sudden case of the nerves? Blowing out a breath, he realized exactly what his problem was. He wasn't worried she wouldn't answer because she was busy; more that, Sonja *would* answer only to hang up on him as soon as she heard his voice, that's what.

Third ring. Fourth. Voicemail. And then…her voice.

Hello, you've reached the voicemail of Sonja Martin, with the law office of Bergman and Bergman. Today is Wednesday, September nineteenth, and I will be at the Midtown Community Court until five p.m. Please leave a message, and I'll return your call as soon as I'm available. Thank you.

Jimmy disconnected the call before the beep. "Bingo."

He glanced at the clock. Two thirty. Plenty of time to grab a shower and head to the courthouse. The prospect of seeing her again set his stomach into a fit of knots. Damn, he never got nervous like this over women. *Get a friggin' grip, dude.* He felt like a teenager, for fuck's sake.

Within an hour, Jimmy stood outside the six-story nineteenth-century building. The place looked carved out of the Renaissance era, complete with tan columns framing the second- and third-story windows and a limestone face on the main level. Running his fingers through his hair to ensure it still held its messy, fell-out-of-bed quality, he took a deep breath and walked through the main entrance. How hard could it be to find one very tall, very beautiful blonde attorney?

After emptying his pockets and walking through the necessary metal detectors and security screenings, Jimmy found it wasn't hard at all. The court had one, and only one courtroom. *Score.* He stepped to the entryway, closing off the courtroom from the main hall and listened. Hearing faint voices, he gently opened the door and peered inside.

There she was, standing at the front, addressing the judge. Jimmy sucked in a breath at the sight of the back of her blonde head and moved quietly inside. Careful to not let the door slam behind him, he stood still, bracing it with his hands until it slid closed. Then he moved to his right and took a seat in the back row.

Sonja spoke with a calculated, direct tone to the judge, and her voice spread over Jimmy's skin like a warm blanket. She sounded different than her voicemail message and also from how he remembered when they met, but then again, they had been in a loud bar. Plus, he'd been a tad intoxicated.

Jimmy grinned, recalling what a bitch she'd been when they first met. She had the same air about her now—stunning, with a hint of the attitude he found so intriguing.

Fire and ice.

She wore a black pencil skirt fitted to her knees and a black blazer with a pale peach blouse beneath it. Her hair was pulled tight in the same twist on the back of her head she'd had in Vegas. And stiletto heels.

Jimmy ran his palm over his chin, smoothing his goatee and smothering a groan. The heels were his downfall. Hell, who was he kidding? Everything about this woman was his downfall, but looking at her long, shapely legs perched on five-inch, black, spiked heels made his blood boil at temperatures that couldn't possibly be safe.

He stretched his legs out in front of him and watched

Sonja-the-lawyer argue the next three cases. The first was a possession of marijuana charge, the next, harassment and the final, prostitution. She debated her points with the judge on every case and got what she wanted for each client. Astounding.

The woman had talent, and you couldn't say it was her looks because the judge didn't seem to notice. The guy barely looked up from the stack of papers in front of him. She had a presence about her, an air of dominance, and strangely, a softness that commanded attention. Considering these were small-time cases, she argued with a skill rivaling his father's. She'd be a force to be reckoned with on something bigger. Did she handle anything bigger? Jimmy wanted to know so much more about her. He wanted to know everything about her…if he could. If she'd let him.

"Court adjourned."

Jimmy looked up at the judge in time to see him slam the gavel on its little wooden disk with a resounding *crack* and rise from his seat. The many onlookers stood and started milling out of the room, some deep in conversation, a few already making calls on their cell phones. Jimmy stayed where he was, catching glimpses of her through the people crossing in front of him in the other rows of seats and the center walkway.

Sonja slung the strap of a large black leather soft-sided case over her shoulder and turned to exit down the center aisle, her focus on the screen of her cell phone. When she got next to him, Jimmy clasped her upper arm.

She stopped, glanced down at her arm and then up at him. Her baby blues widened in recognition. "Well, Mr. Donnelly. I have to say, I didn't think I'd be seeing you again."

Jimmy stepped closer to her. The nervous tension was back, and his mouth was dry. *Chill. You got this.* He had to play his cards right. She'd bolt the first chance she got, and he wasn't going to let that happen. Tilting his head to the side, he took in her prominent cheekbones and her full lips before returning his gaze to her eyes. "Sure you did."

Sonja set her heavy leather bag on the bench. It was a good diversion tactic. She'd take any opportunity to catch her breath and gather her scattering thoughts. James Donnelly was in front of her, and as a result, every part of her body was on fire.

What was it about this young guy that made her feel like she was standing too close to a fireplace? Yes, he was good-looking. *Really good looking.* Yes, he had a nice body. *Really nice body.* But it wasn't like she didn't see attractive men on a regular basis in the City. She did. She saw them often and didn't have this sort of reaction to them.

Sonja pressed her palm to her forehead, looked at him and felt…annoyed.

James had that devilish smile on his face, bringing his dimples front and center. The ones she couldn't quite wipe from her memory. He was wrong. Sonja truly hadn't thought she'd be seeing him again. Hoped, sure. But she wasn't going to admit it to him. That information was between her and her showerhead. Sonja crossed her arms and leaned a hip against the bench next to her. "Presumptuous as ever."

"It's nice to see you again, too."

Keeping this exchange formal and professional was paramount. The last thing she wanted was to continue what'd started between them in Las Vegas weeks ago. "What are you doing here?"

"I told you I wanted to see you again. So, here I am." James put his hands in his pockets and shrugged. "Coffee or something, remember?"

"That was four weeks ago." She grabbed her bag and settled the strap on her shoulder. "I think we're past that now." Sonja turned to walk away and made it as far as the doors.

He cupped her elbow, urged her backward a bit and

pushed the door open for her. "Hey, now. You missed me. I get it."

She ignored the rush of heat from his touch, cut him a sideways glance and walked through the exit. James followed and then moved beside her and placed his hand on the small of her back. Sonja stepped to the side to evade his touch. He needed to stop touching her. She was already burning up—maybe she was having a hot flash? Pre-menopause? She could only hope because the idea that it was his touch making her smolder had her even more agitated than she already was. She simply didn't respond to *any* man like this. "I assure you, Mr. Donnelly, I most certainly did not miss you."

"Liar." He bumped her shoulder with his and pressed the *Down* button for the elevator.

Sonja groaned and shook her head. "I told you in Vegas. I'm too old for you. Don't you have women closer to your age you can bother?"

The elevator doors opened, and James cleared his throat. "As a matter of fact, I do. But I'm thinking you'll be more fun." He held his hand out, motioning for her to step inside the empty car.

She gasped and stepped in. The brushed steel doors closed, and she pressed her lips together. Did he really just say that? Fine. He could be a smart ass all he wanted. It would make this all the easier. "Look, Mr. Donnelly. It's obvious to me our little exchange in Las Vegas meant more to you than it did me. I'm flattered, really. But I think it's best you go play with those other girls. This *woman* has no time for your fun."

The bell announcing the ground floor dinged. *Perfect timing.* Shifting her bag on her hip, she exited the elevator. Sonja didn't look back this time and assumed he wasn't following. Her retort had to have stung. Good. *Damn.*

She didn't care.

Really, she didn't. *Crap.* Did she?

Sonja stepped onto the busy rush-hour-clogged sidewalk

and fanned herself. The evening air was chilly, but it wasn't doing a damn thing to cool her off. Setting her bag down, she removed her suit jacket.

"Let me carry this for you." Jimmy bent and picked up her briefcase. "I think we should have dinner tonight. You look hungry."

"Can't you take a hint?"

James wrapped his arm around her waist and pulled her tight against his chest. Her breath gushed out when their bodies collided. Hard, lean muscles pressed to her chest, stomach and hips. Good God, she was going to burn alive.

"I can take hints just fine, Sonja-the-lawyer." His lips were so close to hers, almost touching, but not quite.

If she breathed too deep, they'd be kissing. Sonja froze. She couldn't kiss him. Could not. "What are you doing?"

"I'm taking every hint you're passing me. You want me just as bad as I want you. I can practically feel it rolling off you in waves."

Sonja licked her lips and inhaled slowly. "I don't..." Despite her frustration, her body softened in his embrace, and traitorous nerve endings vibrated to attention. She cursed herself and dug her nails into his arms. "You can't..."

"You do. And I can." He nipped her bottom lip before releasing her.

Every inch of Sonja's skin came alive, tingling from the contact, and her ability to think straight short-circuited. She let her breath out in a rush and gulped in another, seeking oxygen to fill her body in order to calm down. He stood before her, an intent look in his eyes; their gazes locked. *What the hell am I going to do with him?*

"Let's go get a burger. There's a great place in the Village. You'll love it." He smiled.

Say no, Sonja. Say no. "Fine. Dinner. But that's it. And stop telling me what to do, dammit. I don't know where you get off thinking you can order me around, Mr. Donnelly. I won't tolerate it."

"Call me James." He walked past her to the curb and hailed a cab.

Sonja stepped next to him and smoothed the back of her hair. *Arrogant jerk.* Her heart raced. She ran her tongue over her bottom lip—she could still feel the little sting from his bite. His scent of clean soap with a hint of cologne lingered in her nose—her weakness. But then again, James Donnelly seemed to personify her weakness.

He opened the cab door.

"Just dinner." She took another deep breath and got inside the cab.

CHAPTER SIX

Jimmy sat across from Sonja and watched while she tried for all it was worth to look proper eating a messy, bacon double cheeseburger. She hadn't wanted the layers of sloppy goodness and protested at every turn, but he'd ordered it anyway.

The woman was uptight. Actually, she made uptight look like child's play. Not that it deterred him. After all, he lived in New York City, for fuck's sake. "Bitch" was a theme there among almost all women. The difference with Sonja was the fire burning in her eyes. It was a blaze she kept carefully contained, and Jimmy wanted to set it free and watch it burn. "You got a little something there." Leaning across the table, he swiped the drop of ketchup off her chin with his thumb and then sucked it between his lips.

Sonja froze a moment before visibly swallowing her mouthful. "Thanks." She wiped her lips with her napkin.

He smiled and leaned back in his chair, tilting it back on two legs. "My pleasure."

"You're staring."

"I know."

She widened her eyes. "Stop."

"No." He let the chair fall forward. "Guess you're going to have to get used to it. I like staring at you."

She rolled her eyes and took another bite of the burger.

"So, do you always fight small cases at Midtown, or do you handle anything bigger?"

"Why? Do you need an attorney?"

He laughed. "No. But if I do, I'm definitely calling you."

"I own the firm." She sipped her soda. "I handle whatever I want."

"Nice. What're you doing with those piddly cases then?"

"Once a month, I do pro bono service for the community."

"Why, Sonja-the-lawyer, that's quite generous of you. Someone might think you have a heart." He raised his brows.

"Ha. Ha. Very funny." She shook her head. "Tell me about your art."

"My tattoos or the art I create?"

Sonja wiped her hands on her napkin. "Both, I guess. Start with the art you create."

"Sure." He picked up a french fry and dragged it through the ketchup. "I dabble in a lot of different styles, but most all of it has an industrial theme."

"You weld things. Sculptures and such?"

"I've been known to wield a blow torch on occasion, yeah." He popped the fry in his mouth and then licked his fingers. She watched him. Her gaze flicked from his mouth back to his eyes in the space of a second, but she'd watched just the same.

"Tell me about the different styles." She took the last bite of her burger.

"I like to paint, so I usually construct various items, mount them to a canvas and paint around them. Sometimes I paint the items, too."

"I see. Where do the ideas come from?"

Jimmy leaned forward, crossing his arms in front of him

on the table. "Different things, really. The City's a big muse. The lights, the sounds, the smells—it all plays a part. Sometimes it's music, and sometimes it's people."

She sipped her soda. "The art in the bar in Vegas? Was it all yours or just some?"

"Most everything in there was mine. What did you think of it?"

"I don't have an eye for art, but I found it interesting." Sonja pushed her basket aside and wiped her hands on her perfectly folded napkin. "My tastes are probably too old-fashioned for you."

"I'm sure you think so. Come on." Jimmy stood and held out his hand for her. "I'll show you some. My studio's right around the corner."

"Is that why you insisted on us coming here to eat?" She stood and reached for her bag, but Jimmy grabbed it before she could.

"Not exactly. But now that you're here, I'd love to show you." He took her hand and pulled her toward the door, settling his palm on her lower back.

Jimmy loved how petite Sonja felt beneath his touch, yet it was an illusion. She stood almost eye-to-eye with him. Jimmy's palm itched to wrap around her side and pull her close, but he didn't dare. He'd already pushed her to her limit outside the courthouse when he'd pulled her body close. She'd been so warm and soft against him, Jimmy thought he might spontaneously combust.

And the smarter her mouth got, the faster his adrenaline pumped. It made him want to bend her over his knee and spank her bare ass while she spouted every sarcastic comment she could think of, until finally begging him to stop. Jimmy groaned at the vision the thought conjured.

"Everything okay?"

He stroked her lower back with his thumb while they

waited for the light to change at the crosswalk. "Yup. Every-thing's perfect."

She looked over at him and drew in a breath. He focused on her full lips when she exhaled. A bolt of lust zinged down his spine. Jimmy wanted to taste those lips. The sexual tension was building between them. How he was going to keep his hands off her once they were alone in his studio, he didn't know. They crossed the street, and Sonja's cell rang. Jimmy steered them to the inner side of the sidewalk.

Sonja dug her phone out of her purse and put it to her ear. "Yes, Casey?" They continued walking, but her steps slowed. "What? No. You were supposed to be home thirty minutes ago. Where are you?"

Jimmy turned to look at her when she stopped walking. He pulled her to the side and then turned his back, trying to give her some privacy, but he wasn't going to walk away from her. She'd have to deal with it.

"Are his parents home…? Casey Olivia Martin, I *told* you I did *not* want you going over to that boy's house when his parents aren't there."

He glanced over his shoulder at her. She was visibly upset, her brows drawn together in frustration.

"Get home now… No. No!" She shook her head and turned away from him. "I will ground you if your behind isn't home in the next thirty minutes, and believe me, I will be calling your father about this one. I've had enough of your defiance. Get home now." Sonja pulled the phone from her ear. Her shoulders sank, and her head fell forward.

Jimmy cupped her elbow in his palm. "Hey, you okay?"

Sonja pulled her arm away. "Yes. Perfectly fine." She let out a breath and shoved the phone back in her purse before turning back toward him. Squaring her shoulders, she stood in a defensive stance, ready to take on the world if necessary. "You've got fifteen minutes to show me your studio, but then you'll have to excuse me."

He put his hands in his pockets and gazed over her face, down her neck and shoulders, and to her legs. "That call sounded pretty upsetting. Care to share?"

Her eyes widened and deepened into a slate-blue color. *Fire and ice.* This was how it would be with them. He knew it like he knew his own name, but there was no doubt in his mind she didn't have a clue. Yet.

She turned toward the street. "Don't push me on this, James. It's none of your concern. I should just go now."

"Look, you don't want to tell me, then don't. But I don't want you to go yet. We're already here, so let's keep going. You can fight with me upstairs if you want."

She glared over her shoulder. "I'm not fighting with you."

"Yeah, you are. All good, Sonja. It's our version of fore-play." He smirked and held out his hand to her.

"You're twisted."

"Maybe a little. Come on." He nodded to his outstretched hand, and after a long pause, she finally took it.

They walked the remainder of the way in silence, hand-in-hand, turning the corner at the end of the block. Half a block later, they were in front of his building. He glanced at the metal door. Well, he'd gotten her to his studio. Fuck if he knew what to do with her next.

CHAPTER SEVEN

Sonja stepped through the doorway of his building. It was clean and bright, which was a pleasant surprise. Nervous energy ran like a river from her palms to her chest and down to her stomach. *What the hell am I doing?* Was she really going to his studio? Alone?

They entered the elevator, and she drew in a breath. *It's just his studio, not his apartment or anything.* She'd check out some of his art and be on her way. She had Casey to deal with, after all. Her daughter was really beginning to push Sonja past her limits.

The elevator moved at a snail's pace, and while she watched each floor number light up one at a time, James watched her. In fact, he only seemed to take his eyes off her when necessary. It bothered her. Like she was some sort of bug under a microscope or something. "You're staring again."

"Get used to it."

She smoothed her hand up the back of her hair. "I don't intend to get used to anything."

He chuckled, and the masculine sound of it spread through her like warm honey. The elevator dinged, signaling his floor. *Thank God.* They'd only risen six floors, but the trip felt like they'd gone sixty.

"To your left. Last door."

"All right." Sonja stepped into the hall and walked in the direction he'd directed.

Again, he moved right next to her, his hand pressed to her lower back. She liked it more than she wanted to admit. The warmth of his insistent touch rekindled the memory of how he'd grabbed her outside the courthouse. How he'd nipped her bottom lip. She'd wanted him to kiss her. Which was crazy because, at the same time, she wanted to slap his face and push him away. The man made her mind fuzzy, made her want things she normally never wanted. Especially from someone like him.

When they reached the door, James dug his keys from his front pocket. He unlocked the door and pushed it open, motioning for her to enter. The first thing she noticed in the entry hall was a small side table. A few sculptured clay bowls sat atop it. One bowl held keys and other miscellaneous items. The second thing she noticed was the beautiful, dark mahogany wood floor stretching out before her.

James set his keys in the bowl on the small table. "Can I get you something to drink?"

"You have a refrigerator?" She shrugged. "I guess that makes sense. Water, if you have it."

He moved past her and stepped through a doorway ahead on the left. She followed and peeked inside. It was a full kitchen. *Why does he have a full kitchen in his studio?* Sonja ventured farther down the hall until it opened into a large space. Complete with a small dining table tucked in the corner and beyond, a couch, a love seat, chair, ottoman, coffee table —*holy crap, this is his apartment!*

He placed her briefcase on the table and held out a bottle of water to her. "Here you go."

"I thought we were going to your studio."

"We are."

Confusion boomeranged in her mind. She took the offered bottle and opened it. "This is your apartment."

"Yup."

"James, did you think you could just take me back to your apartment and…what? What *did* you think exactly?"

He sipped his water. "This is my home, Sonja, and it's also my studio. Lighten up, would you? You're always so damn uptight."

"You said *your studio*. You failed to mention it was *also* your home."

"Fine. Guilty. Happy now? Drink your water and relax. My studio is downstairs." He turned away from her and headed for a set of stairs tucked against the wall.

"Fine." With a sigh, she followed and took each step down carefully in her heels. "Has anyone ever told you you're a jerk?"

He laughed. "A time or two, yeah."

"At least you're aware. I suppose there's hope for you then."

He flipped a light switch at the bottom of the steps, illuminating the space. "Sonja Martin, did you just make a joke?"

"It happens on occasion. Don't get too excited about it." Navigating the last step, she followed behind him into a large space with brick walls and a stained concrete floor.

"There's the girl I've barely come to know."

"Please, you don't know m—" A large canvas propped against the brick wall to her right caught her attention. It was smeared with red and yellow paint. Sonja took a moment and looked around, noticing the different pieces of his work in different stages of creation.

Against the far wall, which was made up entirely of windows, was a long table. Several pieces of scrap metal were scattered atop it. Some were car parts, from what she could tell, but others were unidentifiable. She moved to another piece on an easel to her left. There were intricate lines of what looked like copper wires that appeared to be welded together. The lines framed images painted on the canvas. A city skyline with a river in the distance and a bridge. It was almost elegant, in an odd sort of way.

"That's my latest commissioned piece. I need to have it done by this weekend."

"It's beautiful. Truly."

He stepped behind her, his body so close she felt the heat radiating off it. James placed his hands on her waist. "Thank you."

Sonja melted beneath his touch. "What else needs to be done to it?"

"It needs more shaping, more manipulation of the copper with my hands." His breath feathered over her ear, and he pressed his body against hers. At the same time, he ran his hands up her sides and then back down to her hips.

"How?" Her breath eased from her lips. She needed him to stop touching her. She didn't want him to ever stop.

"When I heat the metal, Sonja, it becomes pliable, soft." He moved his hands under her blazer and over her stomach. "It responds to my touch and lets me shape it."

She was shaking, quivering from the inside out. "Then what?"

"Then it becomes what I want it to be. What *it* needs and wants to be." He nipped her ear.

She swallowed past the lump in her throat. The tingle from his tender bite traveled down her neck to her spine, and she let her head fall back onto his shoulder. "Oh God."

"You're so fucking beautiful." He moved his hands up her stomach to under her breasts and kissed behind her ear, then explored her neck with his mouth and tongue, nipping her sensitive skin with his teeth.

Sonja reached back and ran her fingers through his hair. He was treating her like the metal he spoke of. Warming her in order to mold her the way he wanted. Heaven help her, she wanted to let him.

James turned her to face him, and the room spun around her in a daze of heady lust. He cupped her face in his palms. "Let me heat you up." He kissed her neck again. "I'll make you pliable, Sonja." He pressed his lips to her jaw and then her chin. "Say yes."

She'd closed her eyes at some point and only realized she'd done so when she opened them to gaze into pools of warm hazel. "Yes," she whispered.

"There's the fire." He tilted her head to the side and stroked his tongue over her bottom lip.

Sonja gripped the back of his neck, not sure if it was to keep from falling or because she wanted him closer. He moved his hands from her face and ran one palm down the front of her neck. He licked at her upper lip and ran his other hand up her back, pulling her tighter to him. His erection pressed against her through his jeans. "You're shaking."

Wetness coated her panties, and her clit throbbed. "Please…"

"Please what, Sonja?" He moved his hand lower, trailing his fingers over the juncture of her cleavage.

She swallowed. "Kiss me."

He said nothing else, just met her mouth with his own. Parting her lips with his tongue, he delved into stroke and tease. *Oh God. Oh God. I can't. I want. Please. James.* Sonja moaned and moved her hands higher on his neck, gripping the soft strands of his hair.

He backed her against the brick wall and deepened the kiss.

Yes, fire.

CHAPTER EIGHT

Jimmy drowned in the taste and feel of everything that
was Sonja Martin—kissing her, tasting her, seeking more. He
pressed her against the wall in his studio, and her perfect body
molded to his. She lit him up inside and out in ways he'd
never felt before.

In an attempt to slide one leg between hers, he met the
resistance of her long skirt. He moved his hands down her
hips and tugged at the tight material, raising it by inches in
order to allow her long legs to part and make room for
his own.

Sonja gasped against his lips when his thigh hit its
intended target and then shifted her hips forward ever so
slightly and rubbed against his leg. Fucking hell, she was
killing him. The heat between her legs spread over his thigh
and shot straight to his balls. Her little gasps for breath and
eager kitten moans had his prick hardening to a length of steel
in the confines of his jeans. He wanted to taste her everywhere
but couldn't bring himself to leave her hot mouth yet. The fire
that'd started between them was now a raging inferno. And he
wanted more.

Sonja was the first to break the kiss. Gasping for air, she

pressed her forehead against his. Jimmy ran one hand down to her thigh and raised it off the ground to rest against his hip. The movement forced her skirt higher. Perfect. He slid his fingers up the back of her sheer-nylon-covered leg and found bare skin—his knees went weak.

Jimmy glanced down and almost came in his jeans. She had on a set of thigh-high stockings and a garter belt. *Fuck me.* His cock got impossibly harder. And Jesus, her skin felt like silk. With a growl, he raised his thigh flush against her center.

Sonja moaned and rolled her hips. Oh, yeah, this was how he'd hoped she'd be with him. Jimmy braced himself against the wall with his forearm and toyed with the back of her thigh with his free hand, tracing lines back and forth below the crease of her butt cheek. Nipping her jaw, he moved his lips and tongue down her throat to her chest, exploring the skin exposed by the open neckline of her dress shirt. "Fuck, you taste like heaven and hell mixed together."

She said nothing. But he didn't need her to. Sonja's actions and reactions spoke volumes to him. She moved her hands underneath his shirt and scraped her nails up his back. He needed more. He wanted her naked beneath him. He wanted *her*—any way he could get her.

Right fucking now.

Jimmy glanced at her and then nuzzled the side of her neck. "Unbutton your shirt for me."

Her throat bobbed beneath his lips, and he knew her mind was racing, trying to decide which way to go with his request. He moved his thigh higher, forcing her to her tiptoes and rubbed against her core.

"James…" Sonja moaned and bit his shoulder.

"Yes?" He squeezed her thigh and returned his lips to her cleavage. How far would she go? Excitement raced through him, made him want to push further, keep her mindless. She wanted him. It was obvious. The evidence of it scorched him through the denim on the leg pressed to her pussy.

"Oh God. We should stop."

Jimmy slid his hand along her thigh to her hip and then continued up her stomach to the underside of one petite breast. "You really want me to stop, Sonja?"

"Yes. No… Yes." She dug her nails into his sides, and it was his turn to gasp.

He gripped her breast, dragging his thumb over the tight nipple poking through the fabric of her bra and dress shirt. "Fuck, woman! I want you."

She jerked against him, her hip making contact with his throbbing cock. Grinding against her, he squeezed her breast in his fingers.

"Dear God, what are you doing to me?" She rocked her hips, riding his thigh.

He left her breast to grip her ass and moved her against him again. Every muscle in his body was tight with arousal. He wanted her long legs wrapped around him. He wanted inside her pussy, knowing it would be tight like a glove and hotter than a kiln. He'd give anything to melt inside her heat. "I'm doing exactly what you want me to do. What you've fantasized about me doing since the night we met in Vegas. Admit it."

"No."

Panting for breath, he gazed into her eyes. "You're lying. Plead your case, counselor."

"What?"

"You heard me. I'm calling your bluff. You think I can't feel that hot box of yours weeping all over my thigh? Your hard nipples against my chest? I feel all of it. You want me. Say it."

"Fuck you."

"Perfect. Let's go upstairs."

"No." With an inferno blazing in her eyes, she bit her bottom lip and glared at him.

Jimmy moved his thigh from between her legs. She whimpered in protest but tried to stifle it. With a smirk, he cupped her pussy in his palm. "I feel how hot you are."

"So what? It's fucking biology. You're good-looking, and you certainly know how to use it to your advantage. Big deal. Anyone would respond this way."

Jimmy moved her panties aside and ran his fingers through her wet slit. "Is that so?" *What the hell am I doing?* Did he actually think fighting with this gorgeous creature was going to get her in his bed? He couldn't help it, though. Sonja said, "black," and he automatically said, "white". Maybe the fighting between them *was* foreplay. He'd been kidding when he'd said it upstairs, but he was starting to believe it might be true.

Sonja gasped and thrust her hips forward right before her eyes narrowed on him, and she went still as a statue. "It's the truth!" She shoved him away and pushed her skirt down her legs.

Damn, she *was* warm and wet. Ready for him, and he'd blown it. *Fuck!* Jimmy took another step back and rested his hands on his hips. Still panting—dick hard like a rod and heart galloping out of his chest—he swiped his hand over his goatee. "You're gorgeous when you get angry."

"Is that supposed to be a compliment?"

"Take it for what you want. You're beautiful even when you're not mad, but something changes in your eyes when you get angry at me, and it makes me want to pull that skirt up over your hips and fuck you senseless."

Pressing her hand to her chest, she gasped at his harsh words and glared at him. "I don't like you." She stepped away from the wall and walked toward the stairs.

"You may not like me, Sonja, but you want me as much as I want you. That much you can't deny."

"Have fun working off that hard-on. I'm going home, James."

He turned and followed her up the stairs. Christ, he was

an idiot. Her ass, right in his line of sight, made for a pleasant view at least. "I'll send you a text message when I'm done, let you know how good it was and how I called out your name the moment I came."

"You have got to be the rudest, most crude man I've ever met. I have criminal clients with more tact and respect than you."

"That may be true, too, but you still want me. And it pisses you off, doesn't it?"

They reached the top of the stairs, and she retrieved her briefcase. "This conversation is over, and coming here was a mistake I won't make again."

He went ahead to the front door and watched while she made her way down the hall toward him. Little strands of hair had fallen loose from her perfect updo, framing her oval face in perfection. "Have it your way. Next time, we'll go to your place."

She reached around him for the door handle. "There won't be a next time."

Jimmy placed his hand over hers, and when she froze, he stepped behind her, wrapped his arm around her waist and pressed his chest to her back. He ran his lips over the shell of her petite ear. "There will be a next time and many more times after that, Sonja."

She shivered in his arms, her breath leaving her lips in a soft gasp. "Let go of me."

"Never."

"James."

"For now. But this isn't over." He released her and took a step back.

She opened the door and walked out. Jimmy leaned against the doorjamb and watched her walk down the hall with graceful steps, even in her killer spiked heels. Sonja smoothed the back of her hair before pressing the button for the elevator.

She glanced over at him. Crossing his arms, he met her gaze. The elevator opened, she looked away and stepped inside the car. *Gone.* He shook his head, ran his fingers through his hair and went back in his apartment. This wasn't over, nowhere near over.

Jimmy made his way to the primary bathroom upstairs and turned on the shower. Cupping his palms over his mouth and nose, he took in the light trace of arousal and her perfume lingering on his hands. Her elegant scent was all over him, and his dick throbbed in his jeans at the teasing aroma.

He didn't want to wash it off, but he was so wound up he needed the release. And like he told her, he'd be calling out her name when he came. Sonja-the-lawyer had spawned a need in him that he wasn't willing to deny. She might be able to lie to herself and to him about what she wanted, but he knew better.

As he lifted his shirt to remove it, and the fabric passed over his face, Jimmy was subjected to the sweet scent of her once more. God help him. Stepping beneath the hot spray, he let the water roll over his hair and down his body.

Eventually, she'd give in. She had to.

CHAPTER NINE

Sonja spent the cab ride back to her apartment tortured by thoughts of James. Emotions vacillated between anger—at him and at herself—and being so damn aroused she could barely stand it. Shifting her legs, she crossed one over the other and shivered at the feel of the dampness coating her panties.

He'd done that to her. Nearly made her orgasm with only his thigh.

When his calloused hand teased the tender skin of the back of her thigh and then ventured to her breast, the room had spun around her, and she thought she might actually pass out—never mind what the erection pressing hard and eager against her hip did to her. Sonja touched her fingertips to her mouth.

The kiss... His lips, his tongue...

The kiss had been hotter than anything she'd ever experienced. She blew out a breath. When he shifted her panties aside and dragged his long fingers through her folds, it took every ounce of willpower to stop things from going any further. Of course, then he'd gone and pushed her, making it really easy for her to stop.

James had pissed her off. Pricked at her resistance to him. Who the hell did he think he was? That was a question she'd asked herself back in Vegas, too. Worse, why the hell was her body so interested in him? Damn early-forties hormones. Maybe she should sleep with him and sate the desire.

Sonja closed her eyes. The difference in their ages made her shudder. She might be single, but she was eleven years older than him. Forty-one. She was forty-one years old. Logically, there was no real hope of a relationship outside of sex, and maybe that was a good thing. Besides, he was a young, virile, sexy guy who clearly had his pick of any woman in the City.

Why, for God's sake, did he want her? She might not look her age, thanks to good genes, but that didn't really matter when it came down to simple facts. Bottom line? She was too old for him, and he was too young for her. On top of that, they had nothing in common.

It didn't matter how incredible kissing him with his hard thigh pressed between her legs had been. A zing of arousal shot from her stomach to between her thighs at the memory. Sonja stifled a moan and uncrossed and crossed her legs.

She squeezed her thighs together, her clit pulsing with arousal. Sonja licked her lips and inhaled, gazing out at the storefronts and pedestrians. The taste of him lingered on her lips, his scent still present on her clothes. She'd be in the bath tonight for sure, relieving the ache between her legs.

His vow came back to her—he'd be taking himself in hand tonight. Sonja lost her breath and bit her bottom lip. James would stroke himself and call out her name when he orgasmed. He said he'd send her a text telling her so. Would he? She'd acted disgusted when he said it, yet his words hadn't disgusted her at all. They'd only served to make her want him more.

Her choices had been to take him up on his offer or get the hell out of there. Obviously, she'd chosen to flee. Although slight regret lingered at the decision she'd made, Sonja was more than certain James Donnelly was a complication she didn't need in her life.

She had a hard enough time telling the rest of the men in her world "no". She didn't need another one. Even if, at every turn, she found herself wanting to tell him "yes".

The cab pulled in front of her building. She paid the fare through the little plastic slot and stepped out of the car.

Once inside her apartment, she kicked off her shoes and made a beeline for her daughter's bedroom. Without knocking, she opened the door and walked in. Privacy be damned, Sonja wanted answers, and she didn't care if Casey liked it or not.

"What the fuck, Mom!" Casey turned her back and pulled her T-shirt over her head.

Sonja crossed her arms. "Watch your mouth, Casey, or I'll wash it out with soap."

"Can't you knock? God, a little privacy would be nice, you know."

"This is my house, so no, I don't need to knock. Now explain yourself, young lady. Tell me why you didn't come home after school and disobeyed me. Yet again."

"What's the big deal? There isn't one, that's what. Why can't you leave me alone?" Casey climbed onto the center of her queen-size bed and picked up her iPad.

Sonja snatched it out of her hands. "I asked you a question. Answer me."

"I hate you! Give that back. It's not yours. Daddy bought it for me."

"I don't care who bought it for you. I am speaking to you, and you *will* pay attention to me. You are not to see that boy again. Do you hear me?"

"Whatever." Casey let out a mocking laugh. "Not like you can stop me anyway. You're never here, so just stay out of my life and worry about your own."

Sonja let out an exasperated sigh. This kid was going to be the death of her. "Casey, look…you may think you can come and go as you please. You may also think you can do what you want, but I assure you, child, I will make your life a living hell if you continue down this path you've chosen."

"Yeah, what're you gonna do about it? Lock me up in the house? Try it and see what happens. I won't do what you say. So don't waste your time."

Sonja leaned her hip against the doorjamb, baffled and at a complete loss for what to do about her daughter's behavior. What scared her most was that Casey was right. Short of locking her in the house, she couldn't keep her from leaving, or skipping school, or hanging out with that over-privileged thug, Drake. "I don't understand where this attitude has come from. Furthermore, I don't understand why you're so angry all the time. You have a very nice life, you realize. Look around, young lady." Sonja tossed the iPad onto the bed. "Consider yourself grounded for the remainder of the week and into the weekend. And I'm calling your father. I've had enough of this."

"G'head and call him, Mommy. He's just gonna tell you you're overreacting."

"Maybe so, but the grounding still stands." She pointed at her daughter. "You leave this house to go anywhere other than school for the next week, and you can consider every electronic toy you own confiscated." Sonja turned and left the room.

"Fine! I don't give a crap if you take everything away. Daddy will get me more!"

Sonja covered her ears and walked away from her daughter's tantrum. A second later, the typical sound of Casey's bedroom door slamming made Sonja flinch. She buried her face in her hands and shook her head. Fighting with her daughter exhausted her, and now she needed to emotionally prepare for a phone call to her ex-husband, Thomas.

Casey was right about him, too. Thomas *would* tell Sonja she was overreacting. He'd always been the "fun" parent. When they divorced six years ago, Sonja gained full custody of Casey because of his choice to live out of state. Once he'd moved, he went from being the "fun" parent to a Disneyland Dad on steroids.

She wandered into the kitchen and poured a glass of Chardonnay. Alcohol would be necessary to get through the conversation. She loathed talking to Thomas—pompous ass that he was. There was no doubt he'd brush off Sonja's concerns tonight, as he always did, and give their daughter anything she wanted. It was his way of getting back at Sonja for leaving him.

Stepping into the study, a glass of wine in hand, she settled behind what was once her father's antique mahogany serpentine pedestal desk. She eyed the phone at the corner of the leather top and exhaled. "Here we go." Sonja picked up the receiver and dialed Thomas's number in Florida.

"Good evening, Sonja."

The sound of his voice sent a chill skipping over her skin, one coming from disgust rather than desire. "Hello, Thomas. I'm sorry to disturb you. Do you have a few moments to talk?"

"Always. What can I do for you?"

Sonja leaned back in the leather chair and sipped her wine. "It's about Casey. Thomas, she's out of control."

"Oh, I highly doubt that. She's only looking for attention, I'm sure. Have you spent any time with her lately?"

Sonja paused, drawing in a deep breath before answering. She was not going to let him ruffle her feathers. "I assure you, this is not a matter of her needing attention. She never comes home after school as she's told to do, and she's got this boy she's spending too much time with."

"So? Let the child be, Sonja. She's fifteen. It's normal for her to have a boyfriend."

Sonja took a gulp of her wine. He infuriated her, and with

each passing year, it became harder and harder for her to not let her anger get the best of her. Talking to him had become impossible. Especially since Casey started the rebellious behavior. "Thomas, don't you think it's abnormal you're not concerned about your daughter running around with a kid who's almost eighteen?"

"No, *Sonja*. I don't think it's abnormal at all. It's called giving her space. You should try it sometime." There was a pause. "Oh wait, I forget. You give her plenty of space since you're hardly home. One of these days, I'm going to bring her to live with me. She's old enough to choose for herself now."

Sonja let out a sigh and reached for some measure of calm. "Look, I didn't call to fight with you and certainly not to be threatened by you, yet again, over the living arrangements of our daughter. I called you for help. And to let you know, I believe we're heading into trouble with her. I would think that would be more important than trying to get back at me."

There, she sounded reasonable and calm. She could do this, though she knew she'd made a mistake in reaching out to him. Why she kept trying was a mystery to her. Some things never changed, and Thomas Martin was one of them.

"Okay, look. I apologize." There was a pause on the line like he was swallowing down and digesting the fact that he'd made an apology. A rare thing from him. Also, not a good sign. "I have plans to be in Manhattan on Monday. I'll see if I can move my business to Friday and spend the weekend. We can talk about it when I get home."

Home.

He'd never stopped calling her house his home. He never stopped expecting to stay there when he was in town, either. Sonja was willing to bet she would've come home from work on Monday, and he would've been there, sitting in the study, drinking a brandy.

Sonja shuddered and placed her hand on her forehead.

She just didn't have the energy to have the well-rehearsed argument again. "Fine. When will you arrive?"

"I'll let you know. Most likely in the evening. You can tell me all about what you feel she's done after we have dinner."

"I'll have Janissa ready the guest room for you."

"Now, Sonja, that won't be necessary. You know that. Thanks for calling, darling. It's always a pleasure to hear your voice."

"Right. Have a good night, Thomas." Sonja hung up the phone and drank the rest of her wine in one swallow. Darling? She wanted to vomit.

Thomas would come on Friday, and he'd spend the weekend. Not only would he spend the weekend in *her* home. He'd spend it in her bed. That's why the guest bedroom didn't need to be readied for him.

Sonja rose from behind the desk, went back to the kitchen and poured another full glass. Sure, his body was still appealing, and his looks, but she'd stopped having sex with him long ago. Yet he insisted on sleeping next to her. She hated it and in no way desired him anymore.

In the beginning, when he'd first moved to Florida, Sonja let him stay because she thought he'd help with Casey, but it always backfired. The one weekend she'd taken a stand, she'd seen how devastated Casey was by the constant bickering and tension. It was bad enough her daughter had to grow up without a father in her day-to-day life. Sonja didn't want to fill the time Casey did have with him with arguments.

Thomas felt it was better for Casey to see them as the family they always were. Even though they no longer were a family, Sonja didn't argue his point. Sadly, deep inside, she suspected Thomas was likely only trying to stay close to her and merely using their daughter as an excuse.

Bottom line, in the end, giving him what he wanted was better than dealing with the bickering and his constant threats to take her back to court for custody.

Sonja took a large gulp of her wine. She was weak. Always had been. Shame flowed through her, pooling in her limbs, making her stomach churn and bile rise in the back of her throat.

Sonja successfully argued case after case in the courtroom with ease. Standing up for her clients wasn't a problem. But it was just another false front because standing up for herself was a totally different story.

She'd never been able to say "no"—it wasn't in her programming.

She'd give Thomas what he wanted because…it was just easier.

Even if she hated herself for it.

Bottle of Chardonnay and glass in hand, Sonja made her way to her bedroom suite. A bath…a bath was what she needed most. After starting the water in her large claw-foot tub, Sonja went back into her closet and stripped off her work clothes.

Giving birth to Casey over fifteen years ago had changed her body, but she'd regained her figure, mostly. Many women weren't so lucky. Sonja was built like her mother—long and slender. Feline-esque is what Thomas used to say. That was back when she'd loved him. Or at least thought she loved him. Maybe she had.

Sonja ran her hands over her smooth stomach. It wasn't perfectly flat, but it was toned. Working out at the gym helped. There were a few stretch marks from the last months of pregnancy, though they never really bothered her.

Tilting her head forward, she pulled the pins from her hair, freeing the long blonde locks and letting them fall around her shoulders.

Gliding her hands up her torso, she cupped her small breasts in her palms, felt the weight of them and ran her thumbs over her nipples. The light touch tightened her small, pink areolas, and her nipples became erect.

James had touched them earlier that night smoothed his thumb over one of them. Her bra and blouse were no match for the rigid points and proved a weak barrier from his touch. Just like her mind and body had been no match for his drugging kisses. She wanted him. *Madness.* She still wanted him. Why? *Why does he make me want him?* Sonja took a sip of her wine. The reason eluded her.

Stepping back into her bathroom, she set the glass down and pulled her hair up in a hair tie. She gathered a few towels and set them next to the tub, and when she turned to step into the steaming water—her phone beeped on the vanity counter.

Sonja froze and eyed the clock on the wall. Nine p.m. It could be a client. It could be anyone. Picking it up, she saw the text message alert displaying a number she didn't recognize. With shaking hands, she swiped the screen, unlocking it. She took a breath and read the message.

> I can't get the scent of you out of my mind.
> And your name tastes nowhere near as sweet
> as your lips. I'll settle for only that…for now.
> Only your name rolling from my tongue and
> echoing off my shower walls. Your name,
> rather than your perfect mouth. Your name,
> rather than your body. My fantasy of you,
> rather than you…for now. James.

SONJA SAT on the edge of the tub, staring at the words he'd sent her. She read the poem again. Then, once more. No one had ever written her a poem before. On second thought, that wasn't true. Abram Meckler had written her a poem in the ninth grade, but she could hardly compare that to this.

Only your name rolling from my tongue and echoing off my shower walls.

Sonja covered her mouth with the back of her hand. He'd done it, hadn't he? He'd been in his shower and stroked himself to thoughts of her. Of her lips and her body. Of *her*. He brought himself to orgasm with her name on his lips, like he said he would.

Everything inside Sonja went loose. Heat crept up her spine, and perspiration dotted her forehead. He'd know she read the message because of the read receipt indicator on her iPhone; there was no way around that now. But she was *not* going to reply. She couldn't. In fact, she didn't need to. She did, however, save his number in her contacts. Sonja set the phone down and wiped her forehead with her palm. Another swallow of wine, and she stepped into her tub.

James Donnelly…James Donnelly. How could he want her so much?

CHAPTER TEN

Jimmy stood before the commissioned piece of art he'd been working on the whole week. He'd put the final elements together today. Fiber optic, pale-yellow lights now highlighted the windows of the dimmer buildings in the distance and made the whole cityscape come alive.

The piece was softer than his norm, with its copper wires outlining the buildings and the waterway. He was definitely pleased with it. And its sale would pay his rent for the next two months. Not a bad gig. The money was appreciated, but he couldn't help feeling a small attachment to the piece.

Sonja had been drawn to it when she'd been here with him. She'd said it was beautiful, but who knew if she really thought so?

There were a lot of things about Sonja he didn't know. He'd sent her the text on Wednesday night like he said he would. But what he'd sent probably wasn't what she expected to get. He shook his head, pulled the rag from his back pocket and wiped his hands. Tossing it on his workbench, Jimmy grabbed his cell and made a call to the buyer, letting her know the piece would be delivered tomorrow as promised.

He made his way upstairs and then up the circular set to

his loft bedroom. More than ready for a few drinks, he sent a text to his best friend, Andy, saying to meet him at the pub around eight. Jimmy wanted to celebrate plus blow off a little steam in the process.

What had Sonja thought of his text? Jimmy knew damn well he'd been kind of an asshole that night, pushing her buttons, trying to soften the negative tension between them without cooling the sexual heat that had been even stronger than the night they'd met in Vegas. Maybe the poem hadn't gone over too well. He couldn't be sure since she hadn't replied.

She probably thought he was an immature ass. And she hadn't let him forget for a second their difference in age. Regardless, based on her physical reaction to him, the only thing he was sure of was that she wanted him. At least sexually.

Problem was, for the first time since college and the dreadful experience with his ex-girlfriend, Jimmy might want more than just sex. It was a desire he wasn't certain he should entertain, yet it blasted through his mind like a rocket nonetheless.

After getting cleaned up, he headed for the pub. He covered the twelve blocks to Bleecker Street by foot and found his best friend sitting at the bar, nursing a dark amber ale of some sort. Jimmy put his arm around Andy and gave her a chaste peck on the lips. "Hey, doll."

"Hi there. I ordered some wings." Her blue eyes sparkled in the dim light of the bar.

"Sweet. I'm starved."

They moved to one of the wooden booths in the back of the bar. This was Jimmy's favorite pub. It was a unique one in the Village and had been in business for over thirty years. Looking around the dark-paneled walls, he admired, not for the first time, the various bottle-cap art decorating them, the gorgeous stained-glass windows and the many carvings made by patrons in the rustic wooden tabletops.

A table full of college-aged guys erupted into a fit of hoots and hollers, complete with high-fives, drawing his attention. Apparently playing a game of quarters. Jimmy shifted in the booth and leaned his back against the wall. Good conversation and laughs were exactly what he needed.

Andy was his friend—his best friend. He'd met her about two years ago, and they'd been tied at the hip ever since. She was the person he spent his time with when not working. A twenty-six-year-old petite brunette with crystalline-blue eyes and a body a guy would follow anywhere. Skin covered in tattoos, and a few piercings, some visible, some not.

To some, she looked a little hard, but really, Andy was a complete sweetheart underneath the decorative canvas…and she happened to be a lesbian. Broke male hearts all over the state of New York, but he bet the lesbian community was damn glad to have her. God help him if his younger sister, Celia, ever caught sight of her.

Jimmy swirled the shot in his hand before swallowing it in one gulp. Setting the glass next to the other empties, he excused himself and made his way to the men's room. Stepping inside, he pulled out his cell. No messages from Sonja. A beat of impatience rolled through him. He was done waiting. Jimmy sighed, leaned against the sink and typed out a message letting her know where he was. Just the name of the bar, nothing more.

Tucking his phone away, he handled business, washed his hands and went back out to join Andy. *Fuck it.* If Sonja continued to ignore him, he'd go to her office on Monday. He wanted to see her right now, but he'd suck it up and wait her out a little longer.

Another round of beers arrived when Jimmy got back to the table. He was half-buzzed already, and at this rate, he'd be stumbling home in another couple hours. Not the first time, probably not the last. Maybe he should find a cute college chickie to take home.

A sour taste coated his tongue. Touching anyone besides his Sonja made his stomach fold in on itself. Jimmy coughed, then cleared his throat. His physical reaction shocked him. He'd never been a monogamous guy—not since he'd ended things with his ex, Gina, in college. Never bothered even *trying* to be in a committed relationship again after what had gone down between them.

And here he was, not even fucking Sonja—yet—and he hadn't looked at another girl all night. He was done for. Completely screwed without the actual screwing part. *Shit.*

"What the hell's wrong with you?" Andy looked at him over the top of her beer glass.

"I'm screwed."

"Define screwed?" She took a sip.

Jimmy sat back and ran his fingers through his hair. "We need another shot. Fuck me, *I* need another shot."

"Holy shit, you met someone, didn't you?"

"What? Pshaw, no. What makes you think that?" Jimmy took a swig of his Guinness and tried to bury the anxiety springing up like a damn rocket.

Andy leaned forward on her elbows, a grin pasted on her lips. "Dude, you're strung out. I didn't realize it before, but holy shit, I see it now. Who is she?"

"Heh. Look, I'm fine. Let's get some more shots. You should call your girl; see if she wants to come hang out."

"Jimmy Donnelly, no fucking fair. I tell you stuff all the time. Come on!"

He chuckled. "There isn't anything to tell. But I promise, if there is, you'll be the first to know." He winked at her and waved for the waitress. "More shots, Andy. More shots."

CHAPTER ELEVEN

Sonja sat at her long, cherry-wood dining table and sipped her wine, watching her daughter and ex-husband carry on what seemed like endless conversation about every topic under the sun. "Dinner is delicious. Thank you both again for cooking." She smiled at her daughter and took another bite of her pasta.

"You're quite welcome, Sonja." Thomas nodded, a casual smile on his face. She knew better than to take it as genuine or heartfelt.

"Daddy and I love to cook together. It was fun." Casey smiled…at her father.

Sonja swallowed another sip of Chianti. She was glad her daughter loved her father so much, but jealousy still burned in her throat. Of course, Casey loved him. He never did any of the heavy lifting.

Even when they were married, he never disciplined their daughter. From the time Casey was born, he was intent on being the favorite.

She supposed she should be grateful Thomas wasn't like her own father—full of expectation and very little softness. Sonja's father had expected more from her than any parent should. But, as a child, there wasn't much she could do about it. She also knew deviating from *his* plan for her was out of the question.

Thomas was very different from her father, and even though he made Sonja crazy with his lackadaisical parenting style, she knew he loved Casey.

A fit of giggles burst from her daughter, drawing Sonja from her thoughts.

"Mommy, did you hear what Daddy said? Oh, my God, he's so funny."

Sonja wiped her mouth with her napkin. "No, honey. I didn't. Sorry."

"He said we never really grow up, we—"

Thomas raised a brow and drummed his fingers on the table. "Daydreaming? Not like you."

Tension wound its way up Sonja's spine, making her neck ache. "Everyone daydreams, Thomas. Even you."

"Not really. Why bother dreaming when I can just take what I want?"

"There's no fun in always getting what you want. Sometimes, the dream of it is better." Careful to keep her tone even, Sonja set her napkin down on the table. "Please excuse me; I've got some work to do."

Thomas regarded her over his wine glass with a mocking smile. "Certainly. Work is very important."

"It is, yes." She kissed Casey on the cheek. "When do you leave?" she asked Thomas.

"Sunday. I moved my business meeting scheduled on Monday to today. Ready to be rid of me so soon?

Casey shook her head and tucked a lock of hair behind her ear. "Never, Daddy."

"Of course not. It's always so nice when you visit." Sonja forced a smile before leaving the room. She'd had enough, and there *was* work to do. But truth be told, being the third wheel whenever Thomas visited wasn't high on her priority list. It was just easier to excuse herself and give them their time.

Sonja settled by the fireplace in one of the high-back leather chairs in her study. A case folder wide open on her lap, and a glass, along with a new bottle of Chardonnay, on the side table. She wasn't reading the case file. It was one hell of a case, too, and she had a load of work to do on it, yet instead, she sat reading and rereading the poem James texted her Wednesday night.

He'd sent another message earlier that evening. *Peculiar Pub* was all it said. Obviously, he wanted her to come meet him. But she wasn't going—wasn't replying to the messages either. She'd never fit in down at that bar. For the love of all things sacred, it was filled with college students!

There was no way she'd sit there and watch him tease and flirt with all those young girls. Talk about feeling out of place. It was bad enough in the company of all those twenty-some-things in the bar in Vegas; it'd be worse down the Village.

Work. Yes, work.

Sonja focused on the file spread open on her lap and tried to read through the evidence the state was bringing against her client.

She looked up at the glowing blaze in the fireplace and listened to the distant laughing of Thomas and her daughter. Sadness bloomed in her chest, and a lump rose in her throat. Why couldn't she have a relationship like that with Casey? Why was it so damn hard?

Sonja picked up her wine glass and swallowed a large mouthful—forcing it past the swelling of emotion in her throat—and poured more from the bottle. Friday night was a fine night to lock herself in her study, get drunk and have a little pity party. A perfectly fine night. The weekend was going to be hell.

Still unable to focus, Sonja set the file aside. Stepping to the tall bookshelf lining one wall in the room, she perused the titles. Most of the books were her father's. Though, since she'd taken over the house, she'd added many of her own.

Several shelves were filled with countless law books, but there was also some classic literary fiction. Even a few romance novels. She chuckled, finding some old favorites tucked in a far corner.

She'd been a huge Nora Roberts fan during college and read many of her trilogies. She'd loved them. The idea of a happily-ever-after and endless love was a beautiful fantasy, but that time in her life was long gone now.

It'd been replaced by harsh expectations and even harsher realities—a little something called life. Sadness blanketed her vision. Sonja didn't read anymore unless it was a law book or a case file.

She took a seat with one of the paperbacks and thumbed through the yellowed pages. So much creativity packed onto a page. The thought of it brought James to mind…again. Had he finished that piece of art he'd been working on? What would he be creating next? She grabbed her cell phone and read the texts again. She sighed and rested her head against the back of the chair. He'd written her a poem. A beautiful one.

Was he talking to another woman right this moment, or was he thinking of her as she was of him? Clearly, she'd been on his mind at some point several hours ago. Was she still? She wouldn't call him, though. No matter how hard he tried to convince her he wanted her.

Even if he did want her, it was just for sex. The night in his studio played in her mind. The feel of his strong hands on her body, the taste of his lips and the way his body felt pressed against hers. His thigh between her legs and the solid erection pressed to her hip, straining behind his jeans.

Sonja groaned and crossed her legs. Mere thoughts of him sent her body into overdrive, and her libido rose to attention. Her clit pulsed, and she squeezed her thighs together, moaning at the slight pressure. She could have sex with him. Sonja pursed her lips and then sipped her wine. She wanted to have sex with him.

Eyeing the clock, she rose, taking the bottle of wine and glass with her, and headed for her bathtub. A little time with her showerhead was what she needed to take the edge off. The house had gone quiet, and she assumed Thomas and her daughter had turned in for the night.

Sonja entered her dim bedroom. The hall light cast a shadow over the king-size, antique four-poster bed…and the silhouette of a figure beneath the blankets. *Crap.*

Thomas was in her bed. Not like she hadn't expected it, but maybe in a naïve way, hoped for once he wouldn't be there.

She tiptoed past the bed into her bathroom suite and shut the door, locking it behind her. Sonja set her phone and wine down on the counter, lit a few candles and turned on the water to fill the tub.

The shrill ring of her cell startled her, and she jumped, clutching her chest. Didn't it figure she'd get a call from the service on a late Friday night? Technically Saturday, but who cared at that point?

Wait…was she even on call tonight? Sonja reached for the phone and saw clearly who was calling, and it wasn't the off-hours phone service. She sat on the satin settee near the tub, wine glass in hand. "This is Sonja."

"Did you miss me?"

She smiled. "Who is this?"

"Yeah, you missed me." He chuckled.

The sound of his laugh trickled over her skin, and she shivered as she stretched out on the settee. "Did you finish your piece of art?"

"I did. Was hoping you would've come to help me celebrate. Did you get my text?"

"Yes." She sighed. "Congratulations on finishing. Will you be compensated well for it?"

"I will. Thanks. Did you get my text the other night?"

Sonja hesitated. Not knowing what to say. *Just say yes.* But if she said yes, he'd want to talk about it, and she wasn't sure she was ready to address it.

"You still there?"

"Yes, James. I'm here." She pressed her fingers to her forehead. "It was a beautiful and erotic poem."

"Every word was true."

She ignored his statement. "I didn't know you wrote poetry."

"Comes with the whole artist package."

"Yes, I suppose that makes sense. No one's ever written me a poem before. But I bet you write them for a lot of women, don't you?"

"Woman, you wound me again."

She laughed. "Oh, come on, James. You take me for a fool?"

"Nope. I haven't taken you at all. Yet."

A small gasp escaped her lips before she could stop it, and she was sure her cheeks glowed red. She rolled her eyes. He couldn't see her through the phone, so it didn't matter. "You really think you'll get me in bed?"

"Positive."

Instinct told her he was serious. Common sense told her he'd had plenty to drink, too. Maybe he was right. Maybe he would get her into bed, but then what? "Have you been drinking, Mr. Donnelly?"

"Yes, but that has nothing to do with this. Have you?"

She picked up her wine glass and touched the edge to her lips. "I have, yes."

"When you call me Mr. Donnelly, it excites me in a way I can't explain. You say it in your special lawyer tone."

"I don't have a lawyer tone."

"Oh, but you do, Sonja. You do. Makes me envision you with nothing but a bra and panties, garters and stockings like you had on the other day, and those five-inch fuck-me pumps on your feet. You'd be clutching a riding crop in your hand, too."

The image his words inspired had her stomach tightening, and a shot of lust zinged straight to her clit. Heaven and hell, was he nuts? "James..." She swallowed. "That's..." Sonja pressed the cool wine glass to her forehead and raised her knees on the settee.

"That's what, Sonja?" His voice had deepened, sounding raspier than normal with almost a purr to it.

"No one's ever said things like that to me before. I don't know whether to slap you or sleep with you."

"What if I said you could do both?"

"Then I'd say you were crazy, and I should keep away from you. Maybe file a restraining order."

"You won't, though. You know why?"

She could hear the smile in his voice and couldn't help but smile, too. Getting up, she turned off the water spilling into the tub. "You're going to tell me anyway, so get on with it."

"Because you want me as bad as I want you. Because you want to feel my lips on yours again. Because you want to feel my hands on your soft body, too." He groaned. "Because you want to feel my hot mouth while I suck your nipples and then taste every inch of your creamy skin."

Sonja sat back down. "Holy hell."

"Admit it, just once. It's just you and me, and we're a little drunk. Say it, Sonja. Tell me you want me, please."

"And what happens if I do? Will you go away and stop bothering me?"

"Never."

"What do you want from me? Why on earth could you, or would you, want me? James, you're so young...and sexier than a man has a right to be. Why would you waste your time on me?"

"I told you what I wanted. Now, say it, Sonja. I even said please."

"Even if I say it, admit what you think needs admitting, it means nothing. You realize that, right? It changes nothing, James."

"Say it."

His whispered words came through the receiver, and she shivered again, almost completely under his spell. Almost. If she gave in and admitted she wanted him, it might make a difference. But she meant what she said. It wouldn't change a thing.

She swallowed the last of her wine. "I want you. I want all those things you mentioned. And more. And now I'm going to bed. Good night."

Intent on not hearing his reply, she disconnected the call. Sonja didn't want to know what might come out of his mouth next or, heaven help her, she might find herself in a cab and on her way to his apartment.

Her entire body pulsed with arousal, and her breath came in short bursts. *Yes, dammit. I want you!* She eyed the bath, then looked toward the closed door leading through her closet to her bedroom.

With a shake of her head, she set the wine glass on the counter and unplugged the drain in the tub. After blowing out the candles, she opened the bathroom door and moved to the doorway leading to her bedroom. As she stared into the darkness of her room, her ex-husband shifted in her bed, and the sound of his soft breaths reached her ears.

Without a doubt, if she propositioned him, Thomas would make love to her tonight. He'd use her to fill his ego and further prove his point. She hated the idea of it, hated herself more for even considering sex with him again. But tonight, she'd use him instead. Sonja would be in control. For once, she'd get what she needed—even if it wasn't by the man she *truly* wanted it from.

Sonja stripped off her clothes and padded to her bed. Sliding between the sheets, she turned and faced Thomas. He reached for her like always and smoothed his hand down her side to her hip.

Closing her eyes, Sonja sought James's face in her mind. He pressed his lips to her shoulder before kissing down to her breast. She moaned when his mouth found her nipple.

Thomas might have her body tonight, but in her mind, it was James she was giving it to.

It was James she wanted to give everything to.

CHAPTER TWELVE

THE NEXT MORNING, JIMMY MADE HIS WAY UPTOWN IN A borrowed minivan to deliver his client's commissioned piece of art. After dropping off the canvas, he turned up the radio and Stone Sour's "Made of Scars" blared through the speakers.

I want you. I want all those things you mentioned. And more.

Sonja was front and center on his mind and had been all morning. He was still stunned she'd finally admitted she wanted him. He'd been pushing her, daring her. But he hadn't actually thought she'd say it. It could've been the alcohol talking, he supposed, but in his opinion, a drunken man—or, in this case, a drunken woman—told no lies.

He'd debated calling her back but figured it was better to let her think about what she said and then see what she did next. Jimmy rolled his eyes. If anyone had told him six weeks ago he'd be in his bed on a Friday night, half drunk and alone, cuddling only with his cat, he'd have called them a moron. Things had definitely changed.

From the night he met Sonja, he hadn't been interested in anyone else. Was he really ready to settle down in an official relationship again? *Why the hell am I even thinking that far ahead?* Maybe she didn't even want a relationship.

He liked her and for sure wanted to know more about her. And for fuck's sake, he wanted to know what made her smile. She didn't smile often. Always so serious. Too serious, and Jimmy wanted to make her laugh the way he'd done in Vegas.

Letting out a frustrated sigh, he ran his hand over his chin. Irish or not, the Donnellys weren't known for their patience. The need to have what he wanted flowed through him like a tidal wave. This whole wooing-a-woman thing was *not* easy.

He should consider calling his father. Dad knew a thing or two about courting a woman and had managed to hold on to the same one for four decades.

Pulling up in front of his friend's apartment to return the van, he stepped out onto the street, and his phone rang. "Hello?"

"Hello, Mr. Donnelly. This is Janice from Collier Galleries. Do you have a moment?"

Jimmy moved the phone to his other ear and shut the driver's door of the van. "Of course. What can I do for you?"

"Just a courtesy reminder regarding the charity auction Friday night. Have all your pieces you're donating been delivered? We're looking to have everything tagged and catalogued by Tuesday the latest."

"This Friday? Thanks for calling. I did almost forget. You know how artists are." He chuckled.

"Yes, hence the courtesy call. The pieces, Mr. Donnelly, are they all here?"

The receptionist, or whatever she was, was all business. Jimmy snorted and leaned against the van. She reminded him of Sonja. "Right. No, not all of them. I think there are two on-site already. There's one more I'll grab from my studio and bring over to you Monday."

"Thank you. I'll mark the sheet. Mr. Collier asked to

remind everyone it's a black tie event, so please dress accordingly."

"No Chuck Taylors?"

"No, Mr. Donnelly, although it's certainly your funeral if you choose to invoke Mr. Collier's wrath."

"Why, Janice, that was almost a joke." He smiled, tossing the van keys in the air and catching them on their way down.

"Yes. I fear you might be right. Maybe I should get a bite to eat. Take a break."

"Ohh, another! Janice, killing me here. Hey, smile, would ya? It's all gonna be great. See you Monday."

She laughed. "Thanks."

Jimmy disconnected the call and shook his head. Black tie. Good thing he was a grown-up artist and actually had a monkey suit hanging in his closet. A damn expensive one too. Now for the date. Sonja was front and center in his mind, and trailing quickly behind her was Andy.

Except, shit, he'd already asked Andy to go with him before he'd gone to Los Angeles. Thinking quickly, Jimmy sent her a text.

> Jimmy: Meet for lunch?

> Andy: Hell yes. Where?

> Jimmy: Union Square. We'll find something easy.

> Andy: Sounds good. See you in 30?

> Jimmy: Yup

When he arrived, Jimmy scoped out a place for them in the corner of a burger joint. After shooting a quick text to Andy to let her know where to meet him, he sipped his soda and thumbed through the menu.

Andy slid in the opposite seat. "Hey."

"Hi there, gorgeous. You got here fast." Jimmy stood and gave Andy a peck on the lips. "You're looking chipper. Not too hungover this morning?"

"Shit. You kidding me? I just got up when you texted." She laughed. "I will never know how you toss back that shit-ass Jäger like you do and not puke your guts up all night." She pulled the menu in front of her.

"Nice. I'm really hungry now." He scrunched up his face and then raised the menu in front of his mouth and nose. "You're gross."

Andy rolled her eyes. "My best friends are guys. What do you expect? Next, I'll grab my crotch. It'll be a real bonding moment."

Jimmy widened his eyes and dropped the menu onto the table. "Ooh, sexay gurrl. Let's bond."

"Honey, we bonded a long time ago." She snorted. "I'm having two hot dogs and a Mountain Dew." She raised her hand. "Save the crude jokes. I'm not awake enough yet."

"Wasn't saying a word." Jimmy sipped his soda. "Was Steph pissed you got home so late?"

"Nah, it's all good."

"Good." Jimmy nodded and went back to the menu. Turkey club and fries today would hit the spot.

The waiter came over and took their order. Then came back pretty quick with Andy's drink. Jimmy needed to figure out how to ask her about the auction. Damn, he hoped she wasn't going to be pissed.

He looked around the small restaurant at the other patrons. No one remarkable caught his attention. Probably because his attention was everywhere but in the present moment.

"All right, spill it."

Jimmy returned his attention to Andy. "Huh?"

"You're bouncing your leg like you're about to run a damn

marathon and looking all over the place in a daze. Tell me about the girl." She sipped her soda.

"Why do you think there's a girl?"

"It's more obvious than my ass. Now, spill."

"You have a fantastic ass." He leaned back in his chair and stretched. "Fine. There *is* a female. I met her in Vegas when Ry and I went for a quick overnight." He paused as their food was delivered. Ketchup passed back and forth, and first bites taken.

"Go on," Andy said around a mouthful of hot dog.

Jimmy bit into a fry. "She's different. Not my norm."

"Describe, please. Jesus, it's like pulling teeth to get info out of you."

"I'm eating. Damn, girl, a little patience?" He laughed. "She's a criminal defense attorney. Has money. Oh, and she's forty-one." He bit into his sandwich.

Andy almost choked on her drink. "She's forty-fucking-one? Jesus Christ, Jimmy."

"I know what you're thinking." He dipped a fry in his ketchup. "I've already gone through it all in my head. So don't bother."

Andy waved her hands in front of her. "Okay, okay. She's forty-one. What else?"

"She's got a daughter. Age fifteen."

"The plot thickens. Husband?"

He wiped his hands on his napkin. "Hell no. She's divorced."

"Soooo…what's the issue?"

"I like her. I haven't liked anyone in years. Also…we fight." He took a bite of his sandwich and chewed. "And we're not actually dating yet."

Andy laughed and shook her head. "Wait, back up. You fight? What the hell do you mean you fight?"

"It's crazy. I don't know what it is exactly. We rile each

other up. One minute, I'm all annoyed, and the next, I want to rip her clothes off." He took a gulp of his soda.

"Foreplay." She nodded her head to the side. "That's some fucked-up shit, Jimmy."

"Yes! That's exactly what I told her, too." He ran his hand over his mouth. "It is kinda fucked up, yeah, but there's a fire in her, you know? I guess I dig lighting it. It shows up when we bicker. But it's like, unless we're fighting, she won't give me the damn time of day."

"You got it bad. I've never seen you hung up on anyone before. You've been single the whole time I've known you."

"I don't have it bad." He frowned and thought about what she'd said for a moment. "I dunno, maybe you're right. Maybe I do."

"What do you mean you're not actually dating? You haven't taken her on a date yet?"

"No. But that brings me to my next subject." He smiled.

"I'm not done talking about this one. And I sooo don't like that look in your eyes." Andy straightened in her seat. "Lay it on me, Donnelly."

Jimmy raised a brow and chuckled.

She laughed. "Pig."

"Hey, I'm a guy. You shouldn't expect so much. Besides, you know I'm kidding. You're like a damn sister to me, even though I already have a fuckton of them."

"Aww, I love you too." She reached across the table and patted his hand. "Now tell me."

"Remember I asked you to come with me to that charity auction?"

"Yeah, I got a dress. Why?"

Jimmy shrugged and tried to look innocent. "Well…"

"Oh, you're fucking kidding me, right? I got a damn dress!"

"I'll pay for the dress. I'm sorry, but Andy, this is something she'll probably agree to go with me to. Please?"

Andy let out a long and loud sigh. Looked away and then back at him. And rolled her eyes. "Fine. But she better say yes. You're a great guy, you know? Even though you like to pretend you're not. And yeah, you're totally paying me for the dress."

"You're an angel." Jimmy held his glass of soda up for a toast.

Andy raised hers in agreement and nodded. "That I am. And I'm glad you finally recognize it."

"Hey, I'd take you off the market if you weren't already involved. And, you know, a lesbian."

"Liar." She raised a brow. "You'd take me home, fuck me, say you're gonna call and then never bother. Same thing you've done to half the women in the Village."

"Half? Oh, come on. Maybe one quarter, but definitely not half." He grinned at her over the top of his glass. "She'll say yes. I hope."

"Yeah, you got it bad. Keep me posted, playboy."

"Yes, dear."

CHAPTER THIRTEEN

Sonja glanced at her ringing cell on her desk, only to see it was another call from Thomas. He'd called at least four times since nine a.m., and this was the fifth. The man wouldn't quit.

Sonja shuddered, recalling waking up that morning, naked, with Thomas curled around her. Shame had coated her body like a second skin, and she'd almost vomited while she washed the remnants of her stupidity away in the shower. Then, she'd escaped to her office at the law firm before he woke up.

When she'd first divorced him, they'd been intimate a handful of times. After a while, she rebuffed his advances, insisting he sleep in the guest room. He refused, of course, and the argument that ensued over the matter woke Casey, making everything worse. Thomas insisted it was better for Casey if they kept up appearances. Reluctantly, Sonja agreed, and the sex between them continued on and off. That lasted several years, whether to sate her own sexual needs or because it made him easier to deal with, it didn't really matter. At the heart of it, Thomas wanted her to take him back.

Sonja would never take him back.

Eventually, the whole arrangement sickened her, and she flat-out refused him. She might not have been able to get him out of her bed, but she sure as hell *could* keep him from between her legs.

Last night had been different, or so she'd told herself. Last night, she'd been the aggressor, taking what she wanted and using Thomas. Last night, she'd been willing and wanton and warm. Absolutely convinced that having sex with her ex was justified because it was on her terms, but she was wrong. So very wrong.

All because she'd been too hot over James to simply masturbate and get over it.

How stupid.

Sonja leaned back in her leather desk chair, still disgusted with herself and well aware she was hiding out like a coward. But there was no fight left within her to deal with Thomas today—or any day, really.

Her head pounded, and she pinched the bridge of her nose and closed her eyes. Part hangover, part stress. The light from the sizable windows of her corner office was a bit more than she could handle at the moment, too. Sonja blew out a breath and went in search of another cup of coffee.

Traveling the corridor to the firm's break room, she glanced at the bland traditional art hanging on the walls. She'd started noticing the artwork decorating walls wherever she was now. It brought James front and center in her mind, making it difficult not to think of him on a constant basis.

Sonja filled her cup from the Keurig station on the counter. She should've gotten in a cab and gone to him last night. It would have been better to deal with him rather than Thomas and now her self-loathing. A lot more pleasurable, too.

Sonja grabbed a muffin from the refrigerator and made her way down the gray, carpeted hall back to her office. Maybe she should redecorate. Everything looked so drab now.

Odd, because it never had before, or maybe she hadn't really paid attention. Passing over the threshold to her office, she heard her phone ringing. Again. She glanced at it when she reached her desk, checking the caller ID.

James.

Her heart thudded in her ears. The phone stopped ringing, and she took her seat and stared at the device. The tone indicating a voicemail sounded. Sonja scooped up the cell and listened.

Hey, Sonja. It's James. Can you give me a call back? I have something I need to ask you. Talk soon. Yeah?

Sonja deleted the message and set her phone down. She glanced at the case file open on her desk, and then her laptop screen, then back to the cell. Should she call him back? What could he possibly need to ask her? With a death grip on the handle of her coffee mug, she sipped the creamy liquid.

Nervous energy vibrated in her limbs, forcing Sonja to her feet to pace. Around the back of the burgundy leather sofa, past the cherry-wood credenza and back around her desk. Another round. Then another. She paused in front of one of the windows—a perfect view of the Hudson River from there. Giving in, she moved back to her desk.

Curiosity was a bitch, wasn't it?

"I'll call and only stay on long enough for him to say what he needs to say." She blew out a breath and took a seat. Pulling up her missed calls, she selected his number and swallowed hard to drive the knot back down her throat. One ring. Two. Three…

"Sonja-the-lawyer."

"Must you insist on calling me that?"

"What? I think it's cute, and we don't know each other well enough for me to start with the honeys, sweeties and dears, right?"

She laughed and then cut herself off. *Keep it professional.* "I suppose you have a point. Yes."

"I didn't think you'd call me back. I'm glad you did."

The smile in his words was obvious, and her belly tingled. Sonja shook her head and moved to the sofa. "I needed a break from work. What did you need to ask me?"

"Wait, you're working? Why are you working? It's Saturday, Sonja."

"Yes, James. It's Saturday, and I have to work. Anyway, what did you need?"

"You work too much." He sighed. "You're curious, aren't you? I can hear it in your voice."

She paused, trying and failing to stay focused on the "keep it professional" plan. "I'm a little curious. Yes."

"Whoa, I'm winning all sorts of rounds with you. You okay? No. I mean, really?"

No. I slept with my ex last night instead of you, and I hate myself for it. I'm definitely not okay. "Knock it off. I'm fine. Now, what did you—wait, what do you mean winning rounds? You've not won anything."

God, he made her crazy.

He laughed. "All right. You're right. Anyway, I have a thing this Friday night, and I'd like to know if you'd attend with me."

"No." The word was out before she'd even thought about it.

"No? That's it? You don't even want to know what it is? Just, no?"

She'd already made her decision. She wasn't going to relent now. "No is a complete sentence, James."

He went quiet, but she could hear him breathing. His soft breaths penetrated so much more than her ears. She knew what that breath felt like on her skin, on her neck. The tingle was back in her tummy, and Sonja crossed and uncrossed her legs.

"Are you always going to tell me no?" His tone was low and deliberate.

She shifted on the couch, trying to get comfortable. "I don't know."

"Do you tell everyone no, or is it just me?"

His question gave her pause. Was it only him she said no to? She stood and paced, biting on her thumbnail. There were two men in her life she rarely, if ever, said no to: her father and Thomas. Sonja wanted to tell *them* no all the time.

Telling her father no wasn't something she ever did. Sonja learned at a very early age that accepting whatever her father wanted for her or from her was better than fighting him. She wouldn't dare for fear of his wrath.

He'd been dead for four years now, but she could still hear his voice in her mind like he was haunting her from the grave.

Thomas was another issue for her. She *could* say no or defy her ex-husband and had, but it was infrequent, and the consequences to her daughter dimmed the feeling of satisfaction.

James was a different story altogether. He was the antithesis of her father, of authority, and she told him no, even when she wanted to say yes. It was a sort of freedom she'd never had before. But considering he wasn't the kind of man she would, or should ever date, Sonja had a million reasons why she should tell him no. "I... Yes."

"How's that fair?"

She rubbed her forehead. "It's not fair. I'm sorry."

"Make it up to me then. Say yes."

Guilt turned her stomach into knots. "What is the 'thing' you want me to attend with you?"

"It's a charity auction for the recent hurricane victims. I've donated some of my art."

She stopped her pacing. "Really?"

"Yes, really. Why did you say it like that?"

"I..." Sonja let out a breath. "I guess I didn't take you for the charitable type."

"I see. I'm thinking there are lots of things you don't take me for. So, will you go?"

"This Friday night?"

"Yes. It starts at eight."

Sonja stepped to her windows. The sun was setting, and she stared at her reflection. "Yes. But I'll meet you there."

"Sweet! I'll take it. It's formal attire, but I'm thinking that won't be a problem for you."

She looked at her feet. "No, no problem at all."

"Thanks for saying yes. I'll text you the address when we hang up."

"Only because it's for a good cause." Sonja sat at her desk and rested her head in her palm. It was a lie. A bold-faced lie. Her answer had nothing to do with the event being for a good cause. The truth was, she said yes because she wanted to see him.

"Can I see you before Friday?"

She blurted a laugh. "No."

"All right. But who knows, maybe you'll run into me. It's a small city."

"Goodbye, James. I'll see you Friday night."

"Looking forward to it."

The call disconnected, and Sonja leaned back in her chair. *Holy crap!*

Did she really say yes to him? Screw it. She needed a break from everything everyone always expected of her.

A primal need clawed at Sonja's insides. No one expected her to go out with a thirty-year-old, much less someone with tattoos and piercings.

He'd been right in Vegas. She did want to take a walk on the wild side.

Sonja wanted to do something *she* wanted and *not* what everyone else expected her to do. She wanted to be free. It was one small step, but it felt like she'd leaped over the Grand Canyon.

Tamping down the urges somersaulting in her stomach—the very ones she shouldn't allow herself to entertain—Sonja grabbed her briefcase and left the office.

When she stepped inside her Park Avenue apartment, the sounds of Tchaikovsky's "Romeo and Juliet" met her ears. Making her way from the entryway, she navigated the long parquet wood floor of the hall to her daughter's bedroom and glanced inside. Casey wasn't there. Sonja continued in the direction of her study, and the music grew louder the closer she got. Rounding the corner and stepping through the open double-paneled wood doors, she found Thomas sitting in one of the high-back chairs.

He held a crystal brandy snifter, filled halfway, in one hand and the other in the air as if he were conducting the very symphony playing from her CD player. "I missed you today. Where were you?" he said without looking in her direction.

Choosing to ignore his declaration, Sonja laid her briefcase atop her desk. "I had work to get done."

Thomas set his brandy on the small table next to him and stood. He approached her and wrapped his arms around her waist, pulling her into an unwanted embrace. He bent to kiss her, but she turned her head, and his lips landed on her cheek. "Did you miss me?"

Sonja placed her hands on his chest to push him away. Naturally, he didn't move. "Thomas, please don't."

He looked at her. "Please don't, what?" He bent his head and nuzzled her neck.

Bile rose in the back of her throat, and Sonja jerked her head away. She didn't want this. Didn't want him. "You know exactly what." Stepping from his embrace, she crossed her arms. "I realize last night might have—"

His face twisted into a scowl. "Might've what?"

"Don't look at me that way." Sonja turned away and unloaded her briefcase. "It was just sex, Thomas. Nothing more. There is nothing more."

He stepped beside her and circled her wrist with his hand, halting her movement. "I know you don't mean that. You can't even look me in the eye when you say it."

Sonja snapped her head up and leveled her gaze with his. "There is *nothing* more."

Thomas let out a scoff and retrieved his brandy. "We'll see."

"Where's Casey?"

"I let her go out. I thought it might be nice to have some time alone." He sneered, then took a sip of his brandy.

"The Fantasy Overture" played on in the background, sounding quite ominous to her ears, mixed in with the underlying tone in Thomas's words. But it was nothing compared to the anger that lanced her veins like a white-hot poker. Sonja pressed both palms flat on her desk and drew in a deep breath. "You let her go out?" She clenched her teeth, striving for some measure of calm. She was going to kill him. "She's grounded, Thomas. Does that mean anything to you?"

"No. In fact, it doesn't. There's no reason she should still be grounded. You punished her enough all week."

"Damn you!" Sonja raised a hand and slapped it hard on the leather top of the desk. "Get out!"

"Mind your tone *and* your words, Sonja. I will not tolerate you talking to me this way."

"You mind your own damn tone and words, you pompous ass." Fury beat through her in time with her heart, and Sonja grabbed her cell and stormed out of the study. *Bastard!* Would he ever stop doing this? Would she ever learn to stop him?

Sonja entered the kitchen and dialed Casey's cell. Her daughter wouldn't answer, that much she was sure of. Why on earth would she? Casey knew her father was here and assumed he'd handle it. "It" being Sonja...and Sonja was damn tired of being *handled* by her ex-husband, or anyone else for that matter.

Her daughter's voicemail picked up, and she disconnected

the call and tried again. As it rang, Sonja pulled a bottle of wine from the refrigerator and set her phone on the counter, engaging the speakerphone.

Blind with anger, she opened the bottle, all the while talking out loud so her daughter could hear her rage when she picked up the message. "You are going to be grounded for a very long time, young lady. Do you hear me?" Sonja poured a full glass of Chardonnay and managed a long swallow before speaking again. "Get home now, Casey!"

She hit *End* on the screen and turned to find Thomas standing in the doorway.

He eyed the glass in her hand before meeting her gaze. "Go ahead and drink the whole bottle, darling. That'll make tonight even more fun."

"Go to hell." Sonja stormed past him and went directly to her bedroom. Slamming the door behind her, she whirled around and locked it. Over her dead body, would that man be in her bed tonight. So help her God, it wasn't going to happen.

CHAPTER FOURTEEN

THE NEXT MORNING, SONJA STOOD AT THE KITCHEN COUNTER, nursing a hangover and a cup of coffee. Casey had finally replied with a text message stating that she was on her way home. Sonja had been furious last night and remained so this morning. In spite of the mammoth headache she had.

After finishing her coffee, Sonja emerged from the kitchen…and spotted her daughter, clearly trying to sneak into her bedroom without getting caught. "*Casey!*"

She glanced at Sonja, said nothing and disappeared into her bedroom.

Sonja waited, hands on her hips—pissed as hell—for her daughter to emerge. When she finally did, Casey had an impassive look on her face, which only invited more of Sonja's anger. "Get in my study. Now."

Sonja stormed in that direction, and Casey followed. "Where's Daddy?"

"Never mind him. Where in the *hell* were you?"

"I was at Trina's. What's the big deal?"

Sonja closed the door and pointed to the high-back chairs. "Sit."

"Fine."

Well aware Casey was going to toss her a great deal of attitude, Sonja took the seat beside Casey and braced herself. "You did not have my permission to leave this house. You were still grounded. That's what the big deal is."

"Daddy said I—"

"I don't give a damn what your father said. *I* did not say you could go. *I* did not let you off punishment. In case you fail to remember, Casey, *I* am the one who makes the rules." Sonja gritted her teeth and felt her neck and face flush with heat. To hell with "*Daddy*"! She was more furious with her daughter in that moment than she'd ever been in her child's fifteen years of life. Truthfully, Sonja tried to never raise her voice, no matter how angry she got, only slipping on occasion, but she'd definitely never lost her calm, cool demeanor like she was now. Sonja cringed and reached for some calm.

Casey stood, hands on her hips. "I was grounded all week. I wanted to see my friends. You never let me do anything, and you treat me like I'm a baby. I'm not a damn baby!"

"Sit your bottom down, little girl, before I bend you over my knee and spank it. Don't think I won't do it either. I've had it with your attitude. You think you can come and go as you please, huh? I got news for you, you can't, and if I have to restrict you to this house for the rest of the damn year, I'll do it. Don't push me, Casey!" So much for finding calm.

The study door opened, and Thomas rushed in. "Just what the hell do you think you're doing, Sonja?"

"Get out!" Sonja stormed to him. "You have no part of this discussion. I believe you have a flight to catch."

"She's my daughter, too, and I will not be ordered out of my home."

Sonja clenched her fists at her sides and swallowed down the bitter taste in her mouth. He was beyond arrogant, and Sonja had had about as much as she could take. "Your home? *Your* home? This is not your home, Thomas. It never was."

Thomas peered around Sonja. "Casey, where were you last night, honey?"

"I was at my friend Trina's house."

"She's lying." Sonja pinned Casey with a glare over her shoulder. "I tried to reach Trina several times, just like I tried to reach you. I'm quite certain your little friend would lie for you anyway. You were with Drake, weren't you? Did you spend the night at his house?"

"Sonja, back off." He stepped around her.

Blind with fury, Sonja whirled around. "Get. Out. Now, Thomas."

"I'll leave when I'm damn good and ready." He walked over to Casey. "Tell me the truth, kitten. Where were you?" His tone was packed full of softness.

"I was with Trina. We fell asleep and woke up late." Casey looked up at her father and didn't bat an eye while she recited the lie. Sonja would never have believed her daughter was capable of being so deceptive, but there it was, right in front of her.

"Did you see this boy your mother keeps going on about?"

"No, Daddy. I didn't. I swear."

Thomas turned and faced Sonja. She crossed her arms and once again felt her face flush with heat as rage pumped through her veins. He kissed Casey on the top of her head and then brushed past Sonja to the doorway. "She's telling the truth. Enough already. There's no reason to ground her further."

"Go back to Florida and play with your toys. I am quite tired of you thinking you can come in here and tell me how things are going to be. You have no say in this."

"She's not grounded, and that's final. You'll do as I say." He walked out of the room.

Losing whatever control she had left, Sonja followed after him, yelling *and* cursing.

"Keep running your mouth, and I'll have your ass back in court so fast your little blonde head will spin."

Once again, he tossed his favorite threat at her. "Ha! Take *me* back to court? Go ahead and try, Thomas. You and your arrogance should've thought better before you gave me sole custody to begin with. You'll never win. You don't have the resources or the energy. I'll do as I see fit with my daughter, and there isn't a damn thing you can do about it." Sonja looked over and saw Casey, only then realizing she'd followed them from the study.

"*Our* daughter!" Her ex's voice echoed through the foyer of the apartment.

Casey took a step back, eyes wide as tears ran down her cheeks. Casey swiped away the wetness and ran into her father's arms. "Stop it. Daddy, don't go."

He stroked her hair. "It's okay, kitten. I'll call you later. It's all going to be fine." He kissed the top of her head again. "I promise."

Unable to bear any more of this, Sonja tugged on Casey's arm, pulling her away from her father. He needed to go now. "Get out, Thomas. I can't stand to look at you anymore."

Thomas glared at Sonja, looking up and down her body like the sight of her disgusted him, too, before turning and walking out of the apartment. Sonja slammed the front door. "Son of a bitch!"

"I hate you! I hate you for making him leave, and I hate you for never believing me!" Casey yelled between sobs. "I hate you for everything. It's all your fault." She spun and ran toward her bedroom.

"Good. Go to your room. You can spend the rest of the night in there. I don't want to see your face either."

Sonja stormed down the hall to the kitchen in search of a glass of wine. She wasn't proud of herself for losing her temper, but she'd finally stood up to Thomas—in a way she hadn't managed to do since the divorce, and that counted for a lot. Her daughter was out of control, not unlike her ex, and Sonja had no intention of accepting either of their tantrums any longer.

CHAPTER FIFTEEN

JIMMY CHECKED HIS PHONE FOR THE TENTH TIME IN FIFTEEN minutes. Tension filled his limbs, thrumming in time with his pulse while he stood in front of the theatre, waiting for Sonja to arrive. She was late. Or not coming—*she's coming. She has to be.* He blew out an impatient breath and tugged down on the sleeves of his shirt beneath his tuxedo jacket.

Black car after black car pulled up and unloaded couples dressed to the nines for the auction—checkbooks in hand—all in the name of helping out a city of recent hurricane victims. Jimmy paced back and forth in front of the doors while staring at the screen on his phone. The auction was starting in less than twenty minutes. Running his fingers through his hair, he turned and scanned the street again.

And then, she was there.

He froze, feet rooted in place like they'd been bolted to the concrete beneath them. Seeing her was a punch in the gut, and he lost all his breath. *God, she's glowing.* Fear and excitement stole his sanity, and he was no longer sure of…anything.

The silver Towne Car behind her pulled away, and Sonja's pale blue gown fluttered in the slight breeze. She'd worn her hair down, and it also moved from the slight wind as she took one single step toward him. Jimmy had never seen her hair down, and the long blonde locks draping over her bare shoulders, even at this distance, mesmerized him.

With a mental kick in the ass, he managed to get his feet in gear to approach her. *Is this it? Is she the one?* He never figured there could or would *ever* be another for him. Not after what he *had* and lost so many years ago. The thought terrified him, but nothing could've kept him from moving toward her. Jimmy stopped a few feet away, and they regarded each other.

She held tight to the small clutch in her hand. "Are you going to say something or just stand there and stare?"

Jimmy slid his hands into his pants pockets. "I told you, get used to it. You're so goddamn beautiful, staring at you has become my favorite thing to do."

Sonja's chin dipped, and a demure smile graced her lips before she looked back up at him. "Thank you. You look quite beautiful yourself."

He smiled and nodded his thanks for the compliment. "Are you ready to go inside?"

"Yes. No…" She shook her head and blew out a breath. "I suppose."

"I think I could spend the next twenty years trying to anticipate what might come out of your mouth next, and I'd fail every time." Closing the distance between them, he held out his arm to her.

"That's a scary thought, you know. In twenty years, I'll be sixty-one."

"And you'll be as beautiful as you are today."

Sonja looped her arm inside his. "You think flattery will earn you points tonight?"

He led her to the entry doors. "God, I hope so. Either way, my flattery is sincere. You take my breath away, Sonja-the-lawyer."

"If you say you'll need mouth-to-mouth, I may slap you."

Holding the door open, Jimmy chuckled and ushered her

inside the lobby. A server rushed past them with a tray of champagne flutes, and Jimmy snagged two glasses before the guy got away and handed one to Sonja. He winked. "No slapping. You could ruin my devilish good looks."

"As if anything could ruin those." Sonja sipped the champagne and closed her eyes with a moan. "Thank you. This is just what I needed."

"You're welcome. I always know what you need. And… was that another compliment, Sonja?"

She smiled. "Maybe."

"Two in one night? Better pace yourself."

She rolled her eyes, but she was still smiling. A chill ran down Jimmy's spine, and his skin prickled with goosebumps. Her pale blue dress matched the color of her eyes, making them sparkle and shine brighter than he'd seen before. They were utterly captivating. The chill he felt only moments ago turned into a stream of flowing heat, warming his skin, and Jimmy couldn't seem to drag his gaze away from hers. To his surprise, her smile reached deep into his soul and woke something inside him that'd been lying dormant since college. Shaking his head, he pulled himself from his thoughts. "What would you like to see first? There's all kinds of art here for auction."

Sonja looked around the large lobby set up as a gallery and then back to him. "I don't know. You're the expert. Surprise me."

"You don't strike me as the type of woman who likes surprises."

"Perhaps. Yet, since I met you, you've consistently surprised me. Maybe I'm getting used to it."

"Point for me!" Jimmy chuckled and moved them to the fine art photography section.

"Oh, this is beautiful. The lighting the photographer captured is amazing—almost mesmerizing." Sonja stepped closer to the five-by-five-foot piece. "Was it taken locally?"

The picture showcased a cherry blossom tree in full bloom. The sun was setting to the left of it, casting a glow over the side of the tree and its pink flowers. "Yes, actually in Central Park, I believe. A friend of mine, Thad, took it. He's around here somewhere. I'll introduce you."

"And this is up for auction?"

"Everything you see here tonight has been donated by local artists and is up for auction."

She looked back at the piece. "It makes me feel…"

Following his gut instinct, Jimmy stepped behind her, put his arms around her waist and rested his chin on her shoulder, bringing them cheek-to-cheek. Taking a breath, he inhaled her scent. The light fragrance of her perfume mixed with her shampoo made him think of the beach and the sun. "What does it make you feel?"

"Peace." She sighed, and her head fell back against his shoulder. "It makes me feel peace."

"That's rare, isn't it?"

"Yes, especially lately." She pressed her cheek against his. "Show me your pieces," she whispered.

"All right. But I'm betting my stuff won't make you feel peace."

She let out a sigh. "That's okay."

Jimmy brought her to the section featuring the three pieces he'd donated. Two of them were rough-edge pieces with paint on canvas and large metal objects welded together into various shapes. One was a metal sculpture welded using old auto parts. She commented on them, asked him questions, but didn't have the same reaction to his stuff as she had to Thad's photograph.

A flicker of jealousy flew through his veins before he caught it, squashing it. Sonja was delicate, and it made sense the more delicate art would appeal to her. Jimmy's art was anything but delicate. There was no reason for him to be jealous over that. For whatever reason, gaining her approval or praise had become important to him, and he wanted her to feel something when she looked at his art, too.

Many people loved his art. Praised him *and* paid him for it. Yet, he craved that validation from her. Deep down, he believed if he earned her admiration, then he'd know she truly *did* recognize him as more than some irresponsible artist. It shouldn't matter so much, but it did.

They took a seat for the auction. The long gown draped over her slender legs, but the slit down the side allowed a glimpse of her creamy skin. He hadn't forgotten how soft her legs were.

The memory of when he'd had his hands on her upper thigh in his studio slammed into him and ran straight to his dick. Jimmy cleared his throat, smoothed his hand over the back of his neck and blew out a breath.

She caught his gaze, concern evident in her eyes. "Everything okay, James?"

"Yes." He smiled and took her hand in his. "Thanks for coming with me tonight."

"Thank you for inviting me."

Jimmy ran the fingertips of his free hand down her cheek. She froze, closing her eyes, but then leaned into his touch. He wanted her. In his bed, yes. But, more than that. The idea of "more" scared the shit out of him, but ever since he'd met Sonja, Jimmy knew he wanted her.

Sonja was an enigma, but he wanted more than just to solve the puzzle. Jimmy moved his hand to the back of her neck, running his fingers through her soft hair, and pulled her closer. He kissed her. Soft and gentle, a mere brush of his lips over hers.

A soft puff of breath feathered over his mouth from hers, and he kissed her again. She tasted of champagne. Sweet and heavenly. Had she realized the spell she cast over him those short weeks ago in Vegas? Did she realize, even now, the spell was still in full force? "I want you," he whispered against her lips.

She moaned a quiet little whimper and kissed him again. She gripped his jacket sleeve in her slender hand as she pulled away and then pressed her forehead to his. Her breath rushed out in short bursts. "Why? Why do you want me, James?"

"I have no answer for you, Sonja. And at the same time, I have a thousand reasons why." He gazed into her eyes and ran his fingers through her hair again. "I know I'm not what you want, but I can be if you let me try. Will you let me try?"

The auctioneer's voice over the sound system broke their intense moment, keeping her from answering his question. Damn. She smiled a nervous smile at him with lips swollen from his kiss, before facing the stage. Jimmy would've paid any price to know what was in her mind right then. What was her answer? Would she let him try?

The auction ended, and all pieces had been successfully sold at many high bids. Sonja purchased Thad's cherry blossom photo. She planned to hang it in her bedroom. And once again, that twinge of jealousy stirred in his gut. He wanted *his* art in her bedroom, not anyone else's. The possessive nature of the thought shocked him.

The night had been stuffed full of shocking thoughts. What the fuck was he going to do if he actually had the chance to make love to her? He'd barely kissed her more than a few times, and already he was lost in her cornflower-blue eyes and sharp-witted comments. What would he do if she was the whole package and the sex was really good? Which— judging by how they fought with each other—would be an understatement.

What if, right? What if it was bad? What if it was amazing? As it was, he couldn't keep her out of his mind for long. If their chemistry exploded in bed, he'd be lost to her for sure. A forty-one-year-old, divorced, full-time mother had captured his mind—*Wait. Who am I kidding?* She'd gotten a damn good grip on his heart too.

And none of it made a fucking bit of sense. For fuck's sake, he was in the deep end of the pool. Jimmy hadn't been in the pool in a very long time, and he'd forgotten how to swim. What does someone do when they're in the deep end, and panic takes over? They tread water like their fucking life depends on it.

Jimmy was doing exactly that. Treading water.

CHAPTER SIXTEEN

Sonja stood inside James's loft with the soft sounds of Otis Redding's "These Arms of Mine" floating around her. Her lower back still tingled from when he'd rested his broad palm there earlier. The heat of it penetrated the chiffon fabric like a brand on her skin. At the auction, he'd kissed her with all the intense emotion of a thousand thunderstorms. She'd felt it from the top of her head to the tips of her toes.

He wanted her, it seemed, and for more than just sex. Sonja couldn't quite believe it. Regardless, the depth of his desire was evident in his kiss and the way he touched her. Especially the way he touched her tonight. With her arms wrapped around her waist, she gazed out the tall windows in his living room, seeing nothing but her own reflection in the glass.

In the dim light of the room, the events of the week played through her mind. Sonja cringed, thinking about the fight she'd had with Thomas in front of their daughter the prior weekend. She'd tried very hard over the course of their marriage, and since divorcing him, not to fight with him in front of Casey. Regret raced through her. She never lost her temper—yelling and swearing like a crazy woman—as she'd done that evening.

What the hell was wrong with her? Sonja blew out a breath and focused on the many cars parked below. A pale effort at clearing her mind. Her muscles were tight all over, and a knot coiled in her stomach. Nervous energy thrummed through her.

Sonya recalled feeling this way when she decided to divorce Thomas. She'd felt trapped with no acceptable reason to get out, but Thomas had finally given her a credible one. He'd had an affair. Sonja jumped at the opportunity, using it as the reason—rather than her deep unhappiness—to end her marriage. Her father hadn't approved, but she'd braved his disdain for the first time ever and broken free, for the most part anyway, of the life she hated.

Perhaps it was about time to make another change.

The warmth of James's hands returned, and he wrapped his arms around her waist. "What are you thinking about?" His heated breath from his low whisper feathered over her shoulder.

She smiled and let her head fall back against him. "Stuff I shouldn't be."

He kissed her shoulder. "Always a mystery."

His lips were hot on her skin, and she shivered. "Maybe."

Turning her head to the side, she pressed her face to his neck and breathed him in. The scent she hoped to find was present and flowed through her senses. The knot in her stomach broke into a flurry of butterflies, and she brushed her lips against his soft skin. "Show me your bedroom."

"Thought you'd never ask." James stepped away from her body—the loss of his warmth sent an unwelcome shiver through her. One she didn't care to feel again.

With her hand in his, he led her up the spiral metal staircase to the upper floor. It was darker in his bedroom. He let go of her hand, and a moment later, soft, pale light illuminated the space from above. Crown molding bordered the walls, positioned just below the ceiling, and ambient light glowed behind it.

Sonja let her gaze travel down the walls and then focused on his bed...hanging in the center of the room. The mattress sat upon an elegantly carved wooden platform suspended from the ceiling by four large chains. "I have never seen anything like that in my life. It's like a swing."

"I made it a couple of years ago."

"You made this bed?"

"Yeah." He pulled on his tie and removed it. "You don't like it?"

She shook her head in amazement. "What's not to like? I don't think you'll ever stop surprising me."

"I hope not." He stepped in front of her and trailed his knuckles over her collarbone. After a moment, he moved his hand to her neck, then her hair, and tangled his fingers in it.

Sonja's breath caught in her throat when he tightened his hold on her long locks. He tilted her head to the side and kissed her neck, teasing the tender spot with his lips and tongue. He dragged his piercing over the sensitive area. Desire swirled in her stomach, and Sonja's knees went weak. She grabbed onto his arm to steady herself. "James."

"Shh. I got you." He smoothed a palm down her arm. "Just feel, Sonja."

Taking both of her hands in his, he stepped backward toward the bed. When he reached the platform, he sat and pulled her between his parted legs. Sonja gazed into the dark pools of his eyes. The sound of him inhaling a deep breath echoed around them in the near silence of the room.

Turning his head, he rested his cheek against her stomach. Circling her waist with his arms, he pulled her tight against him. Sonja placed a trembling hand on the back of his head and smoothed the disheveled, soft strands with her palm.

He gazed up at her, desire shining in his eyes. "I need you."

A bolt of desire zinged down her spine. Sonja threaded her fingers through his hair and traced his lips with a fingertip of her free hand. Bending forward, she kissed him, and fire erupted in her tummy. He welcomed her inside the warmth of his mouth and stroked over her tongue with his own. With a moan, she deepened the kiss. She needed him, too, but she wouldn't admit it to him. Heaven above, she could barely admit it to herself. James, knowing how vulnerable she felt, would be her undoing.

With his lips and tongue still locked with hers, he ran his hands up her back and stood. He gripped the back of her dress in a firm hold, crushing her body against his. She tangled her fingers in his hair and held him tight to her lips. James's hands danced from her back to her bottom and, then, to her waist and back to her hair. Sonja's body came alive with tingles. Dampness gathered in her panties, and she moaned. She needed more of him—needed to feel his skin.

Finding the zipper on her dress, James tugged it down. With shaky fingers, Sonja fumbled with the buttons of his shirt. She gasped for air when he broke the kiss and moved his mouth down her jaw to her neck. Her gown fell loose, and he rolled the straps down her arms.

He pulled away from her neck, panting for air, and gazed into her eyes. "I love your hair down and how long it is. Did I tell you that?"

Sonja shook her head in response. Swallowing past the sudden lump in her throat, she held the front of her dress in place over her breasts. Fear fueled by insecurity raced through her, putting a damper on her lust. What if he didn't like what he found beneath the gown?

He pulled her hands away. "Let me see the rest of you."

"James…" She looked down, unsure if she could do this.

As if knowing her trepidation, James cupped her chin in

his hand and raised her eyes to his. "Shh. It's all right, beautiful." He kissed her again. Soft and tender, tangling his tongue with hers as he slid her dress to her waist.

The cool air in the room tightened her nipples into rigid peaks. James pulled from her lips and cupped her petite breasts in his palms. Sonja kept her eyes closed—unable to subject herself to the expression on his face when he saw what she felt was an imperfect body.

"You're beautiful, Sonja." His voice was a throaty whisper, and he stroked his thumbs over her nipples.

The light touch shoved her fear away, and pulsing tingles shot down her body, settling in her clit. Sonja sucked in a breath, placed her hands atop his and gazed up at him. Once more, he pressed his lips to hers, this time with more urgency.

Moaning, she finished unbuttoning his shirt and smoothed her hands over his chest. His skin was pure satin beneath her palms, and the need to touch every inch of him shifted into overdrive.

Breaking the kiss, he pushed her dress over her hips, revealing her silk white panties. He ran his hands down her hips and over her bottom. "Holy fuck. My God, woman, look at you."

His rapt gaze upon her body was palpable. She didn't need to see his eyes to know what the expression was laced with—heated appreciation overflowing with desire. It was the balm her ego needed to push any remaining insecurities aside and take that walk on the wild side they'd mused about mere weeks ago in Vegas.

Sonja pressed her lips to his neck and trailed open-mouthed kisses down his smooth chest to one small, flat areola. Teasing the hard tip with her tongue, she delighted in the salty taste of his skin. She ran her thumb over the other nipple, and a bolt of triumph ran through her at his answering gasp.

James picked her up, spun her and laid her on the bed. He

pulled off his shirt and then removed his dress pants. The tattoos on his chest—a dragon on the left side, which extended up his neck, and some sort of warrior with a sword on the right—covered both his pecs. Both arms were covered in various designs, all flowing together.

There were so many that she was in awe. She wanted to spend hours exploring each one with her tongue. Such a shocking desire for her. Sonja wasn't the sort of woman who ever found tattoos appealing, but on James, they worked. More importantly, they worked for her. *Wild side, here I come.*

She had no idea what her face must've looked like, but he gazed at her, a knowing grin on his face as if, again, he could read her thoughts. "Sonja-the-lawyer, you've got a look in your eye I'm thinking I kinda like."

She licked her lips. "James-the-artist, maybe I'd like to take a walk."

He dipped his chin and raised both brows. "A walk, huh?"

"Mmhmm." She scooted to the pillows at the head of the bed.

James gave the platform a hard nudge with his thighs, forcing it to swing backward. On its return, he climbed onto the edge. He stood and gripped the chains in his palms. Using the momentum of his body, he swung them again. "Where would you like to take this walk?"

"It's not a familiar—" the bed swayed faster, and she let out a squeal of giggles, "—neighborhood for me."

"Is it a place that will make you laugh like I make you do?"

Her cheeks warmed, and she grinned. "I believe it's called 'the wild side'. Do you know the place? If so, would you consider being my tour guide there?"

Falling to his knees at her feet, he placed his hand on his chest and bowed. "I'd be honored."

Sonja raised her knees and parted her legs ever so slightly.

James's expression changed from one of jest to something

far too close to reverence. Shifting forward, his gaze traveled from her eyes down her body. With a feather-light touch, he traced a line over the top of her foot to her toes. "When this night is finished, I will have touched and kissed every inch of your exquisite skin."

Sonja's breath caught in her throat at his declaration, and she nodded. He raised her foot to his mouth and pressed his warm lips to the arch. With his other hand, he massaged the muscle of her calf. She moaned, and he moved his lips to her ankle, licking over the flesh there and onto her shin before finding the inside of her knee. He paused and glanced up at her, then ran his warm palm up the outside of her leg and nuzzled her inner thigh.

The tenderness of his touches threatened to pierce the shield that'd long been bolted in place around her heart. Sonja trembled from the inside out, in utter wonder at the rough-looking man—who was turning out to be anything but rough—perched between her legs, touching her like he'd been waiting his entire life for her.

She'd been prepared to deal with rough, maybe even a little eager to experience a night of unhinged passion, but instead, he was treating her with an unexpected gentleness. It made her uncomfortable, birthing an entire new flock of nerves in her tummy. In addition, Sonja feared he might actually breach all her walls. Feelings she had no intention of entertaining stirred in the recesses of her mind. Along with them, something akin to terror raced through her body, making her realize how closed off, how…frigid she'd become.

With a trembling hand, she threaded her fingers through his soft, thick hair. James moaned and gave her inner thigh a gentle nip. Taking his response as a green light, she tightened the grip on the strands and tugged. He growled and gripped her other thigh.

Glancing up, he trailed his tongue closer to her core and tugged her panties down her legs. "Be careful, Sonja."

"Why?" She stroked her fingers down his cheek. "Tell me why I should be careful?"

James rose between her legs and spread her thighs farther apart. His grip was tight on her flesh, but not painful. Running his thumbs up her inner thighs, he stopped before reaching her center. "Because I don't want to lose control with you."

"What if I don't want to be careful?" She ran two fingers over her clit and moaned. "What if I want you to lose control?"

"I'd say you have no idea what you're asking for." His gaze locked onto where she touched herself.

She circled the bundle of nerves before dipping her fingers inside her entrance and drawing the warm moisture up over her clit. "Maybe not, but that doesn't mean I don't want it anyway."

Jimmy ran his palm over his goatee and tried to swallow, but his throat had gone bone dry. Jesus fucking Christ, the woman was going to be the death of him. This was the fire hiding on the other side of the ice he knew he'd find in her.

Sonja rubbed tight little circles over her clit and arched on his bed. "Lose control, James." She returned those slender fingers to the mouth of her pussy and dipped them inside again, but this time deeper.

Fuck! He'd wanted to take it nice and slow with her. He'd wanted to worship every inch of her body. And he would, but seeing her like this—pleasuring her body right in front of him —was his undoing. His dick grew impossibly harder in his boxers.

Oh, yes, he'd worship her body for damn sure. However, it wasn't going to be slow and tender like he'd first intended. Nope. Now, it would be hot, hard and uncontrollable. He stood and slid his boxers off. "Sonja…"

"Yes?" Her voice was a bare whisper, with lids half closed while she pleasured herself.

He fisted his cock in his hand, and her eyes widened. "I want you to play with that perfect little pussy of yours until you come." He cupped his balls in his palm and stroked from the base to the head with the other. God, she was so fucking beautiful laid out before him in this way. A bead of arousal oozed from the tip of his erection, and his sac grew tight. He rubbed the fluid over the head and groaned.

"I don't know if I—" she gasped and arched again, "—don't know if I can do it. I've never done that before."

"Good. You can for me. Fuck, look at that tight cunt of yours swallow your fingers. Show me again, mo chroí." *Shit.* The Irish term his father often used slid past his lips before he had a chance to stop it.

"Wha…" The word slid out on a breath. "What did you just call me?"

He bit his lip and shook his head. "Just an Irish endearment. Keep going." God, what the fuck was he thinking? *My heart.* That's what he'd called her. Thank God she didn't know the words because he was damn sure she would've bolted from the bed.

Sonja met his gaze and nodded before returning her focus to his cock in his fist. When she started rubbing her pussy again, Jimmy blew out a breath and relief washed over him. She licked her kiss-swollen lips. "James, talk to me."

A bolt of lust shot down his spine, and Jimmy went to his knees between her legs. "Dip your fingers inside again. Goddamn, you're beautiful. I can't wait to have you on my tongue."

"Mmm." She curled her long legs around his hips. "I've never had anyone talk to me the way you do."

He ran a hand up her inner thigh. "Do you like it?"

"Yes."

"Spread your lips apart for me. Let me see how wet your cunt is." His focus was riveted on the sound of the soft breaths and little moans escaping Sonja's lips.

Doing as he asked, Sonja spread her folds apart. He took in the sight of her wetness and couldn't suppress the growl erupting from his chest. "Oh fuck, yes, that's perfect. My mouth is watering right now." Jimmy bent over her and took her mouth in a hard kiss, and the head of his dick nudged at her opening.

She whimpered into his mouth and raised her hips off the mattress; the delicious heat from her wetness coated the tip of his cock. Jimmy jerked from the kiss, but his hips refused to follow suit. Sweet, warm heaven began enveloping him. "Sonja. Fuck. Wait!" Unable to stop, he shifted his hips forward and pressed the head a little deeper. "Fuck, woman."

"Oh God. I need you inside me. Please?"

Biting back another curse, he somehow forced himself to pull back. "I need to… Fuck, you're so warm and soft. Dammit, I need to get a condom."

"Crap. I wasn't even thin— Mmm."

He kissed her again, then trailed his lips down her throat. "And I have to taste you first."

Sonja ran her hands over his back and around to his sides; her long nails dug into his flesh. The small sting of pain sent scalding pleasure down his spine and straight to his balls. Jimmy moaned and moved to her breasts, licking between them and then to one taut nipple.

They were flawless. Little quarter-sized, pink areolas with firm nipples the size of eraser tips. Perfect for nibbling on. He'd almost lost his mind when he pulled her dress down earlier and saw them for the first time. He sucked one tight bud into his mouth and rolled his barbell piercing over the tip.

Sonja gripped the back of his hair and cried out, arching against him. Jimmy growled and nipped the peaked flesh and drew it deep into his mouth. She tasted like sweet heaven on his tongue. With his other hand, he massaged its mate and rolled the firm nipple between his finger and thumb. Then he pinched and tugged the tip.

She gasped, tightened her long legs around his waist and raised her hips off the bed. Her hot pussy made contact with his length again. Jimmy unconsciously thrust his hips forward, sliding between her wet folds. *Jesus! Fuck! God, yes!*

"Don't stop." She clawed at his shoulders.

He pulled from her nipple with a growl and moved down her body. He *had* to taste her first. Plus, if he didn't get his dick away from her heat now, he was going to slide inside. Screw the condom. He knew he was clean, he'd been tested, but still, shit happened. And he wasn't about to assume anything. Not until they talked about it.

He dragged his tongue over her velvet skin, and Jimmy's head spun in sheer ecstasy. He was drunk on her. The taste of her. The scent of her. The feel of her body. Her everything was all over him. It was too much to bear, yet he couldn't get enough.

To him, Sonja was the essence of heaven. To him…she was perfection.

Smoothing his palms down her body, he wrapped his hands around her slender waist and kissed and licked a path to her stomach. She moved her hands to the back of his neck. "James."

When he progressed lower, kissing above the thin patch of pubic hair, her fingers tightened, and her nails dug into his skin. Raising his head, he blew a breath over her clit. Her stomach visibly jumped, and a whimper left her lips. The sound made every muscle in his body get tight. Jimmy glanced up her body—she had her eyes closed, her lips parted. "Look at me."

Sonja dragged in a breath and opened her eyes. Jimmy

lowered his head and, keeping his gaze locked with hers, licked over her clit. She jerked beneath him and moaned.

He snaked out his tongue and licked through her slit. Heaven. Fucking heaven. "Don't take your eyes from mine, Sonja."

"Oh God. James. Please?"

Sliding his hands over her hips to her thighs, Jimmy spread her legs and raised her knees over his shoulders. "Please, what?" He ran his tongue through her wet slit again. "More of that? Or this?" He sucked her clit between his lips, rolling his tongue over it along with his piercing.

Sonja shifted her hips forward, and he dived in, gorging himself on her sweetness. Drunk. He was definitely drunk on all that was Sonja-the-lawyer. And it wasn't going to be "last call" anytime soon.

"Yes. Yes!" Her high-pitched words rode out of her between her pants for breath.

Oh, yeah. There it was. This was what he wanted from her.

UNABLE TO CATCH HER BREATH, Sonja kept her eyes glued to the man lying between her legs. His face held a hard expression, and his eyes focused on hers. James licked through her wetness and swirled his tongue around her clit. Every time the warm ball made contact, a jolt of pure electric lust blazed through her, and she jumped and shivered. Tension built, heavy and tight in her stomach.

She was going to come, and soon. Sonja tilted her pelvis forward, seeking more contact with his mouth and tongue, and ran her fingers through his hair. "James. Please. Don't stop."

He groaned against her flesh—a vibration she felt in her core—and shifted his hands beneath her bottom, raising her hips off the bed. Then she felt it. His tongue. Hot and wet, thrusting inside. Oh God. *Oh God!* "More!"

He dragged his tongue back to her clit, circling again. "More what?"

"What?" He licked over her clit again, and she sucked a breath in through her teeth. "God, yes! That."

He raised his head. Which, of course, took his delicious mouth away from her. "More what? Tell me, more of what?"

"No, wait. Don't stop. Please?" Was he crazy? He wanted her to tell him what she wanted more of? Wasn't it obvious?

James blew a warm breath over her clit, and she whimpered. "Tell me what you want more of, Sonja."

She attempted to push his head back to where she needed it to be, but it was useless, he wouldn't budge. Frustration thrummed through Sonja, and she laid her head down on the pillow and closed her eyes. "I can't. Just...keep going."

"Look at me."

Her head snapped up. "I *am* looking at you! And you're baiting me."

He snaked out his tongue and licked along the crease where hip met thigh. "Yes, I am."

"Why on earth would you? You got me here. I'm naked in your bed. You're between my legs...doing what you're—" she motioned with her hand to where his face was between her parted thighs, "—doing. I was quite enjoying it, and you pick *now* to start a fight with me?"

"I want to hear you say the words."

"What wor—" His tongue made contact with her clit again, and Sonja sucked in a hard breath. "Oh, my God!"

But then he took it away. "Tell me what you want me to keep doing."

"Goddamn you! Ugh! Why?"

"Because I know you can, and you want to, and I want you to. Sooo, do it." He grinned and ran his tongue through her folds, never taking his gaze from hers.

Her skin prickled with goosebumps, and her walls clenched in desperate need to be filled. If she didn't come soon, she might get up and kill him. She was damn sure she'd get off on an insanity plea too. "Insane from lack of orgasm." *Your honor, he was deliberately withholding!* It could work.

She made a mental note to research it on Monday, but got no further before his tongue thrusting inside her channel shoved her thoughts into another universe and drew a moan from her throat, sounding so foreign, Sonja couldn't believe it'd come from her. She gripped his hair tight in her fingers. "Tell me what you want me to say, please. I'll say anything, just don't stop…doing…that."

"Say—" James licked through her folds, "—the words. The ones I used. Tell me." He sucked her clit between his lips.

She gritted her teeth. Mindless, with a savage need to orgasm driving her forward and maybe a desire to claw his eyes out, too, Sonja made up her mind. Screw it. He wanted dirty words out of her mouth? Fine. She'd give them to him. He'd better make it worth it because if he didn't, she was definitely going to kill him. Sonja glanced at James. Lying on his stomach, he had her legs draped over his shoulders and a grin on his lips rivaling the Cheshire Cat himself. *Pompous ass.* But that grin? God, that grin did her in on so many levels she couldn't even begin to count.

"Well?"

Decision made, Sonja sat up and took his face in her hands. "James, I want you to eat my pussy like you're a man dying of thirst. Then I want you to make me come." His smile widened, and a swift urge to slap him rose like a storm. She stifled it and lowered her voice. "Now listen carefully. You are not to stop until you've licked every part of me clean." She dipped her head, and instead of slapping him, she kissed him.

He growled against her lips and urged her back to the bed. With a hard grip on her ass, he set to his task.

"Oh, yes. God, yes." Perfect. She licked her lips and rose

up on her elbows. "That's what you want, James? You want to hear me talk dirty for you?"

He nodded and sucked her clit, pressing his tongue against it. Moving his hands from her behind, James gripped her hip with one. As he continued to suck her swollen, now pulsing clit, he dragged two fingers through her folds, then thrust them inside.

"Honey, yes. That's it. Deeper." Sonja rolled her hips, and her walls clenched down on his fingers. God, it felt good. Too good. She was going to come. If he just—

"I feel you. You're squeezing my fingers. Come for me, Sonja." James took her clit between his lips again and curled his fingers inside her, stroking that spot she'd always heard about but didn't believe existed.

Sonja lost her mind, drowning in a sea of sexual heat, and a wave of pure bliss crashed over her, washing all her inhibitions and fears away. Arching on the bed, her orgasm exploded, and she cried out his name.

James kept his hold on her clit with his mouth, and his fingers stroked inside her. Sonja jerked her hips off the mattress, and her channel spasmed around his fingers, over and over.

She gasped, straining to catch her breath with each pulse. Quivers from her climax raced through her, and she trembled from the inside out. The waves were endless.

James pulled his fingers from her and sucked at her opening, then delved inside and licked between her folds. Being the man she'd started to learn he was, he moaned and groaned—completely unafraid to hide his pleasure—breathing heavily while he took in every drop her climax had produced.

As Sonja's body settled from what might be the best orgasm she'd ever had, James rose up between her legs and reached over the side of the bed to the nightstand. When he righted himself, he had a condom in his hand.

Sonja's legs had turned to jelly, and she wasn't sure she

could even move them, let alone any other part of her body. All she could do, in her haze of bliss, was watch while he tore open the package and slid the condom down his hard length.

God help her, but her pussy clenched at the sight.

He was gorgeous. Every inch of his muscled, lean body. His tattoos, his piercings, his cock. All of him…beautiful. She wanted James inside her, and she wanted him there now.

CHAPTER SEVENTEEN

Jimmy settled his hips into the haven of Sonja's parted thighs. The flush on her pale skin, in the dim light, was beautiful. He'd done that to her. He'd made her come hard and cry out his name, and pride welled and spilled over inside him. Call him a caveman, but he seriously entertained the primal urge to grunt and pound his chest.

She tasted like a fucking dream. And once he'd finished taunting her, forcing her out of that damn tight-ass, pedigreed shell she kept herself in all the time, she tasted even better.

Sonja met his gaze, her blue eyes glittering. Dipping his head, Jimmy kissed her, deep but soft, and then dragged his teeth over her bottom lip. Fuck, she'd blown his ever-loving mind. He knew all along she had it in her. And it was by far the hottest fucking thing he'd ever experienced. She took control, told him what to do, what she wanted.

He wasn't submissive. Ever. But the tone of her voice when she commanded him to eat her pussy sent a shudder through his body he hadn't anticipated and had never felt before. It was all he could do not to come on the sheets, he was so turned on. Sonja-the-lawyer had thrown all caution to the wind, ripped off the confining pearls binding her, and had gone all roadhouse-raunchy on his ass. He'd have done anything she wanted. Anything.

Sonja trailed her hands down his back to his ass. "James."

"Tell me again. Tell me what you want." Resting his weight on one forearm, Jimmy brushed her hair back from her face. "Don't ask me why, just give it to me. Tell me." He trailed his lips over her jaw to her neck. "Please?" Moving a hand down her chest, he cupped one breast in his palm and tugged at the nipple.

She gasped, arching beneath him, her warm cunt gliding over his dick. Fucking hell, he wanted inside her, but he wanted her to tell him to do it. He told her not to ask why because the truth was, he wasn't sure he understood the reason why he *needed* her commands so much. He just knew he did.

Sonja bent a leg over his ass. Taking his hand from her breast, Jimmy ran it down her body to her other thigh, raised it and placed it around his waist. He shifted his hips and nudged at the mouth of her sweet cunt with the head of his prick. "Tell me. I need to hear it."

"I'll give you what you need." She raised her head from the pillow and kissed him. Her sweet tongue tangled with his. Jimmy broke from her lips and pressed his forehead to hers. And waited. She tilted her hips forward, and the head parted her folds farther, just breaching her entrance. "I want your cock inside me, James."

Her words crashed over him, and he froze. The head of his cock throbbed, and his dick grew harder. He couldn't believe this. Couldn't believe it was happening like this. He blew out a breath. "More. Tell me more, mo chroí."

"I want it now. Give it to me, but nice and slow. I want to feel every inch of your length as you stretch my cunt."

Fuck yeah! Jimmy nodded, cupped her jaw in one hand and kissed her, keeping his eyes open and locked with hers.

And did what she commanded.

Slow, working the head in and back out, only to press a little deeper inside her tight heat. Sonja moaned into his mouth, and he swallowed it. Sucking her tongue, he groaned when her cunt spasmed around his cock.

She gripped his ass, dug her nails in and tightened her legs around his waist. Then she broke the kiss. "Move inside me, James. Now."

"God, yes. Yes! Anything you want." Jimmy slid out and back in again. He rolled his hips when his pelvis met hers and ground against her clit.

And with each pass, she raised her ass from the mattress and met his thrust, rubbing against him. The base of his spine tingled with his impending orgasm. Every muscle in his body stretched tighter than a suspension wire.

"Faster." She licked up the side of his neck. "Harder, James. Fuck me harder."

Jimmy cupped her ass in his palms. Tilting her hips off the bed, he slid his length out to the tip and then slammed back inside her. "Your cunt is so sweet and hot. Your words are making my dick harder than it's ever been before. Please, don't stop."

Sonja cried out with each thrust and raised her legs higher on his back. He pounded into her, but she felt so delicate and small in his arms it worried him it might be uncomfortable for her. Slowing, he moved his lips to her ear. "Am I hurting you?"

"No. Why? Don't stop. I'm fine." She bit his shoulder.

The sting from her teeth shot through him like a bolt of lightning. The head of his dick pulsed, and he growled. Holy shit, she was killing him. "Because you're s—"

She grabbed him by the back of his hair, pulled his head up and glared into his eyes. Hers were blazing with lust and need. "I said, don't stop. I meant it. You feel incredible. Move your ass, James. I want to feel you pound into me. I *need* you pounding into me."

"Oh, my God." Jimmy gritted his teeth, took her legs and

hiked them high and over his forearms. Rising to his knees, he gripped her hips, slid his cock out and then drove back in. Hard.

"Yes! Yes! Again." She panted, fisting her hands in the sheets.

Jimmy stared down her body and almost lost his mind. Her tight cunt swallowed his prick, and the sound of his pelvis slapping against hers filled his ears. Each time he slammed deep, her tits bounced, and she groaned or whimpered in pleasure. She liked it. No, she loved it.

The look on her face sent a tremble through his body. Fuck, he was getting close. He needed to make her orgasm again before he lost control and couldn't stop himself from coming. Dropping her legs from his arms, he pushed her knees up high and moved over her body again. She spread her legs wider, tilted her pelvis up and took him deeper.

Jimmy lost his control.

Mindless and wild from the feel of her clenching around his shaft, heat spread through his body, his balls tightened, and his orgasm crept up his shaft.

"Oh God, James. Yes, baby. Like that. Don't stop, I'm going to come."

"With me." He sucked in a breath and rocketed into her. "Come with me, mo chroí. I can feel how close you are." Sonja arched on the bed. Her blonde hair fanned out around her like a halo. A damn angel was what she looked like. "I want your eyes on me when we come."

Her gaze moved back to his, and he continued to fuck her. Hard. Fast. And without mercy. Their bodies, slick with sweat, slid against one another. Her tight nipples grazed his chest. He rolled his hips, grinding against her clit. Sonja dug her nails into his ass, and her pussy clenched, spasming around his dick. Barely able to breathe, he stared into her eyes. Her lips parted, and she let out a high-pitched moan, nearing a scream before her lids fluttered closed.

"Eyes, Sonja." He grunted and rode her harder. Her walls clenched again, and he gritted his teeth. Still in the throes of her climax, she opened her eyes and held his gaze. Jimmy's orgasm exploded out of him. He stopped moving and breathing while his dick pulsed inside her.

"I feel you." She tightened her arms around him. "James, I feel you."

"I feel you too, mo chroí." He swallowed, trying to catch his breath.

His heart pounded in his ears, and he knew, without a doubt, he never wanted to have another woman in his bed again. Sonja was the best he'd ever had, and once a person had the best, they sure as hell didn't let it go. Ever.

CHAPTER EIGHTEEN

Sunlight glared harsh through Jimmy's loft windows.
Rolling over and untangling himself from the sheets, he sat up
and called out her name. He glanced over at the bathroom.
The door was open, the light off. Damn. "Sonja, you
downstairs?"

Silence.

At least until Norton jumped onto the bed and answered
with a purr-filled *mmmrrwaawww*. Jimmy ran his palm over the
cat's sleek black fur. "You're certainly not the pussy I was
looking for, but good morning to you too."

Falling back to the pillows, he pressed the heels of his
hands to his eyes. When the hell had she left? And how had he
not felt her go? Jimmy grabbed the pillow she'd slept on.
Pressing it to his face, he inhaled. Yeah, there it was…the
lingering scent of her shampoo and perfume. He might never
wash the stupid thing again. Which meant he needed to get
up right now and put the bedding in the machine. The idea of
trying to preserve her scent on his sheets was way too chick-lit
for him to even allow.

Norton meowed again and nudged Jimmy's leg. "Some
help you are. Why didn't you tell me she was leaving?" The

cat gave him a disinterested look before curling up next to him. Jimmy tucked the pillow under his cheek and closed his eyes. Images of the night with her flooded his mind. His sensory memory went into overdrive. Her taste, her scent, the way her skin felt beneath his hands. Her body wrapped around his while he buried himself inside her heat. All of it flowed through him, drawing a groan from his throat. His body tensed, and his cock twitched, coming to life.

But that wasn't even the half of it. The way she'd been—the way she took control—had knocked him on his ass for sure. Sonja burst from her Upper East Side upbringing and, in doing so, took him to a place he never knew he wanted to go. In all his sexually active life, he'd never felt anything like it. After round one, Jimmy believed he'd died and gone to heaven. Then she completely let loose on him for round two, taking him higher than he'd ever been before.

Sonja had directed him to keep his hands above his head, not allowing him to touch her as she stroked his skin with her fingers and tongue. But then the situation went into overdrive. With his cock buried in the warmth of her mouth, Sonja drove him to the brink of pleasure-induced insanity, refusing to allow him to come. And as Jimmy was swept into a storm of physical bliss, he'd begged and pleaded for her to let him orgasm.

"Please" was the only word he'd been capable of saying. Until finally, she granted permission, and he exploded, spurting his climax down her throat.

Jimmy died a thousand deaths, only to be revived again and again with the sweet power of her words, mouth and hands. The road back from heaven led straight to hell. And what a sweet, carnal trip it'd been.

He burned for her—was still burning. The woman lit an inferno inside him no one had ever struck before. And he knew he'd burn for her forever. There'd be no stopping it now.

A loud bang at the front door ripped him from his

thoughts and also the bed. Jimmy was up and moving toward the stairs before thinking twice. Halfway down the spiral staircase, he remembered he was buck-ass naked. *Shit.* Pivoting, he barreled back up and retrieved his sleep shorts.

The pounding resumed, echoing through the loft in a methodic beat. "I'm coming!" Jimmy hopped down two and three steps at a time, somehow managing to pull his shorts up over his ass. He didn't bother checking the peephole, just threw the door open.

Andy blew past him and hung a left into his kitchen. "'Bout time you opened up. Jesus."

"Come on in." With a shake of his head, Jimmy closed the door and followed after her.

"So?" Andy pulled a couple of bagels from a brown paper bag, sliced them and popped them in the toaster. Jimmy leaned against the doorframe and crossed his arms. She glanced at him with one eyebrow raised before moving to his empty coffee pot.

"I'll get it." Entering his small kitchen, he pulled the filters and coffee from the cabinet.

"Ooh, nice perfume." Andy grinned and pulled a small tub of cream cheese from the bag. "She's got good taste. Tell me what happened."

"Of course, she's got good taste. She's with me." He chuckled and set the pot to brew.

"*With* you, huh? Spill."

"After I've had some caffeine and a shower."

"Dude, I'm not waiting for you to shower before you tell me what happened. Yeah, obviously, you fucked her. That much I can smell." Andy scrunched up her nose and laughed. "On second thought, maybe you should shower first."

"Andy, you're such a girl. And yet...not."

"Dick."

He grinned and pulled two plates from the upper cabinet. "In your mouth."

Andy gagged. "Fucking wrong, dude. Just wrong."

"Hey, don't knock what you haven't tried."

She rolled her eyes, pulled the hot bagels out of the toaster and tossed them down on the plates. Using a butter knife, she slathered each of the halves with a liberal amount of spread. His best friend knew he was kidding, and likely, her silence meant she was contemplating her response. Knowing her, she'd wait until he had a mouthful of coffee or bagel before tossing a smart-ass comment his way, ensuring he'd almost choke to death.

The coffee pot beeped. Jimmy poured them each a cup. Andy took her plate and mug and headed toward his little dinette set in the living room area. Jimmy followed. Sitting across from her, he watched her with caution while she took a sip from her mug, and he took a bite of his bagel.

"A dick is a dick, is a strap-on, is a dick. Whatever works." She shrugged and took another sip of coffee.

There it was. *Shit.* Jimmy laughed around his mouthful of food, covered his mouth with the napkin and did his damnedest not to choke. He swallowed. "I knew it was coming. Only a matter of time." He chuckled. "And thanks for the visual. Christ, Andy."

"Hey, what can I say? You asked for it." She bit into her bagel. "So, are you officially off the market?"

He nodded and added a wink. "Consider me a taken man."

"Noted. But tell me…" She leaned forward on her elbows. "Does your dream girl know this?"

Jimmy stared at his best friend, trying to figure out how best to answer the ten-million-dollar question. Leave it to her to ask him the one thing he didn't know the answer to.

Andy raised her brows. "Go shower. You can think about your answer while you're in there."

"It's complicated."

"Now who sounds like a girl?"

Jimmy grunted and stood. "Eat your bagel. I'll be back in ten."

She grinned up at him. "Yes, dear."

It wasn't a hard question, and one he should know the answer to. How could Sonja not know she'd stolen his heart? Figuratively updating his Facebook status to "In a relationship with…" without him having to do it himself? She must know. And if she didn't, he guessed his next move was to make sure she understood exactly what the deal was between them.

He was a man, after all. Men were hunters by nature and instinctively went for what they wanted. Jimmy wanted Sonja —had wanted her from the moment he met her. Okay, maybe not the exact moment he met her. Technically he thought she was a bitch when they first met, but about five minutes after, and once he'd started plying her with shots of Jäger, getting her to loosen up, he knew he wanted her.

Problem was, he still wasn't sure if she wanted him.

After spending the afternoon with Andy, Jimmy settled on his sofa, his phone pressed to his ear, listening to it ring for what felt like a thousand times.

"Hello, James."

Her sweet voice through the phone line was a balm to the anxiety knotting his stomach in fear she wouldn't answer. Jimmy blew out a breath he hadn't realized he was holding. "How's your Saturday been?"

"Overall, it's been okay. You?"

Slouching down on the couch, Jimmy propped his feet up on his coffee table, crossing them at the ankle. "After waking up in an empty bed, which kinda sucked, I have to say, it got better. Hung out with my best friend for most of the day."

"Surely you didn't expect to wake up next to me. I would think you'd prefer to wake alone. After all, isn't that how things work when you're single?"

Jimmy closed his eyes. She didn't get it. "Yeah, I guess, except…"

"Except what?"

Screw it. He may as well hit her with it straight. "Except I would rather have woken up with you there, that's all."

"I can say your answer both surprises and confuses me."

He chuckled before letting out a loud sigh. Nope, Sonja-the-lawyer did not get it. "And I can say your reaction, sadly, does not surprise me."

"I'm not sure why or what to do with you."

Jimmy dropped his feet to the floor and straightened, rubbing the spot between his brows. "No need to be sure. I have plenty of ideas."

She let out a soft laugh. "Oh yeah, like what?"

Memories of the prior night with her played through his mind—vivid images of her naked body. Her voice echoing in his ears… *Bliss.* It'd been fucking bliss. But really, could you call something you hadn't stopped thinking about since it happened a memory? It was more like a steady stream of awareness of an event he for sure wanted to repeat. He lowered his voice. "Liiiiike…what you did with me last night. That's a fine place to start."

"Hmm…so your desire is to have more than a one-night fling with me?" Her tone was matter-of-fact, almost threaded with disbelief, nowhere near inquisitive.

"Desire? No, Sonja. I *intend* to have much more than a one-night fling with you."

"You sound quite sure of yourself."

"I am." He stood and walked to the loft's big windows. "I know last night was more than a fling for you, too, so don't try and deny it. That kind of chemistry and being in sync with another person is rare, and it *will* happen again."

Silence stretched over the cellular waves between them. Her soft breaths in his ear were the only indication she was still on the line until finally she spoke. "I can't deny there was chemistry between us, but I'm not sure it's wise to continue."

"Wise?" He laughed. "Of course it's wise. It'd be the smartest thing you've ever done. Trust me on that."

"You love to annoy me. You love to pick fights with me. Why on earth should I trust you, James?"

"Tell you what. Come have a drink with me tonight, and I'll explain all the many reasons why you should trust me."

"No."

"No? That's it? Just...no?" Jimmy pinched the bridge of his nose and paced in front of the windows. Jesus, she was stubborn.

"No is a complete sentence, James."

"Yeah, you've said that before and yeah, it is, but I don't get it. Your favorite word to say to me is no. But last night, you said yes. Finally. And you have to admit you're grateful you did. The many orgasms we shared are proof of that."

"I can admit I'm very grateful for the experience of last night."

"Come have a drink with me, Sonja."

"No. But if you must know, I have other commitments tonight I have to attend to."

"Okay, fine, you win. Tomorrow."

"Sunday has its own set of commitments."

Defeat and disappointment warred for first place in Jimmy's heart. Resuming his spot on the couch, he rested his head back on the cushions and closed his eyes again. He thought for sure after last night they'd be past the constant problem of her pushing him off. But, no. "No" was still her favorite answer when it came to him. And that fucking sucked. "You're not going to make this easy, even a little bit, are you?"

"I'm sure I don't know what you mean."

Jimmy blew out an exasperated breath. "Oh, I think you do, but I'll let it go for now."

"Look, I had a very nice time last night."

"Sonja, don't. I'm not going anywhere. No matter how

many times you tell me no, I'm not giving up. So, although I'll concede defeat tonight, be ready for me to call tomorrow."

"Fine. Have a good evening, James."

"You too." Jimmy tossed his phone on the couch beside him.

It was clear Sonja intended to keep him at a distance. Being patient wasn't going to be easy for him, but he'd give it hell. He would show her, at every turn, he was serious. He'd found something that lit his world on fire—he knew it lit hers up just the same.

There was no way in hell he was going to let her rob either of them of that.

CHAPTER NINETEEN

Sonja looked up from the file she was reading at her desk to find James standing in her office doorway. *Damn.*

He smiled that wicked smile of his, holding up a large paper sack for her to see. "Care for some lunch?"

She blinked, straightening in her seat. "Um…"

James strolled into her office as if it were perfectly normal for him to be there. A black T-shirt with some sort of white skeleton-and-angel design on it clung to his chest. A pair of faded blue jeans with a few faint stains on them—might be paint or actual stain—hugged his long legs. Crap, he looked really good.

"Close your mouth, Sonja. It's just food."

She snapped her mouth closed, and her cheeks got warm. Good grief, how embarrassing, but why did he think it was okay to just show up? "I realize it's food, James. I just wasn't expecting you."

He smirked and set the paper bag on the meeting table to the right. "Well, if you checked your text messages once in a while, you might've known I was coming."

She glanced at her phone resting on her desk. He was right. She'd heard her phone beep many times throughout the morning, even noticed his name coming up on the alert notifi-cations, but chose to ignore him. The way she'd been with him the other night had been on a constant loop in her mind. Sonja had been out of control in a very controlled manner; her behavior was far too out of character for her.

She rubbed her arms. But what made it worse was she enjoyed every minute of the dominant actions she'd taken with him. She'd liked it—it made her uncomfortable how much she liked it. With her lifestyle, career and daughter, Sonja couldn't afford such reckless behavior. She had no intention of seeing him again and hoped, perhaps foolishly, he'd simply…go away. "I was busy. Working." She pushed away from her desk and stood, annoyance prickling her skin. "I'm surprised you're awake, really. What is it, twelve-thirty? A little early for you."

He looked her up and down. "Ha ha ha. You say the sweetest things to me. Come on, my uptight attorney. Come eat. I bet you didn't even have breakfast, did you?"

The look in his eyes told her he approved of her chosen work attire. Though she couldn't care less, her skin warmed in excitement, knowing she pleased him. *Stay focused, Sonja.* Smoothing her palm up the back of her hair, she peered at the bag of food. "You shouldn't worry about my eating habits, James."

"And you shouldn't worry about my sleeping habits, Sonja." He pulled out a several cardboard containers of Chinese food. "Unless, of course, you plan on being next to me while I sleep." His eyes were wide, like an inquisitive child asking for a treat. Good grief.

The aroma of the food hit her nose, and her stomach let out a growl. Okay, yes, she was hungry. Fine, she'd eat. People could eat together and have it not be a "thing". Plus, they'd eaten together before, but then again, they ended up at his loft with her pressed against the brick wall of his studio, his thigh nestled between her legs. Sonja stifled a groan and reached for the bag. "Don't count on it."

James tugged it out of reach. "Sit. I got this."

"Okay, fine. As you wish." Sonja pulled out a chair and took a seat.

He winked and set a cardboard plate and chopsticks in front of her. "I wasn't sure what you liked, so I got a bunch of different things. Veggie, non-veggie and a mix. Hope that works for you; I know how picky you are."

It was sweet, even if she didn't want to think of it that way, how he arranged the narrow paper package atop a napkin beside her plate. She didn't want to pay attention to the endearing things he did, like how he wrapped the blankets around her when she was in his bed the other night. Sonja's agitation melted into a warm puddle in her stomach. She clasped her hands together in her lap. "I'm not *that* picky."

"Sonja, you give new meaning to the word picky." He opened carton after carton of food. "Brown rice or white?"

"Brown, please. Can I get you a drink? Water, soda, coffee?"

"That's the one thing you can do. Water works fine."

Sonja nodded, stood and pulled two waters from the mini fridge behind her desk. Returning to the table, she set one in front of his plate and cracked her own, taking a healthy sip.

James deposited a large pile of brown rice on her plate. "What would you like?"

Sonja eyed the cartons. "What do you have that's chicken?"

"Sesame chicken or sweet and sour?"

"A little of both." She held her hand out. "May I serve myself, please?"

"Can you not *let* someone do it for you?"

"Of course I can. But judging by the pile of rice on my plate, you're going to force me to buy a new wardrobe."

He held the container in his hands. "Please, like you have to worry about gaining weight. You're perfect."

Sonja flushed hot from head to toe. The man was delusional. She wasn't perfect. Not too bad for her age, but definitely far from perfect. Especially compared to women his age. Sonja cringed and took the paper carton of sesame chicken from his hand. "I'm not perfect. But, thank you."

"You're also stubborn. Anyone ever tell you that?"

"I prefer to call it set in my ways." She shrugged and scooped some chicken onto her plate, and did the same with the sweet and sour. "You know, because I'm old. Too old for you."

"Boo hiss. Killjoy. Age is a number, and you know it." James filled his plate with white rice, beef and broccoli and then some lo mien noodles, plus an egg roll.

Good grief, where did he put it all, because Lord knew there wasn't an ounce of fat on his delicious body. Sonja opened her package of chopsticks, split them apart and rolled them together in her hands to get the splinters off. "Everyone who's under the age of forty says that." When she looked up, he was beside her chair. Sonja's breath caught in her throat.

He turned her, seat and all, toward him. Placing both hands on the arms of her chair, he leaned forward, coming nose to nose with her. "When are you going to let the age bullshit go?" His voice was a low grumble, vibrating over all her nerve endings.

Still recovering from her loss of breath, she did the only thing she could think of: she glared at him. James gave no ground. He simply glared right back. But then, instead of saying anything else or waiting for an answer from her—the one poised on the tip of her tongue—he kissed her.

Hard, wet, hot and full of everything she hadn't realized she was starving for. Sonja moaned into his mouth. He deepened the kiss, pressing her against the back of her chair. She tangled her tongue with his and threaded her fingers into his thick hair, pulling him closer. Have mercy on her soul, his mouth was a drug. How she had gone two-and-a-half days without it was beyond her realm of consciousness. It was ludicrous to deny herself this. What the hell had she been thinking?

James wrapped both arms around her waist and pulled her up and out of the chair. A frantic clash of tongues lit an inferno inside Sonja, which traveled between her legs and sent her clit pulsing. She pressed her body against him and explored his sides and back with her hands. Finding his hair again, she tugged the thick strands and nipped his lip.

James growled. Grabbing her ass, he hiked her closer and pressed the evidence of his arousal against her abdomen. With a whimper, Sonja reached between them and grabbed for the waistband of his jeans. She needed this—wanted his shaft in her hand. She got the button free, slid the zipper down and pushed her hand inside his pants. The heat of him was like a brand on her palm.

James grabbed her wrist.

Sonja froze.

He pulled away from her lips and pressed his forehead against hers. "Fuck. Does your office door have a lock? Because I'm about to bend you over the table."

They were both panting, and Sonja had to clear her throat before she could answer. "Yes, it has a lock. But we should stop."

He smiled and kissed the tip of her nose. "Then you might want to take your hand off my cock."

Sonja yanked her hand from his jeans like she'd been touching a hot stove. She cringed, and her face flushed hot. Embarrassment filled her like a rising tide, smothering any trace of the lust-infused fire burning a mere ten seconds ago. "Sorry."

James threw his head back and laughed. "Christ, you're

fucking adorable." He pressed a quick kiss to her lips. "Eat, Sunny."

Sonja disentangled herself from his hold and stepped back. "Sunny?"

He took the seat next to the one she'd been in and dragged his food in front of him. "Yeah, short for sunshine."

"Sunshine?"

"Yeah." He popped a piece of broccoli in his mouth. "Sit, eat."

Sonja took her seat and placed the napkin on her dress slacks. "I don't do nicknames."

He chuckled and took another bite. God, he was infuriating! Sunshine? Sunny? Really? Sonja was back to glaring at him again until she pinched a piece of chicken between the chopsticks and placed it in her mouth. With her senses back where they should be, her stomach reminded her she was, in fact, hungry. So, she swallowed her agitation along with the food he'd brought.

After a few mouthfuls, guilt settled like a cold breeze. It was *very* thoughtful of him to bring her lunch. She should be thanking him instead of being a bitch and picking apart his comments. However, the fact she was about to drop to her knees a minute ago and take him into her mouth might've been thanks enough. She rolled her eyes. *Sexual favors for food? Great idea, Sonja.*

They sat in relative silence and ate, and Sonja was grateful for the reprieve from the constant fight with him. Talk about a mental whiplash. One minute, she was agitated and ready to throw him out, the next, she was ready to climb his body like a play gym, and then boom, back to agitation a second later.

Mental-freaking-tennis.

Jimmy rubbed his stomach and leaned back in his seat. Lunch had hit the spot. Making out with Sonja had hit a better one. Eating dessert first had always been his favorite thing to do. True to form, she was fire and ice for him. And he fucking loved it. He loved kissing her and feeling her go all soft and hot against him, and he also loved fighting with her. In his opinion, there was nothing better. Sonja wiped her mouth before folding the napkin and setting it on the table. She had very precise table manners. And he found them beyond adorable. He pretty much found every damn thing about her either sexy or adorable.

He was, in no uncertain terms, fucked.

He took a swig of his water. "Come out for drinks with me tonight."

"I can't."

"Seriously, will you ever stop telling me no?"

Sonja sighed. "Honestly, I don't know."

She wore a pair of fitted black dress slacks. A pale, almost-sheer, mint-green, loose-flowing blouse with what looked to be a green tank top underneath it. And his favorite: spiked pumps. Christ, she was tall already, and those heels made her runway model tall. He wanted to see her in those heels and only those—or any others she had—naked in his bed. "Sounds promising. Maybe there's hope. By the way, you look beautiful today."

She frowned, her brow creasing above the bridge of her nose. "I'm dressed for business and the courtroom. I wouldn't classify this as beautiful."

"Thank you, James. Very kind of you to say." He glanced away toward the floor-to-ceiling windows in her office, then back to her. "You're very welcome, Sunny. But really, I think you would probably look beautiful in sweats and a T-shirt, so yeah."

"I think you may have lost your mind." She chuckled.

"Maybe so. But at least I'm enjoying the benefits of it."

"What would those be?"

"You. You're the benefit, Sunny."

"Stop calling me that."

"No. Ha! See, I can say no just like you can." He grinned. "So, a negative on the drink tonight. What about tomorrow?"

"Hmm, probably not."

"Tell you what. We can discuss it when I come by for lunch again."

"James, you can't just come here when you feel like it. I have work to do."

"I'm well aware you have work. And, yeah, I can. So, I'll see you tomorrow." He stood, gathering the trash from their lunch and folding up the lids on their leftovers. "Gonna put these few cartons in your mini fridge. That way, when you stay too late tonight, which I know you'll do, you can pick at what you want." Sonja watched him—her gaze like a brand on his skin—as he got everything in order and stowed the remainders in her fridge. When Jimmy turned back toward her, she'd gotten to her feet and was still staring at him. He stepped in front of her. "I'll let you get back to work now."

"Thank you." Her lips tilted into a small smile. She raised her hand as if to touch him, but stopped herself.

Jimmy inched closer. "Go ahead. Please. Touch me, mo chroí."

"You still haven't told me what that means." She smoothed her palm up his arm. "Whatever it means, it sounds beautiful."

Jimmy pulled her against him and poised his lips at her ear. "Beautiful is the perfect way to describe it." He pressed a light kiss to the side of her neck. Her breath hitched, and her delectable breasts pressed into his chest. "I want you," he whispered. "And I know you want me. So, think about that tonight when you're working. I'll see you tomorrow."

"Okay." Her words, riding on her sharp breaths, caressed his neck.

He gripped her waist in his hands, pressed a soft kiss to her lips and walked out of her office.

CHAPTER TWENTY

The next day, Jimmy made his way downtown to her office with meatball grinders for each of them. And this time, he remembered the drinks. He hadn't bothered to text her this time—just walked in her office around twelve thirty. His Sunny appeared less shocked to see him. He was gifted with a sweet smile from her when he winked and proceeded to set up their meal on her conference table.

She looked amazing, too. She wore a burgundy blouse and a black fitted pencil skirt hugged her lean hips and long legs to just below her knees. But it was the peep-toe black pumps with a tall chunky heel that made his dick hard. It was all he could do not to pull that tight skirt up and bend her over the arm of the sofa in her office. Stowing his lust-filled thoughts, he managed to eat and carry on a normal conversation with her. It was good—no, it was great, actually. Having basic dialogue between them was fucking priceless.

Once again, he asked her out for drinks. And once again, she declined, but he was confident he'd wear her down. On his way out, he pressed a deep kiss to her lips, making sure to let her know with his tongue how much he wanted her.

She was breathless when he walked out of her office.

Fuck's sake, he wanted her back in his bed the second after he'd woken alone the previous Saturday morning. But tomorrow was another day and another chance with her. He'd bring her lunch again. And for the rest of today and tonight, his only solace was knowing their heated kiss would keep her mind on him, with any luck, as much as his was on her.

Craving him like he craved her. Missing him like he missed her. And horny as fuck because she denied them both what they needed so badly.

SONJA EXITED the double doors of the courtroom into the hall. The morning had been grueling—witness after witness on the stand, testifying against her client, and Sonja cross-examining them. The afternoon would bring her defense. Not that she was worried at all. Her client had an iron-clad case, and the prosecution's was mostly circumstantial. Piece. Of. Cake.

Sonja finished in the restroom and headed back out into the hall. She had a few documents needing review during the lunch break. Heading toward the end of the corridor, her high heels clicking on the linoleum floor, she focused on her phone, perusing the morning's emails from her assistant…and walked straight into James.

"Hiding out from me in the courthouse, I see."

Sonja tilted her head to the side, appraising him and trying not to notice how good he looked. "Yes, that's exactly it. I'm hiding." She moved around him and continued to the benches by the windows. *My word, he really isn't going to give up.*

"It's lunchtime. Let's go grab something."

Sonja took a seat and pulled the two-inch-thick file from her briefcase. "I can't. I have documents to review before the trial convenes again. Work, remember?"

He held his hand out to her. "Yes, work, Sonja. But you

also need to eat. Come on, there's a deli right around the corner. We'll eat, and you can work."

She looked up at him. He had his sunglasses perched on the top of his head, and his lips pursed, waiting for an answer from her. His hazel eyes appeared lighter than normal from the sunlight filtering through the large windows. His goatee was perfectly trimmed. Did he ever *not* look good? Sonja's standard answer for him sat poised on her tongue. *No. No, James, I can't come with you to eat. No, because if I say yes, I'm not sure I'll ever be able to say no to you again.* But she couldn't say the word.

He wiggled his hand, flexing his fingers, waiting for her to grab hold of it. "Come on, Sonja."

Do it. Tell him no. "Fine." *Crap.* She stuffed the file back in her bag and took his offered palm.

James pulled her up from the bench. Still holding her hand, he wrapped their arms around the back of her waist and kissed her. Without giving herself permission, she melted into his embrace and kissed him back. She couldn't help it. He was wearing her down, making her crave his lips…among other things.

A block away from the courthouse, Sonja settled at a small corner table in the deli and ate her grinder while studying the file for her client's case. Or rather, tried to study the file. James was at Sonja's right, instead of across from her, with his hand resting on her thigh. The light touch was making it impossible for her to focus.

As promised, he kept his word and let her work while he busied himself reading a discarded newspaper; however, he kept touching her. In fact, he hadn't stopped touching her since the kiss they'd shared in the courthouse hall. She'd forgotten how good it felt to be touched. She liked it. Much more than she'd ever admit to him. When a person went too long without the intimate touch of another human being, they became numb. Sonja guessed that's what had happened to her

—no longer wanting what she'd become accustomed to living without. However, this man, this young, beautiful and stubborn man, had awoken what she'd long since forgotten about. In spite of her constant attempts to push him away, she secretly hoped he wouldn't stop.

James leaned over and pressed a soft kiss to her cheek, and the alarm on her phone went off, letting her know it was time to head back to court. Sonja sighed. Fastest hour and a half in history. He gathered their trash. She stood, closed the file and placed it back in her bag.

"Dinner tonight?"

She stood and slung her bag over her shoulder. "I can't tonight." James's face fell, his disappointment quite clear. Sonja reached up and cupped his cheek in her hand. "I have something to do with my daughter tonight."

Closing his eyes, he leaned into her touch. "Okay." He turned his face and kissed her palm. "Tomorrow's another day, mo chroí. Come on. I'll walk you back."

"You don't have to."

He smiled and took her hand in his. "I know."

They walked down the block hand in hand. Not an easy trick in Manhattan, yet he didn't let go of her. This time, she had *wanted* to say yes to him. Thing was, James wasn't giving up, and she was running out of excuses. Sonja stared at the cracks in the sidewalk and searched her mind for the reasons why she continued the futile attempts to put him off.

No. Wait. She knew why holding her ground was paramount. He was too young for her. It was foolish to believe he'd remain interested in her for very long. Plus, she had her hands full with her daughter and the law firm and her damn ex-husband. Sonja was just too busy. Continuing this game with him would only lead to heartbreak, likely with her heart being the one broken. She didn't need that on her plate, too.

Simple as that, she was back on track.

No dinner tonight. No nothing with the talented James Donnelly.

The idea she might be making a mistake caused her stomach to knot into a million tangles. Sonja shook off the feeling and smoothed her palm up the twist of hair on the back of her head. She glanced up in time to find they were back at the entrance to the courthouse.

James pulled her into an embrace. She let him. He kissed her. She let him do that, too. Then she watched him walk away, disappearing among the rest of the pedestrians milling on the sidewalk. *Steady. Focus. Keep it together.* Another pass of her hand up the back of her pulled-up hair before she turned and entered the building. Time for work.

JIMMY PULLED the rag from his back pocket and wiped off his hands before hitting the mute button on the iPod speaker dock. Walking to the base of the stairs, he listened again. Sure as shit, another knock echoed from his front door. Taking the stairs two at a time, he glanced at the clock on his cable box before rounding the corner and reaching the front door.

He checked the peephole and—holy shit! Running his fingers through his hair, Jimmy drew in a deep breath. He unlocked the door, took another deep breath, then swung it wide.

"Hi." Sonja adjusted her bag on her shoulder. "Did I wake you?"

Jimmy was so fucking shocked to see her he couldn't talk. But his eyes worked just fine. As he took in her appearance, his lips curled into a grin. She still wore her navy blue business suit...and looked de-fucking-licious in his opinion. Which was the only one that mattered. He shook his head and stepped to the side.

She placed her hand on her stomach and crossed the threshold. "Okay."

Jimmy closed and locked the door. When he turned, she'd moved to his small dining table in the living room area. Without another thought, he was behind her. Wrapping his hands around her waist, Jimmy pressed his bare chest to her back and his mouth to the side of her neck.

Sonja let out a sigh, and her briefcase dropped to the dining chair in front of her. Jimmy tasted the sweet, soft spot behind her ear, taking in her scent. Running his palms around to the front of her suit jacket, he unbuttoned it. She raised an arm, tangled her fingers in the back of his hair and then turned to face him.

Her lips. God, her fucking lips. Jimmy wasted no time taking what he wanted. He dived into her mouth with his tongue, sucking, nipping and devouring what he'd been craving. He could kiss her forever. And he might, too.

Sonja pressed her body against his and circled her arms tight around his waist, digging her nails into the skin of his back. "Fuck," he said against her lips. His cock was hard as a steel rod in his jeans, and he rolled his pelvis against hers. "I can't believe you're here." Jimmy placed kisses along her jawline to her neck and pushed her jacket off her shoulders.

She shook the jacket off and tossed it on the table behind her. "I don't…I just…"

"Shhh…don't, mo chroí." He kissed her again, pulled her blouse from her skirt and unbuttoned it. Parting the two halves, he broke the kiss and ran his gaze over her bra, not missing the hardened points of her nipples. "So fucking perfect." He tugged one bra cup down and sucked one of the rose-hued points between his lips.

Sonja ran her fingers through his hair and arched against him. Jimmy groaned and twirled his barbell over her nipple. Honeyed lust flowed through his veins, settled hot in his balls and made his cock harden more than he thought possible.

Moving to the other nipple, he pushed the other cup aside and bit the tip.

Sonja let out a loud gasp threaded with a moan. Pulling away from her breasts, Jimmy ran the flat of his palm down the center of her chest to her stomach. Her body felt hotter than a kiln, and fire blazed in her eyes when he met them.

"Fuck me, James." Raising her skirt, she slid it up her hips, revealing her thigh-high stockings and garter belt.

And… No. Fucking. Panties.

Unsure if it was the direct order she'd given or the sheer beauty of her pussy bared and ready for him, or maybe the combination of both, Jimmy almost came in his jeans. "Oh, fuck. Fuck, yes." He picked her up and set her on top of his table. "Lie back."

She did as he asked, which was good because he was so wild for her, he wouldn't have tolerated anything else. Bending forward, he raised and spread her legs and licked through her slit, drowning in the pure sweetness of her arousal.

She thrust her hips forward. "Oh God, yes!"

Jimmy pressed her knees to her chest and teased her clit, rolling the barbell in his tongue over the swollen nub. Releasing her legs, he spread her lips and pressed his thumb inside her cunt. He stroked that small ridge of skin within her channel and sucked her clit harder.

Sonja whimpered and panted and writhed beneath his mouth. He wanted her to come hard, and once she did, he was going to fuck her even harder. God help him, this woman owned him. And she had no goddamn idea the power she had.

"James!" His name rode the scream belting out of her, and she arched off the table. Her cunt clenched around his thumb. He kept his mouth right where it was and sucked, knowing he'd driven her over the edge already, but he wasn't done with her yet. The head of his cock throbbed in his pants, and he wanted inside her like a drowning man wanted a life jacket.

But he wanted her begging for it.

She gripped his hair, her legs shaking beside his ears. "I can't…" She yanked his head away, sat up and dragged him to her mouth.

His lips and tongue were coated with her flavor, and Sonja let out another moan, sucking his tongue. He willingly shared the taste of her orgasm with her. "You like that, don't you?"

She didn't answer, just sucked his bottom lip into her mouth. Unbuttoning his jeans, she peeled down the zipper and freed his cock. Scooting forward, she positioned his prick at her opening.

"Babe…wait. Condom."

"Fuck the condom." She grabbed his hips, yanked him toward her and wrapped her long legs around his waist.

Jimmy's dick sank into her heat, and he looked down where their bodies joined. He gritted his teeth and let out a hiss. The warmth of her wet pussy swallowed the swollen head of his cock. "Jesus Christ, look at that."

Sonja reached between them and spread her lips apart, rimming the edges of his shaft with her fingers while he slid in and back out again. He pulled out completely, then pushed back in, slow and with deliberate control, the rim of the bulbous head catching on the tight mouth of her pussy. She moved her fingers to her clit, and the groan that rose out of Sonja sounded like it was mined from deep in her belly.

"Fuck yes, rub your perfect clit for me." Jimmy watched, mesmerized by her actions and by the glistening sheen of her juices on his shaft. "You missed me. Look how wet you are for me, Sonja." He slid out to the head once more, teasing her with short thrusts, just deep enough to penetrate her entrance. A bolt of fire raced down his spine, settling hot in his sac. Having her tight, wet heat wrapped around his shaft was too good, almost more than he could tolerate.

Sonja gripped his chin and raised his head. "Yes, I missed you," she said before thrusting her tongue into his mouth.

A growl barreled out of him, and he slid his hands under her ass, changing the angle of her pelvis before burying his prick deep. "Say it again."

"No! Take me harder." Kissing down his chin and along his jaw, she settled at his neck and bit down hard.

Another growl came out of Jimmy. He could hardly recognize the sound as something coming from him. But then her tight channel clenched around his length—his mind spun, and he lost control. "You want it dirty again, don't you. Fuck, is that it? Tell me."

Sonja ran a hand up the back of his head, tangling her fingers in his hair, and then took hold of the strands and pulled hard. His gaze met hers. And she bit his bottom lip so hard he winced from the sting. Jimmy gripped her thighs, raising them higher and wider. He slammed into her, grinding his pelvis against her clit. "Fucking bitch."

"Yes. Say it again." Still holding him by his hair, she bent her head and bit his shoulder.

Goddammit, that shit hurt! And Jimmy did *not* want her to stop. He'd take everything she wanted to dish out, and he'd fuck her harder with each serving.

CHAPTER TWENTY-ONE

JUST LIKE LAST WEEKEND, WHEN THEY'D HAD SEX, SONJA couldn't believe how she was behaving. It was as if she lacked even a modicum of self-control with this man. She licked her lips, and the salt from his skin tingled on her tongue. Heat sped through her body like wildfire when he called her a bitch —so much so she thought she might spontaneously combust.

Then he repeated it. Oh God, she was going to come…

James gripped her hips and slammed into her so hard she bit her tongue. "So fucking dirty. This what you want?"

"Yes!" Sonja let go of his hair and scraped her nails down his back.

James sank deep inside her and ground against her clit. Her orgasm hit with a force she'd never felt before. Her cunt rippled, and her whole body went rigid. Finding his hard ass, she palmed both cheeks and sank her nails in and bit down on his shoulder once more.

"Fuck! Sonja…goddammit!" At once, James pulled free of her channel and flipped her over.

Sonja's high-heeled feet landed hard on the floor, and with a hand in the center of her back, he pressed her chest to the tabletop. Her orgasm ripped through her like a blazing inferno.

"You want to play rough? Hmm?" James tugged her blouse down her shoulders. Bringing her arms behind her back, he stopped at her wrists and bound them with the shirt. "I'll give you rough."

The wood was cool against her heated skin, and a shiver raced through her. Sonja laid her cheek against the smooth surface and closed her eyes. *CRACK!* James's hand landed on her ass cheek. A scream punched out of her, ending in a gasp, and then he slid his length inside her channel again. Yes! *This* was what she needed.

Like a junkie getting a fix, he'd become her drug. How or when it'd happened, she had no idea, but— *CRACK! Oh God!* Sonja's eyes rolled back in her head, and a moan poured out of her like water. Heat spread from her ass cheek to her cunt, and her channel clenched in response.

"Oh, sweet hell." James rocketed in and out of her, then reached beneath her chest and tugged her bra down to fondle her breasts.

Her hips banged against the table with his thrusts. "Give me more."

"Greedy!" He tugged at her hair, yanking it free of its pins. When it unraveled, he wrapped the length around his fist and pulled her head back, raising her chest from the table. "How much do you think you can take?"

Gritting her teeth, Sonja arched and rolled her hips. She'd lost her mind again, she was quite sure, and she didn't care. She wanted this. Wouldn't go without it again. Lightning raced through her, building the pressure, and she knew she'd come again. "How much can you give? I'll take everything you have."

"I feel you. Gonna come all over my cock again, aren't you? So—" *Slam.* "—fucking—" *Slam.* "—greedy." *Slam!*

The orgasm exploded through her, and she screamed his

name. But he didn't stop to let her come down. Instead, he kept going, slapping his hips into her buttocks, merciless in his thrusts in and out of her. Mindless, Sonja fell into an incoherent haze, and everything around her got fuzzy.

He released her hair, and she collapsed onto the table once more. Pulling free of her channel, James cursed through a loud groan and pressed his shaft between the cleft of her ass cheeks. Sliding his length between them, he climaxed. Ropes of scalding hot semen spurted over her buttocks, lower back and hands. *God yes!* Unable to speak, she closed her eyes and rode the aftershocks of her orgasm while he branded her skin.

James fell over her, breathless. With his face buried in her neck, he blanketed her with his body. Finally sated, Sonja focused on drawing air into her lungs as her heart thudded in her ears. After a few minutes, he raised his head and ran his fingers through her hair. He pulled her hair away from her neck and pressed a soft kiss to the spot behind her ear. Sonja shivered and drew in a deep breath.

Rising off her, he untangled her shirt from her wrists. "Stay here. I'm going to grab a towel."

Craning her neck to the side, she glanced at him and nodded. The haze she'd gone into lingered, and she blinked, trying to focus while he disappeared from her view. Sonja closed her eyes and drew in another deep breath. Never—not ever—had she been like this with another man. A fire had sparked in her belly, and from the moment he laid his hands on her, she burned out of control.

The only remedy being him. His scent. His lips and tongue. His body. Him. Every single part.

She didn't want things to be like this, but she'd found herself at his doorway anyway. She didn't *want* to crave him or smolder inside until desperate, only to give in to the need, allowing him to ignite her once more into a blazing inferno and bring her to heaven so she could drown in the flames.

Sonja opened her eyes when the warm, wet towel swiped

over her lower back and down her bottom. Nudging her legs wider, he wiped between them and down her inner thighs. So tender. Too sweet. A moan poured out of her like thick honey, and lust flowed through her veins when he smoothed the cloth over her clit and lingered there.

James pressed a kiss at the base of her spine. "Still greedy for me." He chuckled, and the sound rippled over her skin.

Sonja's eyes widened, and she cringed. It was all too much, and she had no control. No, she didn't want to want him like this.

CHAPTER TWENTY-TWO

Jimmy walked out of Sonja's office. She wasn't there. And according to her secretary, she wasn't in court today either. Upstate with clients was what they told him, and also, she wasn't expected back until late. Fuck him. He'd tried her cell two or three times already, and she'd yet to reply. She'd gone MIA on him. Again. Fuck him, squared.

True, the work excuse was legit, but didn't mean she couldn't fucking reach out and let a man know what was up— the same man who'd ridden her so good the night before that she screamed his name when she came.

Jimmy shook his head and let out a sigh. It didn't matter. He now knew she couldn't stay away long. Eventually, she'd end back up at his loft and back in his bed. Eventually, the craving would take over, and his Sunshine would show up.

He shot a text to Andy, then made his way to his favorite pub. Once he arrived, he gave his best friend a peck on the cheek, ordered a beer and settled on a stool at the bar next to her.

"You come up with an answer to my question yet?" Andy gave him a sideways glance before taking a swig of her beer.

"Which question is that?"

"Nice try, Romeo. I don't see the lawyer by your side."

"Yet."

"Look." Andy shifted in her seat and faced him. "This woman is going to eat your heart for dinner, and just so you know, I *will* extract it from her stomach and not bat an eye."

He chuckled. "Wow, that was really graphic. And kinda gross, but sweet."

"I'm serious, Jimmy. I've never seen you like this over a chick before, and it's freaking me out."

He gave her a soft smile. "You love me, huh?"

"Yeah, of course I do. And?"

"Andy—" The bartender delivered his beer, and he took a swig. "It's going to be fine. Trust me."

Her eyes rolled in their sockets. "So it's official?"

"Not exactly."

"Then it's not going to be fucking fi—"

"Things are progressing."

"Oh? Well, then. Spill, I'm all ears. What's happened since the weekend?" Andy settled against the low back of the stool and crossed her arms.

"I've seen her every day this week for lunch."

"And?" She pinched his arm. "Dammit, spill!"

"Jeez, you're such a girl sometimes."

She let out an exasperated sigh. "Fuck off. Tell me."

Jimmy threw his head back and laughed, loud and hard. God, he loved his best friend. When he finally got himself composed, she was glaring at him, agitation oozing from her pores. Jimmy had to stifle another laugh. She was so cute, all fired up and ready to defend his honor. He was lucky to have her. Andy was a true friend to him, and he'd pretty much jump in front of a train for her. "Okay, fine. We had a few hot moments in her office. I went to the courthouse and practically had to drag her out to eat during the lunch break. I swear she doesn't even stop long enough to think about it." Leaning back in his seat, he stretched.

"Define a few hot moments?"

"We kissed. Well, more than kissed because while in her office, I swear she almost climbed me."

Andy laughed. "Climbed you? You sure it wasn't the other way around?"

"We might've both been up for a little climbing that day." He grinned.

"So that's it? A few hot kisses, and you think that means things are progressing? Once again, you're the girl."

"No. That's not all that happened." It was his turn to pinch her.

"Well, for fuck's sake, tell me. And ow! Dick." She rubbed her thigh where he'd landed his mark.

"Crybaby. You should know better than to get into a pinching war with me by now. It's an Olympic sport in my family."

She tilted her bottle up to her lips. "Your family is a special kind of sick."

"She showed up at my place on Wednesday night." Jimmy glanced at his best friend.

Andy pulled the bottle away, her cheeks puffed out with the beer she held in her mouth, her eyes wide in wonder, waiting for him to add to the statement. He wasn't going to give the details of what went down, of course—those were between him and Sonja—but he'd let her know the high level. Andy waved her hand, motioning for him to continue.

"Swallow first before you choke."

She did. "Getting juicy now. What happened?"

"Not gonna kiss and tell, but I will say this: Sonja is everything I've ever wanted. In all ways. I don't want anyone else, Andy. Truth."

Andy stared at him. Her face a blank mask. Her mouth closed. Shit, he had no idea what she was going to say. And obviously, she was worried about him. What he'd spoken aloud to her were words she'd never heard come out of his mouth as long as she'd known him. Having no idea what to expect, Jimmy braced for the worst. When the silence stretched longer than he could stand, he spoke up. "Say something, for Christ's sake. You're scaring me."

"I'm sorry. Did you just say you don't want anyone else?"

He frowned at her. "I told you the other day I was off the market."

"Yeah, but…well…I guess I didn't really buy it."

"Andy, you know me well enough to know I don't say shit like that."

"I know, but I figured it was the morning-after-good-sex talking." She shrugged. "Now I'm the one who's scared."

"Don't be."

"I don't want you to get hurt."

"Believe me, neither do I. But this is it for me. I'm telling you, she's it. And if I get hurt, I guess I'll have to deal with it."

Andy leaned over and hugged him. "If you do, I'll be there."

Jimmy rubbed her back and gave her a squeeze.

"After I extract your heart from her stomach, of course."

Jimmy laughed and squeezed her harder. "I love you, too."

CHAPTER TWENTY-THREE

Sonja glanced at the time on her phone. It was just past nine-thirty at night, and she'd worked straight through lunch and dinner, and it would appear well past normal office hours, too. She'd told her assistant no interruptions or visitors today, which meant she had no idea if James had shown up.

All of the day before had been spent with clients upstate, and although she'd gotten a few texts from him and a couple voicemails, she'd yet to reply to any of them. Sonja hadn't been ready to face him after her performance Wednesday night in his loft. On his dining room table, of all places. She cringed and smoothed her palm up the back of her hair. Once again, her mind betrayed her, replaying the heady events of that night, and the cringe fell fast and hard on the heels of the lust that rose and tightened her stomach.

Sonja stood and walked to the windows. She didn't know what she was doing with him. James Donnelly was a harsh contrast to everything in her life, at least everything she'd been allowed to know. Every inch of her skin was tight and itchy, and she rubbed her arms. Her father would never have approved of a man like James. Correction: young man. Sonja could practically hear her father's authoritative voice in her head, scolding her for her choices. She scratched the back of her neck and cringed again.

She was too old for him.

He was too wild for her.

God, but she wanted him. Sonja's insides tumbled with a rage of twinges, and the juncture between her thighs pulsed, hot and ready. For only him. Closing her eyes, she wiped the sweat from her brow. She was detoxing. The only remedy: James Donnelly…her drug. "Dammit." Sonja circled her arms around her middle and bent forward. "Ugh! Dammit! I don't want this."

"Are you avoiding me?"

Sonja whirled around in shock, managing somehow to not stumble backward. James stood, arms crossed over his broad chest, leaning against the frame of her office door.

"What?" Sonja stepped back until she felt the cool window glass at her back. "What are you doing here?" He looked so damn good. His hair was a mess in the perfect way he always styled it. His trimmed goatee framed his lips. A gray button-down short-sleeve shirt covered his upper body, but the tattoos on his arms and the one peeking out from his collar remained on display for her eyes to feast on. Sonja's mouth watered, and she had to swallow a few times.

He took a step toward her. "Are you avoiding me?"

Pressing her palm to her chest, she tried to calm her racing heart. He needed to go. The only way to get over this need was to not be near him. Cold turkey was the best way to beat any addiction. He needed to go now. *Oh God, he looks so good.* "Why would I be avoiding you?" Her words sounded thread-bare to her own ears. No doubt he heard it, too. She needed to move away from the window, away from him.

He stopped barely a few feet away. His hazel gaze roamed over her face and down her body. "I don't know why either. So, would you like to explain?"

Like a physical touch, she responded to his call, going

loose on the inside as molten lava spread through her veins. Sonja moved her hand to his chest. An attempt to hold him back or push him away—either would work.

James took another step closer and then circled her wrist in his palm. His body this close was more than she could resist. The scent of his cologne hit her senses, and she gasped. Her mind screamed what action to take: *Push him away! Tell him to go!* But her heart thudded in her ears and drowned out the voice of reason. Her body, however, dictated exactly what she needed. She needed this. She needed him. With her breath sawing in and out, Sonja gripped the thin fabric of his shirt. Instead of pushing him away, she pulled, closed the small distance separating them and kissed him.

James's tongue sank into her mouth, and a moan bubbled up from deep inside her. *Oh God, yes. There it is.* Sonja wrapped her arms around him, pressed her body to his and devoured his mouth—like a woman starving to death...no, she'd been right before, like a junkie getting her fix. A fucking junkie.

Sonja pushed the thought aside and took what she needed from him anyway. What he offered so willingly to her. Her skin tingled, her stomach tightened, her clit throbbed...but now for a different reason. Now, it was because she was getting what she desperately craved. Him.

His fingers speared into her hair, and he peeled her from his lips. "Two fucking days, Sonja!" He gritted his teeth. "Two days without this." He kissed her again, nipped her lip, then swiped over it with his tongue.

She moved to his neck, kissing and sucking his sweet skin. Screw her doubts. Screw what her father's voice in her head said—or what anyone might think. No, never again would she go without this, without him. She was insane to try. "Never again."

Still holding her hair, he pulled her away from his neck. "Promise me. Tell me right now you won't deny us this ever again."

"I won't. I promise." Sonja pulled at the buttons on his shirt, popping each one as fast as she could. She had to get to his skin. *Needed* to feel more of him. "I need you. Now." Sonja parted his shirt, marveling in the beauty of him. He was right; she was greedy for him. At this moment, she couldn't get enough.

Smoothing her palms down his chest, she followed the path she made with her tongue. His taste and scent permeated every cell of her body, and lightning struck through her, settling between her legs. Kissing down the center of his abs, she went to her knees and then pulled open the button and zipper of his jeans.

James pulled the pins out of her hair. "Fuck, I missed you."

Sonja tugged on the waistband of his boxer briefs, revealing his hard cock. "Fuck, I missed you too." Without a care for the profane words tumbling out of her mouth, she licked her lips, leaned forward and sucked the swollen crown into her mouth. The bead of ejaculate at the tip hit her tongue, and she moaned.

He tangled his hands in the length of her hair, but his body fell still. She didn't want him still. She wanted him wild, as wild as she was. "Fuck my mouth, James." Digging her nails into the skin of his hips, she swallowed him again.

But James didn't move, just tightened his hold on her hair and groaned. With his prick deep in her mouth, Sonja stopped and gazed up at him. She dropped her hands and then held her arms out slightly at her sides, palms up, offering him free rein to control her movements.

She wanted him to do what she asked, yes, but she also wanted to give him what she knew he craved, too. He understood, and she knew it because his cock jerked in her mouth once he registered her actions.

JIMMY COULD HARDLY BELIEVE his eyes. Kneeling before him, she'd submitted and wanted him to take control, yet at the same time, she remained dominant, too. There was a balance to their exchange of power. One he hadn't expected to find. With a growl, he tightened his grip on her hair and drove hard and fast in and out of her mouth. "Mo chroí. You're killing me."

Sonja sucked and rolled her tongue, moaning each time he plunged deep into her sweet mouth. God help him, she was beautiful with her cornflower-blue eyes locked with his and her full lips pulled tight around his shaft. She sucked him in earnest, and it was all he could do not to come right then and there, spurting down the back of her throat. She needed to control the situation just like he did, and she'd found a way to do it. That was good enough for him.

Jimmy gritted his teeth, his balls drawing up tight with each thrust between her hot lips. "Fuck, look at you. Amazing. So beautiful."

The first time they'd had sex, Sonja had taken control. He'd urged her to do so, thinking it was what she might need to be more comfortable. To his surprise, it'd cleaned his clock and aroused him in a way he never imagined possible. The other night, the control had shifted back to him. He'd bound her hands and fucked her hard and fast. Tonight, they were balanced. Without a doubt, Sonja was all he wanted and would ever want again.

Panting, Jimmy let go of the grip on her hair and ran his fingers through the length. He needed to breathe—slow down a bit. This was too decadent to rush. And even if coming in her mouth, like he'd done the other night, had been bliss, tonight he wanted to be inside the heat of her pussy when he climaxed.

Sonja hummed, and her eyes fluttered closed. Jimmy moved a hand to her face and caressed her cheek. "Your pussy all wet for me?" She gazed up at him and gave him the barest of nods. His dick pulsed between her lips. "I want inside your cunt. Will you let me?"

She moaned, her nostrils flaring, and sucked harder. God. Damn. Unable to take it any longer, he pulled free of her mouth and took a step back. Sonja licked her lips and stood, but stumbled. He reached for her, taking her by the elbow, and helped her to her feet.

She pressed her lips to his in a hard kiss, tangling her tongue with his. Turning them, Jimmy pressed her back against the glass and tugged up her skirt. Sweet heaven was what he found when he placed his palm between her thighs. Her panties were soaked through with her juices. He touched his lips to her throat. "Unbutton your shirt," he mumbled against her neck.

Her blouse fell to the floor. Jimmy reached behind her and unhooked her bra. It landed at their feet. Taking her pert breasts in his palms, he massaged them, pinching her nipples between his fingertips. Kissing and licking a line down her breastbone, he went to his knees. Jimmy ran a thumb over her clit through her panties.

Sonja jerked, sucking in a breath as she grabbed his hair. He licked the thin fabric, tasting her sweetness. "Sopping wet for me. I love it." Tugging the material aside, this time, he slid his tongue through her folds and couldn't suppress the groan against her soft curls.

"James! Yes!" Sonja rose on tiptoe, still in her heels, and lifted one leg to rest on his shoulder.

He spread her swollen lips apart with his thumbs and licked her cunt before covering her clit with his mouth. With a tight grip on his hair, she rolled her hips forward. Sucking hard, he kept up the pressure, flicking the tight bud with his tongue and then driving two fingers inside her tight pussy.

"Oh God! Oh God!" She ground against him, then stiffened—the sound of her head hitting the glass resonated around them. Sonja cried out his name and came.

Jimmy lapped at the mouth of her pussy, drinking in her pleasure. Before she stopped moaning, he leaned back and lay on the carpeting. He shoved his jeans down his hips and then held a hand out for her. She stared at him, still panting for breath, the blue of her eyes darker than he'd ever seen them. He freed his wallet from his back pocket and pulled a condom out. "Come to me, Sonja."

"I don't want that." She slid her panties off and stepped forward, straddling his legs, but stayed standing. "I want to feel you, and only you, inside me, like the other night."

Jimmy tossed the wallet and condom aside and took his prick in his hand, stroking from base to tip. He didn't want anything between them either, but they hadn't talked about it. Although it was important, the point was moot. They'd already crossed the line.

She bit her bottom lip and stroked two fingers over her clit. "I like watching you do that."

"And I like watching you do *that.*" Jimmy's balls ached, his dick harder than an iron rod. He wanted inside her tight cunt, but, man, watching her rub her clit while she watched him stroke himself was beyond hot. "You keep doing that, and I might have to pull you down to sit on my face. Taunting me with that gorgeous cunt is just plain cruel...and wonderful at the same time."

"Is that supposed to be a threat or a promise? I could simply sit on your face and suck your cock at the same time. We'd be giving equal punishment then, wouldn't we?"

Jimmy arched, thrusting his pelvis up and fucking into his fist. "I fucking love when you talk dirty. Come punish me by riding my dick."

Sonja sank her two fingers inside her channel. "Say, please."

Jimmy groaned and then chuckled. He loved her like this —loved? *Shit.* He swallowed and licked his lips, giving himself a second to find his voice. "Pretty please?" His words came out in a whisper, which was fine. She'd heard him loud and clear.

Reaching behind her, she unzipped her skirt. Stepping to the side, she removed it before straddling his hips and kneeling above him. Jimmy ran his hands up her bare thighs. Her soft skin made his palms tingle.

Sonja bent forward and kissed him, dragging her tongue against his—wet and full of all the passion consuming him. Still kissing him, she slid a hand between them and took his cock in hand. Positioning him at her core, she lowered herself until he was buried deep inside.

Her wet heat enveloped him, and he broke from her lips, panting for air. Her mouth hovered above his, and she rocked her hips. Smoothing his palms up her thighs to her ass, he gripped it tight, enjoying the slight flex of her buttocks when she undulated forward and back.

With her pelvis tight to his, she ground her clit against him, and her walls clenched around his prick. Jimmy was drowning once again. Lost in all that had become his Sunshine. Her hair fell around them, blocking everything in his peripheral view. All he could see was her. All he could feel was her. And that was all he needed.

She kissed him again, riding him at a lazy pace. Forward and back, forward and back, milking him with each roll of her hips. Her nipples scraped against his chest. Her stomach rubbed against his. Every nerve in his body stood at attention, alive and tingling with awareness of her. And only her.

"Never again," she whispered against his lips.

"Never again what, mo chroí?"

"Never again…" She whimpered and rolled her hips, and he felt her walls spasm around his shaft. "Never again will I suffer without this."

Jimmy squeezed her ass cheeks in his palms and spread them apart enough to make her groan. She moved faster in response, whimpering again.

"I fucking hope to God not. I'll have to paddle your ass till it's bright red with my handprints."

She sat up and placed her hands on his chest. "You'd like that, wouldn't you?"

"Fuck yeah, I would. And I know you liked it the other night."

She let out a breathless laugh before rising up and sliding back down again.

Jimmy bit back a curse, and an evil glint sparked in her eye. Yeah, she had control right now, and he was happy to cede it. Gazing up at the woman who'd stolen his heart, Jimmy knew he'd give it to her anytime she wanted it. Moving one hand from her ass cheek, he found her clit with his thumb. "Ride my cock, babe."

Sonja moaned and rocked her hips forward again. He rolled his thumb over the tight nub, and she moved faster. "Fuck, yes. Yeah." Jimmy shifted his pelvis, keeping in time with her. His orgasm was close, his cock so hard he was going to explode inside of her.

She bounced, her tight nipples begging for attention. "Oh God. James!"

He sat up and sucked one and pinched the other. Sonja seated herself on his prick and ground her pelvis against him. When he slapped her ass and then bit down on her nipple, she exploded. Her whole body seized, and she came.

Unable to hold back, Jimmy's orgasm blazed through him. He closed his eyes, wrapped his arms around her waist and buried his face in her neck. His body vibrated, and his cock pulsed, spurting his release inside her. He was drowning, only to be revived, over and over again, by her.

CHAPTER TWENTY-FOUR

Sonja wandered out to the kitchen in desperate need of coffee and some ibuprofen. After she and James finished their…cardio session—she cringed at the word choice—it felt like she'd run a marathon right there on the royal blue carpet of her office floor. There wasn't a more appropriate way to describe it. Her body sure ached like she'd run a marathon.

Grabbing the freshly brewed pot—*thank you, Janissa*—she smiled and decided she'd simply go with it. The word choice, the marathon session and any that might follow…all of it. After pouring a mugful, she took a seat in one of the cushioned stools at the island. Unfolding the morning paper—also compliments of Janissa—she glanced over the business section. She wasn't really reading the words because snippets of the night with James kept creeping in, blurring the lines into blocks of black print.

Once they'd gotten themselves put back together, he'd taken her to a pub in the Village. Bar food, good music and beer. Not her norm by any stretch, but it didn't matter. The only thing that mattered last night was the man sitting across from her.

She adored his pretty hazel eyes and his intentionally

messy hair—though she'd done a fine job adding her touch to its messiness. She giggled and then sipped her coffee. Also, the way he sometimes brushed his fingers over his mouth and down his goatee made her insides go soft with need. The shapes his lips made when he talked, or the way his scent lingered all over her body, sent lust racing through her veins. A moan slipped out after she swallowed a sip of coffee.

Yes, he was all she focused on last night and all she could focus on this morning, too. Sonja tightened the belt of her satin robe then folded up the newspaper. No point in bothering. Her stomach grumbled, apparently uncaring how distracted she was with all the things she found sexy about James. She pulled a yogurt from a shelf in the fridge, grabbed a spoon and reclaimed her spot at the island.

Shifting, she crossed her legs. The twinge of stiffness in her thighs reminded her she'd forgotten to take the ibuprofen. Sonja smiled and spooned up a mouthful of pineapple yogurt. Screw it, maybe she'd skip the pain medicine and enjoy the discomfort.

Casey wandered into the kitchen, rubbing the side of her head, her long hair a messy tangle of black and blue.

"Good morning." Sonja's smile widened. "Did you sleep well?"

Her daughter shrugged. "Okay, I guess. What's got you so happy this morning?"

"Do you want some breakfast? There's cereal in the pantry, I believe."

"Yeah," Casey said through a yawn.

"Have a seat; I'll get it for you." Sonja moved to the pantry, and Casey took a seat on the stool beside the one she'd occupied. Maybe they could spend the day together. Go shopping or something, have some mom-and-daughter time. "Any plans today?"

"Grounded. Remember, Mom?"

Crap, she'd forgotten. Sonja glanced at her daughter over

her shoulder before pouring milk into the cereal. *Hmm, how to deal with this now?* "Right. Well…" Sonja brought the bowl to Casey, placing it in front of her. "You think you might want to come shopping with me anyway? Maybe stop and get our toes done?"

Casey shot straight in her seat, and her blue eyes got wide as silver dollars. Catching herself, she cleared her throat, slouching in her seat once more. She shrugged. "I guess."

The feigned reaction was so obvious Sonja had to suppress a laugh. Taking her seat again, she rubbed her daughter's back. "Okay then. It's a date."

It felt like forever since she'd had any quality time with Casey. Breaking her own rules, even if it was only for the day, was worth the chance to spend time with her beautiful daughter. Sonja's phone vibrated in the pocket of her robe. Retrieving it, she glanced at the notification before unlocking it to read the message.

James Donnelly: Good morning, Sunshine.

Sonja kissed Casey on the cheek, took her coffee mug and moved to the sink before typing a response to him.

Sonja: Hello. Did you sleep well?

James Donnelly: I did. How about you?

Sonja: Very well, thank you.

James Donnelly: Do you have any plans today?

Sonja: I just made some with my daughter. You?

> James Donnelly: That's good. I have some pieces I need to finish up. Can I reserve a spot on your calendar for later this evening? Dinner?

> Sonja: Should be fine.

> James Donnelly: Wow! Was that a "yes"?

> Sonja: Don't push your luck. 😉

> James Donnelly: LOL Yes, ma'am. Text me when you get back. Have fun.

> Sonja: Thank you. You too.

Sonja swallowed the remains of her coffee and then turned to her daughter. "I'm going to go shower. Can you be ready in an hour?"

Casey glanced up from her bowl of cereal. "Sure."

Before exiting the room, Sonja stopped short and turned around. "It's just a reprieve for the day. Understood, Case?"

Casey rolled her eyes and nodded. "Yes, Mom."

Sonja blew out a breath and headed for her bedroom.

AFTER GETTING THEIR TOES DONE, Sonja called a car to take them to a mall in Queens. Once there, Casey made a beeline for Hot Topic. Sonja wasn't particularly fond of the store or its location, but it was Casey's absolute favorite place to shop, so stopping there was a given. Plus, grounding aside, letting her daughter shop where she wanted gave Sonja more time with her—something she never seemed to get enough of.

As Casey headed for the T-shirts, Sonja stopped in front of a cute little black A-line dress with electric-blue polka dots on it. "Casey, this is too darling. I bet it would look so cute on you, honey."

Her daughter glanced over her shoulder and rolled her eyes. "Ew, no, Mommy. It's a dress."

"Well, yes. I know it's a dress. Is it against the law for you to own a dress?" Unwilling to give up, Sonja held up the garment. "It even matches your hair."

"I guess." Casey shrugged and then went back to the stacks of shirts.

With the dress still in her hand, Sonja moved beside her daughter. "T-shirts, hmm? I think you already own more T-shirts than they have in stock here."

"Seriously, Mom. You can never have too many T-shirts." Casey pulled one from the stack and extended it out in front of her. "Oh, my God! Black Veil Brides! Must have. Must!"

Sonja laughed. "All right then. Make a deal with me?"

"*Mmmaybe.*" Casey grinned and went back to perusing the other shirts. "Name the terms." She yanked another shirt from the stack. "*Yessss!* This one's so awesome. Check out the skulls on it!"

Sonja might not care for the store, the location or her daughter's choice of attire, but what Sonja cared for the most at that moment was the smile that brightened Casey's already beautiful face. Unable to help herself, Sonja smiled too. "Very nice. All right, terms are, you can get four shirts if you let me buy you the dress."

"Seriously?" Casey frowned.

Sonja raised both brows. "Quite."

Casey eyed the dress in Sonja's hand before touching the fabric. "Mmmm…eight shirts."

"Negotiating, I see."

Casey giggled. "It's a dress, Mommy. You leave me no choice."

Sonja glanced down at the dress, then back at her daughter. "Six shirts, and when we're done here, we go back to Manhattan to find me a new dress and shoes."

"Hmm." Casey tilted her head to the side and stroked her

fingers over her chin. "Hard bargain, Mom. But okay. Deal!" She grinned.

Sonja nodded before placing a kiss on Casey's cheek. "Pick out your shirts. I'll be over there by the dressing room."

"Why the dressing room?"

"So you can try on the dress you're getting today." Sonja winked. "Oh, and look? There's an adorable blue tulle crinoline below the skirt."

"What did I just get myself into?" Casey mumbled before squatting down in front of another stack of shirts.

Sonja laughed and moved to the dressing rooms. The day had turned out better than expected, and she was grateful she'd suspended her daughter's grounding in favor of some quality time with her. It was worth it. Later that night, she'd be having dinner with James—a bonus. Yes, the day had turned out better than expected and, with any luck, was only going to continue on its merry course.

CHAPTER TWENTY-FIVE

Jimmy pulled up in front of the sushi restaurant where he was meeting Sonja. The place was uptown from the Village, which worked for both of them. Unsure of any dress code, he'd put on a long-sleeve dress shirt and a pair of black slacks. He'd left the tie but wondered now if he was going to need it.

Jimmy entered and looked around. Like he had a homing beacon in his brain, he zeroed in on her at the bar. Her back was to him. Sonja's hair was up in its twist—he'd be taking that down later—and she wore a little black dress cut low in the back. So low he almost stumbled when he got closer to her. Placing his palm on the soft skin of her lower back, he leaned close and pressed a kiss to her bare shoulder.

She startled, whipping her head to the side before letting out a relieved gasp and then cupped his cheek in her palm. He smoothed his hand up her back. "Sorry, beautiful. Didn't mean to scare you."

She smiled. "It's okay. Did you get your work done?"

Jimmy slid onto the seat next to her. "Not yet—should have it done early next week."

"Is this one sold or something for future sale?"

The bartender approached, and Jimmy ordered a Guinness. "Sold already. You ready for another?" He motioned to the wine in front of her.

"No. I'm good right now. Thank you." She raised the glass and sipped.

Jimmy watched her full lips and licked his own, wanting a taste of her. He glanced back to her bottomless blue eyes, rimmed with a dark kohl. She blinked, slow and languid, her lashes fanning out, teasing him. Gorgeous. So fucking gorgeous. Clearing his throat, he leaned toward her and pressed a soft kiss to her lips. "How was your day with your daughter?"

She sighed. "It was good. Thank you for asking."

"What did you do?"

She smiled and touched the buttons on his shirt. "We went shopping and got our toes done. Typical girl things."

"Shopping, huh?" He trailed the tips of his fingers up and down her spine, loving the feel of her soft skin. "Get anything good?"

"I got this dress." Looking down, she smoothed her hand down the bodice. "Oh, and the shoes too." She angled her foot out so he could see.

Jimmy's head spun, and his dick thickened in his pants. *Dayum!* Black, glittery platform heels adorned her feet. Tall-ass heels! Fuck me pumps coupled with a fuck-me little black dress. *Dayyuuummm!* Leaning forward, he brushed his lips over her ear. "Sonja, you're leaving those on after dinner while I fuck you till you scream my name again." He kept his voice low, but he knew there was a rumble to it. One he felt deep in his chest.

She shivered and gripped his thigh, digging in with her nails. Pulling back, he raised a brow and took a swallow of his beer.

After being seated, they shared several types of sushi. She'd ordered cucumber, spicy tuna and yellowtail rolls, along with some edamame. He liked sushi, just preferred it to be the non-raw-fishy kind. The yellowtail was suspect in his book and pushed some serious limits.

Jimmy wiped his mouth and stared across the table at her. Holding her chopsticks with delicate precision, Sonja dipped a roll of rice in the small tray full of soy sauce. He smiled and took a sip of his beer. "Tell me about your daughter."

Glancing up, she chewed before wiping her mouth with the napkin. "That's a broad question. What would you like to know?" She took a sip of her wine.

"Anything, really." He shrugged. "Does she look like you?"

"A bit, I suppose. She's got dark hair, though, like my ex. Right now, it's blue and black."

"Blue and black?"

Sonja shook her head, rolling her eyes. "She's going through a bit of a rebellious phase, I guess. I don't care for the color, but it's easier to let her do it than to fight with her. In the end, she'll do it anyway."

"Rebellious, huh? Where do you think she gets that from?" He popped a few steamed soybeans into his mouth.

"Not me."

Jimmy chuckled. "You seem pretty rebellious to me."

"Well, you bring it out of me then because it's not normal." She picked up a portion of the yellowtail and ate it. Closing her eyes, she moaned.

Tearing his gaze from her lips, he leaned forward and rested his forearms on the table. "She's fifteen, right?"

"Yes."

"My oldest niece is nineteen. She went through a bit of a rebellious phase, too. I remember my sister, Katie, and her husband, Jerry, were ready to lock her up because she made them so nuts."

"How many siblings do you have?" She took a sip of her wine.

"Nine. You met Ryan in Vegas, if you remember."

"*Nine?* My goodness, that's quite a lot. Yes, I remember meeting him. Your parents must've been saints."

"Trust me when I say they had their fair share of dealing with rebellion. Ry and I got into plenty of trouble as teens. My sisters did, too. My mother is for sure a bona fide saint. I think there's a plaque at our church with her name on it." He laughed.

"How many of each?"

"Six girls and four boys." He raised his hand to count them off. "Katie, Mary, Joe Jr., Cyn, Me, Ry, Angie, Celia, Mark and Beth."

She laughed and then ate some soybeans. "Wow. Catholic?"

"Of course. A fine Irish clan like ours? Definitely Catholic. I'll spare you the list of my nieces and nephews. The clan is growing daily, it seems."

"How many?"

"Nah, it's your turn. What about you? Catholic? Brothers, sisters?"

"If I must." Sighing, she took her wine glass in hand and sat back. "Jewish, and I'm an only child. That's pretty much it."

"Lucky you on the only child part. But you're not getting off so easy. I know that's not all of it. Tell me more."

"My father worked a lot."

"And your mom?" He picked up a piece of spicy tuna roll and put it in his mouth.

"My mother passed when I was sixteen." She took a sip of her wine.

He wanted to reach for her across the table, but knew she'd not allow it. "I'm so sorry. That must've been hard."

Sonja shook her head and waved away his empathy. "It was a long time ago."

"Yeah, and while that may be true, it must've still been hard at the time or even through your early adult years."

"Honestly, I'm fine. Let's change the subject."

"All right." He blew out a breath. Damn, she'd shut him down quickly. Jimmy wanted to press, but let it go. "Have you always lived in the City?"

"I have. I still live in my childhood home."

"That's pretty cool. I'd love to see it sometime."

"Maybe sometime. Sure." She smiled, but it didn't quite reach her eyes.

Jimmy wasn't sure if it was because the topic of her mother had come up or because he'd broached the subject of seeing her home. Either way, he was frozen out. Again. *Damn.* Shifting in his seat, he took a drink of his beer and then ate a little more. The silence stretched between them for longer than he liked. But she was the one to finally break it.

"When did you know you wanted to be an artist?"

"I guess I've always known." He shrugged. "When I was small, I endured a few spankings for drawing on the walls. My mother finally stapled huge sheets of paper to one wall in my bedroom. Every few months, after I'd filled it with various doodles and scenes, she'd take it down and put up fresh."

"That's ingenious." Sonja smiled this time, a genuine one.

"She's pretty smart that way. I guess she had to be creative dealing with so many of us."

"Sounds like you got your creative genes from her."

"Probably. She's a professional chef, so maybe that's where her creative side lives. Dad's a corporate lawyer."

She swirled the wine in her glass. "Interesting."

"I'd love for you to meet them someday." The words were out before he could stop them. And he wished he hadn't said them because he could pretty much guess her answer.

Clearing her throat, she set her glass down on the table. "Maybe someday."

Bingo, he'd guessed right. Jesus, could a man take any more rejection in one night? It stung when it shouldn't have. After all, he didn't really have the right to expect these things from her. But he did, regardless...he still did. He wanted to take her to L.A. to meet them. He wanted to see where she lived, where she'd grown up. He just...wanted.

The waiter came over to ask about dessert and saved them from another uncomfortable stretch of silence. They ordered the twenty-layer German chocolate cake with bittersweet fudge and a side of pistachio ice cream to share. Sonja ordered an espresso—talk about a bittersweet combo. He ordered a regular coffee.

They filled the rest of the time with bites of cake, sips of coffee and chitchat and stayed away from the topic of meeting families and seeing homes. It made the night go smoother for sure and led the way to them ending up back at his loft. In his bed.

Her fuck-me pumps still on her feet, of course.

CHAPTER TWENTY-SIX

Sonja stood before her bathroom mirror, applying the last of her makeup. James had called earlier, wanting to meet for dinner. Since she'd taken care of all her cases the day prior, and Casey was off with one of her friends for the night, she'd decided to go.

They'd been seeing each other now for three months. There had been many lunches in her office or near whichever courthouse she happened to be at for the day, and several dinner dates. They were casually dating, and she liked it that way. Casual being the operative word.

However, the sex… Casual was not a word she would ever use to describe the sexual chemistry and heat between them. The sex had been downright explosive, incinerating, adventurous, mind-blowing—or any other word she could think of to describe it.

Grabbing her purse, Sonja headed out the door and grabbed a cab to meet him. He wanted steak tonight, so that's what they were having. He'd asked her to leave her hair down. She'd done that, too. Twisting to exit the taxi, she glanced at her feet—he'd also requested the red, peep-toe, four-inch pumps. James had a thing for her shoes. It worked for her because she had a thing for them, too. She was no Imelda by any stretch, but she did have an entire six-foot wall in her closet for her shoes.

Stepping onto the sidewalk, Sonja straightened her slacks and headed for the restaurant. She drew in a deep breath when she spotted him standing near the entrance. He always did that to her, made her catch her breath the moment she laid eyes on him. He was…well, he was beautiful in her opinion, and although she was reluctant to admit it when they'd first met, she'd always thought so.

He was too young for her. He wasn't her type. The tattoos and piercings, and also his lifestyle, didn't fit into her world. But the sex? The sex fit into her world fine and dandy. Enchanted by his gaze, she kept her feet moving as if he'd attached an invisible thread to her, and she was unable to do anything but gravitate toward him whenever he was in her line of sight.

His tempting lips curled into a knowing smile. "Hi."

"Hi." Her voice sounded breathless, and she'd given up trying to control it any longer.

James leaned in, threaded his fingers through the length of her hair and brushed his lips over hers. Placing her palms on his chest, Sonja shivered.

"You look beautiful. Did you—"

"Yes…" She stepped back and raised the heel of one foot off the ground, wiggling it from side to side for him to see. "Happy?"

"Mmm. Keeping those on later." He swatted her bottom.

Sonja laughed—another thing he brought out of her. "Feed me first." She kissed him again and turned to walk into the restaurant. James moved around her and held the door open. "Did you get a haircut?"

"I did." He grabbed her hand and approached the hostess stand. "Yesterday. Surprised you noticed."

She threaded her fingers through the shorter length on the side of his head. "Why wouldn't I notice?"

The corner of his lip quirked into a small smile, and he shrugged. "Dunno, just didn't think you paid attention to that level of detail."

Of course, she noticed. Sonja noticed all sorts of things about him: his lips, his goatee, his nose with its piercing, his hazel eyes and how they changed color in the light. His tattoos. His…everything. James was not someone a woman didn't notice. Clearly, he knew that. Smoothing her hand down his shoulder, Sonja shook her head and smiled. "How could I not?"

The hostess came up before she could say anything else and led them to a table close to the back. The restaurant was small and filled with two- and four-person tables, each with a petite oil lamp in the center. Dark paneling lined the walls, and there was a small bar situated in the back. Quaint and elegant. Perfect ambiance, too.

Choosing a seat that let her keep her back to the bar, Sonja sat down. "I'll have a glass of Cabernet, please?"

James folded into the opposite chair. "Guinness, please?"

The hostess nodded and stepped away. Sonja peeked at him over the top of her menu. "Guinness again, hmm?"

James rolled his eyes and let out something akin to a snore. "Yes, dear. Guinness, again." He opened the menu and laid it flat on the table.

"I was thinking you might want to have some wine with me."

He chuckled. "And I was thinking Guinness."

"It wouldn't kill you to stray from the routine once in a while. Step outside of the box." She pursed her lips. "Walk on the wild side."

"I thought that was your job?" He shook his head. "Guinness works fine for my wild side."

Sonja sighed but laughed. Such a stubborn Irishman when

he wanted to be. Good thing, too. Otherwise, she wouldn't be having the sex of her life right now. With some really good food in between.

"How's Casey?"

"Casey's fine. She's spending the night at a friend's house." She glanced back to the menu. "I think I want the filet tonight."

"Hmm."

"Hmm?"

"Filet sounds good." He picked up the menu, and now she couldn't see his face.

"Yoo-hoo? Psst?"

He peeked to the side at her. "Yeeeeessss?"

Sonja leaned forward. "What was the 'hmm' for?"

"Oh, that." He nodded. "Hmm."

Still leaning forward, she pulled her hair over her shoulder and ran her fingers through the ends. "Yes, that. Hmm?"

Setting the menu down, he leaned forward, too, almost coming nose-to-nose with her. "I could do this all night, you know."

Sonja kissed the tip of his nose. "I'm fine with that. I'll keep up with no issue, Mr. Donnelly."

He smiled and sat back, raising the menu up so she couldn't see his face again. Lowering it once more, he peered at her over the top. "I've no doubt you will, Sonja-the-lawyer."

Sonja used to hate when he called her that. As if her being an attorney was the only thing defining her. She guessed at one time there wasn't much more. Yes, she was a mother and, for a while, a wife, but for the most part, she was a lawyer. After all, that's exactly what her father raised and expected her to be.

Things had shifted since she'd met James. It was another addition to the list of things he'd brought out of her that she hadn't realized she'd been keeping locked up. It was the sex with him that'd done it. The chemistry. The fire. He lit her up, and she'd discovered a side of herself she hadn't known was there.

But was that all there was to it? Was that all there was between them? She couldn't be sure. They had *some* things in common, just not a lot of things. There was plenty of conversation with witty banter and debating…always the debating. Foreplay, as he liked to call it.

Regardless, Sonja needed to keep things casual between them—keep expectations low and in check. He'd pressed a few more times regarding meeting her daughter or seeing her home and her meeting his family, but she'd refused to even entertain the ideas. Casual worked for her. If they were to keep doing this, it needed to work for him, too. Simple as that.

JIMMY WIPED his hands on his napkin and pushed his plate to the side. Dinner had been delicious. Having Sonja across from him made it mouthwatering. But then again, she had that effect on everything.

"You look like you're plotting something." She took the last bite of her filet.

"Who, me? Never." He grinned, waved the waitress over and ordered another Guinness.

"Mmhmm. I know that look."

He raised a brow. "You do, huh? I was just thinking…hmm."

"Back to the 'hmm', are we?"

"Maybe." The waitress delivered his drink; he thanked her and took a long swallow, never breaking eye contact with Sonja.

She placed her napkin on the table. "Well, are you going to enlighten me?"

"Maybe." He laughed, and she rolled her eyes.

He knew he was going to end up annoying her; it was

what he did. In truth, he wasn't trying to annoy her tonight and was more serious than she realized. He wanted to ask her a question, had been debating it since they'd arrived. He just didn't want her to say no like she always did.

She stood. "I'm going to head to the ladies' room while you decide."

He snagged her arm before she walked away. Jimmy smiled up at her before pulling her closer. "C'mere."

Sonja bent in front of him. "Yes?"

He kissed her. Once, and then again, tasting her lips and tongue. She moaned, and he pulled away. "Thanks, needed that."

"Mmm. You're quite welcome." Straightening, she swept her hair off her shoulder and walked away from the table. Her long legs in flawless motion on those incredible fucking heels.

Jimmy watched until she disappeared into the ladies' room. The last few months had been the best of his life, and they'd also been the most frustrating. Sonja had a wall up around her he couldn't seem to get through. No matter what he did. They'd fought plenty about the distance she kept between them, too.

The line he'd gotten accustomed to hearing was how busy she was. Always claiming this was all she could give him. He'd taken it, but it hadn't been easy. And it damn sure wasn't enough. He wanted more.

Regarding her feelings about him? Sad truth was he wasn't really sure how she felt. She wasn't real big in the expressing-her-feelings department. However, in bed, she was different. The walls came down, maybe because she wasn't able to keep them up while experiencing the raw passion between them during sex. When they were naked, Jimmy could see with amazing clarity how she felt about him. There was no doubt in his mind that Sonja wanted him as much as he wanted her. He knew it in his bones.

What he didn't know was why she continued to hold back

with him where every other part of their relationship was concerned. In an effort to be patient, he hadn't brought it up in a while, figuring she'd slowly open up. But she hadn't, not truly. And the little patience he had was wearing out its welcome.

Sonja appeared in the hall from the restroom and strode toward him. Her heels clicked on the concrete floor in time with his pulse. Taking her seat again, she crossed her arms on the table and leaned forward. "Well?"

Pursing his lips, Jimmy glanced away from her piercing gaze and scanned the other patrons. After a couple of beats, he met her eyes. *Here goes nothin'.* "You mentioned Casey won't be home tonight?"

"No, she won't be. Why do you ask?" The waitress brought their check, and Sonja reached for it.

Jimmy snagged it before she could. "My turn tonight."

"All right." She tilted her head to the side. "Why did you ask about Casey?"

Pulling out his wallet, he took out his credit card and placed it in the bill folder. "I was thinking maybe we could go back to your place tonight."

"No."

His head snapped up from the check. "That's it? No discussion, just no?"

"Yes. Just, no." She sat back in her seat.

He shook his head and sighed. "Sonja, I don't understand. Why won't you let me come to your place? Like ever?"

"Because I'm not comfortable with it."

"Still? I mean, come on. At some point, you have to—"

"Let's get this straight. I don't have to do anything. I do not introduce people I date to my daughter. Please don't push this."

"I can understand you don't want to bring a lot of men around, but I'm not exactly a lot of men, and from what I figure, you're not seeing anyone else."

"No, I'm not. However, that's not the point."

"She isn't even home tonight, but yeah, what is the point exactly?"

She blew out a harsh breath. "The point is, why can't you be happy with us going to your place? Keeping things casual. Why must you push this?"

"Because it's—" The waitress appeared. Jimmy handed her the check back, and she walked away from the table. "Because it's important to me. Because I care about you. Because I don't understand. And you won't fucking enlighten me. Because I don't even know how you feel about me." His voice had taken on a deep tone, getting lower with each statement. It was either that or he'd start yelling.

Jimmy drew in a deep breath, trying to calm himself. How did she not understand this was important? It'd been three months, for fuck's sake, and they were no closer to being a real couple than when he'd first met her. He didn't get why she still kept the wall up. Or how she could shut off her emotions so easily, like she felt nothing for him. At all.

Talk about feeling like shit about a situation. And half the time, he avoided bringing it up for fear of losing what little time she did give him.

"Clearly, I care about you."

"Clearly? Seriously, Sonja, how do you figure it's clear?"

"Look, let's drop it."

"I don't want to drop it. I want to understand."

Sonja leaned forward again, bracing her face in her hands. She rubbed her forehead with her fingers and then pulled them away to meet his gaze again. He was tired of letting it go. Tired of ignoring the elephant in the room between them and trying to convince himself the situation would change. "You're not going to tell me, are you? You're going to wait for me to drop it and simply continue on like we are. Am I right?"

"I would prefer not to discuss it here, so yes, I'll wait for you to quiet down."

"Fuck that." Jimmy glanced away from her piercing, icy gaze and the waitress returned, placing the bill with his credit card back on the table for him to sign. The poor girl gave him a nervous smile and walked away.

"I'll let you finish up and meet you outside. You let me know if you'd rather go home alone when you're done." Sonja got up and walked out of the restaurant.

Wow. In an instant, the switch had flipped, and clearly, she didn't give a flying fuck if he was upset. And hell no, he was not going to just quiet down. *Shit. Damn. Fuck!* Nor was he going home without her! Their conversation was nowhere near over. If she thought it was, she was in for a damn big surprise.

CHAPTER TWENTY-SEVEN

Sonja could not believe he was behaving in this way. Fishing in her purse, she located a mint and popped it in her mouth. She had no idea why it mattered so much whether or not they were at her house or his. Spending their time together in his domain was preferable for her. In doing so, she could leave when she was ready. On her terms.

James stepped up behind her, and she felt the heat of his presence before he touched her or said anything. He clasped her upper arms, pulling her back against his chest. Pressing his face to the side of her hair, he took a deep breath. "I don't want to fight with you."

Sonja placed her hand on his cheek. "I don't want to fight either."

"Why won't you let me in?"

She exhaled slow and easy before answering him. "I have let you in. But it's not enough for you." Why didn't he understand? Why must he push her...constantly?

"It's not that it's not..." He let go of her, and the loss of his warmth was profound. Sonja glanced at him, and he moved to her side and hailed a cab. "You don't get it, and I don't know if I can explain it to you."

Sonja clasped his hand in hers. "James, I don't know if I can give you what you want."

"What is it you think I want exactly?" His words were soft, almost too low for her to hear, and he didn't look at her when he spoke them.

"You want more than I'm capable of giving."

This time, he did look at her. The expression in his eyes, a mixture of hurt and anger. "Letting me into your life, even a little, is more than you're capable of giving?"

"I *have* let you into my life." She didn't know what else to say to him. Or why he felt so strongly about something that shouldn't be such a big deal.

He turned to her, confusion now mingling with the hurt and anger in his gaze. "How? Tell me, please. How have you let me in?"

Sonja raised her hand to smooth up the back of her hair and then stopped; she'd worn it down. Glancing down at her shoes—her red pumps—she searched for the words she thought he wanted to hear. She'd let him in plenty—an unavoidable consequence of giving in to him and pursuing this relationship. Sonja was doing the best she could and struggling to keep herself grounded. Each time James asked her for something else, something more, it was as though things were skittering out of her control again.

She'd been vigilant in keeping her feelings in check with him and, in the process, kept him at a carefully controlled distance. But he kept changing the rules on her, and she didn't like it. At all. Giving in to his wants felt like she was losing ground, losing the independence she hadn't known existed within her.

Sonja had been giving in to men, being controlled by them her entire life. With James, she'd taken back that control, and she wasn't about to lose it now.

But for God's sake, when they were together in bed or wherever they happened to be having sex, it was impossible to *not* let him in. She'd given in to him during those times, let him take her for many walks on the wild side. All of Sonja's walls tumbled, and a side of herself she hadn't known existed emerged. Even if she'd wanted to, she wasn't capable of keeping him at bay during those times. Nor could she deny herself when it came to taking what he offered.

"You can't answer, can you? You don't have a fucking answer. Dammit, Sonja. What the hell are we doing?"

He couldn't possibly understand what this was like for her, and she wasn't about to share it with him either. "Why is this so important to you? Why does it matter if we're at my place or yours? Shouldn't it matter we're simply together?"

"It matters. If you don't know why, then we have bigger problems than location." He turned away, hailing for another cab.

When he began to step away, a panic that she tried to ignore sped up her heart, and she circled his arm in her hand. "Fine. You want to come to my house tonight? Then fine, we'll go to my house." A cab stopped, but Sonja stood still, waiting for him to turn to her and meet her gaze. "James?"

He glanced over his shoulder. "I hate fighting with you."

She softened her gaze and gave him a small smile in hopes it'd be enough for him tonight. "For someone who doesn't enjoy fighting with me, you sure do a lot of it."

He snorted before stepping away and opening the back door of the taxi. Holding his hand out for her, she took it and moved forward. He kissed her before she slid into the backseat and climbed in beside her. "Foreplay, baby."

"Sick, sick man." Shaking her head, she gave the driver her address.

He nuzzled her neck. "You love that I'm a sick man."

Sonja squeezed his thigh, and he growled against her skin. A shiver ran through her, and every nerve in her body snapped to attention. "Maybe."

He left her neck and stared at her in the dim light of the

vehicle. "Thank you." His words were soft, and his warm breath feathered over her lips.

He pressed a tender kiss to her mouth and swept his tongue inside. Sonja tried to suppress the moan bubbling up but failed. Cupping his cheek in her palm, she deepened the kiss, needing more of him…like she always did. The kiss turned from sweet and soft to one of frantic need, and James slipped his hand between her legs and rubbed her clit through her pants.

Her hips moved forward of their own accord, seeking more from him. Smoothing her palm up his thigh, she found him rock hard behind the line of his zipper. The fierce urge to reach inside and feel his thickness in her hand rose inside her like a tornado. She ran her nail down the outline. James groaned, stroking his deft fingers over her core.

God help her, she wanted this man. If she needed to let him a little farther inside her world, into her home, to keep him, then so be it, she'd do it. She feared the chaos in her mind at the prospect of losing the independence she'd discovered, but she buried it because, in the heat of the moment, nothing was better than this.

Nothing was better than his tongue, his hands caressing her body, the feel of his naked skin against hers, or when he sank his beautiful length deep within her. Nothing. She'd deal with the consequences of her decision in the morning.

He broke the kiss and moved his lips to her ear. "You're wet for me."

Rocking her hips forward—the barest of movement in time with his strokes—she nodded, unable to speak for fear of her words coming out, riding a moan.

"Such a sweet pussy you have, Sonja. I've been thinking about how you taste on my tongue when you come for me, your legs shaking around my shoulders." His breath was hot against her skin, his words a rumbling whisper.

She was going to come right there in the backseat of a cab.

"Come for me, mo chroí." He sucked her earlobe into his mouth, flicking his warm tongue over it and continuing to drive her higher with his fingers.

Sonja ran her palm along his length. "James." She bit her lip—so close to orgasm, her head spun. A whimper escaped. Her channel clenched and spasmed, and her arousal coated her panties. "Oh God!"

He stayed at her neck, and she stared straight ahead, catching a glimpse of the driver's eyes in the rearview mirror. James pressed harder on her clit, circling the tight bundle of nerves faster.

Sonja tensed, and her climax hit. Her head fell back, and her breath punched out of her in short bursts. Whether it was the fact the driver knew what they were doing or simply that James could bring her to orgasm with mere touches and words alone, she wasn't sure. It didn't matter. She only knew her body was at his mercy, powerless to deny him this part of her.

Not that she wanted to anyway.

JIMMY PAID the driver through the front passenger window. She'd given in and agreed to take him to her home. It was a step in the right direction, albeit a small one, but a step just the same. He'd take it. Making her orgasm in the cab had been the cherry on top of the concession she made. He planned to thank her good and proper once they got upstairs.

Once in the elevator, Sonja hit the button for the fifteenth floor but stayed quiet. Figuring she might need the few minutes to compose herself from the orgasm or possibly swallow the fact that she'd conceded to his request, Jimmy didn't bother with small talk.

The doors parted, and he followed her down the hall, the

clicking of her red stilettos on the marble floor echoing around them. Anticipation burned hot in Jimmy's gut—the chance to finally have a glimpse into her mysterious world, and also what he planned to do to her with her pretty feet still encased in those shoes, was more than he could bear.

Unlocking, then opening the door, she stepped inside and tossed her keys into a bowl on an ornate sideboard in the entryway. Jimmy entered and glanced around, absorbing the space. The floor was polished hardwood parquet with decorative inlays made from a dark cherry wood. A bright cream paint, trimmed in white, coated the walls. Various classical artworks, displayed with accent lighting, decorated the long hall ahead of him. Small yet opulent chandeliers hung from the ceiling every few feet, creating a dazzling display on the dark wood.

Jimmy continued, just behind her, trying to process all he was seeing. Being a criminal defense attorney and the owner/senior partner in her firm, he'd figured she had money. He just hadn't realized how much. Her home was the very symbol of Upper East Side old Park Avenue money.

Sonja stopped outside a set of closed double doors. "Do you want something to drink?"

"I don't suppose you have any Guinness, huh?"

She laughed. "Probably not. I wasn't expecting a visitor."

"I see." He moved close to her and pulled her against him. "I guess I'll have to bring some by for next time."

"So sure there'll be a next time, are you?"

"Very sure." He nipped her bottom lip.

Closing her eyes, she moaned and gripped his shoulders. "We'll see."

"Show me your closet." The shit-eating grin he held in place until she opened her eyes probably made him look like a tomcat, but he didn't care. He really fucking *did* want to see her closet, or more importantly, her shoes.

"What?"

"I'm serious." He rubbed the tip of his nose over hers. "I want to see your closet."

She laughed. "You are such a strange man."

"You say the sweetest things to me." He kissed her again before taking a step back. "Which way to the Taj Mahal of shoes?"

"Oh, I understand now. You want to see my shoes, hmm?" She took his hand in hers. "If you insist, James-the-artist."

"I do insist, Sonja-the-lawyer." She led him back in the other direction, past another closed door and stopped.

"Please tell me you're not going to make me model all of them for you."

He grinned, knowing the damn thing stretched from ear to ear. The idea of her modeling all her heels made him feel like a kid in a candy store. Screw lingerie—though he did love her in thigh-high nylons and a garter belt—high-heel shoes on a woman, who was otherwise naked, was all the lingerie he needed. Especially this woman. "Maybe."

She glanced at him and shook her head, almost like she'd read his mind. Maybe she had. He was pretty sure his desire was stamped all over his face.

Swinging the door wide, she stepped inside, and he followed—*Holy shit!* What he'd seen of the house so far screamed elegant, but her bedroom dripped in it. The room was enormous, taking up at least the entire corner of the apartment. Plush, off-white carpeting blanketed the entire space. The one exterior wall was made up of three large windows, showcasing an impeccable view of the skyline. Heavy tapestry drapes hung to the sides of the frames.

A settee, upholstered in the same material as the drapes, sat in the corner near the fireplace with a small side table situated next to it. A pale sage coated the walls, and soft-white crown molding lined each wall where it met the ceiling. A mahogany dresser to the right of the entry, between it and another door, he assumed, led to her closet or master bath, and the matching armor was stationed on the other side of the fireplace.

The focal point was her four-poster king-sized bed, situated on the wall opposite the fireplace. The thick, pale-blush bedding and assortment of throw pillows complemented the drapes and the walls. Jimmy turned in a circle, taking in every inch of the room. This was the soft side of her he adored seeing and feeling. This was the tenderness she held at bay until he captured her in his arms, and it came rushing forward.

This was everything that was Sonja. And Jimmy loved what he saw.

On the mantel were pictures, some small, others bigger. All in silver frames. He moved toward them, wanting to see what images were revered enough to be in her private space.

"James."

The word held the tone of a command. Without a second thought, he halted his movement and looked over his shoulder at her. The expression in her eyes told him with no uncertainty to stop. She didn't want him to look at the pictures. Disappointment bloomed in his chest and settled like a rock in his stomach. And even though it pinched his ass to listen, he had far too much respect for her to push any more than he already had tonight.

She held a hand out to him. "Come here, please."

Jimmy moved to her. "Thank you for bringing me here." Slipping one arm around her waist, he buried the other in her hair, tilted her head back and kissed her. He didn't give her time to answer or time to question what his words of gratitude meant. He took what he needed. And what Jimmy needed was her.

CHAPTER TWENTY-EIGHT

Sonja drowned in his kiss, his scent and his intoxicating presence. She wasn't sure why she stopped him from looking at the pictures on her mantel. She just did. It had been hard enough to let him into her home, but having him in her bedroom was almost too much for her to bear. She was sure if she gave him any more, she'd lose control of everything that had started to make sense.

She didn't understand it completely, only knew she was overcome with a maelstrom of emotion powerful enough to take her to her knees. Sonja's mind twisted around a barrage of memories: Her father's constant disappointment in her, no matter how successful she was, Thomas's consistent disregard for her wants, desires or dreams, and her inability to feel secure regarding anything or to stand up for herself.

As if knowing her mind had gone into a state of pandemonium, James tightened his grip on her hair and deepened the kiss, curling his tongue around hers. Closing her eyes tight, she held on to him and fisted his shirt in her hands—a silent plea for him to save her. Save her from the memories, from the emotion swamping her and from herself.

The rush of overwhelming feelings terrified her, threatening to take her under the surface. But whether she wanted it or not, losing herself in his kiss had become Sonja's safe harbor. With her body pressed tight to his, warmth bloomed in her chest and spread outward through her limbs.

James wasn't supposed to be anything more than a casual fling. He wasn't supposed to mean more. Sonja couldn't allow herself to be irresponsible in such a way and lose the hard-won independence she'd gained. There was no room in her life for this man. No room for more than what he offered between the sheets. No—

With a gasp for breath, she broke the kiss, jerked away from him and took a step back.

He stared at her, his eyes glossy, his lips still wet. "Sonja?"

"It's too much. Too close," she whispered before pressing her fingertips to her tingling mouth.

"Shh. Don't." He reached for her. She took a step back, shaking her head. He frowned, a confused expression on his face. "Sonja. It's okay."

"Too close, James." She crossed her arms. "I don't want things this close."

He sat on her bed. Leaning forward, he propped his elbows on his knees and rested his head in his hands. After what seemed like an eternity, he looked at her. "Why?"

"It doesn't matter why. It only matters I don't want it."

"Bullshit." He ran his fingers through his hair. "You want it. You're just too fucking scared to let yourself have it. Correction, let *us* have it."

"I'm not scared, James. I don't have time for more than this. I don't have room in my life for it."

"That's bullshit too. Why are you making this so compli-cated? It doesn't have to be."

She walked past him and into her closet. Slipping off her shoes, she placed them in their spot on the shelf. When she turned, he was standing in the doorway watching her. "What do you want me to say to you?"

"I want you to answer my question. For fuck's sake, Sonja, I want you to give us a chance."

"There is no us. I have a household and a law firm to run. I have a daughter to raise. I do not have room for an 'us'."

He raised his arms out to his sides. "I'm good enough to fuck, but not good enough to be a part of your life, is that it?"

"I never said you weren't good enough. That's not what this is about."

"Then what? You've got time to fuck me, just no room in your heart for me?"

She shrugged. "I wouldn't put it quite like that, but if that's how you want to say it, yes."

"Wow." He moved in front of her. "So you feel nothing for me?"

Sonja shook her head. "I cannot give you what you want."

"This is fucking insane. I know you can." He took a step closer, eliminating the space between them. "I know you have feelings for me. It's written all over every damn inch of you when we make love."

James stood so close she was unable to look into his eyes without craning her neck. Refusing to give in, she stared at his shoulder and focused on tamping down the burn in her stomach. The words he spoke weren't true. She cared for him, yes, but it wasn't more than that. She didn't have deep romantic feelings for him; she hadn't allowed them. But there was no point in trying to convince him otherwise. Regardless of what he thought he saw, she was putting an end to it immediately.

He grabbed her by the waist and yanked her against him. "Say something. Deny it, or admit it, but fucking say something!"

Her breasts thumped against the hard contours of his chest, and her breath came out in a rush. "I don't have anything else to say. I'm not on trial here!" She glared up at him but then was struck silent. The feral look in his eyes penetrated to her core, inspiring an opposite effect than expected.

I'm insane! Instead of being angry with him for yelling at her and then manhandling her, Sonja's body flooded with arousal, and every inch of her skin tingled with the need to have him inside her.

"Maybe you should be." Though he'd lowered his voice, his tone was laced with fury.

She shivered at the sound. Caught up in her addiction, Sonja was convinced she'd lost her mind again because, dammit, she needed her fix. Having so little self-control where he was concerned disgusted her. In order to keep from saying anything else, she bit her bottom lip. He dropped his gaze to her mouth, then back to her eyes. She didn't care. It didn't matter wha—

"Come on, counselor. Defend your case."

"Fuck you."

"Mmm. Yes, now would be good." His lips curled into an arrogant grin, and she wanted to slap the expression right off his face.

Sonja tried to push him away, but he wouldn't budge. Damn him. "Let me go." She gritted her teeth.

"Ha. Not a fucking chance, babe." James bent his head to kiss her.

Fury boiled inside her veins, and before the process of thought and action connected, Sonja raised her hand and slapped his face.

He reeled back and cupped his cheek in his palm.

Oh shit! Oh God!

Sonja covered her mouth with both hands. Had she really done that? Shame replaced the deep cauldron of fury, and she cringed. She couldn't decipher the expression in his eyes either. She glanced away, unable to bear the sight. "I'm sorry. I think you should go."

Before she could react, James took hold of her waist and locked her against him again. "Not a fucking chance." He pressed a hard kiss to her lips.

She stiffened in his iron grip but wasn't capable of fighting him. The truth was, she didn't want to fight him. She was too busy fighting herself. With a soft whimper, Sonja gave in to the insatiable thirst. The taste of him spread through her like warm honey and erased any lingering fight within her.

This wasn't giving in because it was just easier, like she'd done with everyone else in her life. No, Sonja gave in because he *was* right; she *did* feel more for him than she wanted or ever intended to…even if she could only admit it to herself.

She might really want him, but there was no way she'd actually keep him.

James walked her backward and deepened the kiss while his hands roamed up her rib cage to her breasts. Sonja's back hit the door to her bathroom, and she tugged at his shirt, needing his velvet skin beneath her hands. Frantic, their tongues in a tangle of lust, he did away with the button and zipper of her dress pants and pushed his hand inside.

A loud moan rippled from her throat when he found his target, rubbing over her clit and then slipped two fingers inside her. Sonja rose on tiptoe, and her core clenched around the welcome intrusion.

"Always so wet for me." He moved his mouth to her throat, nipping at her skin, and continued moving his fingers inside her.

Halfway lost in the madness of his touch, she managed to push his shirt up past his pecs. He took over from there and pulled it off. Sonja ran her nails down his chest, and rode the high swamping her mind and making her body hum. She scraped over his nipples, then pinched them.

He groaned and ground his thick erection against her hip. "Why the fuck aren't you wearing a skirt so I could fuck you right now?"

"You didn't ask me—" He sank his fingers deeper, and Sonja cried out. "Oh God…you didn't ask me to wear a skirt."

Raising his head, he locked eyes with her. "Push your pants down. Now."

A shiver rocketed through her from head to toe at his authoritative tone. It brooked no argument. He'd be in control tonight, and she found no issue with it. Emotions were running too high, and although holding the reins in the past had allowed her to keep James at arm's length *and* keep her feelings in check, she didn't have the energy to hold them at bay tonight.

FURY AND DESIRE pulsed through Jimmy's veins in time with his racing heart. He couldn't believe she'd slapped him. Worse, he couldn't believe how fucking granite-hard it made his cock. *Fire and ice...* He should've known she had a few different versions of how that side of her surfaced. Good thing he was okay with all of it, but the slapping would need to be put in check. And he planned to take care of that immediately.

Sonja pushed her pants down her long legs and kicked them off. Holding her gaze, he slid his fingers out of her tight cunt and then pressed them into her mouth. "Panties, too. Now. Or so help me, I'll fucking rip them right off."

Her eyes rolled back in her head, and she whimpered, wrapped her tongue around his digits and sucked.

"Dirty bitch, you love it, don't you?" Sonja nodded with a low moan, sucked harder and slid her panties off. Goddamn, his lust was in overdrive. He couldn't wait to get his dick inside her. Taking his fingers from her hot mouth, he shoved his pants down his hips. Fisting his cock, he stroked from base to tip before rubbing the head over her swollen clit. "Yeah, I know you do. Spread your legs for me."

"Please. I need you." She bit her bottom lip.

"Shirt and bra." He slid the head past her clit, grazing the wet mouth of her pussy, then pulled back, only to repeat the motion, teasing her more. It was a bittersweet torture. With each pass, her wetness coated the tip and shaft, tormenting him, but it was too delicious to resist.

Sonja did as he asked, stripping off the remaining garments. Her little moans and pants for breath, the way her body swayed a little, and her eyes glazed over—every damn reaction made his balls grow tighter and his prick grow thicker. Sonja had no idea how she affected him. And not because he hadn't been clear with telling her or showing her. He had.

But she refused to see it.

Jimmy zeroed in on the pale flesh of her breasts and her taut, pink nipples. All thoughts of their difficulties fled his brain, and his mouth watered. "Play with your tits, mo chroí."

With a nod, she raised her hands to her breasts, cupped them and pinched the tight peaks. Jimmy's head spun, and his cock twitched in his palm. For fuck's sake, she was so fucking beautiful, he could barely stand to look at her. Even more, once his cock was buried balls-deep in her with his name bursting past her lips.

She thrust her hips forward. "I need you, James."

"Need what?" He cupped her chin in his hand. "Tell me."

She tugged on her nipples and gasped. "I need your cock inside me."

"Magic fucking words." Keeping his dick against the mouth of her cunt, Jimmy moved his hand to her thigh and raised it off the ground. Thrusting his hips forward, he slipped inside her heat.

"Oh God, yes. More."

"Greedy." He moved deeper inside her.

"You make me this way." Her channel clenched around him, and he gritted his teeth.

"Yeah, I know, mo chroí." Jimmy grabbed her other leg and raised her off the ground, pressing her back against the door. He rolled his pelvis, plunging deeper into heaven. "Fuck yes. So hot."

"James!"

With a tight grip on her ass, he rocked in and out of her. She rose and fell on his dick and scratched along his upper back, digging her nails into his skin. Her cries and moans grew louder—sweet music to his ears—as his orgasm coiled tight at the base of his spine.

"Don't stop. Please, don't stop!" She sank her teeth into his shoulder.

Jimmy wanted her to keep talking, but the words he wanted to hear were more along the lines of "I want you, I need you, or I can't live without you." He slowed his pace. All Sonja wanted from him was this—just the sex. *Fuck!* Why couldn't he leave it be and just take what she offered? Jimmy let out a sigh.

He only knew that he couldn't, no matter how much he tried. It wasn't enough.

Sonja raised her head and caught his gaze. "James, please?"

His thrusting came to a stop. Unwilling to see her baby blues, Jimmy closed his eyes and kissed her. Then he released her lips and pressed his forehead to hers. *Fuuuuuck!*

She cupped his cheek with her palm. "What's wrong?"

With a hard swallow, he pressed his lips together. He was not her fucking play toy.

"James?"

Unable to speak, he shook his head. He released her legs and let her slide down to her feet, though he was still inside her. *This is all I have time for.* Jimmy shook his head. *Yes, I'll wait for you to quiet down.* She treated him like shit but in a polite sort of way. Just because she masked it with refined manners didn't make it any less painful.

He couldn't do this much longer; it was making his heart ache. But he didn't know how to *not* do it anymore either.

Every time he fought with her, trying to get her to see, to understand, he risked losing what he didn't really have.

With a mental scream, Jimmy took a step back, slipping from her channel. "I think I need to go."

"What? Why?"

Pulling up his pants, he secured them and bent for his shirt. "I'm sorry. I need to go."

"I don't understand." She crossed her arms, shielding her breasts.

"I know you don't." He turned away, heading for the door.

"If you leave…then don't bother coming back."

The threat stopped him dead in his tracks. Could he walk out and call her bluff? *Fuck!* Letting out a deep sigh, he swallowed past the lump in his throat. "Don't say what you don't mean."

"Oh, I mean it. If you go now, then this is over."

Placing his hands on his hips, he glanced over his shoulder at her. She'd grabbed a robe and wrapped it around herself and was now moving toward him. "That easy for you, huh?"

She swept past him to her bedroom. "I don't have time for your drama."

Jimmy flinched at her words. The sting of them singeing his heart more than the slap she'd landed earlier. "Fuck you." He stormed past her, out of her bedroom and continued to the front door.

As he figured, Sonja didn't follow. Didn't call after him. Didn't try to stop him.

She let him go. And Jimmy let himself out.

CHAPTER TWENTY-NINE

Sonja sat in one of the high-back chairs in the study, drinking a glass of Chardonnay, stewing. The evening's events were on perma-loop, replaying over and over again in her mind. Trying to figure out what had happened wasn't working. James was plain impossible to understand. She was giving him what she could manage, yet it wasn't enough. She was sure it never would be.

Picking up her phone, she checked the time. Only nine p.m. Still early. Maybe Ginny was awake, or, knowing her friend, she was likely out having a good time with some handsome man. Kind of like Sonja should be doing right now. With James. *Damn.* She stared blankly at her phone, resisting the urge to call or text him.

Guilt settled like a lead weight in her mind and heart. Their behavior was a clear indication of how screwed up their relationship was. For one thing, she shouldn't have slapped him, but it hadn't seemed to bother him. At all. How could slapping him turn him on? Worse, how could his reaction to it turn *her* on? Sonja shook her head and swallowed a gulp of wine.

Sick and twisted was a perfect definition of them together.

But the guilt—the guilt hung around for a different reason. She shouldn't have been so harsh when his demeanor flipped, and he appeared to be confused and hurting. His reaction had nothing to do with the slap.

No, Sonja knew deep in her gut that James hurt because giving your heart to someone and having them treat it like it meant nothing to them hurt like hell.

The expression on his face and the pain in his eyes had sliced her deep and been far too much for her to process. She'd reacted in the worst possible way. A block of ice had encased her heart, and Sonja was colder than she'd ever been to anyone in her life. Even Thomas. To make matters worse, she let him walk out the door feeling like he did. She wasn't a cruel woman, yet it was clear she'd been cruel in that moment with James.

Sonja cringed, her stomach tying itself into a thousand little knots. Thomas had deserved her coldness and cruelty, but James hadn't. James deserved better, but she didn't think she was capable of giving it to him.

After filling her glass from the bottle next to her, she took another swallow and dialed Ginny. She wasn't a person who shared or did the "girl talk" thing. However, aside from the guilt, desperation was winning the battle in her mind. But the guilt was running a close second.

"Oh, my God, is everything okay?"

Of course, her friend would think something urgent had happened. Sonja laughed. "Hi, Ginny. I'm not sure."

"You're laughing, so it can't be all bad. Why are you…?" Ginny paused, probably checking the time. "Why are you calling me this late? I never hear from you after six at night and *never* on weekends. What's up?"

As predicted, based on the amount of background noise, Ginny was out somewhere. "Do you remember the artist I met in Las Vegas?"

"James Donnelly!"

Sonja pulled the phone from her ear to escape the loud squeal and laughed. She and Ginny had been friends since law school, and although they kept in touch, they led very different lives. Ginny had never gotten married and didn't have kids. She was a successful lawyer and had been involved with some very prominent businessmen over the years, but no one had been able to pin her down. At least not yet. If anyone could give her dating advice, it would be Ginny.

"Yes, James Donnel—"

"Ohmygodddd! Are you seeing him? Where are you? Are you home? Should I come over? Holy shit, I'm so freaking excited! You have to tell me everything! I can't believe you're just telling me this now!"

Sonja took another sip of wine and listened patiently. Eventually, when her friend realized she wasn't answering, she'd settle down and let Sonja get a word in edgewise. When the line finally went silent, Sonja took her opportunity. "Did you get it all out?"

"I'm coming over."

"You don't have to; it sounds like you're out."

"Whatever! No way I'm going to pass up an opportunity to hear what's been going on with you. I'll be there in a few." With that, the line went dead.

Seeing as though Sonja was about to have company, she got out of her robe and into some clothes. The doorbell rang a short time later, and Sonja slid on a pair of flats. After pulling her hair up into a quick twist, she grabbed her glass of wine and made her way to the door.

Before Sonja had the door half open, Ginny blew through it, a paper sack in one hand and her purse in another.

"Sorry, it took longer than expected. I grabbed provisions."

Sonja closed the door and followed after her friend, who was already halfway down the hall toward the kitchen. "Provisions?"

"Is Casey home? I haven't seen that child in forever." She glanced in Sonja's daughter's bedroom when she passed it. "We really do need to get together more."

"No. Casey's spending the night at a friend's house." Sonja eyed the bag Ginny had set on the island. "What did you bring?"

"I brought all things necessary for a good talk. I know you already have wine open and ready to go." Ginny nodded her head toward the glass in Sonja's hand. "Pour me a glass, would you? I'll get this set up."

"Sure." Sonja pulled a fresh glass for her friend from the cabinet and filled it. When she turned around, Ginny had grabbed a platter and was laying out a variety of cheeses, crackers and fruit. "That looks delicious."

"Completely agree." Ginny smiled and popped a cheese square in her mouth.

"Let's go into the formal living room." Sonja held both glasses of wine. "Bring the supplies." She smiled and led the way.

After forcing Ginny to provide the details of what she'd been up to since they'd last seen each other, Sonja was left with no other choice but to share what was happening. She was so bad at girl talk. Always had been. Growing up, she was taught to keep her private affairs just that...private. Even from friends.

She and Ginny had been close, but Sonja never really let her in too deep. Even when she discovered Thomas was having an affair, she hadn't called on any friends to talk it out. On occasion, she'd share with Ginny, but only at a surface level. Sonja had gone through the painful mess of his affair, as well as the divorce, on her own. It was lonely, but it was what she felt comfortable with.

She wasn't sure if she could share now, not the way Ginny shared, but she'd try. Out of all of her friends, Ginny was probably the only one she could open up with. The wine helped, too. "He wants more than I can give him." Sonja bit into a cracker coated with Brie.

"Wait a minute. Back up, please. How long have you been seeing him?"

"A little over three months."

"Three months! God, Sonja, you really know how to keep things to yourself. Has Casey met him yet?"

"No. No way. It's not serious, and there's nothing wrong with keeping things to yourself, Ginny."

Ginny took a sip of her wine. "Sure, there is. It's why you are the way you are."

Agitation pricked at her patience. Ginny's statement felt a lot like an insult. "The way I am?" Ginny sent her a sideways glance and bit into a cracker piled high with cheese squares. Sonja sighed and tucked a leg beneath her. "The point is, there hasn't been much to share. Not really, anyway."

"Are you sleeping with him?"

"Ginny! That's a pretty personal question."

"That means, yes. Is it good?"

Sonja almost choked. Wiping her mouth with a napkin, she pursed her lips and smoothed her hand up the back of her hair.

"Look, we've been friends a long time. Clearly, you're sleeping with him. So, just spit it out. And obviously, something's wrong now; otherwise, you wouldn't have invited me over to talk. So, talk."

"I didn't invite you over. You invited yourself over, but… that's beside the point. Fine. Yes. We're sleeping together. Whether it's good or not is irrelevant." The bold-faced lie left a taste in her mouth so bitter she had to take a long swallow of her wine to wash it away. The sex being good was the whole reason she was in this mess.

Ginny raised a brow. "Yeah, it's good. So what happened?"

Annoyance burned in Sonja's gut. "Why do you do that? I

obviously don't need to tell you anything. You make it up as you go along."

"Am I wrong?"

Sonja let out an exasperated sigh and rolled her eyes.

"Right. See? Sonja, you may not let anyone into your private life, but I lived with you long enough in law school to know you." She raised her glass and shrugged one shoulder. "To me, you're easier to read than a children's book."

Sonja knew her friend was right, but she'd lie down and die before she ever gave Ginny the satisfaction of knowing it. Spreading more cheese onto a cracker, she took a bite, chewing and…stalling. My God, this was harder than Sonja thought it would be. Could she really be this broken, this emotionally stunted? A wave of sadness washed through her, drowning her annoyance.

Her father had molded this side of her. Perfected it to his satisfaction. She didn't want to be this way and damn her father for instilling such a debilitating trait within her. What she wouldn't do to be able to slap *his* face instead of James's. "I'm trying, Ginny. Cut me some slack."

"Always. But I think this is too important to let slide. So what happened?"

Sonja blew out a breath. "As I said, he wants more than I can give him."

"More as in…?" Her friend took a sip of wine.

"I'm not sure, really. I believe he's developed feelings and wants to pursue a relationship with me."

"And what do you want?"

Sonja grabbed the bottle of wine from the coffee table and filled both their glasses. "I want things to stay casual."

"So you're okay with him seeing other people?" Ginny licked some cheese spread from her fingers.

A lump rose hard and fast in Sonja's throat, and her stomach flipped over on itself. The thought of James with another woman made her want to vomit. She stared at her friend, unable to answer. Almost unable to breathe.

"Ah, you're not. So then, why not let it be what it is? You know, go with the flow; see where it takes you."

"Ginny, first of all, he's too young for me. Second, he's this free-spirited artist covered in tattoos and piercings. Hardly someone to be a role model for Casey. I don't even want to get into what I've been dealing with regarding her. The last thing I need is some thirty-year-old playboy complicating my life."

Her friend crossed one leg over the other. "First of all, who gives a shit how old he is, so check that excuse at the door. It's not like he's twenty-one. Second, he's an amazingly talented artist, and from what I know about him, he does quite well for himself. And bless him for being comfortable enough to sport all those yummy tats and piercings. Third—" she took a sip of her wine, "—I highly doubt he'd do harm to Casey. For all you know, maybe he'd be good for her."

"Yes, but—"

"Everything after 'but' is bullshit." Ginny placed her hand on Sonja's arm. "Sweetie, you've been single for a long time. I can't recall you ever dating. Maybe it's time. Does he make you happy?"

"Well, yes. When he's not picking fights with me."

"He picks fights with you? About what?"

Sonja sipped her wine. "He fights with me about everything. Says I need to lighten up, have some fun. I really think he derives a perverse pleasure from getting me fired up. The man is relentless."

Ginny smiled and squeezed Sonja's arm. "Foreplay."

"That's exactly what he calls it, too! I don't get it, and I think it's insane. I just know when it happens, I don't know whether to kill him or take him to bed." Sonja laughed but tried to stifle it, knowing the wine had encouraged her to toss that little tidbit out there.

"Oh, sweetie, *do not* miss this chance. Take it from someone who knows; they don't come along all that often."

"I just don't understand why we can't keep things as they are. Yes, the sex is…well, frankly, it's earth-shattering. But why can't he leave it at that?"

"Because he's not stupid, and he knows he's found a good thing. Because underneath your disease, a little something some of us call 'chronic seriousness', he sees what the rest of us who love you also see: your amazing heart, mind and beauty."

She couldn't imagine how her friend saw those things in her. Sonja sure didn't see them in herself. "So you think I should go for it. Just give in and give him what he wants?"

Ginny raised her glass again. "Absolutely. I think you need to do it."

"And you think I should introduce him to Casey, too?"

"Definitely."

She traced the rim of her glass with her fingertip. "I don't know. This could go very badly, Ginny."

"So what? At least you tried. It's better than missing out and spending the rest of your life wondering, 'What if?'"

"Lord." Sonja pressed her hand to her chest. "What if I can't? It's a risk, especially if I introduce him to Casey. It's a tenuous balance with her right now."

"I think he's exactly what you need, Sonja. Truly. Let yourself have something good for once, honey."

Sonja swallowed the last of her wine. The problem with "something good" was reality eventually hit, and the good lost its shine. Her marriage had been good until it no longer was. If she made this happen with James, the light of reality would shine on it, and maybe the glare would ruin it. It would mean operating on blind faith alone, and Sonja wasn't sure she could do that. "I have to think about it."

"Don't wait too long. Like I said on the plane, I'll take him off your hands." Ginny grinned.

"Like hell! You keep your paws to yourself, lady. You've already dated half the eligible bachelors this side of the Hudson. You can steer clear of my man." Sonja laughed and then covered her mouth. Shock rolled through her at what she said. Maybe she did want him to be hers—even if accepting what she wanted versus what she felt she needed seemed impossible. She certainly didn't want him with anyone else.

"That settles it." Ginny patted Sonja's leg and stood, still wearing her mile-wide grin. "Time for me to go. I need to catch up with one of those eligible bachelors you mentioned. Maybe I'll get lucky one of these days, and one of them'll be a keeper."

Sonja got to her feet, too. "Thanks for coming over and making me talk about it."

"Anytime. I'm always a phone call away. We need to do dinner soon. I want to see Casey and check out what color her hair is now."

"It's purple and pink. Bring your sunglasses."

Ginny laughed. Sonja linked arms with her friend and walked her to the front door. With a hug, they said their good-byes, and then Sonja went in search of her phone. The idea of giving in to James terrified her, but regardless, she needed to call him and apologize for how she'd treated him. It was probably better if she did it in person. She just wasn't sure if she had the courage to face him tonight, or tomorrow even.

CHAPTER THIRTY

JIMMY WALKED INTO HIS LOFT MORE LOST THAN HE'D FELT IN years. Even in college, when he'd discovered his girlfriend—who he'd been about to propose to—was cheating on him, and he'd broken things off so fast his head had spun, hadn't compared to the situation with Sonja. And that'd been some seriously profound heartache he'd suffered.

He still couldn't believe he'd walked out on Sonja like he had. But worse, he couldn't believe she'd let him. Jimmy hadn't left expecting her to follow, but it still hurt like a motherfucker facing the reality that the woman really didn't give two shits about him. Unless he was fucking her, of course. Then she liked him just fine.

Tossing his keys onto the kitchen counter, he grabbed a beer from the fridge and plopped his ass on the couch. Equal parts anger and hurt vibrated through him. The anger was preferable. He picked up his cell and looked at the screen. No messages. He almost laughed at his stupidity. Sonja hadn't come after him, so what in the hell made him think she'd message him? He lobbed his phone aside and turned on the television. Flipping through the channels wasn't much of a distraction, but it was better than nothing.

His phone rang, and he dropped the remote and scooped it up. His brother's picture took up the display. Swiping his thumb across the screen, Jimmy put the phone to his ear. "Hey, Ry."

"What's up, brother?"

Jimmy ran his fingers through his hair. "Nothing I want to get into right now. You?"

"Haven't heard from you in a while. Figured I'd give you a holler."

"I know. Been a little busy. Good to hear your voice, though." He took a swig of his beer. "Oh, damn, wait. I almost forgot. Did you get things settled in court for the visitation crap?"

"Hell, yes. The judge ruled in our favor. Ultimately, I wish they didn't have visitation at all, but at least the Houstons still have to come here to L.A. to see Jacob. I did agree to revisit the agreement after Jacob turns ten."

Jimmy blew out a sigh of relief. "Thank God. I knew the judge would see it your way and do the right thing. Congrats, man."

"Thanks, Jimmy. Maiya and I are both so relieved it's over and settled."

"Speaking of, how is your girl doing?"

"Maiya's awesome. She and Jacob are like two peas in a pod."

"Ah, bro, that's even better news. See, I told you things would be good if you loosened your ass up."

"Yeah, yeah. I know. She moved in, but I'm sure Mom already told you."

Jimmy let out a burp. "Yup, heard about it a while back. Guessing that's what you mean by two peas in a pod."

"Jesus, you're so sexy. How are you still single?" Ryan laughed.

Jimmy slouched down on the couch, letting himself curl up inside the sound of his brother's voice. He missed Ryan more than he liked to admit. He loved his life in the Big Apple, but there were those times, kind of like right then, when he needed his family. "Enough with the flattery. So, you two are good?" Jimmy ran his hand over his jaw. "I mean, you thinking you might take this girl down the aisle?"

"I'm thinking so, yeah. Crazy, huh?"

"No, not crazy. It's a good thing, Ry. You deserve some happy in your life, and she makes you happy. Only a matter of time, the way I see it."

"I haven't popped the question yet. But it's been on my mind a lot lately."

"Mom and Dad know?"

"Not officially, but you know Mom. She always knows. Half the time before we even do."

Jimmy chuckled. "No shit. It's why we never got away with anything as kids. Woman has gut instincts that rival a damn psychic."

"Scary shit. Tell me what's happening with you. Last time we talked, which was forever ago, you were taking that lawyer you met in Vegas to some charity event. You still seeing her, or moved on to someone else?"

Jimmy blew out a breath. May as well spill his guts to his brother. "Yeah, still seeing her, at least up until about an hour ago. Not so sure now."

"She's not your type; I'm surprised it lasted this long. Who's on deck next?"

"No, she's not my type. About as much as Maiya is yours."

"Point. You saying she's got you by the short hairs?"

"You admitting Maiya's got you by yours?" Jimmy moved into the kitchen, grabbed another beer and wandered back to the couch.

"Damn straight. And I have no problem admitting it either."

He took a long swig of the fresh beer. Sonja definitely had

him by the short hairs. No doubt about it. "Bro, I'm fucked here. For real."

"Hang on a second. Hey, baby, can you get him started in the bath? No, it's Jimmy. Yeah, I'll tell him." Jimmy heard the clear sound of a kiss being exchanged. "Maiya says hi."

"Tell her hi back. And fuck me, you sound all in love and shit." Jimmy shook his head, letting out a sigh. "It's a good thing."

"It is. Thanks. Now, tell me what the hell's going on."

"She's awesome. Sonja. She's just…she's awesome. But…"

"But?"

"She's got this damn wall around her I can't get through."

"Shit, I know how that is. Maiya may as well've had the Pentagon surrounding her, she was so closed off."

"I didn't expect it. I mean, she's older, which doesn't matter to me, but I guess I thought…fuck, I don't know what I thought."

"What's her deal?"

"I don't know what's at the heart of it, but she says she's too busy for things to be serious between us."

"She's a lawyer, so I imagine that's pretty legit."

"Yeah, but she's got time to go to dinner and lunch with me and plenty of time to fuck me. But that's where it ends. Hell, tonight was the first time I've ever been to her place, and the only reason that happened was because we had a fight, and she gave in."

"That's weird. Why haven't you been at her place?"

"She's got a kid, a daughter. She's fifteen. Sonja hasn't introduced me to her. Basically, her personal life is kept personal. I haven't been invited in."

"Sounds like you might be wasting your time."

Jimmy stood and started pacing. "I know. But, Ry, when I think about not being with her, my guts turn inside out, and I can't… God, I can't walk away. And the sex? Fuck's sake, the sex is…I can't even describe it to you. It's never been like it is with her."

"I get it. Believe me, I get it. What are you going to do?"

"I don't know. Tonight, I got so upset with her, I walked out of her house. Basically told her fuck you, and left."

"Let me guess, she didn't come after you, did she?"

"What do you think? I'm talking to you on the phone right now, aren't I?"

"Guess not."

"This is fucked, Ry. I'm spun on this woman, and I don't know how to right myself. Hell, I don't know if I'll ever be right again."

"Is she worth it?"

Jimmy stopped and stared out the windows of his loft. Was she worth it? It wasn't a hard question. And his answer was easy. "Yes."

"Then dig in and fight for her. It's what I had to do with Maiya. Of course, when I couldn't take it anymore, I did give up, but she got herself straight and came to me, thank God. I know if she hadn't come back, I'd have spent a long-ass time hurting for her."

Jimmy leaned against the back of the couch. "Was it worth it for you?"

"Hell yes, it was worth it. Even with all the bullshit we had to overcome, I wouldn't trade a damn minute of it."

"Thanks, Ry."

"Shit, don't thank me. It's about time I got to be here for you, for once."

"Give Jacob a big squeeze for me. Tell him his uncle loves him. Give your girl a squeeze, too."

"You got it. Call anytime, Jimmy."

"Will do. Night, bro." Jimmy disconnected.

Tipping back the bottle, he took a long swallow and then checked the time. It was a little after eleven p.m. If he was going to dig in and fight for her, he sure wasn't going to make any ground sitting in his living room, sucking down barley and hops until he passed out. Jimmy grabbed his keys from their resting place on the entryway table and headed out the door.

SONJA SLIPPED on a white silk nightie before pulling the towel from her head. She settled on the settee in the corner of the bedroom, glass of wine beside her on the small table, and combed through her long hair.

The hot bath she'd taken had done her a world of good, helping to ease the tension from her limbs and silence the static in her head. The debate in her mind regarding James and whether or not to give him more of her time had continued, but at a much slower pace.

She wanted to try, at least a little, to let him into her world. She just wasn't sure how to go about it. As Ginny had pointed out, Sonja hadn't dated anyone since splitting from Thomas. Between her ex's constant, unannounced visits, work, and her daughter, it'd been easier not to bother.

Sonja cringed. Everything she'd done, almost her entire life, had been because "it was easier". Going to private school. Attending law school. Marrying Thomas. Taking over the firm. The memories stirred a simmering pot of anger in her belly. All of it had been because it was expected of her and not because she'd chosen it.

The only two things Sonja had decided for herself were having Casey and then, years later, getting a divorce. Her father hadn't wanted her to have a child so soon. Thomas hadn't either. Certainly, neither her father nor Thomas wanted her to get divorced. But she'd done both. At least she could hold her head high regarding those choices. So why was it so hard to choose something for herself again? Why deprive herself of something that felt so damn good? Finishing up her hair, she set down the comb and picked up her wine. Maybe she was punishing herself for stepping out of line... "Well, there's a hundred-and-fifty-dollar-an-hour diagnosis." Sonja laughed and took a sip of her wine as the doorbell rang.

She set her wine on the table beside her, tugged on her robe and then made her way to the front door. At such a late hour, she kept her footsteps light as she approached the door and peered out the peephole. Her mouth dropped open, and she stepped back. No time like the present, she supposed, to talk this through—courage to do so being optional, of course. Apparently, James felt the same because he was standing outside her door, looking as gorgeous as ever, too. *So unfair.*

The bell sounded again, and then he knocked. "Sonja, it's Jimmy!"

Sonja drew in a deep breath, smoothed her hands down her stomach and then swung open the door.

He crossed his arms. "We need to talk."

"Please. Come in." She stepped back, motioning for him to enter. "Do you want a drink?"

"No. I'm good." He ran his fingers through his hair, and her hand twitched at her side, wanting to feel the dark strands herself. "I have things I need to say."

"Okay. I have a glass of wine in my room. I'd like to go get it." She moved to walk past him.

"Fine, we can talk in there."

She stopped. "I'm not sure that's a good idea."

"Really? I think it's a perfect idea." The determined look in his eyes brooked no argument.

"All right then." Sonja made her way to her bedroom. She took a seat on the settee and picked up her glass from the table. James walked into the room and removed his shirt. Sonja's eyes went wide. *Oh shit.* "James, I—"

"Nope. It's not time for you to talk right now. Right now, it's time for you to listen."

She closed her mouth and frowned at him. "Fi—"

"Ah, ah, ah." He knelt before her and pressed a finger to her lips. "No talking."

Sonja sighed through her nose and rolled her eyes. A smirk spread across his lips, and she had to resist the urge to bite his finger. She could be quiet and draw a little blood at the same time. No problem.

After a moment, he moved his hand and ran his fingers through her damp hair. "You smell delicious. Like lilacs." Dipping his head, he pressed a kiss to her chest. Sonja shivered from the soft touch of his lips on her skin. He parted her legs, moved between them and then cupped her face in his palms. "I have things to say to you, and I need you to listen to me very carefully. I don't want you to talk. Do you understand?"

All of this was said in a hushed tone, his lips hovering a bare breath away from hers. She stopped herself from answering and nodded instead.

"I don't know what it's going to take. Or how long. I don't know why you have a rock-solid shell around you. Or if you've always been this way, but it doesn't matter."

Sonja swallowed past the knot rising in her throat. He hadn't moved away, his lips so close to hers she could barely focus on anything but the warmth of his breath while he whispered to her and how intent his gaze was. Her body vibrated in full awareness of him. His hips wedged between her open thighs. His hard, bare chest pressed against her torso. Sonja kept her hands at her sides, terrified if she touched him, she wouldn't be able to stop.

But that didn't mean he refrained from touching her.

"I don't care if you fight me every fucking step of the way." James smoothed his hands down her sides to her hips. "I can take every bit of it. I won't give you up without a fight." Leaning back, he slid his palms to her thighs, running his thumbs along the inside of them, leaving a path of fire in their wake. Sonja's breath sawed in and out of her, and her heart raced in her ears. "Are you hearing me, mo chroí? I'm not giving up."

She tried to focus on his eyes, tried to absorb the things he was saying to her, to understand the gravity of his words. She nodded, then licked her lips. James traced her mouth with a fingertip. "Fucking love your lips."

Sonja snaked her tongue out, touching the tip to his finger, and he groaned. Her belly tightened, and her clit pulsed. He still hadn't told her what mo chroí meant. She just knew the look he got in his eyes when he said the endearment rocketed straight to her heart. She could've looked it up months ago, but wanted the translation to come from him. Somehow, it felt like it would matter more that way.

James kissed her, driving his tongue into her mouth. Opening for him, she allowed herself the luxury of touching him, too. Sonja moved her hands to his chest, smoothed her palms up his pecs and onto his shoulders. His kisses were intoxicating, a drug all on their own. He kissed her like she was the only woman on the planet. He kissed her like she was his.

Her robe had loosened, and he slid his hands inside the soft fabric and up her torso to her breasts. The warmth of his touch penetrated through the thin silk of her nightie, and she whimpered when he grazed her hard nipples with his thumbs. "You're shaking." He flicked over her nipples again. "Why are you shaking, mo chroí?"

"Because your hands feel incredible on my skin through the satin." Tilting her head to the side, Sonja ran her tongue along his neck.

James cupped the back of her head, holding her there. "Mmm. That's what I like to hear."

"I want you." She nipped his earlobe. "Fuck me, James. Now."

"Fuck, that's what I like to hear too." He urged her to lie

back on the settee and then slid her forward so her bottom was near the edge.

Running her hands up her stomach to her breasts, she watched while he unbuttoned and then drew down the zipper of his jeans. Pushing his pants down to his hips, he fisted his cock in his palm and stroked from base to tip. "Raise your legs for me." Doing what he asked, she rested her heels on the edge of the seat. "God, yes, look at that sweet pussy. So wet and ready for me."

A bolt of electrified lust shot through her, hardening her nipples further, and her clit pulsed in time with her heartbeat.

"Spread your swollen lips for me. Show me the heaven waiting for my prick."

"The things you say to me, James."

He rubbed the head of his cock over her clit. She gasped, arching her back off the settee. "What do my words do to you, Sonja?"

"They light a fire inside me only you can control."

James penetrated her opening with just the head. "Oh yeah, there it is. Heaven." He inched deeper. "Fuck yeah, clench your tight cunt on my dick."

"Oh God!" Divine flames of pleasure rippled through her, and her breath caught in her throat. Sonja gazed up at him. A look of sheer bliss graced his features as he watched himself sliding in and out of her, and made him even more beautiful to her than she already found him.

Clarity struck her consciousness like a boulder, and Sonja realized he owned her—every inch of her body and her soul. She hadn't wanted to give him *any* part of her, and she'd been so careful not to.

But like a thief, he'd stolen it. He'd stolen her. In that moment, she hated him, just a little bit, for doing so.

CHAPTER THIRTY-ONE

Jimmy rolled over and reached for Sonja. She wasn't
there. Raising his head off the pillow and blinking a few times,
he realized he wasn't in his own bed. He glanced around the
bedroom—Sonja's bedroom. "Wow." He still couldn't get over
how beautiful the space was. Elegant and soft, a complete
reflection of her.

Hearing a door open, he looked in the direction of her
closet, which led to her bathroom. Sonja emerged, her robe
tied tight around her. "Oh, good. You're up." She smiled and
moved to the bed. "I'm sorry, but I'm going to have to ask you
to head out before Casey gets home."

"Seriously?"

"Yes." She frowned and shook her head. "I need you to
understand."

"I don't understand. Why can't I stay? I want to meet your
daughter, Sonja."

"James, please. I haven't even told her about you. If she
comes home and finds you in my bed—" she motioned with
her hand to his body, "—like that…I—"

"Like what?"

She sighed. "As you can imagine, I don't think it's a good

idea she come home and find a naked, tattooed and pierced man in her mother's bed. Not really the example I'm trying to set."

"All right, fine. I'll get dressed. We can go into the kitchen and have some coffee and—" he rubbed his stomach, "—some breakfast, too."

Sonja's brow creased into a deep furrow, and she crossed her arms. He could tell she was searching for a way to argue her way out of it. And she was welcome to try all she wanted, but he told her last night he wasn't giving up, so it didn't matter. He wanted to be part of Sonja's life, part of her daughter's life, too.

Sonja-the-lawyer might have a thick shell around her, but he was going to break through it, come hell or high water.

"You're intent on getting your way in this, aren't you?"

"Woman, what do you think? Did you forget the things I told you last night?"

Grabbing her hair clip off the nightstand, she pulled the length up. "No. I didn't forget. Honestly, I thought possibly the words were spoken in the heat of passion." She smoothed her hand up the back of her hair.

"I like it down, you know." He smiled. "And no, they weren't spoken in the heat of passion. Every word stands." He pulled her onto the bed, and to his surprise, she let him. "I'd kiss you right now, but I'll spare you the morning breath."

She laughed. "Very kind of you."

"There's my Sunny. Got an extra toothbrush?"

"It's your lucky day. I'll get one for you and leave it by the sink before I go make coffee. But please hurry."

"Yes, ma'am!"

With another laugh, Sonja leaned forward and gave him a quick peck on the lips. She disappeared into her closet and returned after a few minutes. "Get up! It's already after nine." Shaking her head but with a bright smile on her face, she left the bedroom.

Jimmy smiled, too, and then pressed his face into her pillow. Breathing in her scent, he had to tamp down his excitement. Hope was a dangerous emotion, but he couldn't help but feel it. He was about to meet her daughter. And there was no way he wasn't going to be a little hopeful they might actually make some progress forward now.

SONJA ENTERED the kitchen to find freshly brewed coffee and a bowl of fresh fruit and pastries in the center of the island. Bless the housekeeper; she was a saint. Sonja only paid the woman to clean and, of course, help out with Casey if Sonja had to work late, so finding breakfast and coffee waiting for her was a huge treat.

Moving to the cupboard, she retrieved two mugs, two plates and forks and set them on the island. The display before her resonated, and Sonja froze. "Oh no!" What if Janissa heard Sonja and James in bed last night? She covered her face with her hands. "Oh, shoot!"

"What're you 'oh no'-ing and 'oh shoot'-ing about?"

Sonja jerked her hands away and focused on James. "I'm completely mortified!"

After coming around the island, he snaked his arm around her waist and pulled her against him. "Why's that?" He kissed the tip of her nose, then looked to their right. "Oh, hey, that was fast. This looks delicious."

"It does, yes. No!" She swatted his arm. "Wait, pay attention!"

"Oww!" He chuckled with a frown, but then rubbed his nose over hers. "How about you tell me all about your mortification while we enjoy some of the yummy goodness you laid out for us."

"That's precisely why I'm concerned. I'm not the one who laid it out." Disentangling herself from his arms, she grabbed the coffee pot and filled both mugs. "Cream? Sugar?"

"Both. You're going to have to give me a few more details, darlin'."

"My housekeeper did this."

"No shit, you have a maid? Does she let herself in?"

Sonja wasn't sure if she wanted to laugh or cry at his naïve question and tone of voice. Heat crept up her face, and embarrassment reared its ugly head as she looked away from his bright, inquisitive eyes. Talk about a whole new brand of mortification.

She shouldn't be embarrassed.

Or ashamed.

Or anything at all, really. But she was. "She lives here."

"Wow, really? What's that like?" He reached for a cheese Danish and took a bite.

"It's…it's… James, that's not the point. My goodness, use a fork, would you?" He moaned and chewed, a satisfied expression on his face. He really didn't get it, or maybe he did but didn't care. "What if she heard us in bed?"

He took a swig of his coffee. "Seriously? I don't need a fork. And why do you care if she heard us in bed?"

She spooned some fruit from the bowl onto her plate. "Because I just do."

"Oookayy. We're not teenagers having sex in your parents' bedroom, so I still don't see what the issue is." He raised his mug to his lips and paused. "Unless you're ashamed of me?"

"No! Of course not. I just…" Blowing out a harsh breath, she stabbed her fork into a piece of cantaloupe and shoved it in her mouth. Sonja had no idea how to explain this to him. It wasn't that she was ashamed of him, it was just she'd never had sex with anyone in her home other than Thomas.

Considering she was having a hard enough time accepting the growing relationship (dare she even call it that?) between her and James, she wasn't prepared to explain it to her daughter, let alone the maid. On the other hand, she wasn't obligated to explain a damn thing to the maid.

James set his pastry down and pulled her into his arms. "You just what, mo chroí?"

She gazed at him, taking in the softness of his expression. How, or why, this man had come to care this deeply for her was quite difficult to comprehend. But there it was, plain as the nose on her face. His eyes were filled with feeling and concern. Complete, genuine sincerity. "It's fine. Eat your Danish." She kissed him and went to step away, but he pulled her close again and recaptured her lips. Successfully sinking deeper beneath her skin.

"Holy fucking shit! Mom!"

Sonja ripped away from him so fast her lips stung. Casey stood—mouth dropped open like a fish—in the doorway of the kitchen.

Drawing in a deep breath, Sonja ran her palm up the back of her hair as she cleared her throat. This was it, no turning back now. Her daughter was about to meet the man she was —*oh Lord*—dating. "Casey, watch your mouth, please."

"Uhh, hey." James waved. "I'm Jimmy. You must be Casey." He walked toward Sonja's daughter with his hand outstretched.

Casey stared at him, her mouth still open and eyes bigger than saucers. Sonja almost had to laugh. She couldn't remember a time her daughter had been struck silent. Sonja could only imagine what was going through Casey's mind while she took in all that was James Donnelly. Tattoos, piercings, intentionally messy hair…the whole shebang. He was definitely a sight and a damn pretty one at that. Sonja picked up her coffee mug and held it in both hands. "Casey, don't be rude. Say hello and shake Mr. Donnelly's hand, please."

"Mom!"

James looked at her like she'd called him a vulgar name. "Mr. Donnelly?"

Sonja rolled her eyes and took a sip of her coffee. Casey let out a loud scoff, and a blush rose on her cheeks.

"Hey, it's cool. You can call me Jimmy."

Casey finally raised her hand and shook his, and Sonja swore her daughter's cheeks grew a deeper shade of red. "Yeah, thanks."

Well, Sonja sure understood her reaction. As a rule, James had the same effect on all women—apparently, teenage girls, especially ones with raging hormones, were no exception.

"Cool hair."

"Thanks." Casey curled the end of a pink lock of hair around one finger and stared awkwardly at her feet.

Sonja let out a small chuckle and leaned her hip against the countertop. "Casey, are you hungry?"

They both looked over at her, and then Casey answered, "I guess."

"Well, come on then, have a seat at the counter and eat. You too, James."

He smirked and moved to take a seat at the counter. "Why do I feel like I just got mothered?"

Casey took the seat next to him. "Because you did."

"I did not mother you." Sonja grabbed another plate and fork and set them in front of Casey. "Would you like coffee too?"

"Yes, please." Casey grabbed a honey bun and bit into it.

"Casey, manners, please. Use your fork."

"Wow. You're like this with everyone, aren't you? And here I thought it was special treatment for me." James picked up his cheese Danish and bit into it, grinning while he chewed.

"Well, you love to annoy me." She grabbed a mug and poured a coffee for Casey. "Here you go."

Casey took a sip. "Thanks."

James smiled. "No cream or sugar, huh? Hardcore."

Casey gave him a smart-ass grin. "So, how do you know

my mom, and do you always shove your tongue down her throat like that?"

"And direct, too." He pursed his lips.

"Casey!" Well, there it was. The famous attitude had appeared. No hiding it now. Maybe worrying if she was capable of giving James more was a moot point. Maybe she'd luck out, and experiencing her daughter in full rebellious, bad-attitude mode would send him running for the hills. If he did, then they could finally keep things at her pace. Sonja shook her head as she cut into a piece of honeydew. Although he might not spook so easily. Sonja couldn't be sure—especially because despite the fact that she'd been seeing him for the past several months, he'd continued to surprise her at every turn.

"Well?" Casey looked between them.

James chuckled and then winked at Sonja. She didn't know how to approach this with her daughter, but ignoring it wasn't working. Sonja sighed and focused on the fruit in her bowl. Apparently, he was rolling with her daughter's lack of tact. Regardless, after last night, even if he did spook, Sonja wasn't totally sure she wanted things to stay casual.

Casey took a bite of her honey bun, brows raised, apparently still waiting for someone to answer her question.

Choosing to keep it simple, Sonja answered, "Mr. Donnelly and I met when I was in Las Vegas."

"Sonja, please stop calling me Mr. Donnelly. Feels like I'm going to turn around and find my father standing there."

"You met in Las Vegas? That was like three months ago, wasn't it? You've had a boyfriend for three months, and you didn't tell me?"

"He's not my boyfriend."

"Wow." He leaned back in his chair and crossed his arms.

"Sounds like he thinks you're his girlfriend, Mom." Casey laughed and took a sip of her coffee.

"We're friends." Sonja shrugged, doing her best to ignore James's reaction. "I suppose you could say we're dating."

He stroked his palm over his goatee, a look of annoyed confusion on his face. "You're kidding, right?"

"The way you two were kissing when I walked in looked like a whole lot more than 'dating' to me."

"I apologize for that. I hadn't heard you come in." This was getting worse by the minute. Sonja took another bite of her fruit, trying to play it cool.

James stood. "Okay. Yeah. Maybe I should go."

Casey glanced at him and shrugged. "I think you should stick around."

He cleared his throat and paused before smiling at her daughter. "All right, Casey. Since you want me to stay, I'll stay." He focused back on Sonja. "Can I talk to you in private?"

"Fine." Sonja let out another sigh, knowing how annoyed she sounded. A giggle squeaked out of Casey. Apparently, she found all of this amusing.

JIMMY STEPPED out of the kitchen with Sonja in tow. He could not believe his ears. Dating? His ass, they were so much more than just casually dating. He pulled Sonja around to face him when they reached the hall.

"I already know what you're going to say." She looked up at him.

Jimmy crossed his arms. "Yeah, reading minds now, I see?"

"Dating is an appropriate description, James."

"Two months ago, maybe."

"Regardless of what you feel we are doing, my daughter doesn't need to be blindsided. This is precisely why I was concerned about you still being here when she got home."

Jimmy blew out a harsh breath and glanced away from her. She had a point, but it still grated on his already sensitive nerves regarding the topic of their relationship. "Fine. But we're talking about it later."

"Of course." She turned from him and headed for the kitchen.

Frustrating woman. Jimmy ran his fingers through his hair and followed after her. He took the seat next to Casey again, and Sonja moved to the other side of the island.

Her daughter glanced at him. "Staying, I guess?"

"Yup." He smiled and sipped his coffee.

"Your tattoos are cool. I can't wait to get one."

"Thanks." He smiled and glanced at Sonja. Her eyes were wider than a cartoon character's, and she might've almost spit out her coffee. It was clear Casey was all about the shock factor when it came to her mom. "You'll have to wait until you're at least eighteen, but I'm thinking by the look on your mom's face, you might have to wait a bit longer than that."

"Not like she'll be able to stop me. How many piercings do you have?"

"Probably too many." *Holy shit, this kid!* He smirked and took another bite of his Danish.

Casey picked at her honey bun. "I want my nose pierced, maybe my eyebrow too. I don't have to be eighteen for those, right?"

"No, but—"

"You need my permission no matter what the age limit is." Sonja stared over the top of her coffee cup, brows raised so high they almost touched her hairline.

"And that's what I was just going to say." He caught Sonja's eyes and tried to imply through his gaze that he understood exactly the game Casey was playing.

"So, what kind of job do you have that lets you have all those tattoos?"

He looked back to Casey. "I'm an artist."

"Cool. Thought maybe a bouncer in a bar or something." Casey laughed.

"Nope." He chuckled and then took a sip of his coffee. "Not since college, anyway."

"What's your name again?"

"It's James, but you can call me Jimmy."

"Cool. What kind of art? Like drawings or paintings?" She stuffed a piece of bun in her mouth.

He set his mug down. "I do some of that, but my specialty is industrial art. Do you know what that is?"

"Like, with metal and welding?"

"Exactly!" He smiled, grateful the conversation had moved in a safer direction, and pulled his phone from his pocket. "Would you like to see some? A lot of my portfolio is on my website."

"Yeah, that'd be cool. Let me get my iPad, that way the pics'll be bigger." Casey stood.

"Well, Casey, you've surprised me. I wasn't aware you were still interested in such things." Sonja grabbed the coffee pot and began refilling all their mugs.

"There's a lot of things I'm interested in you're not aware of, Mom." Casey left the room.

"Come here, please." Jimmy waved Sonja to him. She did as he asked, and he pulled her between his parted legs. "Deep breath, huh?"

Sonja shook her head and placed her hands on his shoulders. "I'm sorry. She loves to push my buttons."

Jimmy rested his hands on her waist. "She sure does. But it's nothing I can't handle. Big family, remember?"

"I can only guess you must've been the button pusher." Her lips curved into a slight grin, and the urge to kiss her rose up in Jimmy like a tidal wave.

"Beautiful when you look like that." He leaned forward, and Sonja jumped back like he was on fire. What the— He glanced over to see Casey coming back in the room. Sonja stepped away, moving to the other side of the island again.

"Don't be such a spaz, Mom."

"I beg your pardon?"

"Whatever." Casey flipped open the case on the device, unlocked it and handed it to Jimmy.

"Hey, be cool to your mom." Jimmy winked at Casey and pulled up a browser window on the screen.

Casey grunted and leaned closer while he typed a web address into the search bar. Jimmy touched one of the images on the page, and it expanded. Casey bent closer to get a better view. "What the heck is that?"

Jimmy laughed. "What? You can't tell?"

"It sorta looks like a bunch of car parts welded together. But…" She cocked her head to the side. "But it also kinda looks like the ocean and a sunset. That's just weird."

"An ocean and sunset, huh?" He handed the iPad to her. "Here, check it out. Look a little closer."

She studied the image. "Wait! It's a desert scene, right?"

He smiled. "Good eye."

"That's totally freaking cool! How'd you do that?"

"A lot of welding." He took a sip of his coffee. "Go ahead, check out the other stuff if you want."

"It's interesting, isn't it, honey?" Sonja asked.

Casey glanced up at her mom and nodded, then went back to the images on his site. Mission accomplished as far as conversation landmines went, and Jimmy leaned back in his seat and took another deep breath. He was in Sonja's kitchen eating a cheese Danish, drinking coffee and sharing his art with her daughter. What a difference twenty-four hours made. If someone had told him yesterday this would've happened, he'd have said they were smoking something illegal. Granted, they still needed to have that talk about their relationship status, but this moment was where he'd wanted things to go with Sonja and had been holding on to hope by a thread for what felt like forever. And he'd almost given up. Until last night.

Sonja moved back around to his side of the counter and

stood beside him. "Casey, you should show James some of your drawings."

Casey's head shot up. "Oh, my God, Mom. No!"

"You draw? I'd love to see." He wrapped an arm around Sonja, pulling her close, and she stiffened. Jimmy gave her waist a soft pinch, and she wiggled but then settled her arm over his shoulder. *Nice.* A feeling which could only be described as contentment spread through him. He spared a quick glance up at Sonja before returning his focus on Casey. Her eyes were glued to her mother, a mortified expression on her face. *Uh oh.* "Seriously, I'd love to see."

Casey blinked and then focused on him. "I don't know. They're kinda dumb."

"They're not dumb. She's really quite talented, but hasn't drawn in years. Go get them, honey."

"*Mommmm.*"

He gave Sonja's side a squeeze. "It's okay, Casey. Maybe some other time, huh?"

"Yeah, maybe." She frowned and looked back at the screen.

Tension filled the room again for longer than he liked. He glanced at Sonja, and she was frowning too. "Hey, you two feel like doing something today?"

"Oh, I don't know. Like what?" Sonja stepped away and grabbed her mug from where she'd left it on the other side of the island.

He wanted her back next to him again. She drank the last of her coffee and then took her plate and cup and loaded them into the dishwasher. He stood and followed suit, rinsing his cup and—she took it from him before he could load it into the dishwasher himself. He chuckled. Kind of reminded him of his mother.

"What's got you chuckling?"

"Nothing, Sunshine." He kissed her cheek. "A friend is opening a gallery next week and needs a hand getting things organized. Figured maybe we'd all go. Then grab some lunch after."

Sonja smoothed her hand up the back of her hair. "Hmm…Maybe."

"That'd be cool. I wanna go."

Jimmy turned and smiled at Casey. She had a devilish little smirk on her face, her purple-and-pink hair falling over her forehead. Her thickly black-lined eyes narrowed on him before she broke into a full smile. The kid was smart and manipulative, for sure. And apparently, on his side, too. Score one for team Donnelly.

Sonja sighed. "Well, I guess it sounds like we're going. Casey, did you want to change into something a little nicer?"

"No."

"Eh, she's good. I'm gonna put her to work anyway. Her jeans and flannel are perfect."

"Thanks." Casey closed the cover on her iPad and set it on the counter. With a smile, she popped the last piece of honey bun in her mouth.

He looked back to Sonja. "Awesome. This worked out perfect."

"Yes, I'm sure you think it did." She shook her head. "Are you going to put me to work too?"

He bent his head and nuzzled her neck. "Sure. Every job needs a good manager. You can tell us all what to do."

"Very funny, James."

"I'll make it up to you later," he whispered close to her ear and ran his palm down her lower back. Sonja let out a small giggle.

"Ugh, you two should get a room."

Sonja pushed him away and gave him a scolding look before turning her gaze to her daughter. "Go get your things together, please."

Jimmy rested his back against the counter. Casey stood, shot him another sly grin before grabbing her iPad and left the room. When she was out of sight, he pulled Sonja close and kissed her before she had a chance to yell at him for getting too handsy in front of her daughter.

But really, it wasn't like he'd shoved his tongue down her throat—like he was doing now. And clearly based on the grin Casey gave him, she didn't have a problem with it. He wanted Sonja close, and her damn neck taunted him. Half the time, he didn't know if he preferred her hair up or down—the long blonde locks or her milky-white, bare neck—either way, she turned him on.

She was going to have to get used to him being affectionate in front of her daughter. All within acceptable PG-13 limits, of course, but without a doubt, PDA was going to happen. One thing was for damn sure, *not* touching her would *never* be an option.

CHAPTER THIRTY-TWO

Her daughter's text tone sounded, and Sonja glanced at her cell. Picking up the phone, she swiped the screen and read the message.

> Casey: Heading over to Jimmy's place after school. He's working on a new sculpture and said I can help.

Sonja stared at the message, perplexed by the friendship that'd formed between her daughter and James. Since Casey had met him a little over a month ago, the two had been practically inseparable. At least twice a week, Casey was at his loft and either watched him work or helped when he allowed her to. He'd even gotten her drawing again, which pleased Sonja to no end, but she couldn't help but feel a little jealous of their relationship—which was both childish and unnecessary.

They'd bonded in a way Sonja hadn't anticipated, but also hadn't been able to manage herself. She supposed Casey, deep in her rebellious phase, related to James. How could she not, with all his tattoos, piercings and own rebellious nature? Between the edgy art he created and the art covering his body, James was the epitome of rebellion, which she assumed most creative people were. But he'd been lucky enough to forge a successful career from his talents.

After sending a reply to Casey, letting her know what time to be home, Sonja leaned back in her chair and stared up at the tiled ceiling of her office. Her relationship with James had continued *and* deepened. She'd figured once he met Casey, he'd be spooked and back off, keeping things at the pace she preferred. But she'd been wrong. So very wrong.

Before Sonja knew it, he was spending several nights out of the week at her house. He cooked dinner with Casey, watched movies on the couch and slept over many of those nights, too. Sonja had run out of excuses to keep him at bay and gave up trying after a while. Not because it was too much work to fight him and easier to say yes, but because she had to admit, at least to herself, she liked having him there.

She liked crawling between the sheets into his welcome arms at night. She liked having him settle between her parted thighs, giving her the fix she craved while he took her to heaven. She liked waking up in the morning with his warm body pressed against hers, too. Lust blossomed within her, and without giving it a second thought, she called him.

He answered on the first ring. "Hey there, Sunny."

Sonja smiled at the name he still called her on occasion and spun her chair toward the windows. "Hi."

"How's your day going?"

"Pretty well. Was in court all morning and now back at the office. You?"

"Not too shabby. Getting ready to start a new piece. Casey wants to come over and help."

"Yes, she sent me a text. You sure she's not too much trouble?"

"Not at all. She's a great kid. Besides, if she's here, then she's not with Drake Dickfazio and not getting into trouble."

She laughed. "It's Defazio."

"Tomato. Tomahto. From what you've told me, he's a

dick, so there you go." He laughed, too, and the sound trickled over her skin like warm water.

Sonja shivered and pressed her hand to her stomach. "You're so bad."

"You like it when I'm bad."

"Yes. Yes, I do."

"Tell me what else you like, mo chroí?" His voice was a low purr.

Sonja sucked in a breath, and her sex clenched. This was how it was with him, always. Her body responded to his call and came alive, refusing to settle until he sated the craving need for him.

"I heard that gasp for breath. Is your pussy wet for me?"

Sonja crossed her legs, squeezed them together and spared a glance over her shoulder to her office door. It wasn't closed. "Always."

"Spread your legs."

"I can't. My office door is open." But her body did what he asked anyway.

"Even better. Are you wearing a skirt?"

Sonja spun in her chair, squaring herself with her desk. Her clit pulsed, begging for attention. He was going to ask her to touch herself, and every inch of her skin tingled in anticipation of his request. She wasn't going to be able to help herself. "Yes."

"My cock is rock hard for you right now. Slide your skirt up."

She inched her skirt up so she could spread her legs farther apart. "I want you. My hands are shaking."

"I want you too. I want inside that hot cunt of yours. Touch your clit for me." His breath hitched through the phone line, and she knew he'd taken himself in hand.

Sonja bit her lip, trying to keep herself from moaning, and circled her throbbing clit. "I've already soaked through my panties. Oh God...James."

"Oh yeah, babe, rub it for me. I've got my cock in my hand right now. If I were there, I'd be licking all that sweet honey from your cunt."

Sonja whimpered and dragged her fingers over her opening through the wet material, teasing herself. "Tell me how you want to fuck me."

"Pull your panties aside and slide your fingers in your heat. I want to hear your breath in my ear."

Another gasp escaped as she penetrated herself with two fingers. With her eyes locked on her office door, she pressed the heel of her hand against her clit. The idea that she could be caught amped her arousal even higher. "Yes...so good," she whispered.

"You're keeping your eye on the door, aren't you? Does it make your pussy wetter knowing someone could walk in at any time?"

"Yes." Sonja's vision blurred, her channel clenching around her fingers. Her climax built, getting closer every second. "James..." She panted and then swallowed, her mouth dry from her harsh breaths. "I'm close."

"You're my dirty slut, aren't you? Fuck, my cock is so hard right now. I'm going to explode all over my belly."

"Oh God. I love when you call me those lewd names. I shouldn't, but I do." She moved her hand faster, pressing her fingers deeper. "And I want to lick every drop off your belly."

"How about I straddle your chest tonight and work myself up so I can come all over your tits and mouth? I'll even let you suck the head a little while I stroke. You're my filthy come-slut, aren't you?"

That did it. "Oh, my God! Yessss." Sonja's orgasm hit with a force of an earthquake, her channel clenching tight around her fingers. Her clit spasmed, and wave after wave rolled through her body. She bit down on her tongue, panting through her nose while little whimpers escaped between breaths.

"Fuck yes! That's it, come for me. My turn, mo chroí." He grunted and let out a long, throaty moan.

The sounds arrowed straight to her clit, and she knew he was coming too. Sonja also knew how hot those ribbons of creamy semen felt when they spurted on her skin. She shuddered, wanting to feel it again and knowing he'd give her the pleasure later that night. Sonja still had her fingers buried deep inside her channel, sliding them in and out with lazy strokes. If he were there with her, he'd work her up again, nice and slow, until she came once more. "I wish I was there to lick you clean."

"Someday, I'm going to fuck you behind your desk during the day when all your staff is there."

Sonja closed her eyes. It was so depraved, yet she knew she wanted it, too. "You're crazy, James."

"Yeah, and you love my crazy. Be ready for tonight. This only barely took the edge off."

Sonja slid her fingers free and grabbed a tissue. "I think you better be ready, too. That just made me crave you more."

"Sunshine, your hot little box is mine, and I'm going to take what's mine tonight as many times as I want. Now get back to work." With that, the call disconnected.

Sonja pulled the phone away from her ear and stared at the screen. His statement rankled because she knew he was right. *Dammit.* She hated that.

"Ms. Martin, can I get you some coffee?"

Sonja startled at the sudden presence of her assistant in her doorway. The cell slid from her hand and bounced on the desk. "Crap!" Sonja grabbed it as adrenaline spiked through her, then set it back down. "I'm sorry, what?"

Her assistant frowned. "I'm sorry. I didn't mean to startle you. Did you want some coffee?"

"Um. No. No, thank you, Sheila."

The woman pivoted and was gone faster than she'd appeared. Running her hand up the back of her hair, Sonja blew out a breath and almost had to laugh. "Good God, that was close."

———

JIMMY OPENED the door to his loft to find Casey standing in the hall, her backpack hanging off one shoulder. She'd changed her hair color since he'd met her. Now, it was blue with purple streaks on the ends.

She wore a worn-out Type O Negative concert tee under a black-and-green flannel shirt, faded black skinny jeans with a hole in one knee, and a pair of black combat boots, unlaced. At least she had good taste in music, but he doubted she even understood the greatness that was Type O. He'd have to educate her some time. "How's it going, kiddo? You ready to get to work today?"

She smiled and breezed past him. "I'm here, aren't I?"

He closed the door. "Need a snack first?"

"Nah. I'm good." She plopped her backpack on one of the dining chairs.

Jimmy moved to the top of the stairs. "You know where the fridge is if you want a drink. Help yourself and meet me downstairs when you're ready."

"Cool. Thanks."

Jimmy made his way to his studio and wheeled the MIG welder over to the large worktable in the center of the room and then grabbed two masks.

"What're we working on today?"

"Today…" Jimmy handed her a mask. "We're going to build a coffee table. Or at least start it."

"Fuck yeah! Welding!" Casey bounced, a big smile adorning her face.

Jimmy chuckled. "Yeah, it's cool, but watch your mouth."

"Yeah, yeah. Sorry. We need tunes."

"Getting to that, Little Miss Impatient." Jimmy moved to

his workbench against the wall, grabbed the iPod and queued up some Type O, just for her. "Anesthesia" started playing, and he glanced over at her.

She was looking through one of his portfolios she'd picked up off the other table bordering the opposite wall, and gave no indication she knew the band or the song playing. So much for that. He'd for sure be educating her now. "Come on then. Let's get started."

Her head snapped up, and she put the portfolio down. "What do you want me to do?"

"First, we gather the parts we need." He moved over to the inventory of various parts and steel pieces he kept on shelves beside his workbench. Grabbing the biggest piece, which was resting against the wall on the floor, he picked it up and moved it onto the center table.

"What the heck is that?"

"What does it look like?" He moved back to the shelves. "Come here, need you to carry some of these."

"I don't know. It looks like some sort of gear or something." She held out her arms, and Jimmy handed her four metal pipes.

"Take those over to the table, please." He grabbed a few more items he needed and moved next to her. "It's a big gear. Probably used in some sort of factory machine."

"It's huge." She smiled. "By the way, this is a cool song."

"Yeah? Glad you like it."

"Who is it?" She took off her flannel and tossed it onto the workbench behind her.

Resting his hands on his hips, he tilted his head to the side. "You mean you don't know?"

"Should I know?"

He raised his brows and pursed his lips. "Kiddo, if you're gonna wear a band's shirt, you should at least know who the hell they are. Shame on you, Casey Olivia Martin."

"Oh." She looked at her shirt and then back at him. A slight blush colored her cheeks.

Jimmy had to smile. For as tough as she liked to pretend to be, the blush gave her innocence away every damn time. Just like her mom. "No worries. By the time we finish today, you'll be well acquainted with TON."

"TON?"

"And so the first lesson shall begin. TON. Stands for Type O Negative." Jimmy picked up one of the four steel pipes as "Burnt Flowers Fallen" came up next on rotation. "Come on, let's go bend some pipes."

"Okay." She smiled and followed him over to the machine. "What does this do?"

"It bends the pipes to the shape we want them. Watch." Placing the pipe in the track, he clamped it in place, set all the necessary components and started cranking the lever.

"Wow! That's fucking cool! Oh!" Casey covered her mouth with her hand. "Sorry," she mumbled.

"Killing me, kiddo. Wanna try?"

She linked her hands behind her back and rocked on her heels. "Uh-huh."

"Okay, let me adjust the pipe first. Then, when I say you crank the handle. Cool?"

"Mmkay." She rested her hand on the lever and waited, eyes big as saucers.

"All right. Give it a crank." Jimmy stood back and supervised. Casey moved the handle back and forth, bending the pipe as needed. "One more crank, and then we do the others."

"This is so freaking cool!"

"Agreed." He mussed the top of her hair, and she ducked her head, scoffing at him. "Eh, it's just hair. Look at mine?" He ran his fingers through it, messing it further.

"I've seen yours, and that's so not the look I'm going for." She gave the lever one last pull and stepped back. "Next one?"

"Yup, go grab the others. And I'm crushed you don't like my hair. Seriously."

She rushed to the center table, grabbed the remaining three pipes and returned to him. "Nah, I like your hair. It's just not me."

"Riiiiight, because it's *liiiike* one color and stuff." He peppered his words with a mock, girly tone as he twirled a lock of his hair.

Casey rolled her eyes, giggling at him, which was also another betrayal of the sweet girl hiding behind the exterior she'd put in place. She was a good kid, despite what face she displayed to the world around her. Underneath the harsh yet colorful, bright hair were dark brown locks, like her father's. Her heavily black-lined eyes were sky blue, like her mother's. She'd done a damn good job of fooling all those around her, with the exception of the people who knew her best.

Jimmy set up the next pipe in the machine and let Casey do the bending, adjusting when needed. She was like a kid who'd gotten her most coveted toy for her birthday—all giddy with excitement. Seeing her bubbling enthusiasm gave Jimmy a deep sense of purpose in Casey's life.

He understood this kid probably better than most, definitely better than her mother did. Being a rebel himself, he'd tried to assure Sonja, several times since meeting Casey, that her daughter would be fine.

One night, they'd discussed her at length while lying in bed. Sonja had bristled more than a few times when Jimmy gave his opinion on how he thought Sonja should try and view the situation. She wasn't too willing to listen to him. Even tossed out to him that he wasn't a parent, therefore he didn't or couldn't understand. She was both right and wrong. He had a few nieces and nephews, and he had his own experience to draw from, too.

He'd been fortunate because his parents hadn't tried to change him. They let him be whatever he wanted to be and always encouraged him to do what made him happy. Because of their unconditional love and support, he'd pursued all types of art with a vengeance in school. After college, they encouraged him to move to Manhattan and pursue his dream.

Jimmy had blown off his degree in his final year without even considering how much money his parents paid for his education, and yet they'd supported him anyway. If he were in their shoes, he might not have been so accepting or supportive, but for certain, he'd try. He was damn sure Sonja would never tolerate something like that. Finishing up the last pipe, he gathered them together and ushered her to the worktable.

"Do we get to weld now?"

"Yup. We'll do the fitting pieces first. Grab your mask. You watch for the first couple, then I'll let you try, cool?"

"So cool!"

Casey would definitely be expected to go to college. And she'd be expected to graduate with her bachelor's degree, probably with honors, then promptly earn a master's degree immediately after. In his opinion, it was way too much pressure for a kid. But what did he know, right? Jimmy shook his head and put his welder's mask on the top of his head. Flipping the on switch for the welder, he glanced at Casey. "Ready?"

She nodded, pulling her mask over her face. He lowered his mask and welded the first fitting for the pipes to the large gear. Casey squealed, and he could practically feel her limbs vibrating with excitement.

Yeah, God willing, this kid was going to be fine.

CHAPTER THIRTY-THREE

Sonja pulled the garlic bread from the oven and placed it in the waiting basket. Casey was out for the night, staying at a friend's house, and James would be there any minute. After their little phone sex session earlier in the day, she'd been antsy and walking on edge. The orgasm had only served to heighten the almost constant need for him.

The doorbell rang, and she pulled off her apron and headed down the hall. Taking a look through the peephole, she smiled and opened the door. "Hi."

"Hi." James crossed the threshold, took her in his arms and kissed her. Pulling away, he brushed his nose over hers.

She let out a sigh and ran her hands up his arms. "Are you hungry?"

Bending his head, he ran his lips over her neck. "Mmhmm."

Sonja let out a giggle. "I meant for food!"

He straightened and gazed at her. "Oh, food? Yeah, I could eat."

"Good. Because I cooked." Taking his hand, she led him toward the formal dining room.

"It does smell damn good in here. Not as good as you, but a close second for sure."

The lights were dimmed in the dining room. Guiding him to the large cherrywood table set for two, with candles burning in the center, she motioned to the chair she wanted him to sit in. "Have a seat. Dinner will be right out."

"Wow! Nice setup. Can I help?"

"You can open the Chianti. Otherwise, sit right there, James-the-artist, and I shall do all the work."

He grabbed the bottle and corkscrew sitting beside it. "Got it."

She grinned and stepped backward through the butler's pantry door. The rest of the meal was on the table, so she grabbed the serving bowl full of spaghetti and made her way back out to him. "La cena è servita." *Dinner is served.* She smiled and placed the pasta on the table. "Un momento, ho bisogno di ottenere il pane." *One moment, I need to get the bread.*

James snagged her wrist before she stepped away. "I don't know what you just said, and I don't even think I care, but holy fuck, that was hot, and if you keep talking like that, I'm going to bang you on this table right now."

Sonja bent forward, stroking her fingers through his hair. "Promesse, promesse. Si può avere me come vuoi me, James." *Promises, promises. You can have me how you want me, James.*

Pulling her onto his lap, he smoothed a hand over the curve of her hip and onto her backside. "That's beyond sexy, mo chroí. No joke."

"I said, dinner is served." She traced his lips with her fingertip. "Tell me what mo chroí means, and I'll tell you what else I said."

James smiled and then bit the tip of her finger before sucking it between his lips. Fire spread through her veins. Maybe letting him fuck her on the table wasn't such a bad idea. She could always reheat the pasta. Tugging her finger from between his delectable lips, she pressed her mouth to his and snaked her tongue inside. When she pulled away, they were both breathless, and James had one hand up her skirt, tracing little circles on her inner thigh.

He cleared his throat. "No."

"No?"

"No."

Sonja stood and moved to the door. Before passing through it, she looked over her shoulder. "Fine. Don't expect me to tell you either." She walked through the door, leaving him alone at the table. Grabbing the breadbasket, she returned to the dining room, set it on the table and took the seat to his left.

"Oookay." He linked his hands together over his stomach.

Ignoring him, she reached for the bowl of pasta and scooped a large helping onto his plate. Then, added extra sauce and two meatballs. He poured them each a glass of wine. She offered him a piece of garlic bread from the basket, and he took a slice. Then, she served herself. All was done in silence.

Tension filled the room, almost as though they were having a silent argument. Maybe they were. *Hmm.* She intended only to tease him a little by refusing to translate the statements she'd made in Italian unless he told her what *mo chroí* meant. In truth, the mystery surrounding the endearment he used consistently with her made it feel all the more special. Sort of... Sonja went to run her hand up the back of her hair, forgetting it wasn't pulled up. *Dammit.*

"What shall we drink to?"

Sonja's head snapped up to find James had raised his glass. She picked hers up and smiled. "How about a toast to mystery?"

"Mystery, huh?" He shrugged. "Okay."

"Yes, the mystery behind our words."

"I see." He tapped her glass before raising his to his lips.

Sonja blew out a breath and watched his mouth close

around the edge, then his throat bob as he swallowed. Taking a sip of her wine, she swallowed past the lump in her throat. James Donnelly had dug himself so deep beneath her skin she had no hope of extricating him. Why, oh why, did this man want her, and why in God's name did she want him back?

The answer to those two questions had continued to elude her, no matter how much time she spent with him or how many times they had sex. She was beginning to think she'd never figure it out.

"Stop it." He took a mouthful of pasta.

"Stop what?"

He chewed and then wiped his mouth with the napkin. "Just…stop it." He covered her hand with his.

"How's your pasta?"

He leaned over and kissed her cheek. "It's the best spaghetti I've ever had."

"Your mother's a chef, so I doubt that. But thank you."

"Yes, this is true. She is a chef, but this is still awesome. And you should accept a compliment." He took another bite.

"I said thank you." She followed his lead and ate some from her plate. Even she had to admit it was good. The sauce had come out almost perfect.

"Where's Casey?"

"She's spending the night with a friend. How'd she do today at the studio?"

He wiped his mouth and took another sip of wine. "She did awesome. I let her bend some pipes and weld."

"Weld? As in welding, with a torch?"

"No, not really a torch, but yes, welding. Is that a problem?"

"Well, I guess not. I just…" Sonja picked up her wine. "I assume you're using all the necessary safety equipment."

"Of course. Do you really think I'd let her get hurt?"

"No. But accidents happen."

He tossed his napkin on the table. "Why do I feel like we're about to have a fight?"

"Because maybe we are." She took a long gulp of wine.

"Ah, I see. Fucking foreplay, huh?"

Sonja almost choked. "I beg your pardon?"

"Where's the maid?"

"What?"

James stood. "I said, where's the maid?"

"I gave her the night off..." Sonja looked up at him. "James, what are you doing?"

"Giving you what you need."

"What I need?"

"Yup." Bending forward, he turned her chair to face him and knelt before her.

"Oh, dear."

James rested his hands on the top of her legs. "Are you wearing panties?"

Her breath hitched in her throat, and she pushed her hair off her shoulder. "No."

"Good." He tugged her toward the edge of the seat, then scooted her skirt up. "Part your pretty thighs for me."

Sonja slid her skirt a little higher and spread her thighs wide. She knew she was already wet and had been since earlier in the day—even more so since he'd arrived.

"Look at your wet pussy. My God, Sonja. Sweet heaven is right there waiting for me." He gripped her thighs, pressing his thumbs into the tender inner flesh of her legs. "Tell me what you want."

Bolts of lightning rocketed through Sonja, bounced off her insides and made her skin tingle. "Did you want dessert?"

"Only if it's the sweet honey dripping from your cunt."

"Take a taste."

His eyes widened, satisfaction flashing in them before he bent his head and licked through her slit. Sonja's entire body jerked at the feel of his tongue. Her head fell back against the chair, and she raised one leg, resting it on his shoulder. When he latched on to her clit, she gripped his hair with both hands and pulled him closer.

James growled and sucked harder. Sonja's body tightened, and lust pooled in her stomach. He brought her to the edge of climax—and the point of madness—only to change his pace, tormenting her with slow, lazy licks through her slit. She wiggled and rolled her hips, gripping the strands of his hair, wanting more…

Taking hold of her behind her knees, James shifted her farther down the seat and raised her legs in the air, baring her completely to him. "Oh, my God, James!"

With an iron grip on the back of her thighs, he kept them pinned against her chest, and his gaze locked on hers. Snaking his tongue out, he flicked it over her clit. She was mesmerized by him. By the look in his eyes. By the feel of his teasing tongue. By everything he *had* done and *was* doing to her.

"I was going to give you control tonight." He licked through her slit. "But I think, no, not tonight. Tonight, it's my turn."

Her response, poised on the tip of her tongue, was stopped short when he nipped her clit and then smoothed his tongue over it. Sonja arched on the seat, barely able to move due to his unyielding hold, but shifted enough to press against his mouth.

"Ask me to let you come."

She drew in a deep breath when he returned to licking through her slit, then penetrated her core with his tongue. "James…"

"Whose cunt is this, Sonja? Hmm?" He licked again. "Tell me."

His words pierced the lust-induced haze in her mind. Even caught in the maelstrom of an anticipated climax, one she might very well not recover from, she knew the answer. "Yours. It's—oh fuck…it's yours."

"You want to come, mo chroí?"

Sonja rolled her hips. "Yes! Please, yes!"

With an abrupt shift, James moved from between her legs and stood. Shoving the dinner plates aside, he picked her up and placed her on the table. He moved between her thighs. "I think I need to feel your tight cunt ripple over my cock when I let you come. Unbutton your blouse. I want to see your fine tits when I fuck you."

Her hands shook, and Sonja fumbled with the buttons. James opened his pants, freeing his engorged cock. Finally getting the last buttons opened, she removed her shirt and bra. "I want to suck you."

"Oh yeah?" He palmed himself and stroked from base to tip. A bead of arousal oozed from the tip and dripped down the head. He swiped it up with his thumb and brought it to her lips. "Lick it clean."

She moaned and sucked, swallowing his arousal. Pulling his thumb from her mouth, he ran his palm down her jaw to her throat. He gave her neck a light squeeze before continuing to her chest. With the flat of his palm, he pressed her to lie back on the tabletop.

Fire blazed over Sonja's skin when he bent over her and took one tight nipple between his teeth. With his length pressed against her core, she tilted her pelvis back, and his shaft slid across her clit. She moaned, aching for him to be inside her.

James growled against her breast and twisted her other nipple between his fingers. It stung, and Sonja cried out and grabbed hold of his hair, pulling the strands hard. But he didn't move away. Instead, he bit her nipple harder, then sucked it into his mouth while he pinched the other and continued stroking his length back and forth through her folds.

Sonja arched against him, giving over to the insane pleasure the sting of pain brought her. "James, please don't stop. It stings, my God, but don't stop!" She raised her legs and spread them wider. Reaching between them, she took his cock in hand. She positioned him at her entrance and waited.

Releasing her nipple, he dragged his tongue over the tip. "Tell me."

"Tell you what?"

He grinned, then tugged and twisted the other nipple. "Tell me what you want."

His piercing hazel eyes held her captive, and she was terrified she'd drown in them. Sonja swallowed. "I want you to fuck me."

James gave her nipple one last lick before he straightened. Running his palms over her inner thighs, he looked down between them. "Baby, your pink pussy's sucking the tip of my cock." He shifted forward, penetrating a little deeper. "Fuck, yes. So hot how you draw me right in."

Sonja's skin prickled with goosebumps. "James." His name came out on a harsh breath, sounding more like a plea than a command. She didn't care; she needed him inside her. Now. Moving both hands between them, she spread her labia. "I ache for you."

James gripped her chin in his hand. "I ache for you too, mo chroí." He kissed her and slid his length deep with one thrust.

Sonja gasped against his lips and then sucked his tongue into her mouth. James glided out and back in again. Yes! This was what she needed. This was what she had to have.

Her fix.

Her addiction.

The drug she couldn't live without.

He continued to kiss her while he fucked her. Keeping his pelvis tight against her core, James thrust his hips and ground against her clit. Sonja drowned in him—her fear and her salvation—and a million sensations assaulted her body from the inside out. His tongue in her mouth quenched her thirst. His cock buried deep in her core fed her craving.

Her orgasm rose, fast and hard, like a rocket. She exploded, soaring higher than he'd ever taken her. All Sonja could do was wrap her arms and legs around him and hold on for fear she might shatter into a million pieces.

James broke the kiss, and she dragged in a breath. Sliding his hands down her body and then under her bottom, he raised her hips off the table and slid his length out before slamming deep again.

"Oh God!"

"Mine!" He thrust again, bouncing her beneath him on the table. "Say it."

The room spun, and her channel spasmed. "Yours!"

He pressed his forehead against hers and bored his gaze into her eyes with an intensity she'd never seen from him before. Her breath caught in her throat, and with one final thrust, James climaxed.

His shaft pulsed and spurted within her. She closed her eyes, unable to hold his gaze, squeezing him tighter against her. With her eyes shut tight, realization and a little bit of fear obliterated the haze in her mind and struck deep in her gut.

James had already stolen her body, and now, she was more than convinced he was trying to steal her heart. She couldn't let that happen, but Sonja was no longer certain she could stop him.

CHAPTER THIRTY-FOUR

THE SOUND OF JIMMY'S CELL RINGING ROUSED HIM FROM THE deep sleep he'd been in. The kind of sleep that happens after you've had some really intense sex. Speaking of…spooned up behind her, he pulled Sonja's body closer. He must've dreamt that his phone was ringing because the room was silent—until it rang again.

Rolling over, he reached blindly for the device. He squinted at the bright screen. *What the hell?* "Hello," he whispered.

"Jimmy, I need you to come get me!" Casey let out a loud sob, sounding like she was in a complete state of panic.

He could barely understand her. "Slow down, Casey. One sec, honey." Careful to move without jostling the bed, he got up, walked into Sonja's closet and shut the door. "Okay, where are you? What the hell is going on? Are you hurt?"

"No. Well, I don't— Please, can you come get me?" Her voice hitched before breaking into more sobs.

Jesus, fuck. "Calm down, honey. Where are you?"

"Um," She sniffled. "I'm down in the Village in some shit-hole apartment."

"What the fuck, Case? You were supposed to be sleeping

at your friend's house two blocks from here." Jimmy ran his fingers through his hair, and his "duh" moment struck. "You're with that fucking Drake, aren't you?"

She let out another sob. "Yes."

"Did that fucker hurt you? Dammit! Look, I'm hanging up so I can get dressed. Can you text me the address? I'll be there as fast as I can."

"I think so. Hurry, okay?"

"Yeah. You got two seconds to send me that text, Casey. Hear me?"

"I will. I promise."

Jimmy disconnected the call and retrieved his clothes from the bedroom. Moving back to Sonja's closet, he dressed, and his phone beeped with the expected text message from Casey. He replied as he headed out the door to get her. Christ, Sonja was gonna bust an artery over this. He didn't wake her, just snuck out, hoping like hell she'd stay asleep. At least until he got back.

The cab pulled up in front of the address Casey had sent him. After asking the driver to wait, he entered the building. Taking the steps two at a time, he climbed four flights of stairs. Adrenaline coursed through him, and he stalked down the hall with his hands balled into fists. If that douchenozzle-punkdick hurt his girl, he was going to make him suffer. Slowly. Jimmy didn't care if the kid wasn't eighteen yet. He'd had about enough of the asshole.

Banging his fist on the door, he crossed his arms and waited. When no one answered, he pounded harder and again, several more times, until finally, the door swung open.

"What the fu—?" A skinny kid with greasy blond hair greeted him.

"Where the fuck is Casey is what."

"Uhh… Who?"

"Who, huh? Get the fuck out of my way." Jimmy shoved the kid aside and stalked in, hollering for Casey. A quick scan of the small living room turned up nothing, so he moved down the hall to the left. "Casey? Where are you, honey?" He opened a door— And there was Dickfazio, lying on a bed, sheets and blankets hanging off the end, joint halfway to his lips…and some young girl curled around him. *What. The. Flying. Fuck!* "Where is she?" Jimmy rushed forward. "And so help me God, you lie to me, and it'll be the last time your jaw works for a long fucking time."

Drake raised his hands in surrender. "Dude, I swear—Ahhh!"

Jimmy grabbed him by his shirt, hauled him off the bed and then slammed him against the wall. "Wrong. Answer." He yanked Drake forward, then banged him against the wall again. "Now, before I beat you within an inch of your pathetic life, I suggest you try again."

"Christ, wait—"

"Jimmy?"

He snapped his head around to find Casey standing in the doorway. Black eyeliner and mascara streaked down her cheeks from her tears, and her hair was a tangled mess. "Oh, thank fuck." Jimmy blew out a breath. "Get your stuff. Now." Turning back to Douchnozzle Dickfazio, he narrowed his eyes and got nose-to-nose with him. "Listen up, dickhead, and you better hear me good because this is the last time I'm gonna say it. You stay the fuck away from Casey! If you don't, I *will* make you wish your mother'd swallowed the night she got knocked up with you. Get me?"

"Y-y-yeah."

Jimmy had such a tight hold of Drake's shirt, the kid's feet weren't touching the ground. He slammed him against the wall one last time for good measure. "Don't forget it." He dropped him, then left the room and found Casey waiting at the front door. "Let's go."

The retreat out of the building and the entire cab ride to her home was in silence, which was good because it gave him time to cool down. Jimmy was tempted to bring her back to his loft to talk it out, but figured it was better to get her home.

On their way up the elevator of her building, she finally spoke. "Thanks for coming to get me."

"You gonna tell me what the fuck happened?"

She glanced up at him briefly before looking away, twisting her hands in front of her. Dread and fear burned the back of his throat, and he blew out a shaky breath. *Shit.* Maybe she shouldn't tell him because he might end up doing something to Drake that could really land him in jail.

"If I tell you, are you going to tell my mom?"

He stepped off the elevator, and she followed. "I don't know. I guess it depends on what happened, Case."

"Mmkay." She unlocked and opened the door for them.

He patted her shoulder. "Go get your PJs on and meet me in the kitchen. I'll make some hot chocolate."

"Mmkay." She shrugged before disappearing down the hall and into her bedroom.

Jimmy made his way to the kitchen and grabbed the container of gourmet cocoa from the pantry. He set a pan of milk on the stove to warm and then pulled two mugs from the cabinet. Dragging his fingers through his hair, he yawned and glanced at the clock on the microwave. Four fifteen a.m. It was going to be a long night…or morning, rather.

Casey came into the room, clad in her jammies and fuzzy slippers, looking a whole hell of a lot better than when they'd gotten home. Jimmy wasn't sure if she trusted him enough to share what went down, but he hoped so. She'd trusted him enough to call him for help, so maybe he'd get it out of her. Bottom line, he wasn't going to let it go, and not understand exactly what they were dealing with. He spooned cocoa into a mug. "Glad you got all that black crap off your face."

She took a seat at the island and smiled, but he could tell it was forced. "Yeah, makeup remover wipes are like magic."

Jimmy slid the mug her way and then worked on making his own cup. "Magic…I guess that's one way of looking at it."

"Did you grab the marshmallows?"

"Nope. I didn't see any in there."

"I'll get them." Casey stood, shook out her hands, and grabbed the bag of mini marshmallows from the pantry and brought them to the island. After dumping a handful into her mug, she offered some to Jimmy.

"I suppose cocoa *is* better with little puffs of sugar." He smiled and dropped his own handful into his mug. "Although this gourmet stuff you got here is pretty damn sweet all on its own. Haven't you ever had Swiss Miss? It's what us average peeps drink." He winked and took a sip.

They sat in silence for a little longer, both sipping their cocoa. Casey drew in a deep breath and focused on the dark liquid in her mug. After a few more beats, she spoke. "You're waiting for me to start talking, aren't you?"

Jimmy leaned forward, resting on his forearms. "Yup."

"I figured." Casey blew out a breath. "I was at Trina's like I told Mom I'd be, but then Drake texted and said there was a party. Trina didn't want to go, though." She glanced up at him.

Jimmy tried like hell to keep his expression relaxed, calm even, but he knew his eyes probably had a fire blazing in them. "And?"

Casey glanced back down at her mug. "I snuck out after Trina fell asleep."

"Okay, go on."

She shrugged. "Well, the party was fine, ya know? I mean, only a few people there."

"Drinking?"

"Some." She took a sip of her cocoa.

"Drugs, too?"

She flinched. "Some."

Fuck! "Casey, listen, you look like you're crashing really hard right now from whatever you took. Kinda hard to fool me where that's concerned, so just get on with what happened."

"Are you pissed?"

"No. Not pissed. Worried and scared for sure. But not pissed."

She stifled a yawn and rubbed her eyes. "Are you gonna tell my mom?"

"I don't know. Like I said before, all depends on what happened."

"Fine. I took some pills. Two of them. Not sure what they were."

Jimmy grunted but remained quiet. He had no idea if she was being truthful with him. She could be on any number of drugs. He wanted to believe she wasn't, but there was no way to know for sure.

"I guess whatever they were, they're finally wearing off. But I'm okay." She shrugged and avoided his gaze.

Jimmy blew out a breath. "Okay." He blew out another breath and grunted. "What happened with Dic—Drake?"

"It wasn't that big a deal." A tear streaked down her cheek. Turning away, she wiped her face.

Jimmy's heart broke seeing her fall apart. He came around the counter and pulled her into his arms. "Hey, hey. Case, it's okay."

Casey wrapped hers around his waist, buried her face in his shirt and cried. He stroked the back of her head, and when she finally got a grip on her sobs, she pulled away. He handed her a napkin, and she blew her nose. "Well, that was embarrassing."

Damn, he hated that she was hurting, so he did the one thing that always worked with his younger sisters. He cracked a joke. "I'm just glad you didn't blow all that snot on my shirt."

His joke was enough to break a bit of the tension, and Casey giggled. "So gross."

"Psshaw, you're telling me? I've lost a few shirts to female snot before. It ain't pretty, kid." He cupped her chin in his hand, raising her eyes to his. "Whatever it is, you can tell me, Case. Seriously."

"Fine." She blew her hair out of her eyes. "We started messing around. In the room you found him in. But he always pushes me, ya know?"

He took a step back as anger bubbled to the surface. "Did he hurt you?" His voice was a low rumble, and he knew he sounded pissed.

"No." She shook her head. "Not *that* way anyway."

"Okay, then, in *what* way?"

She covered her face with her hands. "God, this is so embarrassing!"

"Casey."

"Fine. He's mean, okay? Because I won't do it with him. He's mean. He started calling me names. Told me I was a tease and didn't say it that nice, either. Why do guys do that?"

Jimmy pulled her into another hug. Jesus hearing this sucked. "Because I'm sorry to say, some guys are assholes. Not all, but some."

"Yeah, well, I guess I picked an asshole." Casey hugged him tight. "Tomorrow, he'll be all sorry about it."

"Uhhh, no, he won't because I told him to stay away from you."

She jerked back from him. "Why did you do that?"

"Because that guy is bad news, Casey, and he's going to get you into trouble. Were you too high to even notice the chick curled up and cozy with him in bed when I got there? You need to stay away from him."

Casey stood. "Well, I'm not gonna. You're not my father. You can't tell me what to do!"

"You're right; I'm not your father. But right now, I'm the

one who's here, and I'm also the one who came and got your rebellious ass. So yeah, you're going to stay away from him." Jimmy stepped back and crossed his arms. She needed to hear this, whether she liked it or not.

She shot him a glare. "Screw you. Screw everybody!" She turned and stormed out of the kitchen.

Jimmy blew out a breath and stared down at his feet. "Well, that went well. Not."

Casey was tired and upset and, by now, probably hung over. It was best to let her sleep it off. He'd try to talk to her more in the morning. As far as telling Sonja, he figured Casey wouldn't tell her mother, and Jimmy planned to decide if telling her was necessary in the morning, too. For now, he and Casey both needed some sleep.

CHAPTER THIRTY-FIVE

In a half-dream state, Sonja felt the warmth of James's body pressed against her back, and then his arm slid around her waist. She covered his hand with hers and scooted her backside closer. "Is everything okay?" she whispered.

He kissed her shoulder. "Yeah, mo chroí, everything's fine. Go back to sleep."

"Mmm…okay." Raising his hand to her lips, she kissed his fingers and closed her eyes.

When Sonja opened them again, the sun was shining through the edges of the drapes. Turning over, she faced him. He was lying on his back, arm draped over his face, still sound asleep. Sonja ran the flat of her palm down his chest to his stomach—and he didn't so much as flinch. She smiled, guessing she must've worn him out more than she thought last night.

Sonja rolled over and got out of bed, heading for the bathroom. She turned on the shower and stepped inside. Pouring a generous amount of shampoo in her palm, Sonja massaged the long lengths of her wet hair into a lather. It was still early, and Casey wouldn't be home for a few more hours. Maybe she and James could go out for breakfast.

Sonja finished up in the bathroom, got dressed, then wandered back to her bedroom. James was still asleep. He looked so peaceful, she contemplated not waking him. Deciding to give him a little more time, she went out to the kitchen and started a fresh pot of coffee.

After having two cups of coffee, reading through the paper and giving in to her hunger by eating a muffin, she wandered back to her bedroom. It'd been about an hour and a half, and he still wasn't up. Maybe he was sick. Sonja moved to his side of the bed—when the hell did she start referring to it as *his* side of the bed? Sonja shook her head and sighed. She supposed it had *become* his side, hadn't it? Smoothing the hair off his forehead, she smiled. Damn this man for sneaking into her life like he had. Damn him for accomplishing what she swore last night she'd never let him do.

Stealing her heart.

Sonja bent over him and pressed a tender kiss to his lips, then placed soft kisses along his jaw to his ear. "Wake up, honey."

James jerked a bit, then cupped the back of her head with his palm. "What time is it?"

She nipped his earlobe. "Just past ten thirty, sleepyhead. You feeling okay?"

"Mmhmm. Just tired." He ran his hand down her back and pressed her closer. "Casey up yet?"

She kissed down his neck. "No, she's at Trina's, remember?"

He sat up. "Wait. She's not here? Did you check her room?"

"No. Why would I check her room?" James got up out of bed, practically shoving her aside and donning his jeans. "What's wrong?" She followed him out of her room. "James? Where are you going?" Sonja stopped when he knocked on her daughter's door.

"Casey?" He knocked again.

"Honey, what's going on? I already told you she's not here." She grabbed his arm, but he pulled away and knocked again. He was in a state of panic.

Before she could stop him, he opened Casey's door and barreled into the room. Sonja went in after him.

"Fuck!" He turned to face her, a look of sheer panic and fear on his face.

"James, for God's sake, what's the matter with you?"

"Shit…I can't fucking believe she did this." He ran into Casey's bathroom and was back out in mere seconds. "Where does she keep her backpack?"

Sonja glanced around her daughter's messy room. Clothes were strewn everywhere. "In the closet. You know what, you're scaring me. Maybe you need to sit down."

He opened the closet door and rummaged around on the floor. "I think she's taken off." He moved to her and grabbed both of her arms. "Casey called me last night. I picked her up from some party with that scum boyfriend of hers, and now she's gone. Her backpack isn't here, and neither is her iPad or phone. So, please, call the police. I'm getting dressed." He turned away from her and ran out of the room.

Sonja took a deep breath to calm down. He was talking crazy. Getting hysterical along with him wasn't going to help the situation. She followed after him to her bedroom. "Are you sure you didn't have some sort of nightmare?"

"Sonja, I did not have a damn nightmare."

"For goodness sake, she's at Trina's. That's why her backpack and stuff is gone. Let me call her, and you can even talk to her. Just take a breath for me, okay?"

"Fine." He pulled his shirt over his head and nodded before bending to put on his socks and boots.

Once she got Casey on the phone, she was definitely going to make him lie back down. He obviously needed a little more sleep. Sonja dialed Casey's cell. Holding the phone to her ear, she took a seat on the settee and listened. It rang and rang, then went to voicemail. Disconnecting, she glanced up at James. He had his hands on his hips, an impatient look on his face. "The girls are probably still asleep. I'll call Trina's mother."

"Fine. Since you're looking at me like I'm nuts, you do that. But I guarantee you, your daughter took off and is probably with that dickhead right now!"

Raising both brows, she leveled her tone. "James, *do not* raise your voice at me."

He let out an exasperated sigh and crossed his arms. "Fine. Make the call."

Sonja shook her head, mostly in disbelief at this whole display. Bringing up Trina's home phone number, she hit the call button and put the phone to her ear. Maybe she needed to rethink that whole he'd-stolen-her-heart thing because this crap was outright unacceptable. Trina's mother answered after the third ring. "Hello, Adrianna. Sorry to bother you, but Casey didn't answer her phone. I assume she's still sleeping. Could you wake her, please?"

"No problem, Sonja. Just a second."

"Thanks." She glanced over at James, who was now wearing a path in her carpet, pacing. "She's going to wake her up. Will you please sit down and relax?"

With his hands on his hips, he continued pacing. "No."

"Sonja, you still there?" Adrianna asked.

"Yes. I'm here."

"Casey isn't here. Trina said she woke up earlier this morning, and Casey was gone, so she went back to sleep. She figured she went home."

She stood up. "Are you certain?"

"That's what Trina said. Is she not home?"

"No, but I'm betting she's wandered down to the Starbucks or something. Thank you, and again, sorry to disturb." Sonja disconnected the call and stared down at her phone.

"She's not there, is she?" He turned and headed for her door. "I told you! Dammit, Sonja, call the cops."

She ran after him. "You still haven't told me what exactly happened last night, and if you would give me a minute, I'll text her. I'm not calling the police. Please stop jumping to conclusions." James walked to the kitchen, and she followed, sending a text to Casey to call her ASAP. "Have a cup of coffee, and you can tell me what happened." She moved to the pot, poured him a cup and handed it to him.

He took it from her, set it on the counter and glared at her. "Call the police, then I'll tell you what happened."

Anger beat through her like a drum, and she slapped her hands down on the countertop. "Call the police and say what exactly?" She'd about had enough of these theatrics. "What the *hell* happened?"

"So much for not raising voices, right? Her room is a mess. Her stuff is missing. And she's not here. Report her as a runaway! You're a goddamn lawyer, you should know this."

"She has *not* run away!"

"I got news for ya, denial's *not* a river in Egypt, sweetheart. Now, call the fucking police."

Sonja flinched like she'd been slapped. The last damn thing she was, was in denial. Her daughter wouldn't *actually* run away. The idea was preposterous. Sonja pressed her lips together. The fact that James accused her of being in denial was offensive and downright insulting. Refusing to even look at him, she cleared her throat and spoke. "You can leave now."

"Like hell. I'm not leaving."

"If you're not going to explain to me why my daughter called you to pick her up last night, then there's no reason for you to be here."

"Fine. You win." He blew out a harsh breath and took a seat at the counter. "She called me from some shit-hole apartment down in the Village."

Sonja's ears began to ring. The Village? She gripped the

edge of the countertop. Casey didn't have any friends in the Village. "What do you mean?"

"I mean just what I said. Around three a.m. I woke up to my phone ringing. Casey was scared and crying and asked me to come get her. So I got dressed and went and got her."

"What the hell was she doing in some apartment in the Village?" Sonja's voice came out in a high-pitched tone. She flinched at the sound and tried to tamp down the panic spreading through her body. She swallowed, and her vision went hazy. James must've gotten up without her realizing it because, in a flash, he was in front of her. She tried to focus on his face as she gripped the front of his shirt. "What the hell was she doing there?"

"Shh, mo chroí, take a breath." He rubbed his hands up and down her arms. "Come on, sit down." Sonja let him lead her to one of the bar stools. After he'd settled in the seat next to her, he turned the chair to face him and continued. "She was at Trina's, and Drake called. Apparently, there was a party. She wanted to go, but Trina didn't, so she left after Trina went to sleep."

Bile rose in Sonja's throat, and she clasped her hands together in her lap. James took her hands in his and squeezed them. "She was a mess when she called, so I made her text me the address, and I went and got her."

Tears filled her eyes, and she blinked in an effort to clear them. How could he take this upon himself, keeping something so important from her? "Why didn't you wake me? You should've woken me."

"Yeah, I know. I'm sorry. But I didn't want you to freak out. I figured I'd grab her and get her back home safe. If she truly wasn't okay, then I would've woken you when we got back. But she was fine, just a bit shaken up."

"You didn't have the right to make that decision. I'm not okay with what you did." She pulled her hands away. "Tell me what happened."

"Look, I did what I thought was right at the time. You don't have to tell me what I have a right to do and not do. You're wasting time and energy taking your fear out on me. What you should be doing is calling the police."

Sonja crossed her arms, and anger beat through her. Who in the hell did he think he was talking to? "First of all, I'm not afraid, and you need to stop telling me what I should be doing in regard to my family. Secondly, you can't just come in here and step into a role no one invited you into."

"I'm not stepping into any role, but if you really want to argue that point right now, consider why she called me instead of you." James stood and turned to leave.

Sonja flinched again at his harsh words and pressed her hand to her chest. "Where are you going?"

"I'm leaving. You're right, I'm out of line. She's your daughter and not my responsibility. You do what you want with her."

Panic ricocheted through her stomach. Jumping from her seat, Sonja grabbed his arm. "At least tell me what else happened, please?"

He stopped but didn't turn to look at her. "She's fine. We talked for a little while once I got her back home, but then she got pissed at me."

Sonja moved around him in order to see his face. "Why did she get pissed at you?"

"Because I told Dickfazio to stay away from her. She didn't like that. She stormed off and went to bed, and so did I. You can get the rest of the story from her if you want."

"James, wait."

"No. I'm tired of waiting. Tired of caring. And always being left on the outside. I'm done." The cold tone and look in his eyes made her blood freeze in her veins. He stepped around her and left the kitchen.

Sonja rubbed her arms, unsure what to do next. A few minutes later, she heard the echo of the front door closing.

She swallowed and wiped the tears from her cheeks. Grabbing her phone, Sonja sent a text to Casey.

With her phone in her hand, she waited another thirty minutes for a reply from her daughter. When one didn't come, she dialed another number and forced herself to say the words she'd never imagined would come out of her mouth. "Hello. Yes, this is Sonja Martin. I need to report my daughter as a possible runaway."

CHAPTER THIRTY-SIX

Jimmy left Sonja's apartment and walked several blocks, trying to clear his head, before finally taking the subway the rest of the way home. He was torn between being pissed off because she reacted the way she did and knowing deep down inside she was right. Unlocking his front door, he entered his loft and closed himself in.

He *was* out of line and *had* overstepped her boundaries. Casey wasn't his daughter. And though he cared about the kid a whole hell of a lot, it still wasn't his place. But dammit, he did what he thought was right…not that he'd thought about it much at all; he just acted.

He'd do anything for Sonja's daughter. Jimmy was only trying to help—not that it mattered. Scrubbing his palm over his stubbled jaw, he blew out a harsh breath. Hell, he'd do anything for Sonja, too, but that didn't seem to matter either.

Setting the coffee pot to brew, he palmed his phone and shot Andy a text, asking her to come by. He needed to talk about it or not talk about it. He wasn't sure which; Jimmy just knew he was worried a fuckton about Casey, and he didn't want to be alone. Twenty minutes later, Andy was banging at his door. Dragging himself off the couch, he let her in.

"What's up?" She strolled past him, giving him a peck on the cheek. "You look like shit, by the way."

"Nice to see you too, sweetpea." He swung the door closed. "Coffee?"

"Yes, please."

Pouring her a cup, he slid it her way and then refilled his own. "So, what's up?"

Andy laughed and rolled her eyes. "Dunno, playboy. You tell me." She sipped her coffee.

"Damn, is it that obvious?"

"Jimmy, I'm your best friend. You're as transparent as a windowpane. What happened?"

"You know I love you, right?" He pulled her into a hug.

She patted his back. "Yup. And I love you too. *What happened?*"

"I don't know if I want to talk about it yet. Can we watch some reruns of some mindless show first?"

She stepped back from him with a grin on her face. "What? No chick flicks?"

"Not today. I don't have any tissues in the house. And you know what a girl I am when it comes to feely chick movies." He chuckled and moved past her to the living room.

Andy joined him on the couch. For the next couple of hours, they sat in silence, their feet propped on the coffee table, drinking coffee and watching old episodes of *Will & Grace*. This was one of the reasons why he loved his best friend so much. She didn't press him, just pulled up a section of couch with him and let Jimmy be a vegetable.

"I think I'm ready for food."

"Are you kidding? It's been—" Andy glanced at her watch, "—two and a half hours. I'm surprised you haven't eaten a throw pillow."

"Duh… They're way too starchy."

"Right? You want to cook or go out?"

"I don't feel like going out or cooking. How about delivery?"

She picked up her phone. "Cool. I'll order a couple calzones from around the corner."

"Sounds good. But I can order. I've got them on speed dial."

Andy laughed. "Ooookay—but let me tell ya—I don't know if you realize it, but you haven't stopped checking your phone the whole time I've been here. I'll order. You go shower. You're stinking up the joint."

"You say the sweetest things to me." He rolled his eyes. He hadn't been checking his phone *that* much. Had he?

"It's all said in love." She batted her eyes and put her cell to her ear. "Maybe consider shaving, too."

"Fine." Standing, he stretched and then headed upstairs.

Jimmy plugged in his phone to charge in the bathroom. He wanted it close in case Sonja called, or at the very least texted, while he showered. Christ, was he even going to hear from her? Anxiety pulsed through him as he turned on the water and then stripped off his clothes. Sonja probably wasn't even going to bother letting him know if Casey came home or not. And that just pissed him off.

After finishing the wash-down, he took Andy's suggestion and shaved. The shower hadn't done much to reduce his tension, but at least he was clean. Grabbing a pair of sweatpants and a T-shirt from his drawer, he pulled them on and went back downstairs, cell phone—with its lack of messages—tight in his hand. A knock sounded at the door when he reached the bottom step.

"Food's here," Andy hollered from the kitchen.

"On it." Grabbing his wallet from the table, Jimmy took out some cash and went to the door. When he returned, Andy was setting the table.

"Oh, that smells soooo good." She took the small boxes from him and set them on the table. "Drinks?"

"I think I have some beer. You want one?"

"Sure, why the hell not? It's Saturday and long past noon, so all good, right?" She laughed.

"True story." Jimmy grabbed two Coronas from the fridge, popped the caps and brought them out to the table. His stomach let out a howl, and he rubbed it. "Damn, guess I *am* hungry."

"Me too." Andy cut into her calzone, dipped it in the sauce and took a bite.

"Thanks for taking care of me, Andy."

"Anytime. But, when we're done eating, you're telling me what the hell happened. Deal?"

He nodded and cut into his food. "Deal."

SONJA PACED THE LIBRARY, half-empty glass of Chardonnay in hand. It was after four in the afternoon already…and nothing. No word from her child or the police.

She'd tried using the "Find My iPhone" feature for Casey's cell. Sonya had no idea how, but it appeared her daughter had shut it off. None of her friends knew where she was either. She'd scanned in a picture of Casey and faxed it over to the police station, and now all there was to do was wait. Talk about feeling powerless.

Sonja wasn't going to call Thomas, not until she was left with no choice anyway. He'd end up hopping the next flight here, and she didn't need that. She cringed. The thought of dealing with him while trying to keep the freight train of emotions plowing through her in check had Sonja on the verge of being sick to her stomach.

Then there was James.

She wasn't even sure what to do about him. He'd just left her there. Taking off as he had was wrong on so many levels —granted, Sonja had told him to leave during the argument, but she'd only said it because she was in a panic and angry. She could barely make sense of any of it now. On top of all of those emotions, she was terrified. Swallowing the last of the wine, she wandered back to the kitchen and refilled her glass.

This time, she settled in her bedroom, but brought the bottle with her. May as well numb the brain a bit while she waited.

Waited to hear from Casey.

Waited to hear from the police.

Waited to hear from James.

Waited...

Sonja frowned before taking a long swallow of her wine. She could do this. She could keep her shit together. Casey would come home. James would show up and tell her how sorry he was, and Thomas...well, he could keep his annoying, misogynistic ass in Florida. Everything would go back to normal. She hoped.

After setting the glass of wine on the table, Sonja turned on her side, stretching out on the settee. She stared at her phone, willing it to ring. She wanted to call James, but she wasn't going to do that. Since she hadn't heard from him, he obviously was no longer concerned with Casey. Or her, for that matter. Sonja sighed and closed her eyes, willing the tears to stay at bay. She'd broken down too many times already, and she simply refused to do it again.

CHAPTER THIRTY-SEVEN

JIMMY TOSSED AND TURNED, TRYING TO SLEEP. GIVING IN, HE went into his bathroom and turned on the water. He cupped his hands under the faucet and swallowed a drink. With his eyes closed, he scrubbed his wet hands over his face. He hadn't heard from Sonja and had no idea if Casey had come home. And it was driving him batshit crazy. "This is stupid."

Jimmy stormed back into his bedroom, grabbed his phone and called her. Halfway through the third ring, she answered. "Hello? Hello?"

"Sonja, it's me."

"What?"

He heard some rustling, like maybe she dropped the phone or knocked something over. He glanced at the clock. Shit, it was late. "Sonja, can you hear me?"

"James? What time is it?"

"It's after one in the morning. Is she home? Tell me she's home, please?" Sonja started to cry. *Fuck.* "I'm coming over." He didn't wait for a reply, just disconnected the call.

The sound of her cries gutted him. He couldn't stand her to be hurting alone like that. The taxi gods smiled down on him because he snagged a cab faster than he ever had before. When he got to her door, he knocked and waited. When she didn't come to the door, he called her cell. She answered, sounding less frazzled but still like she'd been sleeping. And then finally came and let him in.

"Hi." Looking an absolute mess, she turned away, walked through the foyer, and down the hall.

Jimmy locked up and went to her bedroom. She was curled on her side on the settee. Her phone clutched to her chest. Then he noticed the empty bottle of wine on the small table beside her. *Shit.* Sadness blanketed every inch of his heart. She looked so small, so fragile. Moving to her side, he scooped her into his arms.

She pressed her face to his neck and snaked an arm around him. He carried her to the bed. Pulling the covers aside, he laid her down, then sat beside her. She looked up at him with tear-filled eyes.

"Shh, mo chroí, I'm here now. It's going to be okay." He caught a tear with his thumb when it escaped. "She's fine, and she's going to come home."

Her breath hitched on a sob. "Do you promise?"

"I do." Leaning forward, he pressed a gentle kiss to her forehead. "You need to sleep. We both do."

She nodded and pulled him closer. "Don't go. Please don't go."

"I'm not going anywhere. But you have to let go so I can get in the bed with you."

She let out a short laugh through a sob, but he knew it was genuine. She let him go, and he rose, stripped off his clothes and climbed in bed with her. It killed him to see her so raw, but at least he'd be there to take care of her. Once he was settled, Sonja turned over and rested her head on his chest.

Jimmy stroked his fingers through her long hair. The things she said earlier, during their fight, didn't matter. He might still be out of line, but that didn't matter either. She needed him right now, and that was enough for him. He meant the promise he made to her. They'd find Casey, or she'd come home on her own.

Either way, things were going to be fine. Between all of them.

CHAPTER THIRTY-EIGHT

Hot water streamed down Sonja's hair and back. Her head throbbed thanks to the stress and worry, plus the massive amount of wine she'd consumed in the last twenty or so desperate hours. James had come over sometime in the middle of the night—though what happened or what they talked about was still a little fuzzy. Either way, she was glad he was there. Glad to have woken up in his arms, too.

It seemed silly to think his arms around her somehow made all of this easier to bear, but there was no other way to describe it. She was still terrified. Still had no idea where her daughter was, yet at the same time, she knew deep inside it was going to be okay. However, being the logical person she was, Sonja intended to make more calls. She'd harass New York's finest and then go out looking on her own. With James in tow, of course…if he wanted to come.

After finishing in the shower, she dressed, put her hair up and wandered out to the kitchen. James was at the island, sipping a mug of coffee and reading the paper. She approached him and wrapped her arms around his waist from behind.

He glanced over his shoulder at her. "Morning."

Sonja pressed a kiss to the side of his neck. "Thank you for being here."

"I wouldn't want to be anywhere else, mo chroí."

"Good to know." Sonja stepped away, rounded the countertop and poured a cup of coffee. "Did you get anything to eat?"

He flipped the paper over. "Not feeling too hungry. But you should probably eat."

"I don't think that's remotely possible." She took a sip of the hot fluid. "I want to go looking for her today."

"Reading my mind, woman." He nodded, pursing his lips. "Where do you think we should start?"

"I'm glad you said 'we'." She watched him over the rim of her mug. A small smile curved his lips, and he nodded again. She set her cup down. "I was thinking we could take a walk through Central Park. She likes to meet friends there, but she doesn't know I know that."

"All right." He took a drink of his coffee as he moved to the sink. "How do you know she meets friends there?"

"I monitor her phone through GPS. Lot of good it's doing me now, though. She found a way to shut it off."

He shook his head and washed out his mug. "Jesus, this kid."

She stepped next to him, needing to feel closer. Wanting to touch him. His support was going to be critical in order to make it through this without having a nervous breakdown. Giving in to the urge, Sonja smoothed her hand down his back. "I know."

He glanced at her before pressing a soft kiss to her lips. "You ready to get going?"

"Yes." Sonja sighed. "I suppose I should probably call Thomas first and let him know she's run away."

Jimmy raised both brows. "You haven't told him yet?"

She pushed away from the counter, heading for the doorway. "No. I didn't want to deal with him. To be honest, I still don't, so if we can get her home as soon as possible, then I won't have to deal with him at all."

"What's up with that? Tell him to fuck off if he's being an asshole. You do it to me all the time."

"Let's not go there, okay?" She glanced at him as she walked out of the room. He was following, but the look on his face was like a knife in her gut. She had enough to deal with at the moment. Discussing her inability to tell Thomas to keep his comments and opinions regarding her parenting skills to himself was not on the docket today.

He let out an exasperated sigh, and he moved around her to open the front door. "Ohhhkayy."

"Thank you." She gave him a small smile and stepped past him.

They walked, hand in hand, quite a ways through Central Park. The corners and more secluded sections, where she'd mapped Casey to in the past, turned up nothing. They took a seat on a bench, and Sonja went through her list of contacts for Casey's friends. Placing a call to each one, she let them know if any heard from her daughter to please call her immediately. Sonja cringed before and during each conversation, and voicemail left. Being this open regarding her private business was deeply uncomfortable for her, but that wasn't important.

The only important thing was finding Casey.

The last call was to the precinct. They were doing everything they could, or so they said, but Sonja knew it wasn't truly the case. Her daughter was just another runaway; her file added to the already staggering number of kids reported daily.

James massaged the back of her neck. "Let's go get something to eat."

She slumped to her side, resting her head on his shoulder. "My stomach is so upset."

He pressed a kiss to the top of her head. "And that's exactly why you should eat. Come on." He stood and held a hand out to her. "We'll get something light. Besides, it's going to be dark soon. The park isn't safe at night. You know that."

Taking his hand, Sonja stood. He pulled her into an embrace, and she wrapped her arms around him, clinging to him like a life preserver. She supposed that's exactly what he'd become for her today, or maybe what she *allowed* him to become. All her petty crap, the keeping him at bay, the trying to keep the great wall, erected so long ago, around her intact, and the fooling herself into thinking she didn't care about him had all melted away.

Nothing like a frightening situation or an unfathomable tragedy to help a person see what was really important in life. It shouldn't have taken something like her daughter running away to wake her up, but the truth was, it had. Sonja raised her head from his shoulder and gazed at him. "You're right. On both accounts."

He touched the tip of her nose with his fingertip. "Glad you think so."

Tears welled up, and Sonja blinked, trying to force them back. "I'm sorry."

He tilted his head to the side. "For what?"

"For shutting you out." A myriad of things she'd done to him ran through her mind. All the missed opportunities or the times she'd disappointed him. Being so cold and detached… A tear escaped down her cheek, and guilt pulsed through her—she'd slept with Thomas before anything had officially begun between her and James. Sonja cringed. She'd never forgive herself for being so stupid. "For a lot of things."

"Mo chroí…" He cupped her face with his palms. "Thank you, truly. But it doesn't matter anymore. What matters now is

I'm here, and I'm not going anywhere." He brushed his lips over hers.

Sonja circled his wrists with her fingers, closed her eyes and let his soft words warm her. "Thank you."

"Always." He kissed her again. "Let's get you fed." Taking her by the hand, he led her out of Central Park and to the closest restaurant.

CHAPTER THIRTY-NINE

With Sonja just one step behind him, Jimmy climbed the stairs of the apartment building where he'd picked Casey up over twenty-four hours ago. It was a long shot, but maybe they'd get lucky.

The place wasn't bad, but wasn't great either. They continued up the dingy, gray-tinted, white-walled stairwell, and when they reached the fourth floor, Sonja stepped beside him, and he pressed the flat of his hand to her back. It was after nine at night, and Jimmy hoped, this time, when he knocked, a parent might answer.

In front of the apartment door, he glanced at Sonja, then knocked. The sound of a television echoed through the metal panel, but then again, it might be the unit next door. Raising his hand, he knocked again…a little louder this time.

Sonja crossed her arms. "It's late. Maybe they're already sleeping?"

"Dunno. Possible I gue—"

The door opened a crack, the chain lock keeping it from going any farther. "Can I help you?"

It was the same blond boy from the other night, but his

hair didn't appear to be as greasy tonight. Jimmy peered at the kid through the small opening. "Is Casey here?"

"Who?"

"Gonna play this game again? Okay, let me refresh your memory. Blue-and-purple hair? About this tall?" Jimmy raised his hand in the air. "You and me, we met the other night when I showed up. We had a similar conversation, except this time, I'm being a little more polite with your ass."

Sonja cleared her throat. "Excuse me, but is your mother home?"

The kid broke the I-don't-give-a-fuck stare he'd been giving Jimmy and turned his gaze to Sonja. "She's working."

"Oh. Hmm." Sonja dug into her purse, pulled out a business card and stuck it through the opening.

The kid took it and glanced at it. "You're a lawyer?"

"Yes. I'm looking for my daughter, Casey. If you see her or her boyfriend, Drake, can you call me? Or maybe have your mother call me?"

"Drake. Yeah, I know that guy. He's kind of an asshole."

Jimmy barked out a laugh. Maybe the kid wasn't stupid after all. "Listen, kid. I know we didn't get off to a great start, but this is really important. So we'd appreciate it if you helped out."

The kid looked over at Jimmy again and nodded. "Yeah, cool. If I hear from him, I'll let you know."

"Thank you." Sonja let out a sigh, one sounding a lot more like disappointment than gratitude.

The kid nodded again and closed the door. Jimmy wrapped an arm around her waist and pulled her against him. "You okay?"

"Yes. No. Maybe?" She rubbed her forehead. "Tired, I guess."

"Yeah, I know what you mean, mo chroí." He rubbed her back. "Let's go back to your place and get you off your feet."

"All right." She pressed a kiss to his lips.

Jimmy held her tight against his chest. This whole situation sucked, and though he wished it wasn't happening, there was no way he'd trade being able to be by her side through every second of it.

All he wanted was to see Casey home and safe and to know Sonja's fears were put to bed. He didn't ever want to see the look that had taken up residence in her eyes or the frown plaguing her brow again. Jesus, when they got her daughter back home, he was going to wring the kid's neck for putting Sonja through this—for putting them both through this.

Jimmy led her out of the building. Hailing a cab for them, he helped her into the taxi and climbed in behind her. Sonja rested her head on his shoulder while the cab traversed the streets, leading them back to the Upper East Side. He placed a kiss on her forehead and smoothed his hand down her arm. In the darkness of the cab, with her pressed close to him, the city lights passing them by, Jimmy knew he loved her.

He'd fallen completely and totally in love with her. And he wouldn't trade one moment for anything.

She was his sunshine.

Mo chroí. She was his heart.

CHAPTER FORTY

SONJA LAY CURLED UP ON THE COUCH, HER HEAD ON A PILLOW in James's lap. The television was on, but she wasn't really watching. Instead, she was playing out a thousand different scenarios of worry in her mind. Was her daughter okay? Was she with Drake? Had something bad happened to her? Were they ever going to find her?

The shrill ring of her cell phone startled her back to the present moment. Adrenaline spiked in her system. Sonja bolted upright, reached for the device, almost missed the *Talk* button, but then got it and put the phone to her ear. "Hello!"

"May I speak to Ms. Martin, please?"

"This is she. Who is this?" She felt James's hand on her shoulder and glanced at him. A look of concern blanketed his features.

"This is Officer Noellyn from the forty-ninth precinct in the Bronx."

Fear cut through her like a steel blade. "Oh God. Do you have my daughter?" Unable to sit still, Sonja stood and began pacing.

"Casey Martin is your daughter, correct?"

"Yes! Is she okay? Please tell me she's okay." She glanced at James; he'd gotten to his feet, too.

"She was involved in an altercation. She's okay, but we had her taken to St. Barnabas to be checked out. Are you able to come down to the hospital?"

Sonja turned and ran for her purse. James followed, calling after her. "I'm leaving right now. Thank you." She disconnected the call and stopped long enough to grab James by the arm. "She's at St. Barnabas. Let's go." Releasing her hold on him, she turned and rushed for the front door.

The cab ride took forever. James held her hand, and she stared at her phone, debating whether or not to call Thomas.

He gave her hand a squeeze. "It's going to be okay."

"I should call Thomas. But I…" Sonja shook her head and glanced out the window.

"What, mo chroí?"

"I want to see her first. Make sure she's okay. Does that make me selfish?"

"No, of course not." He cupped her chin and turned her face to his. "It makes you a worried mother. Nothing wrong with that." He stroked her cheek.

"I think it does make me selfish because the truth is, I'm hoping she's more than fine, so I won't have to call him at all."

"That doesn't make you selfish either. It makes you smart." He pressed a soft kiss to her lips.

Sonja leaned into him, needing the warmth his presence provided. She had legal and physical custody of Casey, so she really didn't have to tell her ex-husband anything. Regardless, she didn't want to deal with Thomas for a thousand different reasons, and the main one was sitting next to her. Sonja shook her head. She didn't want to think about it. Casey was going to be fine. Any other option wasn't possible. Closing her eyes, she willed the cab to move faster.

When they arrived, James paid the driver, and Sonja

jumped out, ran for the ER door and headed straight for the reception desk. "Casey Martin?"

"You are?"

"Sonja Martin. Her mother."

James came up next to her, and the man behind the desk typed on his computer.

"Ms. Martin?"

Sonja wheeled around to find a short and stocky red-haired police officer there. "Yes?"

"Officer Noellyn." He shook her hand. Then looked at James and shook his.

"James Donnelly."

Enough with the pleasantries. Sonja adjusted her purse strap on her shoulder. "Where is Casey?"

"They're taking good care of her. I can take you back to see her in a minute. But let's have a seat and talk first," the officer said in a thick New York accent.

Impatience beat through her. Sonja glanced back at the receptionist. "Can you let her know we're here, at least?"

The receptionist nodded. "I'll let the nurse know. They should be bringing her back from X-ray in a few minutes."

"X-ray?" Panic flooded her veins, and she glanced back at the officer. "I thought you said she was okay. X-ray doesn't sound okay to me!" James wrapped his arm around her waist, and she leaned into him. "I'm sorry, but I want to see my daughter first."

"Ma'am, I understand you're upset. She's fine, just a little banged up."

"Oh? So, you're a doctor as well?" Her panic gave way to anger, and her heart thudded in her ears. "My goodness, do you have a cape underneath your uniform, too?"

The officer said nothing, just stared at her, his stone features betraying none of the colorful thoughts Sonja assumed were running around his mind. Screw him; she was done putting up with anyone's bullshit. Sonja crossed her arms, daring him to come back at her. She was a fucking lawyer, which meant she was more than capable of dancing circles around him in the argument department.

James gave her waist a little squeeze. "Honey?"

"What?" Snapping her head to the side, she glared at him. Point for him, he didn't flinch.

"Look, Ms. Martin. The sooner we talk, the sooner you can go back and see your daughter."

Sonja returned her focus to the officer and pointed her finger at him. "You get five minutes of my time. No more than that. You have more to say then you can say it after I've seen my daughter."

"Fair enough." He motioned them both over to the waiting room chairs. Sonja took a seat, and James did, too. The officer sat across from them. "As I mentioned on the phone, Casey was involved in an altercation. The young man she was with…" He pulled out his little notepad and glanced at it. "Drake Defazio was engaged in a physical altercation with a Peter Franklin. Do you know either of them?"

"Drake Defazio is her boyfriend. I don't know the other boy."

"I see." He scribbled in his notepad. "Mr. Peter Franklin isn't a boy, and he assaulted a minor."

"Great. How does Casey play into this?"

"According to witnesses, Casey tried to defend Mr. Defazio and was caught in the fray between the young man and Mr. Franklin. After I spoke with her briefly at the scene, I ran a check on her. She showed up in our database as a runaway. Are you willing to take her back home?"

"Of course, I'm willing to take her home. Why wouldn't I be?"

"I mean no offense, Ms. Martin. It's a standard question."

"Well, not to worry. I have every intention of taking her home. Are we done here?"

"Officer Noellyn let out a loud sigh. "Yes. I believe we are."

"Good." Sonja stood and walked back to the reception desk. She knew she was being a bitch, but she truly didn't care. All she cared about was getting to Casey. "I'd like to see my daughter now, please?"

Jimmy followed Sonya into the back halls of the ER. He chose to keep silent; she was a powder keg ready to blow, and saying the wrong thing would for sure set her off. The nurse led them to the treatment area where Casey was being held.

"Oh, my God!" Sonja rushed past the nurse, the curtain flying out in a flourish, and pulled Casey into a frantic embrace.

"Mom, I'm fine—oww!"

Sonja jumped back. "Crap. Sorry, honey. Sorry. Where are you hurt?"

"It's okay. Just don't hug so hard." Casey shifted on the gurney and winced. "I think I sprained my ankle, but that happened last night. And now, maybe broken ribs and my head hurts because I banged it on the ground really hard." She rubbed the back of her head.

Jimmy came around the other side of the bed and clasped her hand. "Had your mom and me really frickin' worried, kiddo."

Sonja stared at her daughter. The expression on her face was like a punch in Jimmy's gut. He let out a slow breath. All things considered, Casey looked pretty good. Her makeup was smudged under her eyes, her hair a bit of a mess, but other than that, she looked fine.

Sonja swiped a tear from her cheek as she bent forward and kissed Casey on the top of the head. "If you weren't hurt, I might take you over my knee and spank the daylights out of you." Sonja let out a small laugh and pressed her nose into her daughter's hair.

Casey shifted her arm and adjusted the IV line attached to her hand. "Mom, seriously? That's not funny."

Jimmy ran his palm over his goatee. "You're right, it's not. But it's true."

The doctor walked into the makeshift room, chart in hand. "Hello there. Mom and Dad, I assume?"

Sonja leaned over and shook the doctor's hand. "Just Mom."

"I'm Doc Scalzi."

"Is she gonna make it?" Jimmy leaned a hip against the gurney, shot Casey a wink, then returned his gaze to the doctor.

"The good news is, yes, she's going to make it." He gave them a small smile. "Her ribs are bruised, and she has a pretty good lump on the back of her head. No concussion. However, she has a hairline fracture at the edge of her fibula. Her ankle. We're going to get her in a Cam boot, and then she can go home." The doctor wrote on Casey's chart. "Any questions?"

Casey let out a groan. "How long do I have to wear a stupid boot?"

"Usually no longer than six weeks unless you heal faster." The doctor clicked the end of his pen and slipped it in his white coat pocket. "It's not so bad. Better than a plaster cast." He smiled before shifting his gaze back to Sonja. "Any questions, Mom?"

"Crutches, I assume?"

"Yes, for a little while. She'll need to come back in a few weeks to have it x-rayed again. The nurse will give you all the necessary paperwork."

Sonja clasped Casey's hand in her own. "Thank you."

"You're welcome. Casey, we'll be in to take you to get fitted into the boot in a few minutes." He smiled again and then stepped out of the room.

"Well, there you go. A boot and crutches." Sonja grabbed the small chair behind her, pulled it close and sat next to the gurney. "Tomorrow, we're going to have a long talk about what's happened. You're going to tell me everything, do you understand?"

Casey rolled her eyes. "Fine."

Jimmy crossed his arms. "Case, the least you could do is pretend to be sorry. Your mom's been out of her mind worried. So have I."

"Yeah, but she didn't even call my dad, so she wasn't *that* worried."

Sonja stood in a huff. "What's that supposed to mean?"

"Why didn't you call Daddy?"

"Because!" Sonja shifted her weight to one foot and crossed her arms, her face a mask of anger.

"Because why?"

"Seriously? Cut your mom a break, will you?" Jimmy placed his hand on Casey's shoulder in hopes his words would serve as some sort of a diversion. He'd rather have Casey pissed and reeling at him than at her mother. She'd gone through enough in the last forty-eight hours, and the last thing she needed was to be questioned by the very child who was the cause of all the turmoil.

Casey turned her fiery gaze on him. "I want to know why she didn't bother to tell my father I ran away!"

"All right, stop! Right now! Whether or not I called your father and why are none of your business. I realize you're tired and in pain, but I will not tolerate another word from you."

Sonja had started out yelling, her eyes wide with rage, but ended up with her voice so low Jimmy could barely hear her. Her tone, however, was laced with fury and warning. A warning he hoped Casey was paying attention to because she was skating on some very thin ice with her mother.

"You don't have to bother now because I called him myself when I got here. He'll be home first thing in the morning."

Sonja's mouth dropped open, shock and hurt blanketing

her features. Jimmy was at a loss for what to do or say. This mess was between her and Casey, and he didn't want to overstep. But, dammit, his instinct to protect his woman was riding him hard, even if it meant protecting her from her own child. Rounding the gurney, he took Sonja's hand. "Why don't we step out for some air?"

"Thank you, Casey. I'm sure his visit will be most enjoyable." Sonja yanked her hand free from Jimmy's and stormed out of the treatment room.

"Nice one."

"Whatever." Casey crossed her arms and winced from the pain. "She should've called him. It's fucked up she didn't."

Jimmy took a seat in the plastic chair. "I'm not going to debate it with you. I'm sure your mother had her reasons."

"Oh yeah? Like what?"

Raising one leg, he rested his ankle on his other knee. "Ohhh, I don't know. Maybe she was praying you'd come home, then she wouldn't have to tell him? I can't imagine they get along all too well." He drummed his fingers on his thigh. "But, ya know? Why should you give a shit about how scared your mom was or whether or not your dad worried for no reason? Or whether they get along well or not? Why should you give a shit about anyone other than yourself right now?" He kept his voice low, mostly because they were in a public place but also because he was beyond furious with her, and if he didn't keep a leash on his temper, he might find himself yelling. There had already been enough of that.

"That's not true. I do care!"

"Lower your voice, Casey. The entire hospital doesn't need to hear your drama."

A nurse entered. She glanced from him to Casey and back again. "Everything okay?"

Jimmy stood. "Of course."

"All right. You ready to get booted up?" The nurse

grabbed the IV bag and hung it on the pole attached to the side of the gurney.

"I guess so." Casey rested her head on the pillow, and the nurse wheeled the bed out of the room.

"See you when you get back." Jimmy shoved his hands in his front pockets and watched her disappear out of the room. After a moment, he resumed his spot in the plastic chair. This was going to be a long night, regardless of what time they got back to Sonja's house.

CHAPTER FORTY-ONE

"I'm talking now. When I'm done, and if I choose, you can speak. Until then, keep your mouth closed. You had no right. None. *You should have called me!*"

Sonja bit down on her tongue and drew on every ounce of patience within her to get through the conversation. Thomas continued his rant, oblivious to anything but the sound of his own voice. She could probably put the phone down and walk away, and he'd never know she was gone.

"I will be on the first flight up there in the morning, and then we're going to discuss Casey's living arrangements. It's quite obvious to me you're not capable of taking care of my daughter any longer. You're too busy with your *boyfriend*, never mind the law firm, to give her the attention she needs."

That did it. Blinding, red-hot rage spiked in her belly and radiated out through her limbs. Sonja gripped the phone so hard she swore she heard the plastic case creak. She hadn't realized he was aware of James. Casey must've told him. Apparently, his jealous bone had been triggered, and now he'd use it as another excuse to threaten custody of their daughter.

"Thomas—"

"I'm not done."

"Thomas—" He continued his tirade right over the top of her. She was so sick of this man trying to rule her life from the ex-husband position. Regardless of what delusions he operated under, Thomas had no power over her any longer. "*Thomas*!" He went silent on the other end of the line. Probably shocked she'd screamed in his ear. Didn't matter. She'd use it to her advantage. "First of all, you want to take me back to court, you go right ahead. You'll lose. Second, whom I choose to spend my time with is none of your business. Third, fuck you." She should've hung up, but instead, she waited for his response.

He was silent for what felt like forever before he finally spoke again. "Sonja, I'll see you in the morning."

The line went dead, and she pulled the phone from her ear and stared at the screen. Wonderful. Fabulous. Spectacular! In no way was she looking forward to the discussion she now needed to have with James. He'd have to go back to his place tonight because when Thomas showed up in the morning, she'd have to deal with him. The last thing she needed was to wade through a bunch of male testosterone clouding the air. James would simply have to understand.

Once she got rid of Thomas, things could go back to normal.

Preparing for the dreaded conversation, she grabbed a water from the vending machine and made her way back to Casey's treatment room. As she walked at a snail's pace, Sonja played the words through her mind, trying to find the right combination. When she rounded the corner and stepped into the room, James was sitting in the plastic chair, legs stretched out in front of him, his attention on his phone. Casey was gone, and she figured they'd likely taken her to get her boot. Sonja watched him for a moment before clearing her throat, gaining his attention.

"Hey there." He scrambled to his feet and came toward her. "You okay?"

She pinched the bridge of her nose. "Not really, no."

"Come on, sit down." He led her over to the chair. "You talked to Thomas, I take it?"

She took a seat and looked up at him. "Not exactly. He did all the talking. Wouldn't let me get a word in edgewise."

"You know, you haven't told me a lot about him, but he kinda sounds like a dick."

"Well..." Sonja took a moment to reflect. She guessed James's assessment was pretty damn accurate. Thomas was, quite simply, a dick. "I think you hit the nail on the head."

James chuckled and squatted in front of her. "Is he still coming?"

She smoothed her hand up the back of her hair. "Oh, yes. He'll be here in the morning."

"All right. We'll deal with it."

"About that..." Sonja glanced away from him, still unsure of how to get this out.

He rubbed her thighs. "Yeah?"

"Look, I don't want you to take this wrong." Straightening in her seat, she gazed at him and placed her hands atop his. "But it's probably best if I deal with him alone."

James tilted his head to the side, pressed his lips together and sighed through his nose. *Shoot.* She wasn't sure if he was pissed, or upset, or annoyed...or all of the above.

How in the hell was she going to get him to understand why it was better this way? He was going to think it was just her trying to shut him out again, but it had nothing to do with that. When it came to Thomas, it was better to just let him come and then let him go without making much fuss. Exhaustion weighed on her, and she felt like she'd just run a 10K marathon. With all the stress, Sonja just didn't need the added drama. She couldn't handle one more thing.

This was just easier.

"Why?"

"Because." Sonja tried to lace her fingers with his, but he pulled them away. "James, please don't."

He stood. "Don't what? Yeah, I fucked up when I walked out that first morning, but I've been by your side through all of this since. And you think I'm going to disappear because your ex-husband, who's clearly a dick, is coming into town? Give me one reason why I can't be by your side through this, too."

"It's not that I don't want you by my side. James, really, you think I want to deal with him on top of everything else that's gone on in the last forty-eight hours?"

"Then don't."

"What do you mean, don't? It's not like I have a choice in the matter. I have to deal with him; he's Casey's father."

"I know he's Casey's father. But you don't have to deal with him—at least not alone. In fact, you don't ever have to deal with him alone again. But you won't choose that, will you?"

"It's not that. You'll want to protect me; he'll want to assert his role as Casey's father. I'm in no shape to deal with the drama of a pissing contest or testosterone war."

He propped his hands on his hips. "I'm not stupid. I know he's Casey's father. But yeah, if he's being an asshole, of course I'm going to protect you. How could I not?"

"Please. It's just easier. Can't you understand that? Why does everything have to be an argument with you?" Sonja stood and started pacing. "Why do you always have to make everything so goddamn difficult?"

"Wow. Really?"

"Yes, really. You don't have to make this such a big deal. It's not a big deal."

He crossed his arms. "Even fucking better."

"What is that supposed to mean?"

"Did it ever occur to you it might be a big deal to me?"

Sonja stopped pacing and faced him. "What occurred to me is you should understand."

"I see. So you believe I should roll over and let you cut me off—again, no less. This will make it what? The third time you've pushed me away?"

"I'm not pushing you away!"

"I dare you to back that statement up and let me be there tomorrow when he comes over."

"Can't you understand this is what I need from you right now? Can you try and see it from my point of view? If you did, you'd see I *am not* trying to push you away."

"The hell you aren't. And I'm over it. I honestly don't know what else to do."

Panic rose in Sonja's chest, and her heart galloped, pounding in her ears. "What are you saying?"

"I'm saying I don't want to deal with being pushed aside anymore."

"James, please." Tears pricked her eyes. "I'm not pushing you aside."

"Yes, Sonja, you are. Otherwise, you'd let me be there, *by* your side, where I belong. I think I need to step away."

A tear slipped down her cheek. Sonja swiped it away and tried like hell to keep the others, waiting to spill out, at bay. "He'll be gone before any time has passed. One, maybe two days at the most. Please, don't do this. Don't walk away." He couldn't mean what he was saying. Not after everything they'd struggled through to get where they were. Sonja reached for him. "Please don't walk away."

James took her hands within his own. "Goddammit, Sonja."

"Please." The desperation in her voice burned in the back of her throat.

"Mo chroí, do you have any idea how much I feel for you?"

"Yes." She gazed at him through blurred vision. The tears

she'd tried so hard to swallow filled her eyes and streamed down her cheeks. Tilting her head back, she caught his lips in a kiss.

She felt for him, too, perhaps more than she was willing to put into words at the moment, but nonetheless, she felt. She felt too much. James cupped her face in his hands and deepened the kiss. His tongue was so sweet, so strong. A lifeline for her. One she needed with an unparalleled desperation.

He broke the kiss and gazed at her as he tucked a stray hair behind her ear. "How about I come over when he's not there? When he goes back to the hotel or wherever he stays. How 'bout that? I mean, at least then I can see you and Casey. Be there for you."

Shit. Sonja bit her bottom lip and broke their eye contact. Once she got done explaining why his idea wouldn't work, he'd definitely leave her.

"Hey?" James placed his finger below her chin and raised her face to his, forcing her eyes to meet his own. He looked at her for what seemed like forever, yet at the same time, it felt like time had ground to a halt.

Sonja licked her lips and drew on what little courage she had left. She was about to lose him, and she knew it. "That won't work."

His face fell, disappointment coating his features, and she cringed. He took a step back. "You want to tell me why?"

"Because...because he doesn't stay in a hotel when he's here." Ice-cold dread flowed through her veins, followed by a generous helping of self-loathing. After all, she was about to commit relationship suicide. Sonja wrapped her arms around her middle as if somehow she could protect or, at the very least, comfort herself.

"Where does he stay?" James placed his hands on his hips and glared at her.

She could tell by the look on his face he already knew the

answer. She didn't need to give it, but she would anyway. "James—"

"Where!"

Flinching, she looked at her feet. Without a doubt, Thomas would never sleep in her bed again, but it made no difference. Her inability to keep Thomas out of her house was proof that her supposed independence was an illusion. One she'd been stupid enough to believe existed. "He stays at my house." The words came out in a whisper. She didn't want to hear them, let alone say them. God only knew what James felt.

But Sonja didn't get a chance to see or hear what he felt because, without saying a word, he turned away from her and walked out.

CHAPTER FORTY-TWO

Sonja stood in her kitchen the next morning, readying the coffee pot and making breakfast for Casey. Running on about two hours of sleep, she yawned and cracked three eggs into a bowl. She'd spent the night steeped in emotional anxiety. Between Casey's antics and the mountain-sized chip on her shoulder, and James walking out on her, Sonja's nerves were shredded to a bare thread.

She glanced at the clock and then poured the beaten eggs into the pan. It was almost seven a.m., and Thomas would be there in the next couple of hours. Sonja wasn't sure she'd survive. Casey wasn't up yet, but she planned to wake her with a nice breakfast in bed. Not that her daughter had earned such a nice gesture, but Sonja hoped—perhaps foolishly—if she started the morning off on a positive note, things might have a chance of being a little smoother.

Glancing at her phone, she checked to see if James had texted or called. He hadn't. Sadness weighed on her like a heavy blanket, making every move strenuous. She'd sent him more than a couple texts and left at least three voicemails since he'd left the hospital last night. Letting out a deep sigh, she layered a pile of cheese on the eggs. With the spatula, she carefully raised one side and folded the egg over on itself. The toast popped in the toaster, and Sonja jumped. She pressed her hand to her racing heart and drew in a breath.

She needed a vacation. A long one. On some beach somewhere, far away from all the difficulties parading through her life. Maybe someplace with just her and James.

James. Sonja frowned.

That option was off the table now, wasn't it? Amazing how he'd become a part of her life in such a short time. Amazing how she'd grown used to him being there. Even worse, she'd been the one to ruin it all. So much for it being easier. "Good God, maybe I should get a few cats and call it a day."

Grabbing the toast, she buttered it and placed it on the dish. She scooped up the omelet, laid it next to the toast and added some fresh fruit. After fixing a cup of coffee for Casey, she set everything on a serving tray and walked it down the hall. Balancing the tray on one hip, she got the door open and stepped inside. Sonja placed the tray on the bench at the foot of Casey's bed and then moved to the side where her daughter was sleeping. "Honey, wake up. I made you some breakfast."

Casey was on her back, her black-booted foot propped up on two pillows. She opened her eyes and moaned. "I don't think I'm hungry." Yawning, she rubbed her hands over her face. "Do I smell eggs?"

"Sure do." Sonja smoothed her daughter's hair off her forehead. "You need to use the bathroom first?"

"No. I'm okay." Casey pressed her hands down at her sides and tried to raise herself up on the bed, but failed and scrunched up her face in obvious pain.

"Let me help you, honey." Sonja wrapped her arms around her daughter's body and sat her forward, then propped two of the other pillows behind her back. "Better?"

"Yeah. Thanks." Casey rubbed her eyes. "Is Daddy here yet?"

Sonja retrieved the tray and placed it on her daughter's lap. "Not yet. But I'm sure he'll be here in the next couple of hours."

"Mmkay." Casey cut into the eggs and took a bite.

"Good?"

Casey nodded and chewed. Sonja smoothed her hand down the back of her daughter's hair before taking a seat at the foot of the bed. "How about you tell me what happened?"

Her daughter glanced up from the food. "Now?"

Sonja nodded. "I think now would be the perfect time. You can fill me in between bites."

"Fine." Casey set the fork down and then took a sip of her coffee. "Drake and me were walking down an alley between two houses, and a dog jumped up on a chain link fence and scared me. I slipped." She shrugged. "It was no big deal."

"Between two houses? Was this in the Bronx?"

Casey picked up the fork and speared into a piece of fruit. "I don't know, Mom. I guess, yeah."

Sonja frowned. "Why were you walking between two houses? Where were you going?"

"Dunno." She shrugged.

Sonja let out a sigh and called on every ounce of patience she had within her. Getting the whole story was going to be akin to pulling molars. "Well, where were you coming from?"

"A party."

"Why didn't you stay there? Did something happen?"

Casey ate another piece of fruit and rolled her eyes. "It doesn't matter. What matters is I got startled by a stupid dog, and I slipped and broke my ankle."

Sonja cocked her head to the side. "Casey, it matters a great deal to me. You were gone. I had no idea where you were. Or if you were laying dead in the street somewhere."

"Well, I'm not dead. I'm fine!" Her daughter glared at her.

"You can stop looking at me like that. Yes, thankfully,

you're not dead, but clearly, you are not fine." Sonja glanced over her daughter's body, then back to her face. "What happened when Drake got into the fight with Mr. Franklin?"

"God, Mom." Casey took another sip of coffee. "We were at a burger place. The guy banged into Drake, and Drake got pissed. The rest you know from the police report."

Sonja rubbed the spot between her brows. "Seems an innocent thing to just bang into someone. Was it an accident?"

"I don't know." She set her fork down. "Drake just freaked out."

"I wasn't aware he had such a temper. I'm definitely not comfortable with you seeing him anymore. Especially after James had to go get you from that other party you were at with him. That boy is trouble, Casey, and now you're getting dragged into it. I won't tolerate it."

Casey stared down at her plate. "Fine, Mom. Whatever you say."

"Casey, you can give me attitude all you want. But there's no way this will continue, so you better just resign yourself to it now." Sonja stood.

"*Goddddd*. I said fine. Just don't expect me to be happy about it." She cut into another piece of egg and shoved it into her mouth.

"Noted. You eat. I'm going to go take a shower. When I'm done, I'll come and help you in the bathroom."

"Mom, seriously? I can manage."

"Not as easy as you think, Casey."

She bit into a piece of toast. "I'll figure it out."

"Promise me you'll wait until I am done before you make your attempt. We don't need any more broken bones."

Casey rolled her eyes and took a sip of her coffee. For sure, there was more to the story than Casey was telling her, and there was nothing Sonja could do about that. With a shake of her head, she ignored her daughter's crappy attitude and exited the room. Going back to the kitchen, she retrieved her cell. She checked for messages again as she wandered to her bathroom.

When she finished the unexpected crying jag in the shower and had gotten dressed, Sonja made her way back to her daughter. As she feared, Casey was already in her bathroom. Sonja tapped her knuckle on the door and opened it a crack. Casey was in the bathtub, her booted foot hanging out of the side. Sonja rushed in. "Oh my goodness, are you even comfortable like that?"

"Mom, it's fine."

"It may be fine right now, but the last thing you need is to get that thing wet. I don't think you want to deal with it getting all stinky. I'll get you a bag."

"Ugh. *Fine.*"

With her nerves jagged and threadbare, Sonja smoothed her hand up the back of her hair and counted to ten. "Thank you."

When she returned, Casey had sunk down into the tub, submerging the entire upper half of her body, including her head. Sonja knelt in front of the tub and got the bag elastic-banded around the boot. Her daughter surfaced and wiped the water from her eyes.

"Tomorrow, we'll take it off so it's easier. You'll have no choice but to let me help you. Do you want me to wash your hair?"

"Nope. I got it."

"Okay, well, I'll leave the door open. Just holler when you're ready to get out." Sonja moved to the door. "Casey?"

"God! Yes, Mom. Stop fussing over me. It's creeping me out."

Sonja chose, once again, to ignore the attitude. Instead, she forced a smile. "See you in a bit."

Grabbing the tray of empty plates, Sonja went back to the kitchen. The housekeeper was already doing the dishes. Hoping for the distraction, Sonja had wanted to do them.

Bidding the woman a good morning, she swallowed the lump in her throat, poured a large mug of coffee and wandered into her study.

As she was about to sit, she heard the front door open. *Thomas.* Agitation rose, fast and hard, like a summer rainstorm. She really needed to get the house key from him or change the locks. Sonja moved out to the hall toward the front door. Thomas hadn't been in town since they'd had their huge fight. It'd been about four months, she guessed. When she reached the foyer, Thomas was dropping his keys in the bowl on the entryway table. Yes, she definitely needed to get the key back.

"Hello, Sonja."

"Daddy!"

Sonja turned around when she heard Casey's enthusiastic call for her father. She crossed her arms and took in the joyful expression on her daughter's face. Sonja would give anything to have Casey look at her like that.

"There's my little kitten!" Thomas moved to Casey and pulled her into an embrace. "Look at you and your big boot. How cool is that, huh?"

Casey giggled. "Dad, it's not cool at all."

"Sure it is! It's like something out of a sci-fi movie."

"I guess. How long are you gonna be here? Think you can come with me when I have to go back for X-rays?"

Sonja stepped next to them. "Probably not."

Thomas glanced at Sonja, then back to Casey. "I'll be here just a few days, kitten."

Casey frowned. "Bummer. Okay. Glad you're here now, though. I've really missed you, Daddy."

"Let's go have a seat in the living room, shall we?" He nodded to Sonja as he pressed his palm to Casey's lower back and led her down the hall. "We have some things to talk about."

Taking it slow, they made their way toward the living room. "Are you mad?" Casey said.

"I was worried. There's a difference."

Once they'd entered the room, Sonja went to the kitchen and prepared a tray with coffee and hot cocoa, along with some cookies. When she entered the living room, Sonja glanced at Casey, who was in the larger chair with her foot propped up on a few pillows atop the ottoman. Sonja settled the tray on the coffee table and filled a cup for Thomas.

"I'm sorry, Daddy."

Thomas bent and pressed a kiss to Casey's forehead. "I know you are, kitten."

Sonja brought the mug of cocoa to Casey, then handed Thomas his cup.

"Thank you." He took a sip. "Perfect."

After fixing herself a cup, she took a seat on the far end of the couch. "You're welcome."

Silence stretched out between them, and tension filled the room. Sonja had assumed Thomas would begin the conversation, and when he didn't, she took a sip of her coffee and then cleared her throat. "I guess I'll break the ice. Casey, why don't you tell your father what happened?"

"Didn't you already tell him?"

Sonja leaned forward and rested her elbows on her knees with her mug cupped between her hands. "I think it's best you inform him of the details."

"Go easy on her, Sonja. I'm sure she's had a rough enough time."

Already, he was going to make this painful. Sonja called what was left of her patience, which wasn't much. "I've been very easy on her, Thomas. Maybe you should consider being a bit more stern?"

A closed-lipped smile spread across his mouth, a muscle in his jaw twitched, and he sighed through his nose. *Interesting.* Apparently, he was having a hard time keeping his patience, too. Good, he could suck it up and deal with her. She wasn't backing down.

"Are you going to start fighting again?"

Thomas turned his gaze to Casey. "No, no, kitten. There won't be any fighting. Why don't you tell me what happened?"

Her daughter brushed her hair away from her eyes. "Fine. But promise me you won't get upset or overreact."

"I can promise you that I will not overreact." He leaned toward her and patted her leg. "You don't have to worry, sweetheart. I doubt you'll even be grounded over this. Your injuries are punishment enough."

Shock and annoyance boiled in Sonja's stomach. Was he nuts? "Thomas, don't be a fool. Of course, she's going to be grounded for this."

"Sonja!" He snapped his head in Sonja's direction, his jaw set like he was gritting his teeth. "Watch your tongue."

She glared at him as anger oozed from every pore in her body. "I beg your pardon? I most certainly will *not* watch my tongue. Now I suggest you start acting like a father instead of a Disneyland Dad."

Thomas didn't respond to the comment, just stared at Sonja. His jaw was set tight—the muscle jumping every few seconds. She let the silence stretch, silently daring him to give her a reason to kick him out again. He must've realized the predicament he was in as they stared each other down for what felt like forever. Thomas's eyes remained stone hard, but Sonja didn't flinch or back down at all. There was no way in hell she ever would again.

CHAPTER FORTY-THREE

JIMMY SPARKED THE TORCH ON THE WELDER, FLIPPED HIS MASK down and fused two pieces of metal together. Restless energy bounced through him and ping-ponged around his entire body, making it almost impossible to sit still. He had a serious case of Sonja-on-the-brain, making for a long night with very little sleep. He could've called Andy, probably should've, but he really didn't want to have to tell her, again, how Sonja had pushed him away. Calling his brother Ryan had been an option too, still was—but instead, he was downstairs in his studio using his energy to create.

He had no clue what he was making, but it didn't matter. The action helped to distract his mind. Sort of. The idea Sonja hadn't wanted him around while her ex was in town had hurt. Worse was knowing the guy stayed in her house. That just plain pissed him right the fuck off. There were too many reasons why she'd let him, and none of them good. Sonja never had a nice thing to say about the guy. As far as Jimmy knew, she couldn't stand Thomas.

Unless…

Jimmy cringed. He didn't want to think she was sleeping with him. But the level of disdain in her voice every time her ex came up *could* indicate residual feelings or passion. And wouldn't that just be a motherfucker? The first time he opened his heart after having it crushed almost ten years ago, and it got crushed again. In the same way.

With a grunt, Jimmy took a step back and observed the start of…whatever the hell this was. Grabbing another strip of sheet metal, he hit one end with the torch, attached it and bent it upward. Then, welded another. Godsmack's "Whatever" blared in the background, fueling his aggressive and agitated mood, which was exactly what he needed. Staying pissed off was easier than wallowing in the heartache.

She'd texted him several times. He hadn't responded, too hurt and pissed off to bother. If he *had* replied, he wouldn't have been nice. In any way. It was better to leave it alone.

Leave her alone, too.

A dull ache bloomed in his chest, and Jimmy rubbed his sternum. He couldn't fathom not having her in his life, but what choice had she left him? None. He wasn't an all-or-nothing type of person, yet that was exactly the line he'd drawn in the sand with her. And she'd made her decision, refusing to give in and let him stay by her side. Either that or she'd been passing time with him until "Daddy" got home. Ugh. No. *Don't go there.* Jimmy grabbed another strip and welded it to the frame of the others.

As he continued working, his mind tripped and stumbled on its journey through the Land of Sonja. God, the woman made him insane. But she had from the very beginning, hadn't she? Shaking his head, he added another strip and stopped mid-weld when the next song came up on shuffle. Jason DeVore's "Wait" rang out around him. Jimmy flipped up his welding helmet and glared at the speaker dock. So much for hard work and hard music keeping his mind occupied. "How in the hell did this song get on *this* playlist?"

Stepping back from his creation, he set the welding wand down and placed his hands on his hips. The words to the song cut through his anger and pierced his heart with a strum of an acoustic guitar. He loved her. She'd become his everything. And he'd walked out on her. Jimmy ran a hand through his hair. When he looked up, he realized he'd been sculpting the figure of a woman. "Goddammit!"

Specifically, his woman.

"Brilliant. I am *so* fucked." Flipping the welder off, he wiped his hands on a rag, shut off the music and went upstairs to shower. He knew he should call Ryan, run this whole mess past him. But he wasn't sure if he could. Telling the story and giving life to the words would somehow make his actions permanent. Which was stupid. Maybe after he showered, he'd call. Maybe.

When Jimmy finished cleaning up, he gathered up his laundry, tossed it in the wash and then forced a sandwich down his throat. He landed on the couch with a beer in his hand and stared at his cell phone. A new favorite pastime, apparently.

He'd listened to her voicemails about ten times and re-read her text messages at least that many times, probably more. He still hadn't responded, but desperation was beginning to win out, for sure. Instead, he pulled up his brother's contact info and pressed "Call".

"Hellooooo, dearest Jimmy," Maiya said.

Jimmy smiled. "How's my favorite redhead?"

"Oh, you know, the usual. Work, Jacob, your brother. Speaking of him, he told me you got yourself a girl. Deets, please."

Jimmy groaned and then slouched down on the sofa, resting his feet on the coffee table. "He did, did he? Typical."

"You know he hates being called typical, but yep, he sure did. He said it's the woman you met when we were all in Vegas together. The lawyer, right? Sooooo...fill me in. I'm dying to hear all about her."

"Yeah, Sonja, but it doesn't matter now because I think we broke up."

"That's right; couldn't think of her name…wait, you *think* you broke up? That's like saying someone's *almost* pregnant. There's not really an in between there, my darling." Maiya snorted. "What happened?"

Jimmy blew out a breath. "It's complicated." He heard the sound of a lighter through the line. "You still smoking?"

"Yes. And don't try to change the subject. I got a fresh coffee in hand and I'm on the back deck, chilling. Talk to me."

"I don't know, Maiya. I don't know what else to do. She makes me fucking crazy, you know?"

"Yep, sadly, I do know."

Jimmy ran through the whole story, giving Maiya the blow-by-blow of the past few days with Sonja and all that'd happened with Casey, which led right into the issue with Thomas. Maiya was easy to talk to—always had been. Now was no different, and once he started talking, he couldn't stop. "She told me I had to stay away while her ex was in town. Can you believe that shit?"

"Whoa…she what?"

"You heard me. It's fucked up."

"Why should you have to stay away because her ex is in town?"

"Good question. She gave me some bullshit line about not wanting to deal with a testosterone war. Oh, and I guess when he's in town, he stays at her house."

"*What* the fuck?"

"Yup."

"That's not cool, Jimmy. What'd you say?"

"I basically told her I was done. That she either wanted me by her side or she didn't, and I was tired of having to work so hard to be there. I walked out of the hospital last night and left her there."

"Did she try and stop you?"

"Yeah, but it doesn't matter. It's not supposed to be this hard, Maiya. And I won't be second to him. I can be second to her daughter, that's to be expected, but I will not fucking be second to him. End of story."

"I get it, sweetheart, I really do, but…"

"But what?"

"It sounds like she's got some shit—kinda like I did—that she needs to work through."

"Yeah, well, maybe she'd rather work that shit out with her ex. Doesn't matter. I'm done. He's there, and I'm not. For all I know, she's still fucking him."

Maiya gasped. "You don't think she's really—"

"How the hell do I know? Seriously, what would you think?"

"I can't even, so let's not go there. And you shouldn't either. He probably just stays there because of their daughter." He heard the flick of the lighter again. "But…"

"But, what, Maiya?"

"You love her, that's what."

Jimmy was quiet for a long time. Per usual, in her way, Maiya had called it dead on. He didn't even need to say the words out loud to her. She just knew. *Dammit.* "It doesn't matter."

"Oh, yeah, it does." He heard her exhale. "Jimmy, you love her, and from what I know about you, you haven't loved anyone in a really long time."

"So what."

"So what? Ugh, really? Look, can I ask you something?"

His beer now empty, Jimmy migrated to the kitchen to grab another. "Sure."

"Promise to answer honestly, yeah?"

He dropped the bottle in the recycle bin and pulled a fresh one from the fridge. "Sure."

"Is she the one?"

"The one, what?"

"Don't play dumb. Is she *theeee* one?"

Jimmy leaned against the kitchen counter, cold beer in hand, and let the question sink in. "I don't know," he lied.

"James Michael Donnelly, that wasn't honest."

"It was. I don't know. Shit… When we're together, there's nowhere else I'd rather be. She's my everything, Maiya. But then she puts up that strong arm of hers, and I think, how could she be, you know?"

Maiya sighed. "Yep, I know, sweetie. But that doesn't really matter, does it? When all is said and done, and it's quiet, she's where you want to be. No matter how much of a pain in the ass she is, she is where you want to be."

Staring at the floor tile, Jimmy's heart rose into his throat. "Yeah, I guess you're right."

"Then go get her, honey. Fuck the bullshit with her ex. Put away your pride and go get your lawyer."

"I'll think about it."

"Jimmy, don't think too long. Life's just too damn short to miss out on what makes us truly happy."

Maiya was right, but how the hell was he supposed to deal with the Thomas issue, especially when Sonja made it clear Jimmy wasn't welcome? "Thanks, Maiya. This is exactly why my brother loves you so much."

"Anytime. But don't forget, I put him through hell, too. And I think he'd tell you it was worth it. At least, I hope he would." Maiya laughed.

"Yeah, he would. Tell him I called, okay?"

"Of course. Night, sweetie."

"Night." Jimmy disconnected the call and made his way back to the couch.

After the talk with Maiya, he was tempted to call Sonja, but maybe he needed to give her the night to handle her business. Or maybe *he* needed the night to decide if he could really deal with the constant struggle it was to stay with her, never mind the shit with her ex—that was a whole other barrel of bullshit. He needed to know if she wanted him. Really wanted him because Jimmy didn't share.

He and Sonja were so different. Almost too different, and yet, when he was with her, none of that mattered. All their differences melted away. Every step of this thing with her had been a struggle. Even the first night he met her. She'd been a huge bitch until he plied her with a little booze and got her to loosen up. That's when he knew…

He knew she was *the one*. She was *his* one.

Sonja sat on the edge of the tub while it filled with hot water. The afternoon and evening with her ex and daughter had been grueling. She'd gone round for round with Thomas, and they still hadn't reached a resolution regarding Casey. Their daughter needed to be grounded for several weeks, or at least until school let out. Thomas didn't agree. Big surprise. There was also the matter of Casey thinking she should be able to skip the remainder of the school year, all because she had a bulky boot on her leg. No way that was happening.

Pouring some lavender-scented bath salts into the tub, she swirled her hand in the water. She hadn't heard from James, and as much as she hated to admit it, it was freaking driving her up a wall. He was right, not wanting to wait around in the background for her to deal with all her life drama. That's exactly what she'd done too—asked him to wait. James shouldn't have to wait for anyone. This was precisely the reason why she'd tried so hard to keep him at a distance. But honestly, why would he, or anyone else for that matter, want to deal with her mess?

James was young, successful and good-looking—young being the most critical point of those three attributes. Someone like him sure as hell didn't need to be with an older woman. Especially one who had a busy career taking up half her time, a troubled teen who monopolized the other half of her time, and an ex-husband who wouldn't go away and stay gone.

Wiping the tears on constant flow for the last few days from her cheeks, Sonja removed her robe, stepped into the tub and stretched out. Lana Del Rey's "Burning Desire" played on low volume, filling her head with dreamy visions of the man she needed to not be thinking of at the moment, or at all, for that matter.

Lord, she'd had the worst luck with men in her life. From her father to Thomas, and now James. Talk about daddy issues. Her father had been dead for four years, yet still controlled her from the grave. Thomas was still very alive and continued to try to control her, though she supposed much of that was her own fault. Thinking about it, her issues with her father were her own doing, too.

Letting out a groan, Sonja wrung out the washcloth floating in the water and covered her face with it. How mortifying to realize she had enough baggage to fill a cargo plane. *What in the hell* did James see in her? He was the only man she'd ever had in her life who didn't try to control her. But instead of moving heaven and hell to be with him, she fought him every step of the way.

What made her think that made her independent? Sadness spread through Sonja like hot lava, and her tears came rushing back. In the end, she'd only screwed up in a monumental, irreparable way.

Sitting up, she wrapped her arms around her legs. She had no clue how to deal with Thomas. She had no idea how to fix things between her and James. And more importantly, she had no idea how to save Casey from herself. "What a damn mess."

After finishing up in the bathroom, she pulled on a night-shirt, wandered out to her bedroom, and stopped short. Thomas was in her bed. Sonja leaned against the doorway, closed her eyes and blew out a weary breath. Whatever made him think this was still okay? In fact, how had he *ever* thought this was okay? Sonja went cold inside with anger. It filled her veins and poured through her bloodstream like ice water. "Thomas. Get out of my bed." When he didn't reply, she tried again. "Thomas! I want you out of my bed."

He glanced over his shoulder at her. "Don't be foolish. Just come to bed."

"Foolish?" She stormed forward. "You think I'm foolish because I don't want my *ex*-husband sleeping in my bed?"

"Yes, I happen to think you're foolish." He patted her side of the mattress, a smug look on his face. "Now compose yourself and come to bed."

No more. *Bastard!* Never again. Sonja was done. Something snapped inside, and a dead calm came over her like a warm blanket. Without saying another word, she lifted her pillow off the bed and, clutched it to her chest and started for the door.

"Sonja, where are you going?"

She opened the bedroom door and looked back at him. "I'm going to sleep in the guest room. Enjoy the bed, Thomas, because tonight is the last time you will *ever* sleep in it." Turning away, she walked out of the room and slammed the door behind her.

Tomorrow she'd put an end to all of this crap with Thomas—she might even burn the sheets. Tomorrow, she'd deal with Casey, too. She planned to look into some private schools for next year, and definitely a private Jewish camp where she could send her for the summer. Getting her daughter away from the city for a while would probably do her a world of good.

She was at a loss for how to deal with James yet. Or even if she should bother. She'd done fine without a man in her life after divorcing Thomas; there was no reason why she wouldn't be fine now. James had been a wonderful and amazing distraction. But now it was over, and she'd move on.

That's what people did who took a chance and dated. When things didn't work out, they simply went their separate ways. Sonja pulled the blankets back on the guest bed and crawled in. But he'd also been a necessary growing experience. Exactly what Sonja had needed to catapult her into taking charge of her life again. Except this time, really take charge and do what was necessary instead of what was easier.

The idea of never seeing James again sent a boulder-sized lump into her throat. She'd never kiss him again. Never touch him again. Never fight with him, either. An ache settled in her chest, and she stared up at the ceiling. "Oh God." Sonja rubbed her breastbone as the waterworks came on full force. "Oh God!"

Sitting up, she buried her face in her hands and wept. There was no way she could let James go, never touch him or fight with him again. There was just no way.

She couldn't do it.

CHAPTER FORTY-FOUR

Jimmy worked on the metal sculpture he'd started the day before. He had no idea what he was going to do with the damn thing when it was done, especially since it was a metal formation of Sonja, but what the hell? Maybe he'd stick it up in his bedroom for a little self-torture. Or not.

After attaching a few more strips of sheet metal, he removed his welding mask and took a step back. Satisfaction, mixed with a healthy dose of sadness, sliced through him. Nothing like a little, or in this case, a lot of heartache to mine and use for creation. Raw emotion made for the greatest pieces.

Jimmy glanced at his phone, checking the time. It was almost four p.m., and he hadn't heard anything more from Sonja. Maybe she'd given up. Then again, he hadn't responded to any of her texts or voicemails, so he couldn't really blame her if she had.

Shutting down the welding machine, Jimmy headed for the shower. Sonja might've gone to work today, and considering the situation, she'd probably be home soon. Call him crazy, but he'd decided in the morning when he woke up, he was going to head over to her place. It was likely the stupidest idea he'd had yet, but with Sonja, if he didn't confront the problem head-on, they'd never get past it.

Finishing up in the bathroom, he got dressed and walked out the door. Jimmy didn't know if Thomas was still in town, and he didn't care. If he was, the guy could fuck off and go get a hotel room.

It was past five by the time Jimmy knocked on Sonja's door. When it opened, the infamous ex-husband stood on the other side. With his white dress shirt—long sleeves cuffed up his forearms—he was a regular *GQ* guy. All he needed was a sweater draped over his shoulders and a set of golf clubs by his side. Jimmy pasted a blasé smile on his face. "You must be Thomas."

Thomas slid his hands into his perfectly pressed tan khakis. "And who might you be?"

"James Donnelly."

"Ah, yes. Please, come in." Thomas took a step back, allowing Jimmy to pass. "What can I help you with?"

"I'm here to speak with Sonja."

"My wife isn't here right now."

"You mean your *ex*-wife."

Thomas smirked. "If you prefer."

Jimmy had the urge to slap the smug expression off his face, but managed to rein himself in. The mystery was confirmed. The guy was a straight-up, grade-A dick, and Jimmy hadn't even been in his presence more than three minutes. "Yeah, actually, I do." Jimmy glanced down the hall. "I think I'll wait and check on Casey while I'm at it."

"Wait—"

Screw it. He pushed past Thomas and walked to Casey's bedroom. Fuck him. Tossing a smirk of his own back at the guy, Jimmy knocked, then cracked her door open. "Hello? Are you alive?"

She looked over from the bed. "Jimmy!" With her lips

curved into a big smile, she swung her legs over the side and reached for her crutches.

"Hang on there, girl, I'll come to you." Jimmy stepped inside and closed the door behind him. When he took a seat next to her and pulled her into a tight embrace, her door opened. *Oh, for fuck's sake!* Jimmy looked over to find Thomas leaning against the doorjamb, arms crossed. "Can we help you with something?"

Thomas straightened. "In fact, you can. I don't find it appropriate for you to be in my daughter's bedroom. Especially with the door closed."

"Daddy! Oh, my God."

"Are you fucking kidding me?" Jimmy stood. "Listen, man. That was completely out of line, not to mention perverted. Casey is like a daughter to me, and the fact you would even insinuate something like that is a testament to what a dick you really are."

"Mr. Donnelly, I couldn't care less what you think. But let's get one thing straight—she is *not* your daughter. She's mine. That means I decide what's appropriate where she is concerned. In my opinion, you are far from appropriate."

"Daddy, please don't." Casey stood.

Jimmy cupped her elbow in his hand. "Case, sit back down. It'll be okay, I promise." After he helped her back onto the bed, he pressed a kiss to her forehead and then turned and approached her father. "You obviously have something to say to me, so why don't we step out of the room and have a little talk?"

"I have nothing to say to you beyond what I've already said. In fact, I believe it's time for you to leave."

Rage boiled below the surface, and Jimmy's skin tingled. If he was going to make his point, he needed to keep a lid on it. Clenching his fists at his sides, Jimmy stepped up to Sonja's ex and lowered his voice. "Go ahead, give it your best. But I'm telling you right now, I'm not going anywhere." Thomas took a step back. Jimmy followed and closed the door behind them. "Come on, Tommy, I think you got plenty to say to me. And, rather than me, I think it's maybe time for *you* to leave."

The bastard laughed, shaking his head. "You do realize you're simply a toy for her to play with in between my visits, don't you?"

Jimmy pursed his lips. "That all you got?"

"I'm sure she's told you about our arrangement, Mr. Donnelly. I mean, you can't be foolish enough to think she'd actually be interested in you. You're practically a child."

Jimmy didn't want to believe one bit of what Thomas was insinuating. But bile rose in his throat anyway. There was no way Sonja was still sleeping with this asshole. "Yeah, see, that's where you're wrong, dude. She's quite interested in me. Also, you disgust her. To be more specific, you make her skin crawl, and she can't fucking stand you. I'm sure she's told *you.* But you don't listen too well, do you? In fact, I'm positive if she were here right now, her choice would be quite clear."

"Whose choice would be quite clear?"

Jimmy snapped his head to the left at the sound of Sonja's voice. He'd been so focused on his "discussion" with Thomas, he hadn't heard her come in. He was willing to bet Thomas hadn't either.

CHAPTER FORTY-FIVE

Sonja wasn't sure what the hell was going on, but she intended to find out. Looking between James and Thomas, she posed her question again and waited for one of them to answer.

Thomas jutted out his chin, an indignant look on his face. "It appears your boy-toy decided to come and piss on my leg."

She glared at her ex-husband. "I beg your pardon?"

James rested his hands on his hips. "Has anyone ever told you you're a pompous asshole?"

"Mr. Donnelly, your insults mean nothing to me, much like your presence."

Sonja stepped between the two men. "Okay, look, I don't know what the hell is going on here, but I want it to stop right now."

James looked around her at Thomas. "The feeling's mutual."

"James, what are you doing here?"

Casey opened her bedroom door. "Mom?"

The three of them turned toward her. Sonja forced a smile. "Hi, honey. I think you should go back into your room."

A look passed between her daughter and James, and then

Casey's gaze moved to her father. Sadness radiated from Casey's eyes. Sonja realized immediately that something had changed while she'd been at work. She moved toward her daughter. "Casey?"

"I got it, Sonja." James moved around her to Casey. "Come on, Case. You look tired. Why don't you lie down for a bit?"

James helped her to the bed, and Sonja watched from the doorway. Once she was settled, he pressed a kiss to the top of Casey's head. Her daughter nodded, and he said something Sonja couldn't hear. Then Casey gave him a hug. Sonja's heart filled to the point of bursting. God, she loved how James treated her daughter and how Casey responded so genuinely to him.

Turning, he walked back toward Sonja. "We need to talk."

"Yes, indeed you do," Thomas said.

Sonja's attention jerked back to her ex. "Mind your own business, Thomas."

"What goes on with my daughter is my business. In fact, whatever goes on in this house is my business."

"Sonja." James's voice was low.

"You're *very* wrong, Thomas. None of what goes on in *my* home is your business. My relationship with James has nothing to do with *our* daughter. Now, if you will excuse us." Thomas looked her up and down, disgust evident in his expression, before he turned and walked down the hall to the library. She waited until the door closed before returning her attention to James. "What are you doing here?"

"Wow! That all you have to say to me? Good to see you too, sweetheart."

"Look…" She blew out a breath. "I haven't heard from you, and now I walk in to find you having a testosterone war with my ex-husband. What the hell am I supposed to say? Besides, did it occur to you that calling first would've been appropriate?"

"For fuck's sake, can we please go somewhere that's *not* the hallway and talk?"

"Fine." Turning, Sonja headed for her bedroom. Even if she was happy to see him, she couldn't believe he was going to give her an attitude simply because she hadn't reacted the way he obviously expected.

When they reached her room, she headed straight for her closet and took off her shoes. When she emerged, James was standing in front of her fireplace, staring intently at a photograph of her and Casey he'd taken off the mantle. "So, you want to tell me why you're here?"

"How old was she in this picture?"

"Two."

"You're smiling. You look happy; you both do."

She walked over to him and glanced at the photo. "Yes, at the time, I suppose I was."

"I like seeing you happy. There've been times over these last several months when I've seen you look that way. Were you?"

"Yes." Her voice was a bare whisper. She didn't know where he was going with this or why, and maybe she was a little afraid to find out.

After placing the picture back in its place, he turned to her. "You're right, I should've called. But I didn't want you to tell me no, so I..." He shrugged. "I don't know; I came over. And all excuses aside, I wanted to meet him face to face."

She reached to stroke her fingers through his hair, but he pulled away. Sonja's heart sank at the rejection. Would they ever get back to where they were? "What did he say to you?"

"Are you still fucking him?"

She gasped, covering her mouth with her hand. Shaking her head, she turned away from him. She wasn't—at least not since she and James started seeing each other. Guilt still plagued her about that. But how could she explain the complexity of the situation to him and have him understand the whys of it? There was no way he'd understand, and she couldn't expect him to.

"Your reaction is answer enough. Goodbye, Sonja."

She jerked around and faced him. "James, wait, please. My reaction is not my answer."

"No? Then what is?"

"It's complicated."

He let out a soft chuckle. "I bet it is. And that's another obvious non-answer."

"I don't know what you want me to say to you."

He crossed his arms. "How about you tell me the truth? Maybe you could start there."

"It's complicated."

"Yeah, you said that already. I'm done. Take care, Sonja."

"Wait…I'm not fucking him." The urge to reach for him raged inside her, and she had to ball her hands into fists to keep from touching him. "I swear to you, I'm not. You have to believe me."

"Nice. You sure as hell could've said that before, but you didn't, did you? And now you expect me to believe you? Fuck that."

"I said it was complicated, and I meant it. It is."

He moved to the settee and took a seat. "Fine. Here's your chance. Go ahead and tell me all about the 'complicated'. I'm all fucking ears."

Fear and frustration raged within Sonja. She wasn't sure where to begin. Should she tell him how things had been with Thomas on and off over the years since their divorce? Should she tell him the last time she'd had sex with him was right before she and James had gone on their first date? Could he even possibly understand, plus understand why she tolerated Thomas for so long, or why she'd given up and given in?

"Yeah, like I thought. The cat's got your tongue, Sonja-the-lawyer, doesn't he?"

She sat on the edge of her bed. "Fine. You want the truth, I'll tell you. Brace yourself because it's ugly."

He plopped his palms down on his thighs and sighed. "Go for it."

Sonja drew in a deep breath and then let it out slow and easy, praying when she got done, there'd be something left of her relationship with James to salvage. "When Thomas and I got divorced, naturally, things were strained. At first, he still lived in the City and would come over a couple nights a week to visit Casey. I made sure to be out of the house when he did."

"See, right there. That makes no damn sense. Why didn't you drop her off at his place like every other divorced couple in the world with kids does?"

"I don't know. I guess…" She ran her hand up the back of her hair. "I guess because it seemed like the right thing to do. It was easier on Casey, and Thomas insisted."

He shook his head. "Fucked-up, Sonja. For real."

"Are you going to insult me the whole time?"

"I'm not insulting you. Merely stating a fact about the situation. But, please, continue."

"Fine." She frowned. "When he moved to Florida, it was even harder on Casey. As you're aware, she's very close to her father, and she missed him terribly. When he would come into town, he…well, he stayed at my house. I didn't want him here. I didn't invite him either, but again, it seemed like the right thing to do for our daughter. I did protest at first, but Thomas can be very convincing and, of course, spared nothing when it came to laying guilt on me for breaking up our family. So, I let him."

"I don't understand you. I swear to God, I *do not* understand you. The word 'no' is like your favorite fucking word, Sonja."

He was using his mouth like a weapon, and his harsh words cut her deep. The hurt morphed into anger, though, streaking through her like a comet. "I realize you're angry and likely hurt by whatever it was Thomas said to you earlier, but I'd really appreciate it if you'd stop tearing into me. I told you it was ugly. I can either finish or not. It's up to you."

Letting out an exasperated groan, he leaned forward and propped his elbows on his knees. "Yeah, I'm angry and hurt. Sorry. I'll shut up and let you talk."

"Thank you." Sonja swallowed past the lump in her throat and willed herself to continue because the next part was worse. "He insisted on sleeping in my room. Again, he used Casey as the excuse. He said it was better for her because things appeared more normal, more like they used to be. Of course, one thing led to another, and we started having sex again."

James cursed and jerked back like she'd slapped him. Sonja cringed. God, this was so hard, but it was too late to turn back now.

JIMMY LISTENED to her tell him all about fucking Thomas for several years *after* they'd divorced as hot lava spread through his veins. It was something he didn't want to know, and although it was hard to hear, at least she was talking about the past so far and not the present. He wasn't sure he had the stomach to listen to her explain what the arrangement was currently.

"After a while, I couldn't stand it. I took a lot of crap from him, but finally, I'd gotten to a place where I couldn't look myself in the mirror anymore. So I put an end to it. I loathed him, and although he flat-out refused to leave my bed, I stopped having sex with him."

Jimmy couldn't speak, let alone look at her. In his eyes, she was an incredible, intelligent and strong woman. It was crazy to imagine her as someone who'd tolerate being treated like

Thomas had treated her. Wrapping his head around it was near impossible. The woman Jimmy knew, and loved, didn't put up with the kind of bullshit she was laying out for him. She sure as hell didn't put up with any shit from him—not that he'd given her any, but still.

She cleared her throat and went on. "The last few years, there's been nothing. Aside from having to sleep next to him when he came into town, I haven't let him touch me."

Jimmy blew out a breath he hadn't realized he'd been holding, and cold relief washed through him, dousing the fire that'd been lit by his anger.

"But then—"

His gaze locked with hers. "Sonja—"

"James, let me get this out, please." She frowned and ran her hand up the back of her hair.

She did that a lot, always when she was nervous or stressed. He'd noticed the habit a while ago but never said anything to her about it. He wasn't going to start now. Rubbing his palms down his thighs, he tried to prepare himself for what she was going to say next.

Her words were killing him, ripping his heart clean out of his chest. This was it, right? Sonja was about to confess to sleeping with Thomas again, which made her no different than Gina. Just because he hadn't walked in on them in bed didn't mean he could handle hearing her say the words. Anxiety filled his chest, and he stood. "No. Stop. I can't do this. I don't want to know."

"James, I need to tell you."

"It doesn't matter. I won't ever trust you again. I've been down this road before, and I'm not traveling it again."

"Wait, what?" She stood and walked to him. "What do you mean you've been down this road before?"

Jimmy needed to get out of there. His heart ached like it was locked in a vise, and his walls had gone up, locking her out for once. "It doesn't matter." He crossed his arms. "I've heard enough."

"Please, I want to finish. I need to explain."

"God, woman! Don't you get it?" He gripped her arms. "I. Don't. Fucking. Want. To. Know!"

Sonja flinched but then caught his gaze—a look of sheer panic in her eyes. "It was once! It only happened once."

He let go of her arms like he'd been burned. Technically, he had. Pain seared through his chest and nailed him right in the heart. Jimmy bent forward, clutching his gut. "Stop. Fuck me, stop!"

"I need you to know the truth. Yes, we slept together, but it was before I went to the charity auction with you. You and I weren't together yet. Please. I need you to understand. I wanted you, but I was denying myself. Thinking nothing would ever happen between us." He felt her hand on his back, and he flinched. "So, I used him. I told myself I was in control for once, and I used him, and I hated every minute of it and—"

A roar from the depths of his stomach and chest boiled out of him, loud enough to stop traffic. Jimmy turned and jerked away from her touch. Just because she and Jimmy hadn't been together yet made no difference to him. They'd had a steamy make-out session in his studio before the auction. If she could do it when things had just barely begun between them but weren't official, then she could do it while they were clearly together. His eyes burned with tears waiting to fall. "Shut up, please, I'm fucking begging you. You've said enough."

"I've said everything," she whispered. "There isn't anymore. I've said it all."

She reached for him again, and he stepped back. Betrayal was betrayal, and she needed to prove to him right now where her loyalty stood. "Him or me, Sonja."

"What?"

"You heard me. I won't play second fiddle to that asshole. And I sure as fuck won't be your boy toy to play with in between visits from him. So you decide, right now… *Him. Or. Me.*"

She swiped away the tears running down her cheeks. "You're giving me an ultimatum?"

"You're damn right I am."

"You're asking me to choose between Thomas and you? How can you do that? Please don't ask me to do that. James, he's her father. I can't cut ties with my daughter's father."

"I can because, yeah, he may be your daughter's father—" he clenched his fists at his sides, "—but he is *not your fucking husband anymore!*" She visibly flinched, and he had to look away. The pain in her face was palpable, but it didn't matter. "You choose, or I'll choose for you."

"James… I…"

When she stalled, Jimmy turned around and walked away from her. For the second and last time, in less than two days.

CHAPTER FORTY-SIX

Jimmy sat on Andy's couch with his head resting back onto the cushions and stared up at the ceiling. His mind was such a mess after leaving Sonja's that he'd gone straight to his best friend's house. Thank God she'd been home, and he was even more relieved to find her girlfriend, Steph, wasn't there.

Anger beat through his body in time with his heart like a damn drum. Among the many thoughts running through his mind, the one screaming the loudest was how stupid he was for putting himself out there again and trusting her. Thinking back, all the signs had been there too. Each and every time she tried to push him away or not allow him to get too close should've been a neon billboard with the word *WARNING* flashing on it. He could sure see that fucking sign now. And man, wasn't hindsight a bitch?

"Here."

Yanked from his wallowing, he looked up to see Andy holding a fresh beer out to him. "Thanks." Taking the bottle from her, he pressed it to his lips and took a long drink.

She sat beside him on the couch. "You ready to tell me what happened yet?"

"Did I ever tell you I was engaged before?"

"What?" Her eyes went wide. "Fuck, really glad I wasn't taking a drink right then. When the hell were you engaged?"

"In college. I guess I wasn't *technically* engaged. I never got to pop the question."

"Holy shit. I had no idea. Who was she?"

"Yeah, sorry. It's not something I like to talk about. Ever." He took a swig of his beer and stared across the room. "Gina, my girlfriend in college. We dated for the first three years. She was an art major, too."

Andy shifted on the couch, curling one leg under her and then took a sip of her beer. "Go on."

"Jesus, I was so fucking in love, thought she was in love, too. I had the ring and everything. Took me months to pay the damn thing off. But when I finally did, I planned on proposing when we graduated."

"Did she turn you down or something?"

"Shit, that would've been easier to take, I think." He tilted his bottle back, taking another long swig. "I had a roommate. I came home early one day and found Gina in bed with him."

"Oh God, honey, I'm so sorry. That must've been horrible."

"Yeah, it was pretty fucking bad." Jimmy slid lower on the couch and rested his feet on the coffee table, crossing them at the ankle.

"Did you confront them?"

"Nope. I walked out. I went to her place and left a note in her room telling her I knew and that we were done. I got out of town, but when I went back to my place a few days later, my roommate tried to apologize. I basically told him to fuck off too. That's when I packed my shit and left. Went home for a while, then moved out here."

"That's the real reason why you didn't finish college. Damn, Jimmy. That's some heavy shit to go through."

"It was a long time ago, ya know? I mean, I guess I'm over

it, but the shit the last few days with Sonja brought it all back to the surface."

"Dude, sorry to say this, but no way you're over it. I've known you what? Two years now? I've never seen you get serious with a woman. Now I know why. You fuck plenty, but you don't date."

"Can you blame me? I mean, Gina ripped my heart out and served it for dinner. Sue me for not being too keen on getting into another serious thing."

"I get it. Really, I do. And I'm so sorry that happened to you. But what does this have to do with Sonja?"

Jimmy sat up and rested his elbows on his knees. "She's fucking her ex-husband, that's what."

Andy touched his arm. "Whoa, whoa. Back the hell up. Are you sure?"

"Pretty much, yeah." He glanced at her. "She wouldn't admit it right away, but yeah, she is."

"Okay, just…tell me what happened, please. I know I haven't met her, which, believe me, I'm not okay with, and I don't always like how she jerks you back and forth, but based on everything you've told me about this woman, I have a hard time believing she's been fucking her ex while fucking you. I thought you said he hasn't been in town for months."

"He hasn't."

"Then, sweetie, how can she be fucking you and him at the same time?"

"I don't know." He ran his fingers through his hair. "He told me I was her boy toy in between visits. Can you believe that shit?"

"He what? *Oh my fucking God.*" Andy went to sip her beer but paused, tilting her head to the side. "Ya know, no, I can't believe that shit. I mean, yeah, no doubt he said that, and you and Sonja have had your share of speed bumps, but I can't believe you're just a plaything for her."

"At this point, it doesn't matter. I won't go through that

shit again. And for fuck's sake, Andy, she lets him stay in her home when he's in town… In her bed! I—no way, I can't do it."

"Okay, yeah, I get it, that's pretty fucked up. Who does that? But… Well, what exactly did she say?"

He let out a chuckle born from bitterness rather than humor. "It's a long, fucked-up story, ending in her admitting she fucked him right before we started dating." He took another swig. "So I told her to choose. Him or me. And she couldn't."

"Damn. But—"

"But, nothing. I'm not doing it. No way. No how. Fuck that. I should've known better than to try."

Andy rubbed his back. "I'm so sorry."

"Me too." He glanced at her.

"Do you think you'll hear from her?"

He shrugged. "Dunno. Half of me hopes I do, but the other half wants her to stay away."

"Listen, she's fucked in the head if she doesn't choose you. Just saying." Andy kissed his cheek. "You can stay here tonight if you want."

"Nah, I'll probably head home in a little bit. Your girl will be home soon, and I'd rather not be here when she arrives."

"Steph won't care if you're here."

"Yeah, it's okay. I appreciate it."

"You know I love you, right?" She took his hand in hers.

"Yup. I love you, too, Andy."

Sitting back again, he slouched down on the couch and reached for the remote. Andy curled up next to him, her head on his shoulder. The Yankees game was on, and he and his best friend watched in silence, both sipping their beers until finally, Jimmy decided it was time to go. Giving Andy a tight hug, he left her place.

Jimmy started on the ten-or-so-block walk back to his place. Pulling his phone from his pocket, he checked his texts.

There were no messages from Sonja. Relief passed through him for a brief second, but then sadness hit him hard, like a punch in the gut.

A broken heart was a fact of life, but it seemed pretty fucking unfair to meet someone who made him feel alive for the first time in years and then fall in love with her only to have it crumble, like an avalanche, around him. Again. Getting burned in this way once was enough for him…twice was way too fucking much.

No way would he be touching the hot stove again. It wasn't worth it.

CHAPTER FORTY-SEVEN

Sonja collapsed to her knees and wept after James stormed out of the bedroom. Her mind had screamed at her to choose him. To tell him and show him how much he'd come to mean to her. But the words refused to come out.

The hard-won decision to truly be independent had dissipated in a flash when she saw Thomas and James together. James's presence should've strengthened that, but instead, it'd weakened it—her fear of dealing with Thomas and what it would mean with James had won. Worse, the fear of taking the leap of faith love required, with the possibility of being wrong, had won, too.

Fear determined and ruled everything in Sonja's life.

As she remained curled up on the floor in the middle of her bedroom, Sonja's tears fell for a long while until the sound of the door opening forced her to take a breath and attempt to compose herself. Wiping the tears from her cheeks, she braced herself and looked up, expecting to see Thomas. But instead, Casey was there, a confused and scared look on her face.

"Mommy?"

Sonja got off the floor. "Casey, honey. I'm sorry."

"No, Mommy, I'm sorry." Her daughter hobbled over to her. "I'm really sorry." Tears welled in Casey's eyes and fell.

Sonja pulled her daughter into her arms and pressed her face into her hair. Her own tears fell again, too. With the things that'd happened in the last several days, Sonja was crying over all of them. James walking out—again—was the icing on top of an already burnt cake. "I love you so much." After a few minutes, she pulled away and looked at her daughter. "What do you say we get you off your feet?"

Her daughter sniffled and nodded. "Can we lay down in your bed?"

Sonja smiled and wiped Casey's tears away. "Sure."

Leading her child to the bed, she pulled the covers back and helped her up and in, and then moved to the other side and joined her. It'd been years since Casey had wanted to lie in bed with her, and considering her raw emotions at the moment, Sonja was hungry for the opportunity to be close with her in this way again.

"I know I worried you and Jimmy when I ran away. I'm really sorry about that."

Sonja looked into her daughter's eyes. "I'm just relieved you're home safe, sweetheart, and relatively unharmed."

Casey scooted closer and rested her head on Sonja's shoulder. "Me too."

Shifting, she wrapped her arm around her daughter's back. Sonja drew in a deep breath and sent up a silent prayer of thanks for this little moment. "Promise me you won't ever do anything like that again."

"I promise."

They lay together in silence, and Sonja ran her fingers through the length of her daughter's hair before Casey finally spoke again. "Mommy, can I tell you something?"

"You can tell me anything you want." Sonja held her breath, curious, yet scared at the same time, of what Casey might say. Her daughter was a teenager. Smack in the middle of the awkward stage of life, where a kid is caught between hormones and still needing to be coddled like a child. Never mind all the peer pressure they were under.

"I don't think it's normal that Daddy stays here when he's in town. And I really don't think it's normal that he sleeps in here with you."

Sonja stiffened before blowing out a breath. She certainly hadn't expected those words to come out of her daughter's mouth. "Well…"

Casey laced her fingers with her mother's. "Do you still love him? Is that why you let him?"

Sonja blew out another breath. "Sadly, no."

"Then, why?"

Sonja stared at the ceiling, wondering how to explain the situation to her daughter. Should she tell her the truth or try to protect Thomas by keeping in place the illusion he believed was logical and solid?

"Mom, it's okay, you can tell me the truth. I'm not stupid. I mean, I have friends whose parents are divorced, but none of them do what you and Daddy do, so I don't get it."

Sonja tugged on her daughter's hair. "Did you just read my mind or something?"

Casey giggled. "No, but I can tell you're debating what to say." She sat up. "Do you love Jimmy?"

Sonja's eyes went wide. "I…" She swallowed. "Where did that come from?"

Casey laughed again. "Sorry, it just seems like when you're with him, you're happy. And when Dad is here, you're not. Like ever."

"I guess you're probably right."

"Well, duh. I mean, it's pretty obvious."

"Does it upset you to know your father and I have been trying to keep up appearances for you?"

"No. I mean, a little, I guess… But I never really paid attention. I think I started to notice the last visit when you

guys had that huge fight. I guess I didn't want to see it before."
Casey shook her head. "But I see it now, and I don't know… I
tried to ask Daddy about it this morning, why he stays here
and not in a hotel or something, and he acted like it was
normal. Like it was okay. But I know it's not, and it really
bothered me that he tried to play it off that way."

Sonja frowned. What on earth had they talked about?
"I'm sorry, honey."

"It's okay. I think that's just how he is." Casey shrugged.
"He even asked me if I wanted to spend the whole summer in
Florida, which is crazy, Mom. I told him I'd think about it, but
I don't think I want to do that. Not the whole summer,
anyway. I mean, I still love him. He's my dad."

Sonja shifted to her side. It was so typical of Thomas to
pitch a full summer visit on their daughter—probably hoping
he'd be able to convince her to stay for good. "You don't have
to go for the whole summer if you don't want to." She sighed.
"He loves you too, and he will always be your daddy, honey."

"I think Jimmy is awesome, Mom. He's really cool. And
he's easy to talk to. Even though I got mad at him the other
night—you know, the night I left? Anyway, I guess what I like
most about him is he makes you happy. You're better when
he's here."

Sonja stared at her daughter, listening intently to her
words, and watched the happy expression on her face. As
adorable as she found Casey at that moment, she knew her
only child was being completely serious. "I'm glad you like
him."

"He's funny, too. Plus, I think it's kind of cool how he
fights with you."

Sonja rolled her eyes. "He loves to fight with me."

"Yeah, but you love to fight with him too. And it's a
different kind of fighting than when you fight with Dad."

Sonja had to hold back a laugh. "What makes you think I
love fighting with James?"

"Come on, seriously, Mom; it's so totally obvious you love it. You get this dreamy look in your eyes when he's poking at you, and when he's not looking, you stare at him like you love him."

Sonja couldn't believe her ears. But she finally let the laugh out because her daughter was one-hundred-percent right.

"Do you love him?"

The repeated question made Sonja's stomach drop. She swallowed. "I don't know—"

"It's okay with me if you do. I mean, I think you deserve to be happy. I think you'd be crazy not to love him."

"I guess you have a point there." Oh, hell. Sonja sat up and placed her palm on her daughter's face. "What's not to love?"

Casey smiled but then frowned. "Mom, I heard the stuff Daddy said to Jimmy tonight, and it was really screwed up. Is that why he left?"

"No, honey. He left because of something I said."

"What did you say?"

"Well, it's complicated."

"I think you should kick Dad out, then go make up with Jimmy."

"Casey, he's your father."

"So? He shouldn't be here. Jimmy should." Her daughter nodded as if her mind was made up.

Sonja sighed. "I wish it were so simple."

"Seriously, Mom. It *is* that simple. Tell Dad he has to leave in the morning and then go see Jimmy. You should spend the night with him tonight, too. Dad can spend the rest of the night hanging out with me, and you can go be happy."

Apparently, the charade she'd tried to maintain all these years was not only foolish, it was a huge waste of time. Her daughter had finally seen through the lie and blasted an enormous hole in the façade. Moreover, her daughter was probably right about Sonja deserving to be happy. She'd suffered long enough at the hands of her father and then Thomas. Not to mention herself because Sonja wasn't the victim she once believed herself to be; she'd participated and allowed all of it to happen. Jimmy made her happy, and Sonja not only needed that—she wanted it. Sonja touched the tip of Casey's nose with her fingertip. "When did you get so smart, hmm?"

Her daughter scrunched up her face and giggled. "Good genes, I guess."

Blowing out a breath, Sonja got up from the bed. "I guess I need to go have a talk with your father. Maybe you should go to your room and turn your music on. Loud."

"You think there's going to be yelling?"

"I hope not, but your father doesn't usually do well when I put my foot down. So, unfortunately, there might be."

Casey got up and balanced on her crutches. "It's gonna be okay, Mom. No matter how he reacts, don't back down." She made her way to the door.

"Casey, are you sure you're okay with this?"

Her daughter smiled at her. "Yeah. Besides, I'll be going to see Dad this summer. I'm good, Mom."

"I love you, Casey."

"I love you, too, Mommy." Casey turned and walked out of the room.

How crazy her life had become since she'd met James. Yet, at the same time, it was so much better. Her daughter had pushed the boundaries, run away and got hurt. Then, once home, in a matter of twenty-four hours, Casey's perception of her home life had shifted and shattered into pieces. Sonja supposed it was a good thing, and although Casey said she was fine, Sonja worried the backlash from the mess she and Thomas had created was yet to come.

Sonja moved into her bathroom and splashed some cold water on her face. It was time to have a talk with Thomas. When she was done, things would change forever. She'd take the keys from him, and he'd never again be allowed to stay in her home, much less her bed, when he was in town.

She wasn't sure yet what to do about James or if he would even consider giving her another chance. But she had to try. Without a doubt, Sonja knew she loved him. From the petty bickering and his pain-in-the-ass persistence to the off-the-charts sex, he was everything she hadn't known she wanted and everything she needed.

A once-in-a-lifetime kind of love, and she wasn't about to give it up without a fight.

CHAPTER FORTY-EIGHT

Sonja knocked on James's door and waited. She'd let three days pass, trying to give him some time and space to cool off before she couldn't take it any longer and decided to go see him. When the only answer was silence, she knocked again. It was a little after two in the afternoon, and she thought for sure he'd be home. Knocking once more, she waited. Maybe he was downstairs working. Still, the door remained unanswered.

Disappointment boomeranged around her insides, and she frowned. *Dammit.* Defeated, she turned away, making her way down the beige hall, staring at the wooden planked floor on the way to the elevator.

As she was about to push the Down button, the compartment doors parted, and there he was. Her heart skipped, and she sucked in a breath. When their gazes locked, James froze mid-step. Time slowed to a screeching halt, but then he blinked and just…walked past her.

She caught his arm in her hand. "James…please stop, we need to talk."

Yanking from her grip, he glanced at her. "There's nothing more to talk about." He continued down the hall.

She followed. "Oh, yes, there is. There's plenty to talk about."

"Fuck that, Sonja. Save your argument for the courtroom. I'm not interested." He stopped at his door.

She was so caught up in the maelstrom of emotions running through her she almost plowed into the back of him. Gripping his shoulder, she halted her momentum. He glanced at her and then jerked away from her touch. *God, that hurt.* "This isn't over."

"Yeah, it is." After turning the key in the lock, he opened the door. He tried to close it on her, but she blocked it with her body. He didn't even look back, just continued down the entryway hall of his apartment to disappear into the kitchen.

"Dammit, James!" She slammed the door behind her. When she made it to the kitchen, he'd already pulled a beer from the refrigerator. With his head tilted back, he drank deeply from the bottle, his throat bobbing with each swallow. Sonja stood motionless, her eyes riveted on his features. Even pissed off and hurting, James still took her breath away.

He was so damn perfect.

Perfectly imperfect.

Several months ago, she'd had no intention of giving him any of her time, and here she was praying to God he'd now give her more of his.

He brushed past her. "Say what you need to say, then get out."

Panic rose inside her like a flash flood, and she moved to the hall. "I love you."

James stopped short but didn't turn to face her.

The words spilled out before she had a chance to censor them. But she meant them. With all of her heart, she meant them. "Did you hear me? I love you."

"Please…" He raised one hand in the air as if to warn her off. "Please don't say that."

She approached him but kept her shaking hands at her sides. "Why not?"

"Because I'll want to believe you." His head fell forward, and his shoulders followed suit. "And I can't because there's no way you mean it."

"What?" Sonja moved around him so she could see his face. "You think I would say those words to you if I didn't mean them? How could you think that?"

James looked at her. The expression in his eyes so harsh she felt it like a physical slap. "Because everything has been a struggle. Always a fucking struggle. Because you fought me every damn step of the way, from going on a date to fucking me to seeing your home, right down to meeting your daughter. Christ, you've never even met my best friend. You pushed me away at every turn, and now…" He ran his palm over his jaw and mouth. "Now, I find out it's because you're not willing to give up your pretend life with your ex to have a real one with me. I just… No." He shook his head. "No."

Ouch. That stung. Sonja blew out a breath. "That's not true. I do want a life with you."

"Bullshit."

"Look, I know things have been hard between us, and I know that was my fault. But none of tha—"

"What about after? Did you fuck him after we were together?"

Gasping, Sonja took a step back. She hadn't been prepared for the question, though she should've been. "No. Never. It's only been you."

"I don't trust you."

"How can you say that?"

"I can say it because it's true. You lied to me."

"I beg your pardon?"

"You heard me." He took a swig of his beer.

"I most certainly did not lie to you!" Anger and frustration raced for first place in her mind. How dare he accuse her of lying? She never lied to him. "I lied to me. I lied to my daughter. But I did not lie to you."

He brushed past her and took a seat on the couch. "Omission is the same as a lie. So, sorry to break it to you, but you lied to me, too."

"I can't believe this." She walked around the sofa and stood in front of him. "I can't believe you're going to use me *not* telling you something that happened before we were even together—which, by the way, was none of your business at the time—as an excuse to end this. That night had nothing to do with you and everything to do with me believing I was stealing some control back. I was stupid and blind, and it was a damn mistake. One I've regretted since the moment it happened."

"It doesn't matter anymore." He blew out a breath. "This isn't going to work. We don't work, and I don't want to play this game with you anymore." Stretching his long legs out in front of him, he tipped his beer back for another swallow.

The panic was back, and this time, it boiled over and spilled through her limbs. This wasn't a game to her. She needed to open up and tell him everything, and it terrified her. Sonja didn't know if she could be so raw and risk losing him anyway. But she had to try. He wasn't going to let her off the hook so easily, and she supposed he probably shouldn't. "If you think I'm going to give up after everything that's gone on between us and all that I feel for you, you're sadly mistaken.

"James, listen to me, please. You are the antithesis of how I was raised. You represent everything I was never supposed to want or have. Meeting you was a surprise. Being attracted to you was an even bigger one." He snorted and glanced at her, and she continued. "You think I'm some independent, strong woman, but I'm not—in the courtroom, maybe, but not in my personal life. Truth is, I'm a coward."

Sonja turned away and sat on the arm of the sofa. Looking at him and saying the things she needed to say felt impossible. "For as long as I can remember, I never stood up for myself. After my mother died, it wasn't possible. My father would've never tolerated it." She let out a bitter laugh. "After law school, he delivered me down the aisle to a man *he* approved of. One that would continue what he started, which was to control my choices, my thoughts and my desires…my everything. Didn't matter what I wanted or what I thought.

"Thomas fit the bill for sure, and I believed I loved him. At least I'd convinced myself I did, and it was easier to just go along with what they wanted." She looked down at her hands. "I stood up for myself when I got divorced, but even that was cowardly because I used Thomas's affair as the excuse instead of my own unhappiness."

"Sonja, look, I don't—"

"Please, I need to get this out." She stood and paced, but kept her gaze trained on the floor. "When I met you, it was easy to tell you no. You were not someone my father would approve of. Even from the grave, I heard him expressing his disdain. But more than that, telling you no was freeing. I could stand up to you. I *made* things hard because I could—because I needed to. Rather than ducking my head and doing what was expected, I could be independent with you. I'd finally found my backbone…or so I thought." Sonja stopped pacing and blew out a breath. "So stupid. So foolish." She ran her hand up the back of her hair and turned to look at him. "You were the first person who never wanted to control me. You only wanted to be close to me, and I just crapped all over you. I was so wrong. I never should've done that."

"Listen, I'm glad you've had this great realization, but it doesn't change anything." He put the beer bottle down on the table and sat back again. "We. Still. Don't. Work."

Frustration exploded inside her and propelled her forward. She didn't stop to think, just went where her emotions led her. Sonja knelt on the couch next to him, slid her skirt up, then swung a leg over his lap and straddled him. "The hell we don't. I'll prove it to you."

"Sonja—" He raised both hands in the air. "Don't do this."

"Do what?" She rolled her hips, grinding against him. "This?"

He grabbed her waist. "Oh, Jesus. Stop!"

"Make me." She pressed a kiss to his neck. "We work, James. We work perfectly." She nipped his ear and felt him shiver beneath her. There was no way in hell Sonja was losing this argument.

It was quite possibly the most important one she was ever going to have.

CHAPTER FORTY-NINE

Jimmy froze as she rolled her hips, grinding against his now rapidly rising erection. *Goddammit!* Confusion from all her words filled his mind, and now arousal was taking up space, too. Refusing her wasn't in Jimmy's DNA; there was no way he could battle his desire for her.

Never mind that he was beyond angry with her for more reasons than he was sure she realized. But he knew she was being real and raw with him. And also that she was being honest, probably for the first time with herself, even. Maybe he could forgive her, trust her again.

A moan slipped out of him, and he had to stop himself from tilting his hips forward. She licked along the side of his neck. Sonja hadn't been unfaithful to him, not technically, but she sure as hell had been unfaithful to herself for too many years. That little tidbit had him pissed at her for sure. In addition, he wanted to strangle her for making things more than difficult for them for all these months, and *now* she'd done a one-eighty and wanted to make it easy?

Things were *not* going to be easy.

She kissed along his jaw until reaching his lips. Pausing, she pressed her forehead to his. Unable to take it anymore,

Jimmy gave in, wrapped his arms around her and pulled her closer. "I'm so fucking angry at you."

"I know." She pressed her lips to his for a kiss.

He jerked away. "Dammit, Sonja. No. It's not that easy."

"Yes, I know." She frowned. "But I'm not going to let you take this away from us. Nothing about us is easy. I don't want the 'easier' path anymore. I want you. I want real. I want…" She rolled her hips again. "Fire and passion. I want us, and I was an idiot to ever pretend I could be okay with anything less."

"It's too late."

She leaned forward, her lips hovering above his. "It's never too late. I love you, James."

His heart melted, and it was torture. He wasn't sure what was going to happen or if he could stay with her. He wasn't sure of anything except that he loved her. He loved this woman with every fiber of his being. But he needed to know about Thomas. Jimmy cupped her face in his hands. "Is he gone? For good gone?"

"With the exception of Casey going to visit him, yes. He's gone."

Fuck! Jimmy arched up, closing the distance between them, and kissed her. Thrusting his tongue into her mouth, he groaned, and she opened for him. Fucking hell, it felt like forever since he'd last kissed her. The taste of her washed through him like a warm summer rain, cleansing all the anger away and nourishing his soul.

Jimmy broke the kiss, leaned forward and spun her onto her back. Settling between her thighs, he gritted his teeth and rolled his hips forward, grinding against her. "Damn you, Sonja. You're fucking killing me." He ran his hand down the front of her blouse, seeking her breast. He rose to his knees between her legs. "Get this off now. I need to feel you."

"Oh God, yes!"

After pulling his shirt over his head, he watched as she

released each button and then parted the two halves of the pale pink fabric. Sitting up, she slid the shirt off her shoulders and arms, then unhooked her bra and removed that, too.

"My sunshine, so beautiful."

She ran her hands down his chest. "Touch me."

"It's not your turn." Pulling her palms away from him, he looked at her. "Take your hair down."

Sonja did what he asked and laid back on the couch, and her long hair fanned out around her. Leaning forward, he took one rose-tipped areola between his lips. Her sweet scent permeated his senses and sent his brain spinning. She arched beneath him, and he pinched the other hard point, tugging a bit before rolling it between his fingers. He bit the taut peak in his mouth, and she gasped. He loved when she was like this, giving herself over to him completely. His rock-hard cock throbbed behind his zipper, and Jimmy rocked his pelvis, grinding against her clit.

With a whimper, Sonja ran her fingers through his hair. "I need you inside me. Please?"

Looking up at her, Jimmy smoothed his palm down her stomach and then lower. He cupped the heat between her legs. "Whose is this?"

"Yours."

He pressed the butt of his hand against her mound and rubbed. "Tell me again."

She bit her bottom lip. "Oh God. It's yours."

Dragging his fingers over her wet panties, he teased her opening. "That's right. Tell me what you want next."

Sonja rolled her hips. "I want you inside me."

"Inside where?"

"My pussy. I want you inside my pussy."

"That's my girl."

Rising from between her legs, Jimmy stood and removed his pants. He cupped his sac in his palm and stroked his length. "This what you want?"

"Yes," she breathed.

"Show me how wet your cunt is."

Without hesitation, she slipped her skirt and panties over her slender hips and down her long legs. Lying back, she spread her legs and then her glistening folds. Lust hit him like a bolt of lightning, sending tingles along his spine. Good thing she wanted him inside her because Jimmy was pretty sure he might die if he didn't feel her wrapped around him in the next two seconds. He took a seat on the couch. "Jesus Christ, I'll never get tired of seeing you dripping for me. C'mere."

Sonja moved immediately and straddled him. He cupped her ass in his palms and held her above him. With her sweet nipples perfectly in line with his mouth, Jimmy took the opportunity to taste them again. She arched, and he sucked one between his lips, then moved to the other. Gripping her bottom, he spread her buttocks and slid his fingers to her core.

Her wetness coated his fingers, and she moaned. Jimmy groaned and pulled away from her breasts. Having a taste of the sweet honey coating his fingertips would have to wait. Wrapping her arms around his neck, Sonja pressed her lips to his, and he lowered her down on his cock. Her wet heat enveloped Jimmy, and everything melted around him. There was no ex-husband, no worry of a daughter running away… nothing but the two of them. "Mo chroí…" Jimmy smoothed his hands up her back and wrapped them around her shoulders. "I love you."

Sonja closed her eyes and sank down on him, seating him fully inside her. "Stay with me?"

"Look at me." She opened her eyes, and Jimmy took her face in his hands. "You're my sunshine." He touched his lips to hers. "You're my heart, my everything. And I'm not ever letting you go."

"I'm so sorry, baby." She kissed him, and her tears wet both of their cheeks.

Was it possible to have your heart broken and then healed

in the same breath by the same person who'd caused the break in the first place? Jimmy was pretty damn sure that's what had happened. Her pain and fear of losing him were as palpable as the love he felt and saw in her eyes. "I'm sorry, too."

Sonja rose and fell, riding him with languid movements as he drowned in her. The feel of her hot core wrapped around him, the taste of her lips, and the scent of her skin—every part of Sonja healed his heart, giving him air to breathe again.

As her pace quickened, Jimmy broke from her mouth and grabbed her hips. Buried deep inside her core, she slid back and forth. "Fuck, yes. Rub that sweet clit against me."

She gripped his hair and rode him faster. "James!"

Her tight cunt spasmed around his prick, and Jimmy groaned. "Woman, that pussy... Jesus—" He bit down on her shoulder, and she whimpered, her cries growing louder with each sway of her hips.

"I need to come. Oh God, James, make me come."

For God's sake, he was about to shoot sky-high. Lacing his fingers in her hair, he yanked her head back. Jimmy rolled his hips, holding her tight against his pelvis. "Look at me when you come all over my cock. Come for me, Sonja."

With her eyes locked with his, she shuddered above him, gasping as her orgasm hit. Her channel squeezed him in quick little spasms. Rolling her over, he perched above her and flung her long legs over his arms. Jimmy lost all control and slammed in and out of her with reckless abandon until every muscle in his body seized. His climax exploded, and he let out a guttural moan. He spurted over and over inside her core, filling her as endless waves of pleasure spread through him.

She dug her nails into his hips. "James!"

"Fuck! Fuck, yes!" With his cock still jerking inside her, Jimmy gasped for breath and released her legs, collapsing onto her.

Wrapping her limbs around him, Sonja pressed her warm lips to the side of his neck. "I love you."

He lifted his head and gazed at her. "I think you could tell me that a million more times, and I'd never get tired of hearing it."

She tilted her lips in a small smile. "Promise?"

Jimmy stroked his thumb over her bottom lip. "Yes, mo chroí…my heart." He smiled. "I promise."

Fire and ice was what knew he saw in her when they'd first met. He'd been right, but little did he know that what he saw was only the tip of the iceberg, and the tiny smoldering embers, which appeared harmless, burned hotter than the actual flame.

So much more than he ever expected. So much more than Jimmy ever knew he wanted and definitely needed. He'd found the best, and when a person found their match—found the best—they didn't let it go. Ever.

And Sonja was hands down, no questions asked, the best.

ABOUT THE AUTHOR

Dorothy F. Shaw lives in Arizona, where the weather is hot, and the sunsets are always beautiful. She's a self-proclaimed sex scene snob and is proud of it. When she's not writing, she's thinking about writing.

With her ever-open heart, bright red hair, and many colorful tattoos, she truly lives and loves in Technicolor!

Get in bed (and read) with your favorite redhead!

Newsletter sign-up: Yes, please!
Join *Dorothy's Ruby Readers* on FB:
http://bit.ly/DFSRubyReaders
www.dorothyfshaw.com
DorothyFShaw@Gmail.com

facebook.com/AuthorDorothyFShaw

instagram.com/authordorothyfshaw

bsky.app/profile/dorothyfshaw.bsky.social

tiktok.com/@authordorothyfshaw

threads.net/@authordorothyfshaw

goodreads.com/dorothyfshaw

amazon.com/stores/author/B00DPRI5HK

bookbub.com/profile/dorothy-f-shaw

ALSO BY DOROTHY F. SHAW

Head to my site to find all links to my available backlist:

www.DorothyFShaw.com

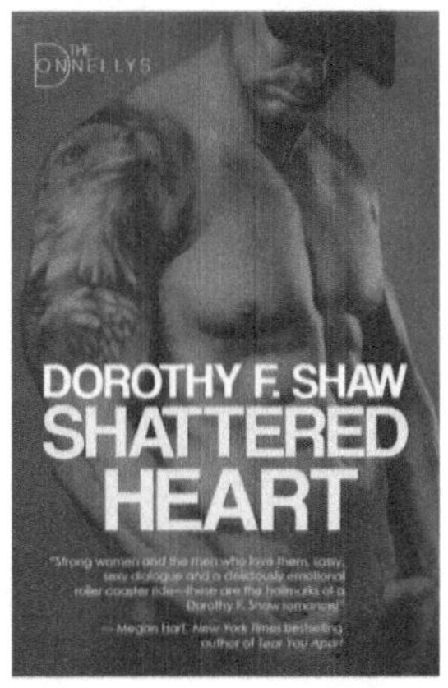

A crush is just a fantasy. The real thing packs some serious heat.

When Cynthia Donnelly lays eyes on her high school crush at her brother's wedding rehearsal, she regrets her self-imposed, one-year moratorium on dating. If possible, he's even hotter now than when they were teens.

Back in school, Shane made a point to ignore his best friend's cute, sassy little sister. Now that she's grown into an incredibly sexy woman full of Irish spunk, resisting her is out of the question. Besides, in his book, all "hands-off" rules have expired.

One sizzling night together should have been enough. Instead, the heat rises, tempting Cyn to take a chance on a long-distance relationship and making Shane consider pulling up stakes and moving back to L.A.

Cyn's recently dumped ex, however, has other ideas. His quest to get her back escalates into violence, shattering Cyn's faith in herself, and in anyone else of the male persuasion, and leaving Shane with his work cut out for him to repair the damage—or lose his shot at a once-in-a-lifetime love.

Turn the page for a sneak peek…

Shattered Heart

Chapter One

"Oh my God, Maiya! You look fucking incredible!" Cyn Donnelly scrambled to her feet and ran to her future sister-in-law's side. She smiled in awe of how beautiful her brother's future bride looked in her gown. "I thought it was gorgeous when you settled on it a few months ago, but now that it's been fitted? Yeah…*in-fucking-credible.*"

"I can't even…" Maiya cupped her hands over her mouth, tears breaching the edges of her eyes, and gazed at Cyn in the large mirror in the bridal shop. She swished the tulle skirt from side to side. "I can't believe it's me."

"Cynthia, please…language." Cyn's mother, Roseanne, frowned at her as she came to Maiya's side, too. "Maiya, you look perfect." She stroked her hand down the back of Maiya's hair. "An absolute angel, honey."

Maiya stroked her fingertips over the strapless sweetheart neckline of the gown and then smoothed her palms down the beaded and sequined bodice. Cyn rolled her eyes at her mother, then took Maiya's hand in hers and nodded. "Mom's right, you're an angel."

"A tattooed angel, maybe?" Maiya giggled.

"Those are the best kind, especially in a mermaid gown that shows off all your amazing curves. Ryan is gonna pass the hell out when he sees you coming down the aisle." Cyn squeezed her hand.

"Do you really think he'l—"

"Crap! I'm late! Where is she?" All three women turned around to see Jodi, Maiya's best friend, come barreling around a rack of wedding gowns, blonde curls billowing behind her before skidding to a halt. "Oh sweet Jesus and the Blessed Virgin…" Jodi pressed her hand to her chest. "Maiya, you're an angel."

"That's exactly what we said, too!" Cyn laughed.

Jodi stepped in front of Maiya. "I don't doubt it, Cyn. It's like she fell from heaven or something. Turn around, Maiya. Let me see the back."

"Oh my God, stop!" Maiya pressed her hands to her cheeks. "You guys are totally embarrassing me now." With a laugh, Maiya rolled her eyes and turned around, facing the mirror again.

"I'm going to have them bring out your veil, too." Mom stepped away.

Settling in the seats behind them, Cyn watched as Jodi doted on Maiya, a giggle or two bubbling up in all the excitement. Ryan and Maiya's wedding was this coming weekend, and Cyn couldn't be happier for them. A little over a year ago, her brother had met a woman who made everything in his life make sense, and in the process, his precious son, Jacob, would finally have the mother he so deserved.

For lack of a better word, it was a fairy tale. And although Cyn knew life wasn't really like that, Ryan and Maiya came pretty damn close. Sure, they argued. Sure, they got on each other's nerves—after all, they were as opposite as two people could get. But in the end, they connected and, in Cyn's book, that equaled happy. She sighed and rested her chin on her fist. If only she could be so lucky.

Her mother returned and placed Maiya's veil on the back of her long, thick red hair. The tulle hung to her lower back, turning an already perfect dress into an absolutely perfect ensemble. Maiya beamed, staring at herself in the mirror, and then her tears made another appearance. Jodi hugged her best friend, and Mom held Maiya's hand.

Yup, happy was exactly what this was.

Cyn's phone chirped from her purse, the text tone letting her know exactly who it was before even having to check the screen.

Carlos: Not gonna make dinner.

Cyn: Are you serious? Carlos, this is really important to me. Why can't you be here?

Carlos: Something came up at the office.
Sorry. Will text later if anything changes.

She didn't bother replying. Her boyfriend was blowing her off…yet again, and even if he really did have a valid reason, it didn't matter because there was *always* some excuse, some reason why he couldn't do whatever he might've committed to doing with her. Guaranteed, he wouldn't text her later either, even if something changed.

Closing her eyes, Cyn swallowed down the golf ball-sized lump of disappointment in her throat. She and Carlos had dinner plans with her other brother, Jimmy, and his girlfriend, Sonja. The couple had arrived last night from New York with Sonja's daughter, Casey. Ryan and Maiya were coming, too. It was supposed to be the six of them, but now, because Carlos was a grade-A flake, Cyn would be the fifth wheel at the table with four other happy people. Damn him.

For the life of her, she couldn't understand why she put up with his shit. Yeah, the sex was decent, but that was beside the point. It wasn't about the sex for her. Worse, for the last few months, the only time the man showed up for her was when his dick was hard, but even that had tapered off. At least before, she could tell herself it was worth it. But now? Cyn took a moment and thought back to the last time they'd actually had sex…two weeks ago? Wow.

"Cyn, you've got that look on your face again. And your phone's in your hand. Not a good sign."

She looked up from the screen at Maiya and sighed. "Yeah, I know."

Maiya put her hands on her hips. "He's not coming, is he?"

"No." Cyn slid her phone back into her purse and stood. "But it doesn't matter because today is your day, and we are *not* talking about my drama." She kissed Maiya's cheek.

"Roseanne? Can you please order your daughter to dump this dude? Please?" Maiya pulled her veil off and handed it to Jodi.

"Sweetheart, I wish I could. You know as well as I do, my kids do what they do, and I let them because if I didn't, they'd never find their way. Cyn knows I don't particularly care for Carlos, and she also knows no one else does either. But she's going to have to learn in her own time."

"That's what I always say, Roseanne. We're raising adults, not babies. Best they learn their lessons in their time." Jodi raised a hand in the air. "Not that y'all need me to put my two cents in. You've raised ten, but I'm just saying it's nice to know I'm going about it the right way."

Agitation prickled the skin on the back of Cyn's neck. *Learn in my own time, whatever.* She crossed her arms and cocked one hip to the side. "Excuse me, but I'm standing right here."

"And?" Maiya laughed. "Whatever. Not like it's a secret how we all feel. Carlos is an asshole—sorry, Roseanne, for cursing—and you deserve better, Cyn. Now help me out of my dream dress, and let's go get our nails done." Maiya turned and headed for the dressing room.

Cyn glanced at her mother, who was wearing a smile wider than the Grand Canyon. Jodi was, too. *Awesome.* With an exasperated sigh, Cyn followed after Maiya. "Fine."

Yeah, Carlos was an asshole, she knew it. But Cyn still loved him. Eventually, when it got painful enough, she'd let go and walk away. She just wasn't there yet.

Want more?
Head to my site to find all links to my available backlist:
www.DorothyFShaw.com

Available from all major e-sellers in digital and print.

Start at the beginning of
The Donnellys series with:
Unworthy Heart

The Donnellys Book 1
© 2019 Dorothy F. Shaw

Opposites not only attract, sometimes they spontaneously combust.

Ryan Donnelly's past relationship may have failed, but he's determined to make single fatherhood and his career a resounding success. He's got his eye on the top of the ladder at an L.A. marketing firm when his gaze snags on co-worker Maiya Rossini.

She's a feisty, witty, tattooed redhead who's nowhere near his type, but she pushes every one of his hot buttons.

Maiya clawed her way out of her dysfunctional, trailer-park childhood to earn a college degree and establish a promising career. Her future dreams are big, bright and packed with full-throttle fun, but when it comes to matters of the heart and men—especially stuffy corporate types like Ryan —her past slams on the emotional brakes.

In the office and in the bedroom, Maiya and Ryan rub each other in all the right ways. Though Maiya is everything Ryan didn't know he wanted, he's got his work cut out for him convincing her she's worthy of love—or the bright light she's brought to his life could slip through his fingers.

Publishing History.
Digital/Print 1.0 edition / May 2015
Digital/Print 2.0 edition / August 2017
Digital/Print 3.0 edition/ November 2019

Red Queen
Publications

9 780997 831023